Helen Lacey grew up reading *Black Beauty* and *Little House on the Prairie*. These childhood classics inspired her to write her first book when she was seven, a story about a girl and her horse. She loves writing for Mills & Boon True Love, where she can create characters and stories with soft hearts and happy endings that remain with readers long after their happily-ever-afters. Find out more about Helen on her website, helenlacey.com

Carrie Nichols grew up in New England but moved south and traded snow for central AC. She loves to travel, is addicted to British crime dramas and knows a *Seinfeld* quote appropriate for every occasion. A 2016 RWA Golden Heart® Award winner and two-time Maggie Award for Excellence winner, she has one tolerant husband, two grown sons and two critical cats. To her dismay, Carrie's characters—like her family—often ignore the wisdom and guidance she offers.

THE NIGHT
THAT CHANGED
EVERYTHING

HELEN LACEY

THE SERGEANT'S
MATCHMAKING DOG

CARRIE NICHOLS

MILLS & BOON

First Published in Great Britain 2021
by Mills & Boon, an imprint of HarperCollins*Publishers* Ltd
1 London Bridge Street, London, SE1 9GF

www.harpercollins.co.uk

HarperCollins*Publishers*
1st Floor, Watermarque Building,
Ringsend Road, Dublin 4, Ireland

The Night That Changed Everything © 2021 Helen Lacey
The Sergeant's Matchmaking Dog © 2021 Carol Opalinski

ISBN: 978-0-263-29982-3

0621

MIX
Paper from
responsible sources
FSC™ C007454

This book is produced from independently certified FSC™
paper to ensure responsible forest management.

For more information visit: www.harpercollins.co.uk/green

Printed and bound in Spain
by CPI, Barcelona

THE NIGHT THAT CHANGED EVERYTHING

HELEN LACEY

For Robert
Soul Mate…Best Mate
I love that we share this life together.

CHAPTER ONE

"I'M GETTING MARRIED!"

Grant Culhane pulled his cell phone away from his ear for a second in disbelief.

Winona. Getting married? Since when?

They spoke most nights, around dinnertime, and had done so for years. Growing up, Winona Sheehan was the best friend he'd ever had—and that hadn't changed much as they'd gotten older.

He digested what she'd said, got a twitch in his gut he didn't waste time registering and then scowled again. "Who the hell to?"

Grant heard her soft sigh. "To Dwight, of course."

The boyfriend. More accurately, the long-distance boyfriend, a marine who was currently deployed in Bahrain. "Winnie, you haven't seen him in nearly a year. Don't you think you should spend some time together before you start planning a wedding?"

"I'm not *planning* anything," she said. "We're eloping."

Grant's back immediately straightened. "What?"

"I'm heading to Nevada tomorrow and meeting Dwight in Vegas on Thursday. He's got a few days' leave."

She sounded happy. Happier than he'd heard her in a long time, actually. But still, marrying someone who had been in another country for over *ten* of the eighteen months you'd been dating didn't seem like such a great idea.

"Winnie," he said, dropping his voice an octave and using the nickname, funnily, that only *he* called her. "Don't you think you should—"

"I'm tired of thinking," she said, clearly exasperated as she cut off his words. "I overthink *everything*. That's why I work in a boring job and have never ventured past the South Dakota state line. I'm sick of playing it safe. Dwight asked me to marry him and I said yes, so you could at least pretend to be happy for me."

"Of course I'm happy for you," he lied, since he wasn't feeling that way inclined at all. Damn if he couldn't figure out why.

"Are you gonna be there or not?" she asked abruptly, cutting him off again. "Dwight's bringing his best friend from his unit, and to be honest, I'd like my best friend to be there, too. Can you get the time off work?"

Grant pushed back in his chair. He looked around at the four bland office walls. He'd been working fourteen-hour days on the same job for over a week and suspected he could certainly use a break. Plus, there was the current family drama that was taking up way too much of his thinking time lately.

Still, he wasn't sure how he felt about seeing Winnie get married, either!

But how could he say no to her?

"Of course I can be there by Thursday," he said, surprising himself a little.

He heard her relieved sigh and then felt better about

his decision. If he was there, at least he had a shot at trying to talk her out of it, or maybe he could have a word with Dwight and get the other man to see that eloping wasn't a great idea. For starters, Winona's grandfather would certainly have something to say about his only grandchild racing off to marry a man she had only seen in the flesh a handful of times.

"Have you told Red?" he asked.

She sighed. "No. You know how he is. He's going to ask me to wait so we can have a proper wedding."

"He'd have a point."

"It *will* be a proper wedding," she replied. "All that matters is that Dwight and I want to do this now. Besides, he's only got four days leave and Papa wouldn't be able to travel that far on such short notice."

That was true. Red Sheehan's health wasn't the best. The older man had been the foreman on Grant's family's ranch for years before a series of strokes forced him to stop working altogether. He still lived on the ranch, though, and helped out where he could. Grant's oldest brother, Mitch, would always offer a home for the Sheehans on the Triple C.

"I'll call you tonight," Winona said and ended the call.

Grant slipped the phone into his pocket, got to his feet and walked to the window, staring out to the street below. He stretched out his shoulders, thinking about Winnie, his concern quickly gathering momentum. Of course, after nearly twenty years of friendship, he'd never known her to be impulsive—Grant didn't even know if she really loved the guy. Sure, she regularly talked about the marine, but he wasn't convinced she was doing the right thing by marrying him.

He wondered whether he should have tried to talk her out of it, or at least tried harder to get her to hold off for a few more months. The truth was, he probably should have seen it coming. But he'd been distracted lately—with work, with family stuff—and maybe he'd been too preoccupied to focus on what was going on in his best friend's relationship. He'd try and get to the bottom of things once he saw her, he told himself— even if that was going to be on her wedding day.

He pushed back at the niggling jolt racing up and down his spine and worked out his next move—go to Vegas and try and talk some sense into her.

After that, maybe he'd go home for a while. He'd lived in Rapid City for seven years, moving there after completing four years of college in Sioux Falls. But Cedar River, South Dakota, would always be home. Situated in the shadow of the Black Hills, it had once been a vibrant mining town. Now, it was mostly a stopover for tourists and commuters heading for the state line. There were several tourist attractions, though, including the famous O'Sullivan Hotel, numerous dude ranches and a couple of the old mines, now operating as tourist centers. Grant loved Cedar River and, more importantly, he loved the Triple C Ranch and his family. The second youngest of six children, he looked up to his older brothers, particularly Mitch, who had gained guardianship of them all when their father had bailed. Grant had been just twelve years old at the time, and still remembered the day his father left. He'd raced after his father's truck, begging him to take him with him. It was a memory Grant tucked away, determined to keep buried.

If only Billie-Jack would let him.

Billie-Jack Culhane had been a deadbeat dad twenty years ago and Grant had no reason to think he'd changed. Except that two weeks earlier, out of the blue, he'd received a call from his long-lost father.

He hadn't recognized the number and let it go to voice mail. The message was short and to the point—Billie-Jack wanted to reconnect. Numb, he hadn't a clue how to react to the memories that he'd struggled for years to hide and which had quickly resurfaced. Three days later, Billie-Jack called again. But Grant wasn't going to be pushed into seeing him. And he knew any of his four older brothers and younger sister, Ellie, wouldn't be interested in seeing the old man, either. No, it was better he kept the information to himself for a while. Besides, now that Winona had dropped her bombshell he had other things to think about.

Grant sighed, stretched out his shoulders again and walked back around the desk. It was going to be a long afternoon, he figured, and sat down. He usually had no trouble concentrating on his work. He liked his job and the company he'd been employed with for the last few years. He'd loved gaming as a kid, but in high school, one of his science teachers noted his skills and encouraged him to pursue computer science as a career. Intrigued, he took the teacher's advice. Now, he worked wherever the company sent him, doing program design and sometimes high-end tech support and program installation for companies up and down the west coast. He had an apartment in Rapid City and spent most of his time there, traveling when needed. And he liked his life. He had a nice home. Good friends. Money in the bank. Yeah, life was sweet.

Except…his father wanted to make a comeback.

And Winnie was getting married. To some guy she hardly knew, no less.

Well, he'd just have to talk to her again—to make sure she was certain that marrying the marine was what she really wanted.

With his mind set on a plan, Grant got back to work and managed to push through until the end of the day.

He was home by six, showered and eating a swiftly put together stir-fry by seven-thirty. Nothing he did, though, could push thoughts of Winnie from his mind.

He wasn't sure why, but the idea of her getting married made his insides churn. It was just his protective instincts jumping into action, that's all, he figured. Of course he wanted to make sure she was safe. He cared about her. After all, they'd grown up together on the Triple C. They were best friends. They knew everything about each other. And he certainly would never have expected this kind of bombshell from her. Most days he forgot she actually had a boyfriend, since the marine was half a world away and she hadn't seen him too often during the months they'd dated.

He and Winnie had been there for each other for as long as Grant could remember, for everything. She taught him how to throw a curveball in middle school; he'd taught her how to ace a math quiz. He'd been the shoulder she'd cried on when she was dumped by her first boyfriend. She'd been the first person he'd called when he'd discovered he was valedictorian in senior year. He teased her when she got braces; she dissed his taste in music. They talked about everything, from bad dates, religion, the environment, to her insistence that one of his work colleagues had a thing for him. The plus one for weddings and parties. That one friend who mattered above all others. They'd supported one another through loss, grief, heartbreak and failed romances. Yeah…they were best friends, and even if he didn't agree with her planned elopement, he'd still be there for her. Because no matter what, she would do the same for him.

Not that Grant had any plans to get married…*ever*.

After dinner, he booked a flight to Vegas and then picked up his cell and called her. She didn't answer and he didn't bother leaving a message. He was just starting to type out a text message when she called him back.

"Hey, there," she said. "Sorry I missed your call. I was in the middle of sending Dwight a message."

Grant bit back a comment. "No problem. Okay, I'll be at the hotel around three o'clock," he told her. "I'll text you when I'm there."

"Okay, great," she said and then hesitated, her voice scratchy.

"What's wrong?" he asked.

"I feel bad for not telling Papa. And Ellie," she added. "You know how she loves organizing things like this."

That was true. Grant's little sister was a party-planner extraordinaire. "They'll get over it," he assured her, ignoring the sudden and ever-present twitch in his gut. "Once they see how happy the marine makes you."

She laughed. "You know, he does have a name."

"I know," Grant said humorlessly "I'm just giving you a hard time about it. I hope he appreciates you, Winnie."

"He loves me," she replied and sighed. "That's all I want."

Grant figured that's all anyone wanted. But he'd

never been a great believer in the idea of true love. Sure, he believed in attraction and lust and he liked sex as much as the next person, but love always seemed to fade. And worse, ruin lives. He'd watched his father fall to pieces when his mother had died. He'd witnessed his brother Mitch endure divorce from the only woman he'd ever loved. Even though Mitch and Tess were back together now, that didn't erase the years of pain in between. And when his other brother Joss had lost his young wife to cancer, he'd been put through hell by his in-laws as they tried to gain custody of Joss's two daughters. Yeah…love wasn't for him.

"Winnie," he said after a moment. "Are you sure you're—"

"Positive," she replied, cutting him off. "And promise me you're not just coming tomorrow to try and talk me out of it?"

Grant held off for a second, figuring she'd know exactly what he planned on doing. "Well, I only—"

"I know what I'm doing," she assured him. "Please support me in this."

Grant's gut plummeted. Despite his misgivings, he knew he would absolutely support Winnie if she wanted to tie herself to the marine. It was her life. Her choice. And as her friend, he'd support that—even if the idea tied his stomach into knots.

"Okay," he relented. "I promise."

He heard her relieved sigh. "Don't tell Krystal you're heading to Vegas, though," she teased, "or she'll be booking herself on the flight with you."

Krystal Heller worked for the same company he did and although she was nice enough, pretty and friendly, and had made it clear she was interested in him, he

wasn't feeling anything other than a respectful working relationship. And he'd never believed in messing
around with someone he worked with—it had complication written all over it.

"Give it a rest, will you."

She chuckled. "I'll see you tomorrow," she said and
chatted on excitedly for another few seconds before
signing off. "Love ya," she said, the same words she
ended the call with every night.

"Ditto," Grant replied, as he always did, and then
realized something that was oddly unsettling—that
it might be the last time he said it to her. She would
be married—another man's wife. She'd move to a
new town. Probably a new state. And he would rarely
see her. Their nightly phone calls would cease. She
wouldn't be the last voice he heard before he fell asleep
each night.

And he couldn't figure out why the mere idea of that
cut through him so hard that for a moment he could
barely breathe.

Life was about doing what made a person happy, Winona Anabel Sheehan thought as she looked around
the Las Vegas hotel room.

And taking chances.

Not that she'd taken a lot of risks over the years, but
that was about to change. She had a lot to be thankful for. First and foremost, she loved three things. Her
grandfather, Cedar River and Grant Culhane. Well, of
course she actually loved all the Culhanes—but Grant
was extra-special to her. He was her best friend.

Four things she loved, she corrected, shaking her
head as she carefully draped her wedding gown across

the bed. She loved Dwight Kelly, too. He was good-looking and funny and she'd fallen head over heels for him eighteen months ago. He'd been in Cedar River visiting a friend and they'd met at Rusty's bar, hitting it off immediately. Originally from New Mexico, he'd joined the marines at nineteen. He was finishing his current tour in three months, but insisted he didn't want to wait that long to get married. Winona had accepted his proposal via Skype without a second thought. When he finished his tour they would settle at Fort Liggett, California, for a while and Winona was looking forward to the move. She'd lived in Cedar River all of her life, only venturing as far as Sioux Falls for a couple of years to attend a community college there. Yeah, she was about as *hometown* as a girl could get, and at twenty-six was more than ready to venture out into the world.

Papa will understand, she said to herself. Red Sheehan had raised her since her mother ran out when she was nine. Winona didn't know her father, only that he was Brazilian and her mom had hooked up with him in Reno for a weekend and she was the result of that tryst. She knew his first name, which was Paolo. But no surname. No picture. She'd accepted his absence from her life long ago—just like she'd accepted having a mother who didn't really want her. But she had Red, the greatest grandparent in the world. And she had the Culhanes, too. Particularly Grant, and Ellie, who was more like a sister than a friend.

And now she had Dwight—her future husband.

Winona stared at the satin-and-lace gown the saleswoman had said flattered her figure, and pushed down the hankering she had for something more traditional.

It didn't matter what she wore. All that mattered was that she would be standing at an altar with the man she loved.

With both of them!

Oh, God, snap out of it, girl!

Winona shook off the thought. As a teenager she'd secretly and longingly pined for Grant Culhane to look at her as something other than his best friend—only admitting the truth in the diary she wrote in—but never letting Grant know how she felt. As she grew up, she accepted that she was in the friend zone and that's where she would stay. She stood by and watched him fall in love with a girl in high school, and then fall out of love just as swiftly. She remained his sidekick as he hooked up with one woman or another over the last decade, always ending the relationship within a couple of months. Grant didn't do serious. He didn't do commitment and he certainly would *never* do marriage. But he was the shoulder she always cried on. And she did love him—but she wasn't *in love* with him anymore, like she had been back in high school. That would be an obvious waste of her time. Now she was in love with Dwight. It had worked out exactly as it should have.

Her cell pinged and she grabbed the phone, recognizing Grant's number.

I'm in the foyer and all checked in.

Winona's heart skipped a beat. The hotel wasn't the flashiest in Vegas—but it was the best she could afford. She'd told Dwight she would make all of the arrangements, including booking the honeymoon suite. The room was huge and almost hideously decorated in shades of lime green, gold and red, with embossed velvet curtains and ornate furnishings. She was sure Grant would have something to say about the outrageous color scheme—not that she expected him to see the suite. No, she'd be sharing the room with her husband in just over five hours. Dwight was on his way. He'd called her that morning and they spoke briefly, making arrangements to meet at the chapel. Winona had thrilled at hearing his voice, and suggested they catch up at the hotel first, but he'd teased her, saying it was bad luck to see one another on their wedding day.

She grabbed her key card and tote and quickly left the room, heading downstairs to the foyer. The place was busy, and she noticed a bride and groom walking toward the elevators. Newlyweds were certainly in plentiful supply in Vegas. Winona spotted Grant immediately—he was hard to miss! Well over six feet, dark hair, broad shoulders and dark green eyes that were blisteringly intense. She saw a few women glancing at him appreciatively. He was hot, no doubt about that.

He hauled her into a hug the moment they collided and held her close. His arms had always made her feel safe and she hung on tightly for a few extra seconds. He smelled good, too, his cologne woodsy and familiar.

"What?" he said when he released her, holding her a little away, and looking at her jeans and shirt. "No bridal gown?"

"It's upstairs," she replied and laughed. "Don't want to get it wrinkled before the big event."

He glanced at his watch. "Countdown in two hours. Enough time for us to have a drink and catch up."

She gripped his arm. "As long as you keep your promise not to try and talk me out of it?"

He sighed. "I'll do my best. Where's the marine?" he asked and looked around.

"Dwight will be here soon," she assured him, thinking that he never used the other man's name. "He's meeting me at the chapel. He said it was more romantic that way."

Grant rolled his eyes a little. "Okay, Winnie, let's find a cozy spot at the bar over there and you can tell me exactly why you want to marry this guy."

"You know why," she refuted and walked him toward one of the bistros. "He loves me. I love him. That's why people usually get married."

The hotel was busy and several people were milling outside the bistro, but Grant quickly wrangled them a booth seat inside. He ordered drinks—an imported beer for himself and wine spritzer for Winona, her usual when they went out.

"Did you tell anyone?" she asked once the waitress left their booth.

Grant tapped several fingertips on the table. "You asked me not to breathe a word of your plans, remember?"

One thing she knew for certain—she could trust Grant. "Thank you."

"So, what happens after the wedding?" he asked. "Are you coming back to Cedar River?"

"In a few days," Winona said and nodded. "Dwight has to head back on Monday, so I'll return home then and probably stay for a couple of months. His tour finishes in seven weeks. After that I'll move with him to Fort Liggett."

"California?" He raised both brows. "That's a long way from South Dakota."

"It's only for a couple of years. After that, we'll probably come back to Cedar River and settle down. Dwight plans on leaving the army and, once we have kids, I want to make sure we're close to Papa. I think I told you that Dwight's parents are divorced, and since he hardly sees his dad and his mom got remarried, he's happy to live in Cedar River."

Grant leaned back in the seat, one hand around the untouched beer. "Sounds like you've got it all figured out."

She didn't miss the judgment in his tone and shrugged. "I've got plans for the future, like *most* people."

His mouth flattened. "If that's a dig, I'm not biting."

"I guess some people just aren't the marrying kind," she said and sighed. "But I am."

"Which is why you've agreed to marry a guy you haven't seen for the last ten months," he said quietly.

Winona frowned. "I know what I'm doing. Dwight is a good man. Once you get to really know him, you'll think so, too."

He didn't look convinced and it was exactly what she expected. Grant was concerned about her and she understood why he had reservations. To an outsider, it might look as though she didn't know Dwight all that well. True, they hadn't spent a lot of physical time together since they first met, but he'd visited her in Cedar River a couple of times in the first six months of their relationship. And they talked every week, and texted almost every day, while he was deployed.

"We'll see," Grant said and sipped his beer and then sighed heavily. "Okay... I'll try."

"And you'll behave yourself when we're at the chapel, won't you?" she urged, feeling a little panic rise up and curdle in her belly. Since she'd been surprisingly calm since Dwight had proposed, the sudden attack of nerves startled her. She didn't want to have doubts. She didn't want to live a life with her glass half-empty. She wanted stability, family, real love. And she wasn't going to let her commitment-phobic best friend make her feel any different. "I mean, you are kind of my maid of honor, after all."

He looked appalled by the idea. "If that's what you wanted, you should have invited Ellie along to this gig."

Winona loved Ellie like a sister, but the other woman had a reputation for speaking her mind. "Ellie would have blabbed to your family and to my grandfather. You know you're the only one I trust."

Her words made him stare directly at her. "I just don't want to see you get hurt."

"I won't," she assured him. "But I appreciate that you're looking out for me."

"I always will."

She knew that. "You know, Dwight knows how important you are to me."

That much was true. Although her fiancé wasn't entirely thrilled about her close friendship with Grant. For a while she suspected Dwight wasn't convinced that their relationship was strictly platonic. But it was. It always had been.

"Where's your engagement ring?" he asked, looking at her bare left hand.

Winona shrugged. "There wasn't time for that. And the chapel said they could supply wedding bands."

He raised a quizzical brow. "Did you purchase the complete bridal package online?"

She smiled. "Something like that."

"Organized down to the last detail, I see," he said and grinned.

She smiled. "You know me."

He nodded. "That I do. You know, I'm gonna miss you when you leave for California."

Winona met his gaze and her throat tightened. She'd been so caught up in the excitement of Dwight's on-line proposal, she hadn't taken much time to think about the consequences. Like living in another state, or being away from her grandfather for the first time in years, or being separated from the only home she'd ever known. From her grandfather. From her friends. Especially Grant.

"I'll miss you, too," she said, feeling the meaning of her words down to the soles of her feet. "More than I can bear thinking about. We've been a part of each other's lives since we were kids."

"Since Red took in his wildcat granddaughter," Grant reminded her. "You were what…eight years old?"

"Nine," she corrected. "And you were twelve. Do you remember finding me in the hayloft that first day?"

He nodded. "Yeah…you were angry at the world."

"But you understood," Winona said as the memory kicked in, tightening her throat. "Because you'd been there yourself. And you're right, I was angry and hurt. My mom had just left me. But you were kind to me that day. You talked me down from the loft and taught me how to halter a horse."

Winona recalled the moment as if it were yesterday. Her mother had dropped her at the ranch, with nothing but a pink backpack and her favorite books. It was just for a few weeks, she'd said. Looking back, Winona knew her grandfather didn't believe it. And when her mom finally made contact over twelve months later, Winona chose to stay with her grandfather after that. Looking back, it was the right decision—even though at the time she'd experienced the range of emotions associated with being abandoned by her only parent. And still did, she suspected. But rationally, she knew she'd had a much happier childhood growing up at the Triple C with Red than she would have had she stayed with her mother. The first day had been hard—but Grant had made her feel so welcome, so much a part of things—and from that first day she developed a little bit of hero worship.

Over time, that turned into a serious crush—and by her thirteenth birthday she was convinced he was the love of her life.

Silly, she supposed, to think about that now, just as she was about to marry Dwight.

Thinking about her fiancé made her sit up straight and then shuffle out of the booth. "I have to get ready," she said. "Meet me in the foyer in an hour."

"How are we getting to the chapel?"

She checked her watch. "Taxi."

Winona took off and headed back to her room. Once she was inside, she showered, slipped into the white lace underwear she'd splurged on, before doing her hair and makeup. Not too much, since most days she went makeup free, but she swept her long black hair into an updo and added the pearl earrings Grant had given her for her eighteenth birthday. She stepped into her lace gown, which was long and figure hugging, off the shoulder in design, and pushed her breasts up in a flattering way.

Giving herself one final look, she double-checked her purse to make sure she had all the documentation she needed and then headed downstairs. Since brides in white gowns were obviously the norm for the hotel, she barely got a glance from the people she passed in the corridor, or in the elevator. Although one older lady did smile and say she looked lovely.

Grant was waiting for her in the foyer and gave her a long and appreciative look.

"You look beautiful," he said when she reached him.

Winona took in his dark suit, white shirt and tie and raised a brow. "You look pretty good yourself."

He smiled. "Do you have everything?"

She nodded and rattled her purse. "Just need to get to my groom."

"Lead the way," he said and grasped her elbow.

Ten minutes later they were at the Love Is All Around Wedding Chapel. There was a couple just finishing their ceremony and Winona watched from the waiting area, nerves settling big-time in her belly. She looked around, noticing how quaint and nicely decorated the place was, and thought it looked exactly like it had online.

The couple at the altar came out arm in arm, laughing happily, and nodded in their direction, with the minister and a well-dressed middle-aged woman following in their wake, throwing confetti. Once the other couple were out of the chapel, the minister approached her and she confirmed their appointment.

And waited for her future husband.

At ten minutes to four, when Dwight still hadn't

turned up, Winona got twitchy. "I'm sure I told him 3:45," she said to Grant and looked at the time on her cell again. "The minister said we needed about fifteen minutes to fill out the paperwork."

"He's only five minutes behind schedule. Maybe his flight was held up, or he's at the hotel changing into a suit."

She shook her head and called Dwight's number. "He's wearing his dress uniform. But you're right, he's probably caught up in traffic or something."

When the call went to his voice mail, she left a message and then sat back down, the uneasiness in her stomach increasing as the minutes ticked by. And then, after she tried his cell twice more and the time clicked past four o'clock, Winona knew something wasn't right.

The minister approached her at ten minutes past four and said he had another ceremony booked in twenty minutes and couldn't hold the spot much longer. Winona was about to call his number again when her cell pinged with a text message. She looked at the caller ID. It was from Dwight. Her stomach churned and then she took a breath. She was imagining the worst for no reason. He was late, that's all. He was stuck in traffic or his flight was delayed. Right?

Except, when she read his message, her hopes were crushed.

I'm so sorry, Win, I just can't do it. I'm not ready for a commitment like this. I know you probably hate me right now, but this is for the best. I'm sorry. D.

Her hand shook and she gasped, pressing her other hand to her chest.

"Winnie?"

Grant's voice. Suddenly, he was sitting beside her and she turned to face him, her hand still shaking. She held the phone up and shuddered out a reply. "He... he's not coming."

"What the hell are you talking about?" he asked in disbelief.

She shoved the phone at him with a shaking hand. "Read it."

He took a couple of seconds and then wrapped his hand around hers, placing the phone in her lap. "Winnie, I'm so sorry. But...maybe this *is* for the best."

"I don't understand...he promised..."

Winona's insides hurt so much she could barely breathe. And then, somehow, Grant's arm came around her and she dropped her head to his shoulder. He held her, murmuring that he'd take care of everything, he'd make sure she wouldn't be alone. Oddly, despite the hurt and the chaos screeching though her brain, she felt better.

Because Grant's arms were exactly what she needed to shelter her from the pain of being abandoned.

Again.

CHAPTER TWO

GRANT COULDN'T REMEMBER the last time he'd had a real hangover. Maybe never. Even in college he'd been too focused to ever let loose and party hard. His brothers often told him he was too uptight and needed to relax. And yeah, maybe he was. But he liked being in control. He liked knowing exactly who he was and where he was 24/7.

But even though he knew all that about himself, the heavy-limbed sensation he was feeling, along with the headache that pounded at his temples and the lethargy that had hold of his entire body, had all the markings of the hangover from hell. For a moment he considered not opening his eyes for a while and letting sleep do its job. The big bed was comfortable, after all. A few hours, he figured. Then a shower. A change of clothes. And food when his rolling stomach allowed it. That was the sensible course of action. And he was nothing if not sensible.

And he would have done it, if at that precise moment he hadn't realized that he wasn't alone in the bed. He turned his head a little, ignored the pounding that now traveled to the base of his skull and pried his eyes open a fraction.

Right...

A woman lay on the other side of the huge bed, on her side, her glorious black hair spilling down her naked back. Grant's eyes opened a little more and he admired the smooth skin, catching himself where the sheet lay draped across the curve of her hip. She was asleep, he registered, listening to the soft rhythm of her breathing for a moment.

Recognition fluttered through his brain, and he tried to remember who he was with and what they had done. Images flashed, of skin on skin, of kissing and touching, of sex that was out of this world. The memory made him wince, and the hellish hangover went a couple of rounds in his head. He glanced around the room and then back to the sleeping woman. She stirred, moaning a little, and then rolled, taking the sheet with her as she moved to face him, and he instantly reeled back in shock.

Holy freaking hell... Winnie!

Grant's already addled brain went into overdrive and then his libido did a leap when he noticed her breasts were bare and were so close he only had to move a few inches and he could...

Snap out of it!

Because...well...what the hell was he doing in bed with *Winnie*?

For one, they were both naked. And the sheets were messed up. And her mouth was full and red and the pinkish mark on her neck looked suspiciously like a love bite.

He spotted a couple of empty bottles of champagne on the table near the window and lifted his head a little to notice other things—like his suit and shoes scattered on the floor and a wedding dress draped over the back of a chair.

More images bombarded him, settling in his memory banks, and he remembered fractured events of the past eighteen hours. Arriving in Vegas. Seeing Winnie in her wedding gown in the foyer and his jaw almost dropping to his feet. Waiting in the chapel. The marine bailing on her. And then…she was crying. He remembered holding her, he remembered offering her words of comfort, he remembered telling her everything would be okay.

And then he quickly remembered other things—like doing way too much drinking. He also remembered being in her hotel room. And then he remembered kissing her, touching her, doing a whole lot of things with her he'd certainly never done before. He remembered the way she'd felt in his arms—her eagerness, the pleasure of her touch, the soft sighs she uttered against his mouth in between kisses. The way their bodies had moved together. He remembered the heat, the sweat, the desire that had taken hold of them both for so many hours.

He tried not to look at her and failed. Because it was impossible to ignore the fact her lips were redder than usual, or that her hair was cascading over her shoulders and back, or the pinkish marks along her collarbone and neck that looked like a beard rash. He touched his jaw and felt the culprit, letting out a long groan. The sound was enough to stir her a little more and he watched, mesmerized, as she stretched, moaned and then opened her brown eyes.

She stared at him, adjusting her sight to the morning light beaming through the spot at the window where the drapes didn't fully meet. And she instantly jerked back when she noticed him, tugging the sheet up to cover herself.

"Grant?" She said his name in an almost bloodcurdling whisper. "What… I don't…"

He swallowed hard, unable to move. "Winnie…we should probably…you know, get up."

She nodded and inched away, taking the sheet with her. Grant grabbed the duvet at the end of the bed and covered himself before she got far off the mattress. Not that it mattered, he supposed, since he was pretty sure she'd seen everything there was to see. Because, as much as he didn't want to admit it, there was no hiding the fact that they had spent the night together.

"Oh, my God," she breathed and stumbled from the bed, taking two steps back once her feet hit the floor. "What did we do?"

"I think that's pretty obvious," he replied, trying to not sound as mortified as he felt, and also ignoring the way the sheet slipped down a little, exposing her breasts again. He looked away for a moment while she adjusted the sheet and wrapped the duvet around his waist as he stood, almost falling back onto the bed as the room spun and he swayed.

Great.

"We drank champagne," she said and motioned to the empty bottles on the table. "Lots of it. And tequila."

Grant put a hand to his temple. "Way too much. I never drink like that."

She walked a few paces and then slumped into a chair, keeping the sheet tightly wrapped around herself. She was breathing hard, as though every time she inhaled it actually pained her. She looked up, meeting his gaze, her brown eyes darker than he'd ever seen them, the deeply slanting brows above them adding to the query in her expression. She was beautiful, that's for sure. Her Brazilian heritage had gifted her smooth olive skin, a mane of riotous dark hair, deep chocolate-colored eyes and striking features. She was smart and stunning and had inherited her quick temper from her grandfather. But in that moment, she looked so vulnerable and unsure he was lost for words.

"We had sex," she said, clearly horrified by the idea.

He sighed, then winced a little as his head throbbed. "We did. But it'll be okay, Winnie."

"How is it going to be okay?" she shot back. "We crossed a line."

It was true…they had. The one line that he suspected they both believed they would never cross because they were best friends and that was *way* more important that hooking up for a night of casual sex. And not that it was casual, either…because it was Winnie and they were more than a simple meaningless hookup.

Which meant one thing…*complicated.*

"Winnie, we can move on from this. Last night was…" His words trailed off and he saw the way her eyes glistened. "It doesn't change anything between us."

"Are you kidding?" she shot back quickly. "It changes everything."

"Only if we let it," he added. "And we won't, okay?"

She shook her head. "Sex complicates everything."

"Not for us," he said, trying to put her at ease, despite knowing she was right. And despite the way his stomach churned and his brain felt like it was about to explode. "Our friendship is unbreakable."

She didn't look convinced. "I think I'm going to throw up." Their eyes clashed and she shrugged. "From the alcohol, I mean. Not from…" She waved a hand as her words trailed off. "You know…*that*."

He was stupidly pleased to hear it. For one, this was Winnie and he hated to think he'd done anything to hurt or offend her. And two, he had as much ego as the next guy. He looked at her, noticing everything, the way she bit down on her lower lip, the way her naked shoulders were held tight, the way her tousled hair looked as sexy as hell.

Sexy… Jesus…what the hell is wrong with me?

He shook himself and took a breath, trying to ignore the snapshot of images toying with his brain. Memories of kissing her, of touching her in places he'd never dared imagine he would touch, of lying between her thighs and being inside her in the most intimate way possible. And then, as the images gained momentum and he experienced a deep-rooted churning way down low, Grant noticed something else—a gold band shimmering on her left hand.

"Ah… Winnie," he said, the words almost collapsing his throat. "You're wearing a wedding ring."

She looked down and gasped, her face turning ghostly pale. She shot her gaze back to his as she held up her hand. Her gaze didn't waver from his for a few excruciating seconds and then she tilted her head to the side and glanced down.

"Oh, my God," she whispered and jumped to her feet, pointing to his left hand. "So are you, Grant!"

His lids dropped and he looked to where his left

hand was clutching the slipping duvet. Holy crap! She was right. The bright gold band on his ring finger was plain to see.

No...it couldn't be...

He searched his memory banks, trying to remember, pulling on his recall...and slowly, piece by piece, the fragments began to merge. They'd been at the chapel, Winnie was upset, crying over the jerk who'd dumped her. Grant had her in his arms, holding her, soothing her, telling her how everything would be okay. And then later, they were at the hotel, back in the bistro and drinking a pitcher of mojitos. After that they had done a few rounds of tequila shots. She'd cried some more, then once her bravado set in, began to curse her ex-fiancé, using words he'd never heard her speak before. They walked the strip for a while, laughing, arm in arm, stopping at another bar for a drink and a bowl of pretzels. And then, somehow, they were back at the chapel.

Do you take this woman...

To have and to hold....

'Til death do you part...

The memories banged around in his head. Taunting him, awakening feelings he wasn't sure he knew what to do with. Feelings he didn't want. Because he didn't do feelings—not these, that was for damn sure.

He strode three steps across the room and snatched up a couple of pieces of paper that were on the table by the window. He looked at the documents, scanning them quickly, and the uneasiness in his gut increased as the seconds passed. He saw names, signatures, a blurry stamp in dark ink...and he knew exactly what he was looking at.

A marriage license.

His name. Winnie's name. Two signatures he recognized in the bride and groom section, and a couple he didn't were scrawled in the witness section. It was undeniable. Unimaginable.

They were married.

"We've got a situation," he said quietly, glancing at her and then looking at the damning document in his hands. "It looks like we got hitched last night."

Color leached from her face and he could see that her hands were shaking.

"That's impossible," she said, almost croaking out the words.

He shook his head and then took a few steps across the room, holding out the paper in his hand. "Take a look."

She grabbed the page and the crackling sound reverberated in his ears, reminding him of the headache and hangover he was so desperately trying to forget he had. He wanted some aspirin, a shower, shave and coffee in that order. Grant looked around the room and spotted his clothes and shoes.

The bridal suite, he figured, taking in the over-the-top decor and huge bed.

The marriage bed.

Where they had foolishly consummated their union. Damn…the situation quickly spiraled from bad to worse when he realized what that meant. Married *and* lovers. Which made the idea of annulment unlikely, right? Which of course is what they would do. Winnie wouldn't want to be married to him any more than he wanted to be married to her. Hell, he didn't want to be married to anyone.

"How could we let this happen?" she said as she scanned the page and then thrust it back into his hands. "Yesterday I was..."

Dreaming of marrying someone else...

Oddly, the notion irked him and he couldn't understand why. Sure, he didn't think the marine was good enough for her and believed they should know one another better, but that didn't mean he wanted to step into the other man's shoes. But he had...in every way possible.

He let out a weary sigh. "Well... I guess we'll have to get a divorce."

Winona had never been more confused in her life. Twenty-four hours ago her plans had been set—marry Dwight, move to California, start her new life with her new husband.

Oh, yeah...she had a husband, all right...just not the one she'd planned on!

Winona Culhane...

Simply thinking the words made her head hurt. And her heart hurt, too.

She looked at Grant, absorbing every inch of him in a microsecond. Naked from the waist up, the duvet wrapped haphazardly low on his waist, he looked as sexy as sin. His broad shoulders were smooth and tanned, his chest covered in a light dusting of hair that tapered down his belly and disappeared beneath the duvet. Of course she'd seen him shirtless before. But never like this. Never after sex. She considered the way her body felt, the ache in the backs of her thighs and the heavy lethargy seeping through to her bones, and the haze her brain seemed to be in. She'd had two other lovers in her twenty-six years—her high school boyfriend and Dwight. Casual sex had never interested her.

But Grant, she knew, only did casual.

He'd never had a long-term relationship. A couple of months and he was out. She knew the drill. He'd meet someone, they would date, she wouldn't move into his apartment—as far as Winona knew, he wouldn't even let a toothbrush be left at his place. He wasn't a player and never cheated in his relationships, but he wasn't exactly known for going the distance.

And yet, here they were—married!

The nausea returned, clutching at her throat, and she put a hand to her mouth. The last thing she wanted to do was throw up in front of him—that would be too humiliating. She had to get a grip, to prove she was in control and able to deal with their current situation.

"Divorce?" She repeated his suggestion and stared at him, not wanting to think about how much she was stung by his quick solution. "Why not an annulment?"

He raised both brows and pointed to the rumpled bed. "Er...not that I'm an expert on South Dakota's marriage laws, but I think we may have botched that option when we...you know...spent the night together."

Winona's insides crunched up. She didn't know how to feel or what to think.

She walked across the room, clutching the sheet, passing him without taking a breath as she headed for the bathroom. She closed the door and pressed her back against the wall, the cold tiles making her wince a little. Winona took a couple of long breaths and then stared into the long mirror.

Oh, my God... I look wrecked.

Her hair was everywhere, her eyes bloodshot, her grayish pallor indicative of way too much alcohol consumed. She jumped in the shower for a couple of minutes, washing quickly, ignoring the throbbing sensation at the back of her head. Aspirin would be good, she figured, and once she'd dried off and wrapped the sheet back around herself, she rummaged through her toiletries for the painkillers. She found them, took two, left another couple on the washbasin and then opened the door. Grant was still standing by the bed, still draped in a duvet, still looking so hot she had to swallow a couple of times to get her lady parts out of the way of her brain so she could stop remembering, thinking and fantasizing about her new husband in any way whatsoever!

Because she loved Dwight, right? At least, she *had* loved him until he dumped her so heartlessly and left her standing at the altar. Of course, she hated him, too, since he had no right to treat her so badly. This time yesterday she had been dreaming of her wedding and her new life. Now, she was living an actual nightmare—with a seminaked Grant playing center stage as her husband!

"We should get dressed," she said flatly, searching for her suitcase among the discarded clothes on the floor. "I left some aspirin for you in the bathroom."

She found her suitcase by the window, opened, and her belongings a jumbled mess.

"What?" he asked, obviously noticing her scrunched-up expression.

"I can't believe we did this."

"Which part?" he remarked. "The drinking, the wedding, the—"

"All of it," she snapped, cutting him off. "Yesterday…"

"Yesterday your idiot ex-fiancé abandoned you. You needed to forget about it *and* him. That's why we—"

"It's no excuse," she said quickly, rummaging through her bag for suitable clothing. She found jeans, fresh underwear and a red shirt and pulled them into her arms. "We've got to fix this."

"Of course," he said quickly. "Once we get home I'll go and see Tyler Madden. He'll know the best course of action."

Tyler Madden was a lawyer in Cedar River. Winona had met him briefly when he'd looked after her grandfather's will.

"I'd like to get dressed," she said quietly. "You can have the bathroom."

He hesitated for a moment, as though he wanted to say something, but instead he nodded. "Sure," he said and grabbed his clothes and shoes, struggling to hold the duvet with one hand. "Good idea."

He disappeared quickly and Winona relaxed a fraction. She used the sheet as a makeshift tent as she wobbled on her feet, slipping into her underwear and jeans. She remained on point, dropping the sheet for a few moments, her gaze fixed firmly on the bathroom door as she thrust her arms into her shirt and quickly did up the row of buttons. She found her shoes and then gathered up her scattered clothing, taking a second to look over the crumpled wedding gown. A few of the pearl buttons were missing and she remembered the way she'd rushed to get out of the dress in her eagerness to have sex with Grant, the way she'd clung to him, begged him, kissed him like she was starved of touch. And was instantly mortified by the memory. She was a predictable cliché...a woman who'd pounced on her best friend the moment she'd needed a rebound lay. Appalled, she rolled the gown up and pushed it into the suitcase, along with shoes and anything else she found on the floor.

He emerged from the bathroom a few minutes later, dressed in his suit, his jaw still raspy with a five-o'clock shadow. She tried not to stare, keeping herself busy by unzipping and then rezipping her bag.

"My plane leaves at 10:40," he said and tossed the duvet in the middle of the bed. "Would you like me to arrange a flight for you? I'm guessing you don't want to hang around here for any longer than necessary?"

That was true. Winona had a flight booked for Monday. It was now Friday morning—she certainly didn't want to be alone in Vegas for three days, pacing around the honeymoon suite, her mind a mix of memories, thinking about Dwight *or* Grant. She rummaged through her bag and pulled out her airplane ticket.

"Thank you," she said and passed him the ticket.

"I'm gonna head back to my room for a shower and change of clothes. I'll be back soon."

She didn't say anything else and waited until he was gone before she sighed and managed to relax a little. She made coffee and drank it as hot as she could stand, and paced the room until he returned about twenty minutes later, carrying his overnight bag.

"We're all set for our flight," he said, unsmiling. "And the concierge has arranged for a car to take us to the airport at nine. We have time for breakfast in the restaurant downstairs. Or we could order room service."

Winona glanced at the clock on the wall: 7:50. The last thing she wanted was to be cooped up in a room with Grant for the following hour. "Downstairs," she said and picked up her suitcase and handbag, sweeping the room one last time for anything she might have left behind, before she collected her toiletries from the bathroom.

She glanced down at her hand and realized she still wore the wedding band. She looked at his hand and noticed it was bare, thinking that removing it was probably the first thing he'd done when he got to his room. She met Grant's gaze and let out a long sigh. "I should take this off."

The ring came off easily and she dropped it into the small pocket inside her tote. Shame pushed down on her shoulders again and she swallowed back the tightness in her throat. She wanted to cry, but absolutely would not fall apart in front of him.

"Let's go," she said flatly and walked from the room.

Once they were downstairs, they left their bags with the concierge and headed for the restaurant. There were plenty of tables free and Winona was relieved to see it was a buffet-style arrangement—it meant she had time to linger by the buffet table and avoid sitting down with him for any length of time. She piled up her plate with fruit and toast and headed for their table, conscious that Grant was still selecting his food. She poured herself a glass of water, drank it in a few seconds and then poured another, grateful that the aspirin she'd taken earlier was now kicking in.

By the time he sat down at their table she was struggling to digest a second piece of cantaloupe and looked up. It was time to get serious about their situation. "So, we need to make a pact," she said and grabbed a napkin.

He looked at her. "A what?"

"Pact," she repeated. "Agreement. Arrangement. You know, a pact."

"About?"

"To not tell anyone what we've done."

"Which part?" he queried, one brow up.

"The married part," she replied as heat crawled up her neck. "The sex part. Promise me."

"Of course," he said quickly and sipped coffee. "But you know what my family is like, Winnie, and I hate the idea of keeping secrets from them."

"Sometimes secrets are necessary," she said.

"Don't I know it," he shot back.

Winona stared at him. "What does that mean?"

He shook his head dismissively. "Nothing."

"Perhaps we should get a lawyer in Rapid City. You've lived there for years, surely you know someone?"

He pushed his untouched plate away. "Maybe. You know Len Pearson—he got divorced last year, so I could ask him."

Winona knew all of Grant's friends, including Len, who she didn't particularly like. "It will probably be easier just to go and see Tyler, then. He's a good lawyer and we'll just need to make sure we're discreet. And we should deal with it before word gets out. I don't want anyone knowing about this."

"Winnie, I don't think—"

"I feel so ashamed I can barely breathe," she admitted as she cut off his words, holding her shoulders so tight her bones ached.

He exhaled heavily. "I do understand how you—"

"No, you couldn't possibly," she said, cutting him

off again. "Just yesterday I was going to marry the man I loved and start my new life and now it's all—"

"Loved?" he questioned, both brows now up. "You said that in the past tense. So, what…you don't love him anymore?"

"How could I possibly—after what he did to me?"

"If that's all it took, then his leaving you at the altar was clearly the best thing for you both."

Winona glared at him. "How dare you say that. What do you know about anything? Your idea of a real relationship is allowing your date to order dessert."

He scowled, clearly stung by her words. "At least I have sense enough not to marry someone I haven't seen for the last ten months."

It was a cruel dig and one she didn't deserve. Grant knew how much her relationship with Dwight meant to her—since she spoke to him about it most nights when they talked on the phone.

She met his gaze. "Why are you being like this?"

He sighed heavily. "Because I'm tired, and when I'm tired I act like a jerk. Sorry."

"You're right, though," she admitted and shrugged. "I was clearly not thinking straight when I agreed to marry Dwight. And what was last night if not a complete lapse in judgment?" she added a little hotly, so annoyed with herself she could hardly breathe. "We got drunk, got married and had sex… I'd say as far as lapses go, that's the lapse of the century."

He laughed. "I don't think I've ever been called that before."

"It's not funny," she retorted. "This is the worst day of my life. Which is a strange irony, because it should have been the best day. I've done some foolish things over the years, but I've never had rebound sex before, have you?"

"Is that what it was?" he asked quietly, looking at her over the rim of his cup, his gaze unbelievably intense.

"Of course, what else?"

He shrugged, but Winona saw the tension in his shoulders. She suspected he was acting cool because he thought it was better for them both, but she knew him too well—she knew he was faking. He wasn't cool, he wasn't okay, he was as wound up, as confused, as completely out of sorts, as she was. He was simply better at disguising it. He was the master of it, in fact.

"Can't you just admit that you're as freaked out about this as I am?" she challenged him.

His gaze didn't waver. "Would it change anything?"

"For starters," she said and huffed, "it might stop me being mad at you for acting like the Tin Man."

"Well, we're certainly not in Kansas anymore," he replied and drank some more coffee and then checked his watch. "We should get going."

Relief scored down her back. "Great idea."

Winona got to her feet and pushed the chair in, grabbing her tote. She was halfway around the table when Grant grasped her hand. She felt the connection. The burn. The tingle his touch always evoked. And any other time she wouldn't have thought anything of it—like when they were at the movies and he led her to their seats, or if they were out to dinner and he pulled out her chair, or if they were dancing, or if they were mustering cattle at the ranch and he helped her mount her tall gelding. But this wasn't any other time. This was now. They were married. They were lovers. And everything was different.

She pulled away, weirdly missing his touch the second their fingertips were apart.

In that moment she knew why she was so overwrought; it wasn't because Dwight had dumped her. It was much, much worse.

It was because she was terrified that, amid it all, she'd lost her best friend.

CHAPTER THREE

BACK IN CEDAR River late that afternoon, Winona imagined things might be better. But they weren't. After an awkward flight, she and Grant had parted at the airport in Rapid City with barely a goodbye as they headed toward their cars, both parked in the long-term parking lot.

Now, she was curled up on her sofa, a mug of green tea pressed between her palms, staring through the window of her one-bedroom apartment above the bakery. The sweet scent of sugar and cinnamon from that morning's bake still lingered in the air and gave her some comfort. She'd lived in the apartment for a few years, and mostly enjoyed the solitude. She had a few friends in town, like Grant's sister, Ellie, and his cousin Leah, but since Grant was her closest friend, most of her spare socializing time was spent with him.

Not anymore...

The terse way they had parted company at the airport made things abundantly clear—after almost twenty years of friendship, their relationship was forever changed.

And it hurt...in some ways, more than Dwight bailing on their wedding. Of course she was deeply wounded by her fiancé's behavior, but she realized now she'd get over it. She was strong, resilient. She'd been left before and survived. This, however, was something else. Grant had said they were unbreakable, but she wasn't so sure. He'd always been there to help her through tough times—but how could he help her through *this*? How could they help each other?

She didn't understand how things had taken such a turn, and after the drama of the past couple of days, she was too emotionally drained to figure out just what in the hell they'd been thinking when they'd exchanged vows—and ended up in bed.

If Dwight had shown up, things would have been very different. She'd be on her honeymoon. She wouldn't be broken inside. But maybe she *was* really better off, since Dwight obviously didn't want to marry her. Maybe he never had.

She got to her feet around six and changed into a pair of shorts and an old green T-shirt and then unpacked her suitcase. The crumpled wedding gown was quickly shoved into a garment bag and hung up at the back of the closet, and the matching shoes received similar treatment. She piled the laundry in the hamper and then headed to the kitchen. She ate a noodle cup standing at the countertop, took some more aspirin for the lingering headache and was back on the sofa by eight o'clock.

Noise from the street below filtered through the open windows, mostly people walking toward JoJo's pizza place down the block. Laughter echoed and she experienced a deep sense of loneliness through to her bones. Lately, it seemed as though loneliness was a frequent companion. Silly, she supposed, when she had her grandfather and Ellie and the rest of the Culhanes in town. And yet, it was that hunger for company that had drawn her toward Dwight, wasn't it? He was nice and friendly and low maintenance as a boyfriend—since he lived in another state and was then stationed overseas. Winona wondered if that's exactly why she had started their relationship in the first place. He'd been physically absent from her life for the most part, which meant she didn't have to invest much of herself.

On reflection, it wasn't a particularly flattering picture.

Her phone rang and she looked at the number. *Grant.*

She picked up on the fifth ring, after several agonizing seconds considering letting it go to messages. "Hello."

"Hey," he said after a second's pause. "How are you?"

"Fine," she replied. "You?"

"Same," he said and then sighed. "I was worried about you."

"Like I said," she remarked, her throat tightening. "I'm fine. And actually just about to make it an early night."

He was silent for a few long seconds. "Winnie," he said, his voice so soft she pressed the phone closer to her ear. "I hate this. We've never had trouble talking, not ever."

"We've never been married before, either," she reminded him. "So, I'm not sure the usual rules apply."

He expelled an exasperated breath. "Can't we just… I don't know…move on from this?"

His ability to compartmentalize their relationship so easily both infuriated and hurt her. "Do you mean before or after the divorce?"

Another sigh. "You're being difficult, you know that, right?"

"I'm being realistic. You're acting as though nothing has changed. As though this doesn't mean anything."

"Of course it means something," he said quickly. "But, Winnie, does it have to mean *everything*? Can't we just get past it and move on?"

Winona sucked in a breath. He didn't get it.

"Good night, Grant," she said impatiently.

"Winnie...don't..."

"I'm not like you, Grant... I can't just switch off my feelings."

"I don't do that," he said, his tone lowering an octave.

"Sure you do," she replied. "That's how you've managed to avoid loving anyone your whole life."

He was silent and she knew she'd hit a nerve. Her own nerves rattled, too. Because talking about Grant loving someone made her insides ache in a way she'd avoided thinking about for years.

"I don't...*not love*...people," he said, and she heard his voice crack a little.

"I don't mean your brothers or your sister or even..." Her words trailed off for a moment and she swallowed hard. "Or even me. I only mean..." She stalled again, desperate to backpedal. "I mean...you know...you've never really had a serious relationship."

"Like yours and the marine?" he asked. "Is that what you mean?"

Heat surged through her. "Actually, I don't know what I mean. I'm tired and I need to get some sleep. I'll talk to you tomorrow."

He sighed. "Sure. Good night, Winnie."

She ended the call and swallowed back a sob. It was

the first time in forever that they'd ended their conversation in such a way. There was no saying *I love ya*. There was no *Ditto*. There was nothing but thick, relentless tension.

Winona turned in around nine o'clock and spent several hours staring at the ceiling. Her bedroom had one window that overlooked the street and she left the curtains open so she could see the colors from the traffic lights below. The changing hues were oddly comforting as she endeavored to drift off to sleep. She woke up at seven and puttered around the apartment doing a few chores and, at eight, dressed in jeans, shirt and light jacket and headed downstairs.

The bakery was busy and she slipped through the rear entrance, waving to the three women behind the counter. The owner, Regina Drake, was clearing tables as she talked to patrons and Winona smiled as she waited in line for service. The other woman had purchased the bakery about two years earlier and they had become quite friendly over that time. Winona even helped out occasionally, when one of the staff called in sick. It was a busy change from her regular job doing admin at the tourist center in town.

She ordered a latte and her favorite bagel to go and was waiting for her order when she saw Grant striding through the entrance. Of course he knew her usual Saturday routine.

"Hey there," he said and shrugged when he reached her. "How'd you sleep?"

"Lousy," she admitted, trying not to look at him. "You?"

"About the same," he replied and quickly ordered a black coffee. "I stared at the ceiling for most of the night and gave up around five-thirty. I went for a run," he said, not quite looking at her. "And then I thought I'd try and meet you here for breakfast."

"I'm getting mine to go," she said, looking as un-enthused as she could.

He gazed at her for a moment, then asked, "Winnie, is every conversation we have from now on going to be a hard one?" He was frowning a little.

"Maybe. Look, I need some time to digest things," she said.

"Well, how about we digest things over breakfast," he suggested.

Winona shot him a skeptical look. "Black coffee isn't breakfast."

"I had a protein shake earlier and that's all I can stomach," he admitted. "I'm still recovering from the champagne and tequila the other night."

She wasn't surprised. He rarely drank and was very health conscious, having been a vegetarian since he was fifteen. She knew he worked out at the gym sev-eral days a week and ran three miles every morning. He traveled a lot for his job, which was mostly seden-tary, but certainly kept himself in shape.

"You should eat something," she found herself say-ing. "Food is good for a hangover."

His brow rose. "Only if you'll stay and keep me company for a while."

Her order arrived and she relented, finding a quiet table in the corner of the bakery. She sat, spooned a little sugar into her latte and waited for him to join her, carrying his coffee and a muffin on a plate. She looked him over as he approached—in dark, low-rise jeans, a gray twill shirt and cowboy boots, he looked sexy and wholly masculine—and her heart skipped a couple of beats. Winona knew she was foolish, but couldn't help herself. Green eyes, dark brown hair, a strong, square jaw—she couldn't help but find him attractive!

He sat down and pulled in the chair, resting his elbows on the table. "I thought we could hang out and talk for a while."

"Great," she said with fake enthusiasm. "What would you like to talk about?"

He chuckled and the sound hit her directly behind the ribs. She really did need to pull herself together. With her resolve galvanized, Winona stared at him, one brow up, waiting for his response.

Which didn't come, because Regina approached their table and laid a hand on his shoulder. Winona pushed back the surge of green-eyed monster and took a breath. As far as she knew, Regina was madly in love with her longtime musician boyfriend and wasn't the sort to covet another woman's husband...even if that husband was a huge secret and an even bigger mistake!

"Hey, you two," Regina said. "Isn't it beautiful out there today? Grant, you seem like a persuasive sort of guy—see if you can finally get Winnie to agree to come into partnership with me, will you?"

It was a long-standing conversation between them—Regina wanted a partner so she could step back a little from the business and spend more time having a personal life. Winona wasn't totally against the idea—in fact, she was sorely tempted. She simply didn't have the funds to cover the investment. Her job at the tourist center just didn't afford her the luxury of saving a large nest egg once her rent and utilities were paid each month, and she wasn't prepared to borrow the money from a bank or any other avenue. Including Grant, who'd offered several times to loan her the money. Truth be told, he'd *give* it to her in a heartbeat if she asked.

"I'll see what I can do," he said and grinned, waiting until Regina headed off before speaking again. "You know, it's not a bad idea. You've been saying for ages how bored you are with your job."

"Which doesn't mean I'm going to jump into a risky business venture," she countered, sipping her latte.

He looked around the busy bakery for a moment. "Looks like a pretty safe investment, though. And I'm sure Regina would be a good business partner. Sometimes you have to take a leap of faith."

She laughed. "That's rich, coming from Mr. Über-cautious-About-Everything."

He scowled. "I'm not like that."

"Ha," she flipped back, "you're as predictable as the sun setting every night."

"No," he countered. "I don't think so."

Winona raised both brows and began counting off her fingers. "One, you go running every morning at 6:15. Not ten past six, or twenty past six, but 6:15 precisely. Two, you own half a dozen pale blue shirts and team them with a darker shade blue tie and wear that to work every day—no exceptions. I know this because I have given you three or four humorous ties over the years and you've never worn them." She counted on another finger. "Three, you stir your coffee five times counterclockwise. Four, you've used the same cologne for the last decade. Shall I go on?"

"What, because I like blue shirts and can stick to my schedule and wake up in time to go running every morning, that makes me predictable?"

"Yep," she replied, enjoying his scowl. "You wouldn't take a risk if your life depended on it."

It came out sounding like an insult, as though she was making some huge character judgment and found him lacking. Which, of course, was ridiculous. She loved the fact he was predictable and calm and rock solid. It's why she had gravitated toward him when they were kids. He knew who he was, what he wanted, where he was going. At sixteen he'd begun planning his future career, at eighteen he'd gone to college and at twenty-one got his first job in program design. Now, he flew across the west coast for his work. He was well regarded in his field, highly sought after and very good at what he did. Whereas, most days, Winona felt like a complete failure in the career department.

"Sorry. I didn't mean to come off like that. You know what I mean," she said and sighed. "You've always known who you are and what you wanted. Not like me," she added and made a face.

"You just haven't figured out what you want to do for a career," he said quietly. "That's not a crime. It takes time to figure out what makes you happy."

She knew he was right, and she also knew she needed to make some changes. She'd studied history in college before switching to an undeclared major after a couple of semesters, knowing the subject wasn't for her. After her grandfather had his last stroke, he was diagnosed with Parkinson's disease, and Winona decided to take time off from school to make him a priority. At first she'd moved back into their cabin, but eventually she felt he was strong enough for her to find a place of her own in town. He'd supported her moving from the Triple C Ranch, knowing she needed her own life independent of the Culhanes, but he was happy to stay on the ranch and live out his days there. She helped out on the ranch when she could, during mustering and branding seasons, and often assisted Mitch with the horse breaking and training. Her job at the tourist center was simply a way of paying her bills—certainly not her dream job.

"When I said you were predictable and wouldn't know how to take a risk, I didn't mean it to sound like I was criticizing you," she said and took a sharp breath.

"I'm pretty sure no one would have predicted that we'd get married," he said quietly, his voice so low she inched forward in her seat to hear him.

But suddenly she didn't want to talk anymore; she didn't want to talk about their nuptials or impending divorce. And she didn't want to think about the other thing, which was raging like a giant red flag between them.

Sex...

They'd crossed a line. There was no going back.

Grant had spent the last twenty-four hours in a kind of daze. He knew he and Winnie needed to talk, but she wasn't making it easy. He also knew she was upset, hurt and probably embarrassed by what had transpired over the past couple of days. He'd experienced most of those feelings himself in one form or another.

The thing was, he didn't know how to talk to her when she was in such a bad mood.

He also didn't want to keep thinking about her in the way he was.

Because now that his memory was clear, he remembered the sensational sex they'd had. He remembered how she'd responded to his touch and the memories

were acute, distracting him from the issue at hand—
namely, their impromptu wedding and the quick need
for a divorce. He'd do as he promised—arrange for
them to see a lawyer on Monday and try and get the
whole thing straightened out as soon as possible. In
the meantime, though, he wanted to make sure Winona was okay about what had happened between them.
Especially before he had to take off again for work. He
was flying to San Francisco on Wednesday.

"Are you staying in town for the weekend?" she
asked.

"I was thinking I would. Mitch is always nagging
me to come home more often. I'm sure there'll be the
usual family gathering at the ranch this weekend."

She shrugged. "I planned on seeing my grandfather
this morning, but I'm not sure I want to face a crowd.
He might want to talk about Dwight and I don't think
I'm up for it."

"You'll have to tell your grandfather that the marine is out of the picture at some point," he remarked.
"Better sooner than later."

She sighed heavily. "I suppose so."

"You don't have to say anything else," Grant said
quietly. "Just that you guys broke up."

"I guess I don't," she said on a sigh. "No one needs
to know I was dumped at the altar, right?"

"No, they don't," he replied, feeling the twitch in
his gut sharpen because she looked so unhappy and he
knew he was part of the reason for her mood. Sure, the
marine had a lot to answer for, and in the cold light of
day Grant was sorely tempted to contact the other man
and have it out with him for being such a jerk. "You'll
get through this. You're stronger than you think," he

assured her. "We're not the first people to make a mistake, Winnie, and we won't be the last. We just have to get through it. And we can."

"Can we?" she queried, her eyes huge, the irises turning a deep chocolate brown.

He reached across the table and grasped her hand. Something he'd done countless times before. She resisted, not quite pulling away, but looking like his touch was the last thing she wanted. The twitch in his gut increased and he gently closed his fingers around hers. "Sure we can."

"I don't have your confidence," she said quietly, moving her hand away and tucking it in her lap. "The thing is, any other time, any other situation, you'd be the person I wanted to talk to if I was feeling like this."

"Then talk to me," he insisted.

"I can't," she said and pushed back the chair, her eyes glittering. "I'm so appalled and embarrassed and…disappointed. In Dwight and in myself and in…"

Her words trailed off, but he got her meaning. "In me, you mean? Believe me, Winnie, if I could undo the last couple of days, I would."

The glittering in her eyes turned into tears and he fought the battle he had going on in his head—the one that instinctively made him long to soothe her, to be the balm for her pain and hurt. It's what he'd always done. What *they'd* always done for one another. Until now.

"You can't," she said dully. "This one isn't an easy fix, Grant. This one includes lawyers and divorce, and the very idea of that makes me sick to my stomach. Instead of marrying the man who proposed to me, I find myself married to a man who's acting as though this situation is just a blip on the radar, something we can pretend never happened. Well, it's more than that to me. Because it *did* happen. It happened to *us*, Grant," she implored, tears on her cheeks. "And I know you think we can get past this, but I don't share your confidence."

She walked away, leaving her untouched breakfast on the table. Grant watched as she slipped behind the counter and headed upstairs. He considered following her and then abandoned the idea. He left the café and walked to his car, which was parked outside. He drove slowly down Main Street and headed for the highway.

The trip to the ranch took about twenty minutes and as he drove through the gates he relaxed a little. It was home. Regardless of where he lived, the ranch and everything on it reminded him of who he was and where he came from. Culhanes had lived on the Triple C for generations and the ranch was in good hands under Mitch's guidance. His oldest brother was honest and hardworking, a man who'd put his own life on hold at eighteen so he could take guardianship of his five younger siblings. Without Mitch, they would have been forced to leave the ranch and been farmed out through social services. But Mitch would never have allowed that. Even now, nearly twenty years later, his brother was the glue that held the family together.

He spotted his brother coming out of the house the moment he pulled up. The quintessential cowboy, Mitch's familiar swagger made him smile. Grant liked horses well enough and helped around the ranch when he could, but the life wasn't ingrained in his DNA like it was with Mitch.

His brother greeted him with a bear hug. "It's good to see you. Tess and I were just talking about you last night."

"You were?" Grant queried. Tess was Mitch's wife. They'd been married once before, got divorced, then reconnected again a couple of years ago. Now they had a son, Charlie, and were happily remarried and thoroughly in love. It was a complicated story, but Grant was pleased they had managed to work through their troubles.

"We were hoping you'd come for a visit this weekend," Mitch said as Grant grabbed his bag from the trunk. "Joss and the girls will be here soon. Sissy is having trouble with an assignment for her computer science class and Ellie was going to give her a hand with it. But now you're here," Mitch said and grinned, "all the better."

Grant had always been the geek in the family. "Sure, no problem."

They entered the house and Grant was filled with a heavy sense of melancholy. It always hit him, every time he came home. Memories, both good and bad, bombarded his thoughts, no doubt amplified by Billie-Jack's recent message—a complication he didn't have the head space to think about, not when he had so much going on with Winnie.

Tess greeted them in the hallway and gave him an affectionate hug, pulling him from his thoughts.

"Where's my nephew?" he asked and returned the embrace.

"Napping," she replied and exhaled. "Poor little guy has his last couple of teeth coming through, so we've had a few sleepless nights." Tess eyed him curiously. "Everything okay with you?"

"Sure," he lied. Tess was an intuitive woman and he suspected that if he didn't pull himself together she'd figure out something was wrong pretty quickly. "Great. Is Ellie around?"

"I think she's in the office at the stables doing a stock feed order," Tess replied. "I was just about to make coffee and put out some of Mrs. B's famous banana-and-walnut loaf."

He grinned. Mrs. Bailey had been the housekeeper on the Triple C for about seventeen years and was considered part of the family, and Grant loved her cooking. She lived in one of four cottages behind the main house. Ellie lived in the largest; Wes, the ranch foreman, lived in another, and Red Sheehan lived in one, while the last was left for guests. Grant had moved from the ranch for college and had never permanently returned, but he liked knowing there was a room upstairs that was his any time he wanted it. His childhood room was now the nursery and he passed it once he headed upstairs. He dumped his bag on the end of the bed in the guest room and walked back downstairs, stopping in the stairway to glance over the family photographs.

Generations of Culhanes stared back at him. His grandparents, Aurora and Henry, and his mom, Louise, who looked so pretty in a blue dress and heels. There was even an old snapshot of Billie-Jack with his arm looped around his mom's waist. Happy times. Back then Grant had worshipped his father. But then Grant's mother had died and Billie-Jack went off the rails. He couldn't handle the loss of his wife, and instead of helping his children cope with their sorrows, he drowned his own in a bottle. Worse—he became an abusive drunk. Jake got the brunt of it, since he would antagonize Billie-Jack so the old man would leave the rest of them alone.

Then, when Grant was twelve, a drunken Billie-Jack drove his truck down an embankment. Grant had been in the back seat, and Hank, two years older, had been in the front beside their father. He remembered Jake tailing them on his motorbike, and how his older brother had pulled Grant out of the truck just before it caught fire. Billie-Jack, not wearing a seat belt, had been flung clear of the burning wreck. But Hank wasn't so lucky and had suffered burns to over twenty percent of his body. Over the next few years, Hank spent most of his time in the burn unit in the Rapid City hospital, enduring countless surgeries and skin grafts.

By then Billie-Jack had bailed. He left them all with Mitch and handed over custody without a fight.

At the time, they'd been stunned—by the painful loss of their mother, and now by the desertion of their father. Looking back, though, Grant realized his leaving was probably the best thing for everyone. Billie-Jack had messed up and didn't deserve the family he'd abandoned. But still, Grant often wondered what life would have been like if his father had resisted his demons and accepted his responsibility to his family.

Maybe they'd all be screwed up. As it was, they'd all turned out okay. Mitch had looked after them. Made sure they all went to school, and that they all stayed together. Now he ran the Triple C and had a family of his own. Jake, who'd gone into the military after high school, had reconciled with his high school sweetheart a year or so back after discovering he had a seven-year-old son. Hank was chief of police in Cedar River. In an eerie echo of his father's experience, Joss was a single dad raising his girls after losing his young wife to cancer. Except that

Joss was a wonderful dad. And Ellie still lived on the ranch, helping with the horse-breeding program.

In hindsight, they were lucky Billie-Jack left and Mitch took over. Grant was very grateful his brother sought full custody and then stepped up to raise them. He thought about Billie-Jack and the two calls he'd ignored from the old man in the last few weeks. He thought about what his brother would say—about what *all* his siblings would say—and then decided to keep the information to himself for a while longer. They didn't need to know just yet.

Grant lingered on the stairs for a few more moments before heading downstairs. He walked into the kitchen and chatted to Tess and Mrs. B for a few minutes, then headed through the mudroom and outside. It was a warm and sunny day, and after all the hours he spent at a desk, being outdoors always reenergized him. He considered taking one of the horses out for ride and was halfway into making the decision when his sister, Ellie, emerged from the stables and strode across the yard. As a child she'd been sassy and adorable; now, she was five feet four inches of spirited, redheaded beauty, yet he still loved calling her Brat.

"Where've you been hiding these last couple of days?" she said as she hugged him. "I've left three messages on your cell since Thursday."

He'd gotten the messages, but had been too caught up in other things—namely Winnie. "Sorry—I've been busy."

She frowned. "I need some help with this new DNA mapping system we've started using and Alvarez is breathing down my neck to get all the information input before the end of the month."

Ramon Alvarez was an ex–reigning champion and horse trainer from Arizona who Mitch had gone into partnership with several years ago. Grant suspected Ellie didn't dislike the other man as much as she protested, and happily dissed her about him whenever the chance arose.

"Boyfriend trouble?" he teased.

She made a face. "Spare me. You know very well the only thing I like about him are his horses, that's all."

"I dunno, Brat," he teased again. "You know the old saying about protesting too much?"

Ellie smiled extra sweetly. "Have you seen Win?" she asked and linked her arm through his.

"This morning," he replied, his gut tightening. "Why?"

"She's also been off-grid for the past few days," Ellie replied. "Which isn't like her."

He shrugged vaguely, ignoring the damning *also* in his sister's words. "Maybe she's working."

"Nope," Ellie said. "I checked at the tourist center. And she's not answering my calls, either. How was she when you saw her?"

"The usual," he said and quickly changed the subject. "I thought I'd take one of the horses out while I'm here."

"Take Bianco," she said and grinned. "He hasn't been ridden for a month."

Bianco was a big, bad-tempered overo gelding that bucked everyone off. Him included. Grant had no idea why Mitch didn't sell the animal. "No one can ride that thing."

"Alvarez can," she admitted and scowled again. "The man certainly knows how to ride a horse, I'll give him that."

Grant laughed and felt some of the tension leave his

system. The ranch and Ellie were always good medi-
cine. As they walked across the yard, a car appeared
coming up the driveway. The classic, bright orange
VW was unmistakable.

Winnie...

His insides constricted instantly. He wasn't used
to feeling tense around her. It didn't sit right. The car
pulled up beside his and she got out, her glorious black
hair flowing around her shoulders, her hips swaying as
she walked, and the uncharacteristic twitch in his gut
amplified, turning into something else...something he
didn't want to acknowledge, something that had been
tormenting him for days.

Awareness...

Attraction...

Sex...

He swallowed hard, pushing back the feeling. He'd
not experienced it before. Or at least, he hadn't allowed
the thoughts to enter his head. But their relationship
had changed, and Grant forced himself to admit one
undisputable fact. Without knowing how, without even
knowing what it meant, the truth was suddenly and
glaringly obvious to him.

He was, without a doubt, hot for his wife. And that
could mean only one thing.

Trouble.

CHAPTER FOUR

OF COURSE WINONA knew Grant would be at the ranch. It was his home, after all. But she'd promised her grandfather a visit and she would never intentionally let Red down. So, she gathered up her courage and walked across the yard and toward the corral.

There were a few cars parked out front of the main house and she recognized Joss's SUV. She waved a hand in Ellie's direction and barely spared him a glance. She was still mad at him for being such a jerk about the whole marriage situation. She didn't want him to be so in control—she wanted him to fall apart at the seams like she was. At least then she'd know he was *as* affected by what had transpired between them.

And she was annoyed that he looked so good, too. Why the hell couldn't he be a troll? She wished he didn't have a gaze so blisteringly intense she could barely meet his eyes. She wished they hadn't ruined everything by having sex. Even the marriage thing didn't seem so bad compared to the sex thing. Because having sex with Grant had definitely ruined everything.

"Hey," he said as she approached, and Winona managed a tight smile in his direction.

"Hi," she replied and stood beside Ellie, who was now hooking her arm around her elbow.

"Where've you been for the past couple of days?" Ellie asked.

Winona shrugged. "Just busy with work. Feel like going to Rusty's tonight? There's a good band playing."

Rusty's was a tavern in town—a little less formal than the O'Sullivan Hotel and not quite as family friendly as the Loose Moose. It was where the younger crowd hung out and a good place to have a couple of drinks and dance and unwind.

"Sounds like a great idea," Ellie said and looked toward her brother. "You in?"

His brows came up. "Am I invited?"

Ellie laughed and Winona ignored the dread settling in her belly. "Since you two are usually joined at the hip when you come home," Ellie said and jerked a thumb in both their directions. "I can't see why not."

Of course, her friend couldn't have known that her words would imply an intimacy that hadn't been there up until days ago, and when heat crawled up her neck at the idea of being joined to any part of Grant, Ellie gave her an odd look.

"Something wrong, Win?"

"Not a thing," Winona replied and shrugged. "I'm going to hang out with Papa for a while—catch you later," she said and untangled her arm, not looking at Grant as she walked off toward the cottages behind the main house.

Her grandfather's home wasn't the biggest of the four cottages, but he was incredibly house proud and had planted an amazing garden around the perimeter. She smiled when she saw he'd repainted the wishing well and the ornamental fairies placed around it. Situated beside a flowering arbor, it had always been one of her favorite spots to think and unwind when she was a child. She needed that thinking space more than ever at the moment. She was one step away from the porch when her grandfather opened the front door and greeted her, shuffling outside with the help of his walking stick, managing a lopsided grin.

"Hey, there's my favorite girl."

"Hi, Papa," she said and rushed up the steps to give him a hearty hug. He'd lost weight, she noticed, and frowned a little. "Have you been skipping dinner again?"

He tutted. "Now, don't be fussing around me. I eat plenty. Mrs. B brings me a plate every evening and I've got plenty of treats in the freezer for snacks. I haven't heard from you for a few days," he said, slurring his words a bit, a sign that he probably hadn't been resting enough. "Everything okay?"

I got dumped by my fiancé, then married my best friend on a drunken rebound and slept with him!

"Everything's fine," she fibbed. "I thought we could do some gardening today," she suggested. "Last week you said you wanted some help planting in the vegetable patch."

"Nah," he said and grinned. "Ellie helped me out during the week."

Guilt pressed down on her shoulders. She'd been so busy screwing up her life in the past few days she'd neglected the one person who truly loved her. "Sorry."

"No need to be sorry," he said and waved a hand as they headed inside. "I know you're busy."

Her grandfather's cottage was neat and Winona felt

immediately at ease the moment she crossed the threshold. They hung out for a while, chatting about Red's garden and the deck planking he'd planned on getting down now it was spring. She moved to the kitchen to get them both a drink and he asked about her job, and then, inevitably, about Dwight.

"Ah—well, actually," she said and poured lemonade, "Dwight and I broke up."

Her grandfather went silent for a moment, then regarded her with his usual kind expression. "Well, can't say I'm surprised. I mean, you haven't seen each other for a while."

Winona swallowed the burn in her throat. As mad as she was with Dwight, and no matter how much his no-show at their wedding still hurt, she also felt a portion of relief. "I guess we both wanted different things," she said and shrugged. "It wasn't to be."

"Then I'm glad you broke it off," he said and sighed.

I didn't. He dumped me. Left me. Abandoned me.

"So," Winona said and quickly changed the subject, "what can I do to help around the place while I'm here?"

He made a few suggestions and they got busy cleaning and polishing the pieces inside the trophy cabinet. Most of them were from Red's early years as a bronc rider, but there was one shelf that stored Winona's scholastic accolades. Looking at the trophies, it seemed like such a long time ago—when she'd been filled with dreams of a real career. She'd always struggled with math, but once Grant took her under his wing and began tutoring her, she discovered a knack for numbers and imagined she'd have a career in the business sector. She didn't really know why she'd cho-

sen to study history over business when she finally got
to college. And she knew it was simply excuses that
kept her from finishing her studies. She'd had the same
conversation with Grant many times over the years.
Of course, he was always her staunchest supporter,
but he didn't hold back his opinion, either. Like questioning her resistance to going into partnership with
Regina at the bakery. It made sense. She could stay in
Cedar River and be close to her grandfather, work with
someone she liked and respected and sink her ambi-
tion into a thriving business. Yeah…it made complete
sense to go for it.

But…

What if it didn't work out? What if the business
failed and she lost everything she'd invested? Thinking
about it made all her insecurities rush to the surface.
Because logically, Winona knew it was fear holding
her back.

Once they were done with the trophy cabinet it was
lunchtime. She made sandwiches and poured apple
cider and after they ate her grandfather went off for
his daily nap. Winona hung around the cabin for ten
minutes before finishing her drink and then heading
outside. The sounds of the ranch were comforting and
she made her way down the steps and walked around
the house, and then toward the orchard.

She'd been sitting in a spot near the apple trees when
she heard Grant approach and say her name. Winona
turned and sighed, knowing her solitude was over.

He sat down beside her, stretched out his long legs
and crossed his arms. The aftershave he wore was as
familiar to her as any scent on the ranch and she inhaled sharply, quickly evoking memories she knew she

needed to forget. Skin, sweat, sighs, kisses that made her spin. *I shouldn't be remembering this.* But she did. So acutely it filled her with a kind of nervous energy.

"You know," he said, looking straight ahead, "you can't ignore me forever."

"I'm not ignoring you," she denied. "I'm spending time with my grandfather. At least, I was, but he's napping now. Did you want something?"

"Just to talk," he said easily. "Like we've *always* managed to do without complication for the last eighteen years."

The reminder made her throat ache. "Times change. Things change."

He uncrossed his arms and reached for her hand, holding it firmly within his own. "Winnie, we don't have to let this situation change anything."

She snorted. "Is that what we are? A *situation*?" she said and pulled her hand from his.

He let out a long sigh, clearly ignoring her question. "So... have you heard from the marine?"

Winona blinked. "No. And I don't expect to. He dumped me at the altar, remember?"

"I remember. Lucky escape, then?"

She laughed humorlessly. "Yeah...because things are so much better for me now."

"I'd never abandon you, Winnie, whatever the circumstances."

His words cut her through to the core. Of course she knew that. Grant would never make a promise and then not see it through because he possessed an innate integrity that defined him. Even with the women he dated, he was always honest about his intentions. Or rather, his *lack* of intentions.

"This must feel weird for you," she said and shrugged. "I mean, you've made it clear you never wanted to get married. I mean, not that we're really married…"

"Oh, we're *really* married," he corrected. "We've got the license to prove it. And everything else," he added and glanced her way.

Winona's skin heated as the memory returned. "Well, it wasn't that big a deal," she lied, recalling every blistering moment. "I think that's best forgotten, don't you?"

"I've never been good at pretending," he remarked and got to his feet. "And neither are you," he added and held out his hand. "Come on, Winnie, let's not worry about it for today and try and enjoy ourselves."

She hesitated, looking at his hand, thinking it was an olive branch of sorts, his way of keeping them connected and *normal*. But her fear was that they would never be normal again. Still, she took his hand, felt the warmth of his fingers linking with hers and a familiar sense of connection that, despite everything, forced her to admit that she needed him in her life. *Wanted* him in her life. Even when it seemed impossible. Or when she hurt deep down to her bones.

"So, you're going to see the lawyer on Monday?" she asked as they headed for the main house.

He nodded and gently swung their arms in a companionable way—much like they had done when they were kids. "That was the plan. Do you want to come?"

"I'm working Monday. But I have a break at one o'clock so I could meet you there if you can get an appointment for that time."

"Okay."

"It shouldn't be too complicated, should it?"

He shrugged a little as they headed for the back door and walked through the mudroom. "I don't think so. It's a no-contest divorce, so it should be simple enough."

The news should have cheered her up; instead, all she experienced was a deep-rooted wave of disappointment and unhappiness. Instead of being on a honeymoon, of sharing days and nights with her husband, of intimacy and soft whispers, of strong arms holding her, she was talking about divorce.

She pulled her hand from his as they entered the kitchen and were greeted by the sugary scent of baking and Mrs. Bailey's broad grin. The kitchen at the Triple C was the hub of the house, with its Shaker-style cabinets and long countertop, and she'd spent much of her childhood listening and learning recipes from the older woman.

"I wondered if I'd see you today," Mrs. B said and smiled, gesturing to a baking tray she was taking out of the oven. "I played around with that cookie recipe this week, you know, the one with the ginger pieces. I think they turned out much better with the secret ingredient."

Grant, who was very open about his cookie fetish, looked at them both. "What secret ingredient?"

Mrs. B chuckled. "Well, it wouldn't be a secret if we told you."

"Are you holding out on me, Mrs. B?" he teased and held a hand to his heart. "You know I'm addicted to your cooking."

She laughed again. "Enough with the charm. I remember the day you told me you were a vegetarian. I don't think your brothers believed you. You were, what, fourteen?"

"Fifteen," he replied. "So, about these cookies…"

Mrs. B continued to chuckle and placed the baking tray on the other side of the countertop, and away from Grant's swift hands. "I promised Joss he could have this batch."

Grant looked suitably affronted. "And here I was thinking I was your favorite?"

"Of course you are," the older woman replied and quickly passed him a cookie. "Now, off you go, the pair of you."

He devoured the cookie in two bites and then Winona ushered them from the kitchen. It felt nice to laugh, she thought as they headed up the hallway and toward the living room. Joss's daughters, almost thirteen-year-old Sissy and ten-year-old Clare, were sitting on the sofa, an electronic tablet in hand and earbuds in their ears. Joss had lost his wife eight years earlier and had raised his girls as a single dad ever since. They had always treated Winona as an honorary and much-loved aunt, and she relished the role. Joss and Mitch were also in the room, and Winona made her way toward the girls while Grant hung out with his brothers. She loved spending time with the girls and they were quick to show her their latest downloaded movies on their tablets. She'd been their babysitter countless times over the years and always helped out Joss when she could. Family was like that, she thought, and now more than ever she felt as though she needed them. Perhaps she could reach out to Ellie, or Mitch's wife, Tess. She was sure either woman would understand her predicament and offer consolation and sensible advice.

And yet…she didn't want to overstep. She didn't want to assume anything.

They were Grant's family. Not hers. She had her grandfather. And since she wasn't about to burden Red with her troubles, Winona knew one thing.

She was alone.

Grant watched Winnie and couldn't ignore the heat churning in his belly. Things were so tense between them and he didn't know how to fix it. Strange for him, because fixing things was what he did. Well, in his work at least. He'd always figured he was missing the gene that his brothers had—the one where they made getting close to people look seamless. At least, that's how nearly all of his siblings made it look. Well, all of them except for Jake. But even his second oldest brother had embraced family, fatherhood and responsibility since returning to town nearly two years ago. Sure, Grant loved his siblings, but deep down he believed that losing his parents when he was young had switched off something inside him. He wasn't sure how to define it, how to explain the sense of disconnect he experienced whenever Mitch, Jake or Joss talked about being married, or being a father.

It made him think about Billie-Jack and for a moment he was tempted to spill to his brothers that the old man had reached out. In his heart, he knew exactly how his siblings would react. *If* he decided to meet with his father, Grant knew he had to do it alone—at least at first.

He caught Winnie's gaze, and when she raised a brow he realized he was frowning. Of course, she knew his moods better than anyone. But it went both ways. She was unhappy and Grant knew he was partly responsible for the way she was feeling. He left his brothers and walked across the room to where she sat with his nieces and plonked in the chair opposite.

"What?" she demanded sharply.

"Nothing," he replied and stretched out his legs. "Just hanging out with my favorite girls."

Sissy and Clare chuckled and quickly bombarded him with computer questions, perching on either side of the chair. They stayed like that for a while, until his brothers left the room in search of snacks, with Joss quickly calling his daughters to the kitchen as they left.

Grant rested his elbows on the chair arms and looked at Winnie. "So, I was thinking about what Regina said this morning."

Her gaze narrowed. "You were?"

He nodded. "Well, yeah—I was thinking that if you're interested in taking on the bakery and you need funds, I could—"

"What? Be my financial backer?"

"Why not?" he said, shifting in the chair. "Wouldn't you do it for me if the situation was reversed?"

She sat farther back. "Well...yeah...but this isn't the same—"

"Of course it's the same," he said, cutting her off. "And for the record, we've been having this same conversation for the past twelve months. But if you're so hell-bent on doing things by yourself, we could make it official and draw it up like a proper loan with interest and a payment plan. Don't let your pride stand in the way of getting what you want."

"No."

Grant sighed. "I don't understand you, Winnie."

"Understand what?" she shot back and sprang forward in the seat. "That I want to make my way in the world on my own terms, without taking handouts from friends or family? You did it—why is it so hard to comprehend that I want to do the same?"

"If you remember, Mitch paid for my college tuition," he reminded her.

"That was different," she said and exhaled heavily. "The Triple C is as much your legacy as your siblings' and Mitch is your brother."

"And you're my best friend," he said flatly. "Plus, I might add, my wife."

She shushed him quickly, looking around to make sure no one else heard his words. "Technically, not literally."

Grant smiled a little. "You don't think? So, how long do two people have to know one another and how much sex do they have to have before they are *literally* married?"

He saw color rise up her neck. "Can you *not* joke? This isn't funny."

His smile increased. "I'm just trying to lighten the mood, Winnie. But I'm right, though, about the bakery. Unless you want to work at the tourist center forever?"

"Of course I don't, but it's a job. Besides, since when have you been such a job snob?"

"I'm not," he replied. "If working at the tourist center satisfied you and it was the job of your dreams, I'd support you one hundred percent. But I've seen you baking here with Mrs. B and I know how happy it makes you. Plus, you're much more savvy when it comes to numbers and retail than you realize." He sighed. "Look, just promise me you'll at least think about it."

She stopped scowling and tossed her hair in a way

that struck him as sexy. Had she always done that? He'd never noticed before. But something about the action hitched up his awareness a notch or two.

"Okay, I'll think about it," she said and then excused herself, leaving the room quickly, the scent of her fragrance lingering in the air.

Once he was alone, Grant tried to compartmentalize his feelings. True, he'd always known Winnie was beautiful. But something had changed, like there had been a cosmic shift in his thinking. There was something in the way she spoke, the way she moved, that brought other feelings to the surface. Like a slowly building desire that amplified every time he looked at her. There was memory, too—of holding her and touching her and having her in his arms. It was a shock, thinking about her in any other way than as his best friend. He figured he should feel as guilty as hell, but oddly he didn't.

It will pass...

He said the words to himself a couple of times, trying to clear his head, to forget the memory and get on with the present. He had a job in San Francisco coming up, for a large hotel that had recently switched management software and were having all kinds of tech problems. Grant had worked on a couple of hotels in the past and expected to be gone for at least a week. Maybe the time away would be good for his relationship with Winnie. She'd have a chance to think about his offer to help her invest in the bakery and get accustomed to their impending divorce.

Thinking he had it all figured out, Grant got to his feet and joined his brothers and nieces in the kitchen. Winnie wasn't there and he figured she'd returned to her grandfather's cabin. Ellie was sitting at the counter beside Tess, and Mitch was also there, holding his young son, Charlie. He tapped his oldest brother's shoulder affectionately. The truth was, even though there was little more than six years between them, Mitch was more like a father than their own had ever been. He both loved and respected his brother and owed him a debt of gratitude for keeping him on the straight and narrow during his school years. It had been hard at first, and Grant had rebelled, skipping classes, missing assignments—but by the time he hit sophomore year, Grant pulled himself together and took his studies seriously, making plans for a future career in software engineering. Now he got paid a lot of money to do something he loved, and he knew Mitch had played a huge part in his success.

He watched his family interact and again thought about Billie-Jack's sudden resurfacing. Mitch, he knew, would calmly warn him away from making the connection. Jake would probably tell him to say go straight to hell. And Hank—who had more reason to hate Billie-Jack than any of them—would advise him to do what he felt was right. He figured he should start with Joss, who always said what was on his mind, and could always be relied upon for a dose of honesty.

Grant hung around the house for the remainder of the afternoon and it was past six o'clock when Ellie reminded him that they were heading to Rusty's. Joss had dropped his girls off at his in-laws' that afternoon and said he'd meet them there. He knew Winnie had left the ranch around four and figured she was also hooking up with them at Rusty's. Or maybe not. Perhaps hanging out with him was the last thing she wanted to do?

He and Ellie headed into town and pulled up outside Rusty's around seven that evening. There were a
few cars out front and he recognized Joss's tow truck
in the parking area. He pulled up beside the truck and
Ellie was quick to get out. Grant glanced around for
Winona's car and when he realized it wasn't there his
gut dropped.

"Did you say something?" Ellie asked when she
came around his car.

Grant shook his head. "No."

They headed inside and Ellie waved to Joss the
moment they spotted his brother by the bar ordering
drinks and chatting up the pretty bartender. Grant was
following Ellie toward one of the booth seats when he
spotted a woman in jeans, boots and a bright colored
halter top, with long dark hair. She was standing by the
small stage, laughing and talking to one of the band
members. Winnie. She looked incredible. For a moment he felt as though his heart had stopped beating.
It didn't make sense. He'd seen her dressed up countless times. Sex had messed up his brain—there was
no other explanation. The band began playing and she
quickly joined them at the booth, sliding across the
seat opposite him.

"I didn't see your car outside," Grant remarked.

She shrugged lightly. "I came with Regina. Her boyfriend is the drummer."

Grant vaguely remembered and his gut relaxed a
little when he realized that was why she looked to be
so friendly with the band.

"The bass player is cute," Ellie said and grinned as
Joss joined them with a round of drinks.

She shrugged again. "He's okay."

"Does your boyfriend know you have a thing for bass players, Win?" Joss teased and sat down beside her.

"Dwight and I broke up," Winnie said flatly, not looking at anyone.

"What?" Ellie squealed. "When did this happen?"

"A couple of days ago," she replied and briefly met Grant's gaze.

Ellie grabbed a drink. "What happened?"

Winnie shrugged. "Oh, you know, long-distance relationships never work out."

"That's true," Joss said agreeably and winked. "So, the bass player?"

"I don't think so," she replied. "I'm not in the market for a rebound relationship just yet."

Ouch.

Grant felt the sting of her words and shifted in his seat. He drank some beer and listened to his sister prattle out more questions as the band changed songs, doing a slow cover of a Creedence classic.

"So, who broke up with who?" Ellie asked. "Is he seeing someone else? Do you think he was cheating on you and that's why he—"

"Winnie," Grant said when he saw her pinched expression. "You love this song—let's dance."

She looked startled for a second and then quickly agreed, shimmying out of the booth and heading for the dance floor. Grant met her in the middle of several other couples and grasped her hand. They'd danced before—at weddings, at Rusty's, even in her small apartment above the bakery when she tried to teach him how to rumba. But he experienced an odd sensation rippling through his limbs as they moved closer together. Her fingers curled around his shoulders and he rested his hands around her waist, settling on her hips.

"Thanks," she said, speaking closely into his ear. "I wasn't in the mood for an inquisition."

"I figured," he said, ignoring the way his knee brushed between her thighs. "I know Ellie can be relentless when she wants intel."

She relaxed a little. "People will be curious, I guess."

"How did Red take the news about the marine?"

"Oh, you know Papa—he was cool about it. Probably relieved, although he would never say so."

"Well, he undoubtedly thinks no one is good enough for his little girl," Grant said and grinned. "Maybe he's right."

"Oh, I don't know," she said and swayed. "He's a fan of yours, so would probably welcome our, you know, *situation* with open arms."

Grant heard the tremor in her voice and felt every ounce of the obviously mixed emotions in her heart. It pained him. He never wanted to see Winnie hurting.

"We'll work it out," he assured her. "I promise."

She nodded, resting her head against his shoulder. "I hope so."

It felt good to have her so close. Like they were still as connected—as tightly bound together in friendship—as always. And he liked the way she felt in his arms. Her perfume, some floral scent he would recognize blindfolded, swirled around them and the familiarity of it strangely settled his frayed nerves.

"We'll see the lawyer Monday and by the time I get back from San Francisco it will be well on the way to being finalized."

"Oh, that's right, you're leaving soon," she said and sighed.

"Wednesday," he confirmed. "But I'll call you while I'm away. As usual."

But he knew she wasn't convinced. There was nothing *usual* about what was hanging between them.

And they both knew it.

CHAPTER FIVE

THEY HAD AN appointment to see the lawyer at 1:15 p.m. on Monday afternoon and Winona greeted Grant outside Tyler Madden's office right on time. She'd met Tyler a few times and had always found him to be polite and professional. He didn't offer any opinion about their situation other than give them quick and concise advice on the steps they were required to take towards dissolving their marriage.

She sat quietly beside Grant, noticing how tight his shoulders were as they listened to the lawyer and when Tyler asked the obvious question.

"And you're sure this is what you both want?"

"Absolutely," Grant replied.

Winona's insides contracted at the swiftness of his reply and then she got mad at herself for being so ridiculous. Of course, divorce was what they both wanted. There was no other option.

"Yes," she said. "Of course."

When the meeting was over, she felt oddly drained, like she needed to sleep, or at least to shut her eyes for a while and not think about the chaos that had suddenly become her life.

Once they were finished at Tyler's office, she quickly said she had somewhere else to be.

"Do you feel like getting coffee?" he asked. "Or maybe—"

"No, sorry, I gotta go."

"Sure," he said, clearly aware of her need to rush away. "Ah...so I'll call you while I'm out of town," he reminded her.

Winona *did* want to get away—from him, from *them*, from the ache that had suddenly lodged in her chest. "Yeah...whatever."

Then she bailed, hightailing it along the sidewalk as fast as she could without looking like she was running. And knowing that he'd remained where he was, watching her as she disappeared from view.

But true to his word, Grant called her while he was in San Francisco. Not every night, but enough to maintain a connection. That didn't mean Winona actually looked forward to his calls. Because it wasn't like before.

Before Vegas.

Before her world had turned upside down.

He was annoyingly upbeat about everything when he spoke, and Winona tried to be the same. She tried ignoring the word *divorce* and didn't think about the time they were together, dancing at Rusty's, pretending as though everything was normal between them. Instead, she pretended that he was on any other work trip and it was any other moment in time. But it wasn't. Because the tension between them was undeniable.

In the meantime, as the week ended and another week dragged along, Winona had decided she needed to make some serious life changes. A new career—or a career, full stop—was definitely a priority. Making a decision about the bakery. Talking to the bank and her accountant. Perhaps even getting a bigger apartment or even a house once she was more financially settled. And yeah, maybe a dog or a cat. Finding some new friends.

Yes, she needed to make plans and see them through.

And would have done exactly that if not for one tiny wrench in her works.

One huge wrench actually.

Her period was late.

Four days late. And she was *never* late.

Which was why she was sitting on the edge of the bathtub in her bathroom, staring at the pregnancy test she'd taken thirty seconds earlier. Waiting. The longest five-minute wait of her life.

By the second minute, she'd convinced herself that her late period was simply a reaction to stress and she had nothing to worry about. By the third minute, she began to worry. By the fourth minute, she was on the verge of a panic attack. When her phone's alarm pinged at the five-minute mark, Winona snatched up the test and stared at the results.

Two lines.

Positive.

Pregnant.

Oh, my God!

She sucked in a few quick breaths and clutched the edge of the bathtub.

Could it be real?

She looked at the test again. She was really pregnant. A baby. Motherhood. Life-will-never-be-the-same-again. Her brain felt like it was going to seriously overheat, and she took another succession of breaths, desperate to calm her pulse. She had to think clearly.

This can't be happening...

But she knew it was. In her heart, she'd known it for days. From the first day her period was late. Because she was never late. And now, unlike never before, she was paying the price for her foolishness. Which included her quick decision to accept the marriage proposal of a man she'd barely spent any time with since they started dating, and then rushing off to Vegas with some silly notion of the whole thing being romantic. As though Dwight was the great love of her life. When she knew he wasn't, even before she'd agreed to marry him. It wasn't love that drew her to Dwight. It was her need to be loved. To be wanted. To be a part of someone's life. Her behavior was foolish and impulsive. Grant was right. She should never have done it.

Grant! God, how was he going to react?

She stared at the results again and shuddered, turning cold all over.

Her life was now irrevocably changed. And so was his.

Winona got to her feet, still clutching the pregnancy test, and headed for the kitchen on the shakiest knees she'd ever experienced. She tucked the test in her pocket, washed her hands and made tea. Decaf, she figured, and rummaged in the cupboard for the right tea bags. She found them, made tea and sat on the sofa by the window, staring out at the darkening street.

It was Monday evening and she'd worked for most of the day, the uneasiness growing within her each hour when she thought about the test she'd discreetly purchased at Talbot's drugstore during her lunch break. The tourist center had had a busy day, with several busloads of travelers coming in to pick up brochures about local events and Black Hills memorabilia. By the time she was home she was exhausted. And now, looking out across Main Street, watching the solitary set of traffic lights change every few minutes, seeing commuters driving home, or stopping outside JoJo's for pizza pickup, that somehow amplified her exhaustion and loneliness. Normally, she'd just call Grant, explain she was feeling *blah*, and they'd talk for a while. But she couldn't call him without *telling* him, and she simply wasn't ready to face it.

She wasn't sure how long she sat like that, just staring out at the street, but when her cell rang after eight, she quickly glanced at the number, saw that it was Grant and let it go to voice mail. She waited ten minutes before listening to the message.

"Hey, it's me. Just checking to make sure you're okay. I'm wrapped up here and will be home tomorrow. My boss has given me a few days off, so I'll call you when I'm in town. We really need to talk. I miss you."

Winona listened to the message again. And then again. It was similar to other messages she'd received in the past week and she shouldn't read any more into his words. He couldn't possibly know anything was wrong. So, he wanted to talk. Probably about their impending divorce. She responded with a thumbs-up emoji and headed for the shower, determined to get thoughts of him out of her head for a while.

When she returned to the living room she grabbed her laptop and starting searching for information about the early stages of pregnancy. Since she was just over two weeks along, she wanted to ensure she was prepared for what was to come. However, she knew one thing—Winona had every intention of having her baby. Of course, she knew it wouldn't be easy and had never anticipated she'd be a single mom. But she didn't care. Now that the initial shock had subsided, she was thinking clearer with each passing moment. She was facing the ultimate responsibility and now, more than ever, needed to make some significant changes to her life.

Firstly, though, she needed to tell Grant.

And she knew, without a doubt, that he would freak out at the news.

He didn't want to be a father. He'd made his feelings about marriage and fatherhood clear to her many times over the years. He wasn't interested in commitment. She knew his feelings were wrapped up in what had happened with Billie-Jack and she supposed she couldn't blame him. She had her own abandonment issues, after all.

So, she'd tell him and he could make up his own mind about what level of involvement he wanted. Plenty of people juggled parenthood without being in a real relationship.

She went to bed with a semiclear head, knowing she had decisions to make. When she got up it was past seven. She had a short shift that day and didn't start until eleven, so she cleaned up a little around the apartment, spent an hour or so looking at Instagram pictures of nursery rooms, made an appointment to see her local GP and then headed to work after she had a late breakfast.

The afternoon dragged on, though, and she was pleased when her shift ended. She dropped by the supermarket to pick up a few much needed groceries and got home around six o'clock to find Grant standing by his car, which he'd parked outside the bakery. He wore work clothes and she wondered if he'd come directly from the airport.

"Hey," he said as she approached and quickly took the grocery bags from her.

"You're back?"

He nodded. "I said I would be."

She looked him over. "Did you come straight from the airport?"

"Yes. I was hoping you'd be free for dinner. Feel like pizza?"

"Sure."

He followed her up the stairs, and once they were inside she unpacked the groceries while he called JoJo's and ordered their dinner. Winona busied herself in the kitchen while he left to collect the pizza, and when he returned she had the table set and two sodas opened.

He dropped the pizza box on the table. "Are you okay?" he asked, his expression narrow and concerned.

"Fine," she replied as she sat. "How was the trip?"

"Long," he said and slid into the seat opposite. "Ten days in a hotel room is way too many."

Winona nodded agreeably and served out the pizza, picking the extra peppers off her piece and adding them to his slice. "You look tired."

He exhaled heavily. "I feel tired. What about you, what have you been up to?"

Winona caught the breath in her throat and the truth teetered. The longer she put it off, the harder it would be. "So, you said in your message last night that you wanted to talk?"

He nodded. "Yeah…ah…the lawyer has the papers ready. I managed to get an appointment at nine tomorrow morning, so if that works for you we can sign them and get them filed in the court."

Winona's belly sank. She didn't know why. She'd been expecting it. She wanted it.

"Sure, no problem. I'm not working until eleven tomorrow morning."

He nodded again and she noticed his tightly drawn expression. She knew him too well to put it down to simple fatigue. He was tense and conflicted—just as she was. She thought about the baby growing inside and wondered, as she'd been doing all day, who he or she would look like. Would their child inherit Grant's green eyes, or would he or she be darker, with black hair and brown eyes? Would their child grow up to be calm and controlled, like he was, or quick-tempered and reactive? Would their child have horses and ranching in their blood?

Winona knew so little about her own father and wondered if she'd made a mistake by not pushing her mother for details when they spoke. Communication with her mom was so rare and sporadic she figured there was little point in dredging up the past, but now that she was having a child of her own, she did have a deeper curiosity.

"What are you thinking about?" he asked, picking up on her faraway look.

"My father," she said before she had a chance to snatch the words back. "I was just wondering, you know, what he was like. Or if I should try and ask my mother about him again."

He shrugged lightly. "You could. Do you think she'll tell you any more than you already know?"

"I'm not sure, but the older I get, the more curious I get. Then again, if I did find him and he rejected me…" Her words trailed off painfully. "I don't think I could bear that."

"We both got screwed over in the father department."

There was a coldness in his voice she hadn't heard for a long time. When they were kids, she knew how much his father's departure had wounded him. Over the years he seemed to have found peace with it. But maybe not. She watched him, felt the tension emanating from the stillness in his jaw and tight, unmoving shoulders.

"At least you knew your dad," she offered and drank a little soda. "That's something."

"He was an abusive drunk," Grant said, eyes down, not seeming to focus on anything in particular.

"Perhaps he's changed."

He looked up sharply, meeting her gaze. "He left us, Winnie. There's no coming back from that."

"I guess the trick is to break the cycle," she said, almost holding her breath. "You know, being a better parent than the ones we've got."

His shoulders relaxed fractionally. "Well, my brothers seem to be doing a better job." He sighed, dropped the pizza slice in his hand and stared at her. "Sorry to be such a killjoy."

She managed a gentle smile. "You don't seem like yourself."

"I've got things on my mind."

He wasn't the only one…

She took a breath, spotting an opening even though she'd had no intention of announcing anything over dinner. But there was no time like the present. And he needed to know the truth. "Well, actually, there's something I need to—"

"Billie-Jack called me," he said flatly, cutting her off, his words almost freezing the air between them.

Winona reeled back. She knew Grant's feelings for his father were conflicted—she also knew he was aware of the fact. It was a complicated situation for the whole family. "What? When?"

"He's left a couple of messages in the last month," he replied. "He wants to reconnect."

Winona swallowed hard. "What are you going to do?"

He shrugged tightly. "I have no idea."

"Have you told your brothers or Ellie?" she asked.

"Nope."

Winona looked at him, saw the tension tightening his shoulders and knew that it wasn't the right moment to tell him about the baby. For one, he looked beat, and it wasn't the kind of news he needed to hear when he was tired, mentally exhausted and clearly had so much else on his mind.

"Do you think he wants money? Or something else?" she asked quietly.

"I'm not sure what he wants. I haven't seen him for eighteen years," he said and ran a weary hand through his hair. "Can I crash here tonight? I don't feel like being at the ranch when I'm in this mood. Or driving home."

It smacked of familiarity. A familiarity she wasn't sure was such a great idea. But of course she would never turn him away. He was her friend. *My husband. The father of my child.* As she thought the words, a heavy ache weighed down on her chest, but she managed a tight smile.

"Sure," she said and motioned to the couch. "It's all yours."

They finished up the pizza, drank the soda and managed to get through the following hour with very little conversation. He headed downstairs to grab his bag and was back a few minutes later.

"Okay if I take a shower?" he asked.

Winona finished clearing the plates and nodded. Once he was out of sight and she heard the water hissing, she relaxed a little. It had never been like this between them. Usually, she could deal with him being in her apartment, in her bathroom, in her life. He'd bunked over countless times. But so much had changed between them and she couldn't quite compartmentalize her feelings.

When he returned, he wore low-slung jeans, a white T-shirt that clung to his chest and loafers. He looked much more relaxed, though, and she managed a tight smile in his direction.

"Better?" she queried.

"Much," he said and rounded out his shoulders as he moved into the kitchen to stand beside her. "Thanks again."

"No worries," she replied. "Would you like coffee? Or tea? I have beer in the fridge."

"No, I'm good. If it's okay I might chill out on the sofa for a while and watch a little TV to try and clear my head before bed."

Winona glanced at the clock on the wall. "Of course.

I'm going to take a shower and go to bed. See you in the morning."

"Sure," he said and grasped her hand, rubbing his thumb over hers for a moment. "Winnie, once we get through this, everything will get back to normal. I promise."

Winona drew in a long breath and pulled her hand from his, then reached up and touched his face. His eyes were brilliantly green and regarded her with burning intensity. She stayed like that for a moment, connected to him, feeling the pulse in his jaw beneath her thumb.

"The thing is, Grant," she said and dropped her hand, "you can't make me that promise. Not now. Not ever again."

Then she walked off, her heart so heavy in her chest she actually ached.

Grant woke up the following morning with a crick in his neck and pain in his hip. He stretched out on the sofa, groaned and swung his feet onto the floor. He checked his phone, saw that it was 7:20 and stood. Looks like he *wasn't* going for his predictable 6:15 run. The apartment was quiet and he figured Winona was still asleep, so he headed for the kitchen and was filling the coffee filter when the front door opened and she came into the apartment carrying take-out coffee cups and a brown bag.

"I bought breakfast," she announced and then made a face as she placed them on the countertop. "Well, actually, Regina didn't charge me this morning. I *have* breakfast," she corrected. "How did you sleep?"

"Lousy," he replied and rubbed the back of his neck. "I prefer a bed to a couch."

She looked at him oddly, and he wondered if she found his statement provocative. He hadn't mean it to sound that way. The truth was, he was tired of trying to make everything sound normal between them.

"Pecan Danish for me, and some kind of vegan-friendly muffin for you," she said after a moment.

Grant grabbed his coffee and muffin and walked to the small dining table. "Thanks."

She remained by the counter, watching him, and he felt her scrutiny down to the soles of his feet. "We'll head to the lawyer's office and pick up those papers first thing," he said and sipped his coffee.

She nodded and moved to the table, taking a seat opposite, placing her cup in front of her.

Then she took a breath, as deep as he'd ever heard. "I have to tell you something."

Grant's gaze narrowed. She looked pale, he noticed, and out of sorts. Had she been like that last night? Had he been too wrapped up in his own thoughts he hadn't realized? He recalled their phone conversations over the last week or so and realized they'd spoken about very little. Concern burrowed deep and he tried to lighten his expression. "What is it?"

"It's important. Really important."

"Okay," he said, uneasiness pooling in his gut. "Go ahead, I'm listening."

"Well, I'm...the thing is... I'm..." Her words trailed off and she sighed heavily. "Oh, hell, there's no easy way to say this."

She reached into her jeans and pulled something from the pocket, then slid it across the table. It was about five inches long and white, and the moment he registered what it was, Grant's stomach plummeted. He stared at it, then looked at Winnie, and then again at the damning piece of plastic. He'd never seen one up close, of course. He'd never been in that situation. But still, he knew exactly what it was.

"That's a pregnancy test," he said and swallowed hard, white noise suddenly screeching between his ears.

"Yes, it is."

He took a breath, as deep as he could, trying to get some air into his lungs. "Is it positive?"

She nodded. "Yes."

"You're pregnant?"

Grant couldn't believe the hollow voice asking the question was his. But he was in shock, the kind of shock that started at the feet and worked its way up, polarizing movement. His chest tightened and for a fleeting moment it was impossible to breathe and he wondered if he was going to pass out.

"Yes, I am," she replied quietly.

Grant met her gaze. "I don't... I can't... It's not..." He stopped speaking before he said something stupid and got to his feet, pacing the room, hands on hips, head spinning. *Pregnant.* He inhaled and turned to face her, registering what it actually meant. "It's mine?"

She nodded again. "Yes."

"You're sure?"

Her beautiful mouth thinned. "Am I sure I'm pregnant, or am I sure that it's yours?"

He quickly realized how bad the question sounded. "I didn't mean to—"

"What?" she shot back, her voice so quiet he knew

she was annoyed. "Accuse me of lying? Question my integrity?"

"Of course not," he said raggedly. "I'm just…you know…in shock."

"The baby is yours, Grant," she said flatly. "My boyfriend was deployed overseas, remember? Then he dumped me at the altar. Then we got drunk, got married and had sex—you recall all that happening, right?"

"I…we used birth control," he said, the memory rushing in and out. "At least, I think we did."

She shrugged. "Well, it mustn't have worked, because I don't sleep around."

Grant finally managed to take a breath, dropped into the love seat by the window and swore softly. Of course he knew that about her. "Sorry. I'm kind of reeling here… I can't quite believe it."

She pushed back her shoulders. "That's how I felt when I found out the other day. Today, I see things a lot clearer."

"You do?"

She nodded. "I'm going to have this baby, Grant… if that's the next question you intend on asking me."

He wasn't sure what he was going to say. A baby? Winnie was having his baby. It seemed too surreal to believe. "Like I said, I'm in shock. So, do you feel okay? Not sick or anything?"

"No," she replied. "I feel fine. I made an appointment to see my GP on Monday. I'm a couple of weeks along, so it's too early for an ultrasound. But I'll let you know when I get one—I mean, if you're interested."

Grant stared at her, more confused than he had ever been in his life. Interested? What did that mean? She doubted him? She wondered what he'd do? Or wouldn't do? "Do you think I won't step up?"

She shrugged. "I don't know what to think about you anymore. Let's face it, the last couple of weeks haven't exactly been business as usual for us, have they? The truth is, all I've really thought about for the past couple of days is the baby I'm carrying. And you're right, it's a shock, but I'm not going to lie and say I'm *unhappy* about it. Scared out of my mind, yes. Terrified I'm going to screw it up, absolutely. But, Grant, you have to make up your own mind about how you feel about it," she said levelly. "I can't tell you how to feel. I can't make you react a certain way. I can't force you to be a father to this child. Step up, or don't, it's completely up to you."

The conviction in her voice was resolute and unwavering. He knew that about her. Knew that she could be stubborn and hard-nosed about things. Like not borrowing money to invest in the bakery. Like eloping with the marine. She would do it without him—that was very clear.

"We have to go," he said, suddenly impatient to clear his head and take some time to think about what she'd told him. "We have an appointment with the lawyer, remember?"

"I remember," she said flatly. "And don't forget to take your stuff with you when we leave. If you're going to be staying in town for a few days, we can sign the divorce papers right away. I think we both know that the quicker we fix this, the better."

He nodded, barely able to draw in breath, and then quickly changed his clothes. They left her apartment shortly after, without speaking more than half a dozen

words to one another, and dumped his bag in the car
before they walked to the lawyer's office, two blocks
away. Even though Winnie was at his side and he
could feel the tension vibrating through her, the walk
did him some good and managed to clear his head a
little.

A baby?

He'd never thought about fatherhood much in rela-
tion to himself—only in an abstract kind of way. Since
he wasn't convinced he was a marriage-and-white-
picket-fence kind of guy, the idea of being a parent
rarely crossed his thoughts. No doubt his resistance
had something to do with his own screwed-up relationship with Billie-Jack.

A baby with Winnie?

That was the killer. Of all the turns he might have
expected their relationship to take, having a kid together had never been on the radar. Losing her to the
marine—well, yeah—of course he'd thought about that
possibility. Being friends for life? Yes, he'd thought
that, too. He'd even thought she'd have kids one day
and maybe make him their godfather. But having a
baby together, that was bigger than big.

He remembered their night together in Vegas, and
then was quickly pleading with his brain to switch off
the images suddenly bombarding his thoughts. Skin,
heat, sweat, kissing and touching, pleasure on a cosmic scale. He knew it was foolish and irresponsible
behavior. He knew he should have pulled on every
ounce of his self-control that night and ignored the way
his body reacted to her. He shouldn't have kissed her
when she'd asked him to. He shouldn't have stroked
her skin and gotten lost in her touch. He should have

shown strength. And hell, the *character* he'd always considered made him the man he was.

But he hadn't. He'd shown weakness. She'd kissed his neck, touched his chest, pressed herself against him, and he was quickly reverted to putty. Sure, they were drunk and that had clearly impaired their senses. But somewhere during that night reality *should* have checked in. He should have been able to drag himself away from her—no matter how much it would have cost. Because even though he knew she would have felt rejected and alone, that risk should have outweighed everything else.

And now they had a baby coming.

It was mind-blowing and too much to think about. They were two doors away from their destination when he spotted his brother Joss coming out of the drugstore. He wasn't in the mood for family just yet. Telling anyone seemed irresponsible. And the way Winnie dug him in the ribs with her elbow made it clear she felt exactly the same way.

"Hey, you two," Joss said as he greeted them and quickly looked toward Grant. "I didn't know you were in town. What's going on?"

Grant's clear head quickly disappeared and suddenly he felt like he was on the verge of a full-blown panic attack. "Ah—just taking a few days off. What about you?"

His brother held up a small brown bag. "Clare's asthma medication. Being a dad is a 24/7 job," Joss said and grinned. "But I love it."

Grant's insides crumbled. How could he possibly match being father of the year like his brother? Joss had the parenting gene ingrained in his DNA, like

Mitch. Grant didn't even own a cat. He had friends. A job he enjoyed. He dated when he felt like it. Nothing serious. There was nothing *edgy* about his life. But in that moment, he felt like he was about to fall off a cliff.

"Are you okay?" Joss asked with a frown. "You look like crap."

He heard Winnie suck in a breath and hated that his brother could work out his moods so easily. Grant quickly shook some life into his limbs. "I'm fine," he lied. "Just tired. I gotta go, errands to run, but I'll catch up with you and the girls while I'm in town." He shook his brother's hand and waited for a second while Winnie gave Joss a brotherly hug and then they headed down the street, not looking back, and hoping that Joss didn't notice they took a left turn and walked into Tyler Madden's law practice.

"That was close," she breathed once they were in the small waiting room.

"Yeah," he replied. Too close. He loathed sneaking around. With Billie-Jack resurfacing and the situation with Winnie, Grant felt as though he was being suffocated by secrets.

Ten minutes later, after a short consult, Tyler gave them the documents they needed to sign. "So, that's it?"

Tyler nodded. "Yes. It's a fairly straightforward process. It's a no-contest divorce and there are no assets to divide and no children."

Grant was sure his heart stopped beating. He looked at Winnie, pale and rigid in the chair beside him, her back so straight it looked as though it might snap. "If there were kids…things would be different?"

The other man nodded again. "Of course. Children

change everything. Once you've both signed the forms, bring them back and I'll file them in court. About sixty days after that, the marriage will be over."

Over...

Children change everything...

They left the office shortly after, the envelope in his hand.

"You sign it first," she said, her hands clutched together. "Drop them off when you're done."

"Winnie, I—"

"Let's just fix this, okay?" she said quietly. "I have to get ready for work. I'll talk to you...whenever."

She walked off, her shoulders so tight he knew she was barely hanging on. But she would, that was her way. There was a resilience to Winnie, a strength she possessed that never failed to amaze him, even now.

Grant headed to his car. He knew Winnie didn't finish work until three so he had a few hours to fill before they could talk again — something he knew they needed to do. Instead of heading out to the ranch he stayed in town, driving around, buying coffee and sitting in the park for a while, answering emails on his phone, thinking about anything and everything except the reality staring him in the face.

His future.

His child.

His wife.

He got back to her apartment at 3:25 that afternoon and tapped on the door. He had a key, but it seemed oddly invasive letting himself in. She answered the door quickly and he was struck by how beautiful she looked. Her hair was down, flowing over her shoulders, and her wide brown eyes seemed huge in her face.

"We really need to talk," he said quietly.

She stared at him. "Tomorrow."

"This can't wait," he said and strode past her. Once he was in the apartment, Grant turned to face her, holding out the envelope. "I don't want to sign the divorce papers."

She gasped. "What?"

"We can't get divorced, Winnie," he said, hearing his own voice like it belonged to someone else. But still, he knew it had to be said. "Not now. We have to stay married."

CHAPTER SIX

WINONA STARED AT Grant in disbelief. He'd clearly lost his mind and was making zero sense.

"Stay married?" she echoed incredulously. "What? Why?"

"Because of the baby," he replied and exhaled. "Why else."

Winona drew in a shuddering breath. "You can't be serious?"

"Perfectly," he said. "I think our child should be born to parents who are married, don't you?"

Of course divorce wasn't ideal. But neither was staying married for the sake of the baby. "I don't think that matters much these days."

"It matters to me," he said. "And since we're married anyway, what difference will it make? It's not like we have to plan a wedding or do anything."

She took a moment to digest his words and then sat down. "So, you're saying we should *stay* married, not that we should *be* married, correct?"

He scowled. "What's the difference?"

"Night and day," she replied, ignoring the heat filling her blood. "If we stay married, we just go about our business as usual. If we *are* married—that's a whole different ball game."

"I don't see how."

She huffed a breath. "Because it means living together, *being* together, sleeping in the same bed, arguing over who gets the remote. You know, marriage."

He quickly looked like he'd been smacked in the face with a truth stick. "Well, yeah, but I think—"

"No buts," she said, her hand instinctively settling on her belly. "You don't really want to be married to me, right?"

"I want to do the right thing," he replied earnestly.

Winona didn't know if she wanted to hug him or hit him. But she knew that about Grant; she knew he oozed integrity and had probably spent the last few hours considering his options and coming up with one clear winner—that a baby meant they should stay in their marriage. But Winona wasn't so black and white. She might not be the most world-wise woman on the planet, but she knew a potential disaster when she saw one.

"You can be a father," she assured him, "without being a husband."

His expression blanched. "You mean part-time?"

"Plenty of men do it," she replied.

"Doesn't mean I want to be one of them," he said, firmer this time. "Look, I know you think you have it all figured out, but be sensible, Winnie, we're talking about a child. Our child. Don't you want the best for him or her?"

"Of course I do," she retorted.

He waved a hand to their surroundings. "And a one-bedroom apartment above a bakery is the best? I don't think so."

Her temper quickly flared. "Well, I didn't plan on raising the baby here. I'll get a new place. A house, with a yard and a fence."

His brows came up and she knew what that meant. "And how do you propose to pay the rent on a bigger place? With good intentions?"

Winona fought to keep her temper in check. "You can be so obnoxious when you want to be," she said and jumped to her feet. "Do you think I haven't spent the last few days thinking about how I'm going to do this? I've been thinking about Regina's offer to buy into the bakery. Until then, I plan on taking on more hours at the tourist center and I have a little nest egg saved. Not much," she added when she saw his brows shoot up again. "But enough that I won't be relying on good intentions to feed and clothe my child. Anyway, I don't want to talk to you when you're in one of these moods."

"I'm not in a mood," he said quietly. "I just want to work this out."

Winona stalked across the room and opened the door. "For the record, you are the last man on earth I want to be married to."

Of course it was a lie. But he'd never know that.

"Too late," he said and tucked the envelope under his arm, "because you *are* married to me, Winnie. Remember that while you're trying to stay mad at me for believing this is the best solution for everyone."

She closed the door loudly behind him, stormed across the room and waited by the window, watching as he got into his car and drove off. He was being impossible. And absurd. They couldn't stay married for the sake of the baby.

Winona sunk down in the love seat and pressed

her fingers to her temple. The last couple of weeks had been the most confusing of her life. She glanced at the collection of framed photos on the sideboard. There were a couple of her with her grandfather, another with Ellie and Leah and a couple of herself with Grant. She focused on her favorite one, taken a few years earlier at the spring fair. They were sharing a seat on the Ferris wheel; his arm was loped across her shoulders and she had one hand against his chest. They were laughing, heads close together, her hair whipping around them. She'd loved the selfie so much she had it printed and framed. Grant had the identical picture in his apartment.

And as loath as she was to admit it, she knew that Grant was right—she couldn't raise a child on good intentions. She had some savings, having spent a portion of her little nest egg on a wedding dress and a gaudy hotel room, leaving less than three thousand dollars in her checking account. She did plan on asking for more hours at the tourist center, and talking to Regina about the bakery. At least she had some time to save up and get a new place, and of course she'd stay in town.

She was tidying her herb rack in the kitchen late that afternoon when her cell pealed. It was Grant.

"What do you want?" she asked sharply.

"You were angry earlier," he said calmly. "I'm just making sure you're okay. That *we're okay.*"

"I'm fine," she said.

"Can I see you tonight?"

"No," she replied. "Where are you? At the ranch?"

"Outside O'Sullivan's," he said, "planning on getting takeout. Abby's working tonight and said she'd make risotto. Can I bring you some?" He paused.

"Please, Winnie, I really don't want to leave things like that between us."

His words faltered her resistance and she made an irritated sound. "Okay, but you can't stay long."

"Just dinner, I promise."

She hung up. Forty minutes later he was back on her doorstep, leaning one shoulder against the jamb, carrying a bag of food. She was hungry, and for a second, as she took in how good he looked in low-rise jeans and a white polo, she wasn't sure what she was hungrier for—dinner or Grant. She swallowed hard, ignoring her weakening will, and let him inside.

"That smells good," she said as she inhaled.

He grinned. "Luckily my sister-in-law is the head chef at the best restaurant in town."

Winona grabbed plates and set the table. "What did you do this afternoon?"

"Drove around," he admitted. "Avoided my family like the plague."

She sat down and dished out their dinner. "So, you haven't told anyone?"

"No," he replied. "I'm not quite sure what I'd say at this point."

"Well, we probably shouldn't say anything until I reach the second trimester," she said, voicing something she'd been considering all day. "Just to be sure."

"Are you worried?" he asked, looking uncharacteristically uncomfortable. "I mean, that you might lose the baby?"

"No," she replied. "It's just a precaution. Once I go to the doctor I'll know more. I'll probably get vitamins and brochures on pregnancy—the usual."

"There's a usual?" he asked and shrugged. "You

seem relaxed about it. I envy that. I'm way out of my comfort zone."

"I'm not relaxed," she admitted. "I'm faking it. But I've had a couple of days to get used to the idea. Plus, once I skipped my period, I had my suspicions, so I was semiprepared for the test results. And actually, you seem pretty calm right now. Did you sign the divorce papers?"

"No," he replied. "I had other things on my mind."

"What?" she asked. "Your loveless marriage idea?"

He sat back in the chair, watching her intently. "It wouldn't be loveless. We care about each other."

He cared. Of course Winona knew he loved her, she'd never doubted it. But it wasn't enough. She wanted more from marriage. She wanted everything.

"There's a big difference between *loving* someone and being *in love*, Grant."

"Is there?" he shot back with a loose shrug. "Maybe there's not. Maybe it's all the same and we just have this insatiable need to put a label on it. I'm sure there are marriages that have started out with a lot less."

"Probably," she remarked. "But I'm not prepared to sell out. And you shouldn't be, either, just because you don't believe in romantic love."

"I don't think that."

"Sure you do," she said and pushed some risotto around on her plate. "Do you remember when I fell for Callum McCrae in senior year? You told me I had sawdust in my eyes and that it was merely simple chemistry. Just lust. Desire. Sex. And that being *in love* was a fantasy."

"He was a jerk, anyway," Grant said and scowled.

"Maybe. The thing is, I know there's a difference…

and that doesn't make me a schmuck. It takes guts to fall in love. And yeah, when it doesn't work out it hurts like hell, but that isn't going to stop me and the rest of the world from trying to find it."

Grant didn't want to waste any energy remembering the guy she'd had the hots for in high school. By then he was graduating college and planning his future. Winona falling for some jock Grant never thought was good enough for her was a distraction he hadn't needed back then.

"He was your first boyfriend," Grant said and realized he'd spoken out loud.

She regarded him curiously, her brown eyes darkening. "He was my first everything. First kiss. First..." She blushed.

"You lost your virginity to him in the back seat of his pickup," he reminded her, and wasn't sure why the memory sat like cement in his stomach. "Classy guy."

Her mouth curled at the edges. "I called you that night, remember? You gave me a lecture about birth control. Ironic, really, considering the way things have worked out."

Heat crawled up his neck. "You were a girl back then. Now you're a woman. And I never liked the guy."

"You didn't like Dwight, either. Look, I know you were only trying to protect me," she said quietly. "And still are in your own way. But you don't have to be a hero here, Grant. Plenty of people co-parent children without being married."

"But we *are* married, Winnie," he said. "There's the difference. And we should tell your grandfather the truth as soon as possible."

"I would prefer—"

"I'm not good at pretending. Or lying, even if it's by omission."

He watched as her expression grew taut. "What will people think?"

"I don't much care," he replied. "I care about what you think. What I think. I care about doing what's right. I care about my family."

"They'll be shocked."

He shrugged loosely. "So, what? Let them be shocked—they'll get over it. The only thing we can control is how we respond to things. I'm not going to let you raise this child alone when I can do something about it. I'm not going to see you living in a tiny apartment when I can afford to buy us a house." He put his hand up when she opened her mouth to retaliate. "I know you think this is me being bossy...but it's not. It's me being sensible and pragmatic and a more honorable kind of father than my own ever was. I won't shirk my responsibility to you or our baby. Call me old-fashioned, call me anything you like, but I'm not walking away."

He felt better once he'd said it, once she knew exactly how he felt about the situation.

By now their dinner had turned cold and she looked as though her appetite had gone with it. Grant pushed both their plates aside and reached for her hand, grasping the edge of her fingers and linking them with his own. They stayed like that for a moment, gazes connected, fingers touching, ignoring everything else in the room and the rest of the world.

Finally, she pulled her hand away. "We've been friends a long time, Grant, so I'm not about to rush and make a decision that will impact the rest of our lives. We have plenty of time to work out how we want to co-parent this baby. Plenty of time to figure out how we want to manage…*us*. Until then, I think we need to go through with the divorce and try to get our lives in order."

He saw the resolute determination in her expression and suspected he'd lost a round, despite his impassioned speech about doing the right thing. Winnie was as stubborn as a mule when she wanted to be, so making demands wasn't going to work. He had to get her to see that staying married was the best option— even if he wasn't really sure what that would look like.

He shrugged agreeably. "We'll take things slowly. But I won't compromise in one area."

"Which one?" she asked suspiciously.

"Telling your grandfather, and my family. I'm a hopeless secret keeper, you know that," he said and offered a rueful grin. "It will feel too much like a lie and I've got enough secrets going on with the whole Billie-Jack situation. So, compromise…yes?"

She exhaled, taking her time, and then shrugged. "All right," she agreed. "We'll tell them soon."

"I'm heading back to Rapid City tomorrow, and Friday I'm traveling to Denver and will be there for about five days. A company conference," he added when she regarded him curiously. "You know, building team morale and that kind of thing."

"Oh, Krystal will have you all to herself for five days."

He had no idea why she said it. Or why her voice sounded like she was having an attack of jealousy. Normally she laughed about it. But she wasn't laughing at that moment. She looked lethally serious. It sparked something inside him—something he couldn't define.

"What?"

"Nothing," she said quickly. "Ignore me."

"I can stay if you're worried about it."

She shook her head. "I'm not worried. And I know you have the kind of job that involves traveling and conferences and things like that."

He still wasn't convinced she was okay with the idea. "It's just for five days. How about we tell everyone when I get back?"

She got to her feet and cleared the plates. "Sure, if that's what you want... I may as well endure complete humiliation in one fell swoop."

It sounded like an insult, as though being married to him and carrying his baby was the worst possible scenario imaginable. Sure, he hadn't been expecting it, but she didn't have to make it sound like it was a life comparable to being slung into the depths of hell.

He stood up and pulled his keys from his pocket. "Are you working tomorrow?"

"I have a short shift that starts at two."

He nodded. "I'll call you in the morning."

"What for?"

His gaze dropped to her flat belly. "Just to say hi— isn't that reason enough?"

She sighed and then nodded. "I guess. Good night, Grant."

"Night, Winnie." He hesitated. "Sweet dreams."

It's not what he wanted to say...nowhere near it. He wanted to tell her everything would be okay. That they'd work through it together. That they were unbreakable. But the promises got stuck in his throat.

He left her apartment quickly, taking his mood with him, although he didn't go straight back to the ranch. He took a detour to Joss's house. His brother owned a big brick-and-tile place on a leafy, peaceful street not too far from town and he pulled up outside. It was after eight and by the time he got to the porch the overhead light flicked on and his brother was at the door.

"Hey," Joss said agreeably, his blondish hair shimmering under the light. "What's up? You looking for a place to crash?"

Grant crossed the threshold. "No, I'm staying at the ranch tonight. I just thought I'd stop by for a while. Are the girls asleep?"

Joss chuckled. "At eight o'clock? No. But they are in their rooms and probably won't surface for the rest of the evening since it's a school night. I was just about to do some ironing."

Grant followed his brother down the long hallway and into the kitchen. "Sounds like a wild night ahead."

His brother laughed again. "I reserve my wild nights for every second weekend when the girls go to the in-laws' place."

Grant spotted the ironing board set up and a huge basket of clean laundry on the table. The kitchen was spotless, with everything where it should be, and his admiration for his brother amplified. Joss was one of those people who managed to be good at everything. He had a successful business, owned several rental properties in town, was raising two girls and seemed to juggle his entire life without any hiccups.

"You make all of this look easy," Grant remarked as he accepted the beer his brother passed him. "How do you do it?"

"It's not easy," Joss replied. "But I have to keep it together for the kids, you know. They were so young when Lara passed away, and this is all they know now. Routine is the key. So, what's up?"

Grant took a long breath. "Billie-Jack contacted me."

It wasn't what he intended to say. It wasn't even close. He wasn't even sure he'd planned on saying anything. He also wasn't sure why he'd stopped by his brother's place. Usually he tackled things on his own—particularly girl trouble. Although this wasn't the kind of trouble he'd ever found himself in before. But a niggling sense of loyalty to Winnie kept him from saying anything about the convoluted state of their relationship in that moment. It was best he talked about something else—like their father.

"Son of a bitch!" Joss said and shook his head. "What the hell does he want?"

"I don't know. He called my cell a few weeks back and I haven't replied to his message."

His brother scowled. "How the hell did he find your number?"

"I don't know that, either. I guess he probably looked me up online. Let's face it, tracking someone down these days is not hard."

Joss took a long swallow of beer and rested his behind on the counter. "You gonna call him back?"

"I'm not sure what I'm going to do," Grant replied. "I suppose I'm curious, but I also know that it's kind of like disturbing a hornet's nest."

"Ain't that the truth. Do yourself a favor," Joss warned. "Don't tell Jake. Or Hank. And for God's sake, don't say anything to Mitch. Or Ellie," he added with a rueful expression. "You know how she gets when any-one mentions Billie-Jack."

Grant exhaled heavily. He did know. Ellie had a load of unresolved resentment for their father, like he did. But out of all of them, he suspected Ellie was the one who had the most abandonment issues—especially since she could barely remember their mother. "That's why I'm telling *you*," Grant said and grinned.

Joss looked at him seriously. "Maybe he wants money."

"It's possible. Or he could want to make amends. Neither is out of the question. Eighteen years is a long time."

"Smart move on the old man's part, though," Joss said quietly. "Contacting you first."

"Smart? How?"

"Because you're the most sensible one out of all of us. Jake and Ellie can be hotheads, Mitch is overpro-tective, I'm too cynical and of course Hank has every reason to hate the guy until the end of time. Whereas you are perfectly reasonable and levelheaded. You don't screw up anything. Freakin' annoying, really," Joss said and laughed a little.

Grant almost laughed back. Almost. But he couldn't stop thinking about Joss's words. Reasonable and level-headed. Someone who never screws up in life. It made him sound as dull as an old shoe. But he figured it wasn't too way off the mark...mostly. For all everyone knew, he was the guy who got his act together when he was a teenager, studied hard, was valedictorian in high school, finished college with honors and had his pick of top employers when he graduated. He'd never gotten a speeding ticket, never spent a night in jail, never did drugs. Yeah…he was levelheaded, all right.

Except for the situation he was now in.

Grant stayed for a while longer, talking mostly about Billie-Jack, and he listened to his brother's sage advice. He said goodbye around nine, lingering by the bottom step off the porch.

Hell, everything was such a mess.

"You know," he said as he kicked at a pebble on the path. "I do screw up sometimes."

Joss regarded him curiously. "You do?"

He nodded. Then, realizing Joss couldn't see his expression in the darkness, he sighed and said. "Sure. Big-time."

"Like what?"

Guilt pushed down on his shoulders. "Nothing… forget I said anything."

Joss stepped forward. "Not likely. What's going on?"

He made a self-derisive sound, the words suddenly tumbling out. "A couple of weeks back I went to Vegas with Winnie because she was going to elope with that marine. He didn't show up. So instead, we got drunk, got married, spent the night together and now she's pregnant," he announced, his voice sounding hollow as it carried on the breeze. "Oh, and even though she's having my baby, she still wants to go ahead with the divorce. How's that for a screwup?"

Joss teetered on the edge of the top step. "You're serious?"

"Yep."

"Holy crap. I take back what I said. That's a big pile of trouble you got there."

"The biggest of my life," he admitted.

"If she's having your kid, why does she want a divorce?" Joss asked the obvious question.

"Because she doesn't want to be married to me. She went to Vegas to marry the marine, remember?"

"She still loves him, then," Joss said, voicing what Grant had been stewing silently on all day.

"I guess," he replied flatly. "People don't just switch off, right? Anyway, keep the news to yourself, will you? We were hoping to tell the family and Red together, this weekend. And I promised Winnie I wouldn't say a word, and here I just spilled my guts to you."

"I won't say anything," Joss replied. "Discretion is my middle name. Take care of yourself. And call me if you need me."

Grant nodded as he turned and walked down the path, through the gate and back to his car. He was halfway back into town when he decided against crashing at the ranch for the night, and instead headed for the hotel. He was checked in, showered and trying to sleep by ten o'clock.

Despite the turmoil of his dreams, he actually had a better night than the previous one cramped up on Winnie's couch, and managed to get a run in early the following morning. Afterward, he ordered room service and tried to ignore the niggling thoughts going through his mind.

She still loves him...

He had no idea why his brother's words were hanging around in his head. The marine was history. But since she'd told Grant point-blank that he was the last man she wanted to be married to, he wondered if she was still thinking about her ex-fiancé. She'd pretty much said she was over Dwight…but how could he be sure?

The whole situation was messed up…but he had to fix it, to make it right, to get Winnie to see that staying married was the best solution. So yeah, maybe he hadn't imagined he'd be married with a baby on the way a few weeks back, but since he was, there was no turning back. He had to step up and do what was right. They both did. A Culhane did not turn his back on family and responsibility. If he did, he'd be no better than Billie-Jack—and that wasn't a legacy he intended carrying on.

He rummaged through the side pocket in his overnight bag and found the wedding band he'd ripped off so quickly a couple of weeks earlier. So much had happened since then. He stared at the ring, thinking about the simple significance of the small circle. And knew instantly what he had to do.

He was back on her doorstep by nine, and when she answered the door she almost looked as though she'd been expecting him.

"I'm not staying, I promise," he assured her and exhaled. "But please, let me say something."

"What?" she asked, looking as though she'd had very little sleep.

"I know this isn't our idea of an ideal situation. But here we are, together," he reminded her and saw her wince. "So, we need to take a breath and think about what this really means for our future and our child's future. Family…" he said, his words trailing off as he fought the urge to take her hands, to connect with her, to make her see that their child was worth fighting for. "You were right when you said I've never really thought about getting married. Or having kids. But you're my best friend, Winnie, and the fact is we're also husband and wife. And I can't believe we're not going to try to make this work. I believe we care about each other enough to at least give it a shot, don't you?"

The color leached from her face and she crossed her arms tightly. "Marriage is—"

"Not final," he said quietly. "We both know that. And since we've got eight or so months until the baby comes, we've got time to try and figure it out." He lifted his left hand and fiddled with the wedding band that was now back on his finger. "I'm going to wear this from now on, or at least until we know for sure that being married isn't something we can do. Because I don't know that for sure. Neither do you. This might turn out to be the best thing that happens to either of us."

"Or the worst," she added.

"Maybe," he said and shrugged loosely. "But you know what I don't want to do, Winnie? I don't want to look into the eyes of our son or daughter when he or she is born, or on a first birthday, or a tenth birthday, or graduation, or wedding day, and admit that we didn't give it a chance. That we bailed because we were scared to fail or afraid of commitment or were pining after something or someone else or thinking of some foolishly romantic ideal about what a successful marriage looks like. If we screw up, at least we screw up without excuses. Please say you'll consider it?"

He grasped her hand and urged her close, holding her against him, and she came willingly, looking up at him, her brown eyes wide and warm. And he kissed her. Not hot and heavy. Now wasn't the time for that.

It was a simple, almost chaste kiss, just their mouths fleetingly together, tasting each other for a few moments.

When he pulled back and lifted his head, she was breathing hard, still looking at him. "Okay," she said softly. "I'll think about it."

Grant released her and stepped back. "I'll call you."

"Don't," she replied. "I need some time to sort this out in my head. I hear what you're saying, Grant, and a part of me knows you're right. But I *am* scared. And confused. Things used to be so simple between us and now everything is completely different. This is a new reality for us both. And even though you might think it's okay if we screw it up, I'm not really wired that way. I need to be sure."

The thing was, Grant thought as he left, they both knew there were no guarantees.

CHAPTER SEVEN

WINONA SPENT THE next week in varying states of indecision. Grant didn't call her. He texted, though, asking how she was, keeping the messages brief and lighthearted. She responded each time with a simple emoji, not wanting to get bogged down with more conversation, more explanation, more…anything. And she made it her mission to not think about the Krystal factor. He'd told her plenty of times that he wasn't interested in the other woman and she had no reason to disbelieve him. The only thing she couldn't believe was her own reaction.

She also avoided the world for the following days, hanging low, taking on extra hours at the tourist center over the weekend to avoid Ellie's invitation to go horse riding at the ranch. She even bailed on her catching up with her grandfather, pleading a headache and promising to drop by the ranch soon. On Monday she went to her doctor's appointment and her pregnancy was officially confirmed. She was given a list of vitamins and supplements to take, and the name of an obstetrician in Rapid City. The community hospital in Cedar River had a good birthing unit and she took down those details, as well.

And she thought about Grant…a lot. Some days it seemed that he was *all* she thought about.

She thought about their last conversation and tried to make it right in her head.

Stay married. Be married. Try to make it work. Do the right thing.

And that kiss. A kiss that had her yearning for her secret dreams. A kiss that reminded her of everything they weren't. A kiss so sweet it held the promise of more…but she knew in her heart that he didn't have more to give.

He turned up on her doorstep on Thursday morning, dressed in cargoes, a pale gray shirt and dress shoes. She gestured to his overnight bag. "Are you planning on moving in?"

He shrugged. "Gotta start sometime."

"That's presumptuous. I haven't given you my answer."

He walked into the room and sat on one of the kitchen stools. "I know. I guess I was hoping you might've had some time to think about things and maybe make a decision."

"I *have* made a decision," she said. "And you can sleep on the couch."

His mouth twisted. "Now who's being presumptuous?"

"Just keeping things manageable," she said and glanced at his left hand, spotting the gold ring instantly. "I bet that put a dampener on any hooking-up opportunities this week."

His brows shot up. "Is that what's been keeping you up these nights, Winnie? Worried that your brand-new husband was straying?" He laughed, but there was little humor in his tone. "Rest assured, I was not. You know me better than that."

She did. He wasn't a cheat or a liar. He was the most honest man she knew. And she immediately felt foolish for saying it, let alone allowing herself to wallow in the idea for the previous few days. And he was right about the other thing, too—she had made a decision... perhaps the biggest of her life.

"We'll try this marriage thing for sixty days," she announced, arms crossed, her heart almost in her throat.

"Sixty days?"

"That's how long it takes to get a divorce, right?"

"Yes," he replied and scowled. "So let me get this straight. You want to sign the divorce papers and *then* try to make this relationship work? That doesn't make a whole lot of sense."

"It does to me. By then we'll definitely know if we've done the right thing or not in plenty of time before the baby arrives."

"So, we go into this with our expectations as low as possible, correct?"

It sounded like a coward's compromise, but Winona wasn't prepared to commit to anything more. She didn't share his confidence that they could make it work. And she knew why. Grant had a barbed-wire fence around his heart. He looked at it purely from an economical point of view. They had a baby coming, they were already married—presto, problem solved.

But she...she was different.

She tucked her tote in her lap. "Well, if we *can* make it work, we'll have enough time to stop the divorce going through."

"Well, since I'm not in any real position to make demands, sure."

Winona nodded. "Thank you. Although maybe we should postpone today and—"

"Winnie, I told Joss last week," he admitted guiltily. "I'm sorry, I know I said we'd wait until I got back. But I needed…"

His words trailed off, but she knew what he was going to say. He needed to talk to someone. And it pained her. Because up until a few weeks ago, she would have been his go-to person. Now their relationship seemed to be altering daily. Every time they spoke, the tension between them grew. Tension that was manifested from all angles.

"I understand," she said, thinking she needed her own confidante, and experienced an acute rush of loneliness. "Although I think I should be the one who tells my grandfather," she said.

"Maybe we should do it together."

"And then?" she asked. "After we've told everyone, what then? You said you were staying for a few days… and afterward?"

"House hunting, I guess. We can stop by the Realtor in town and check out some places."

"Move in together right away? That's your great plan?"

He looked at her and nodded. "Married people usually live together, Winnie. There's no point in making it some soft transition." He glanced around the apartment. "And there's not a lot to pack here."

"What about your place in Rapid City?" she inquired.

"I can find a tenant," he replied quietly.

"Well. If you're sure it won't be too hard to find someone, I guess it's settled. So, how was your conference?" she asked, changing the subject. "Did you get plenty of team building done?"

He shrugged. "It was fine."

"Normally we talk about it," she reminded him.

"Normally we do, yes. But you don't seem like you're in the mood for chitchat," he said quietly.

"I always want to hear about your work stuff," she said and smiled a little.

He did the same. "Well, then, yeah, it was okay. Just a typical work conference. Interesting meetings, crappy buffet and some attendees drank too much. Nothing out of the ordinary. We should get going."

"And the Krystal factor?"

His brows rose questioningly. "She was mostly well behaved."

Winona scowled and smiled. "Well, she's only human and you can be very charming."

He laughed. "Do you think? I thought I drove you crazy?"

"We were discussing Krystal, not me. But since we've decided to try and make this marriage work, I'm glad she kept her hands to herself."

"You know, fidelity's not a huge price to pay," he remarked.

It seemed an odd comment, but she didn't dwell on it.

When they got to the Triple C, Winona waited for him and they walked toward Red's cottage together. As expected, her grandfather was delighted to see her, and happy to see Grant, too.

She hugged him for longer than usual, and once

they were seated she took a deep breath and spoke, her hands shaking so badly she pressed them into her thighs. "Papa... I've got something to tell you."

"*We've* got something to tell you," Grant corrected gently and grabbed her left hand, holding it within his.

Strength seeped through her and she nodded, taking another galvanizing breath. "Well, the thing is, a few weeks ago...we... Grant and I, we...eloped."

"Eloped?" Red echoed.

She nodded. "Yes, Papa, we got married."

Grant cleared his throat a little. "We know it seems...sudden. And we probably should have spoken to you about it. But we're going to get a place in town, so Winnie won't be far away from you."

Winona waited for her grandfather to respond, and when he did, Red's face creased with a smile. "Well, congratulations. I'm thrilled for you two."

She nodded and swallowed hard. "Ah...there's something else."

Red's eyes seemed to twinkle. "More good news?"

Grant squeezed her hand gently, and she nodded. "We think so. You're going to be a great-grandfather, Papa. I'm having a baby."

"Damn," Red said and clapped his hands together. "That's just wonderful."

In a way, he almost seemed relieved, as though some great burden had been lifted from his shoulders. She didn't want to read too much into it, or overthink his reaction, as she was prone to do. He shook Grant's hand and congratulated them both again and, oddly, didn't ask too many questions about their plans, their intentions or anything else. He actually seemed to accept the marriage as a done deal. He said he was looking forward to being a great-grandfather and nodded agreeably when Grant said he would make sure she and the baby were cared for.

"That was easier than I thought it would be," she remarked as they walked toward the main house. "Too easy. He almost seemed relieved."

Grant chuckled. "Well, I'm clearly quite the catch."

She jabbed his ribs with her elbow. "Don't you think it's odd that he wasn't… I don't know…surprised?"

"We've known each other forever," he said and smiled. "It's not such a big stretch, is it?"

"How about the fact that you treat me like an annoying little sister?"

He stopped walking, grabbed her hand and brought her close to him, linking their fingertips. "Annoying best friend, maybe," he corrected. "But believe me, Winnie, there's nothing remotely brotherly about my feelings for you right now."

Winona looked up, her eyes wide as they met his. They were so close she could feel the heat coming off his skin. His cologne swirled around her, an intoxicating blend of spice and sea, and she shuddered a little too breathlessly. The pulse in his cheek throbbed as his irises darkened. A flash of memory assailed her, thinking about Vegas, about the way he lay above her that night, his weight on his elbows, their gazes connected with the same intense intimacy as their bodies. She remembered his kiss, the taste of him, the way his mouth and hands had explored her, the way she'd sighed and moaned and experienced pleasure so acute it was impossible to stop the heady flush rising up her neck. She remembered touching his face, his shoulders, his back. She remembered clinging to him, feeling every part of him against her, lifting her hips to meet his, pleading, urging, whispering words she'd never dared imagine she would have the chance to say.

"Winnie," he said quietly, one hand reaching up to touch her cheek. "For the sake of my sanity, can you please ditch the X-rated look in your eyes?"

She inhaled sharply. "I didn't mean to—"

"I know," he said, cupping her jaw as he softly sliced through her words. "This is all rather unexpected, isn't it?"

"This?"

The pressure of his touch increased a fraction and he traced his finger down her neck. "The foggy brain that comes from having sex with someone."

She smiled, knowing exactly what he meant. Yes, *foggy brain* certainly described how she was feeling.

"Hey, you two!"

It was Ellie, her voice ringing out clearly from where she stood on the veranda. Grant released Winona immediately and she turned, ignoring Ellie's curious expression as she climbed the steps.

"Hey, Brat," Grant said affectionately. "Mitch and Tess around?"

Ellie nodded. "What's going on?"

"Come inside and find out," he said and ushered Winona into the house.

His brother and sister-in-law greeted them in the hallway and moments later they were all in the living room, talking to and over each other as usual. Winona had the urge to hold his hand, to seek comfort, protection. Then she scolded herself. She didn't need protecting from the Culhanes. They were friends. *Family.* They would understand. Winona looked at them all amid the hubbub, noticing how Tess was watching her with a tiny smile on her face, almost as though she had guessed their news before the words were spoken.

It took Grant about ten seconds to break the news of their situation, so matter-of-factly it was over before she realized.

"Winnie and I got married and we're having a baby," he said before he looked at her, offered a reassuring nod and waited for a response.

"You're what?"

It was Ellie who spoke first, Ellie who was regarding them incredulously.

"Married," Grant said again, looking as cool as always. "And having a baby."

Winona wished she had his calm demeanor. She did have a tendency to let her feelings show in her expression, and she suspected this was one of those times.

"This is rather sudden, isn't it?" Mitch asked, looking at them both in turn.

Grant shrugged. "It is what it is."

Ellie was on her feet, clearly not buying it. "I don't understand. Where does Dwight fit into this little scenario?"

"He doesn't," Winona replied, looking at her friend and seeing the disbelief in her expression. "We broke up."

"And now you're married to my brother and having a baby?" Ellie asked, brows up, clearly suspicious. "Oh, my gosh, is it Dwight's?"

"Settle down, Ellie," Grant said and perched on the edge of the sofa. "Stop jumping to conclusions. It's my—"

"It's Grant's baby," Winona said, her tone unequivocal, and she stood, straightening her back. "If you want details, I *had* planned to elope with Dwight in Vegas," she admitted, heat coursing through her veins. "But he was a no-show. He dumped me. Your brother was there to walk me down the aisle, but instead we got drunk together, got married and had sex. Now I'm pregnant. And seeing as I hadn't seen Dwight for ten months, you do the math."

"Couldn't have said it better myself," Grant added and got up, grasping her hand. "Look, we're not asking for approval or advice. It's done. We're married. We're having a baby. What we choose to do from now on is our business. What we would like, though, is for you to share in the good news."

"You must have expected us to be surprised," Ellie said, still looking suspicious.

It was Tess who spoke next... Tess who was the calm voice among the building family chaos.

"Congratulations. Babies are always a wonderful way to bring people together. We should have a celebration," she suggested and smiled. "A post-wedding get-together for the whole family. How about I arrange something for next weekend? Ellie would love to help me, wouldn't you?" she asked and grasped Ellie's hand.

Ellie was quickly agreeing and a minute later the date was set for the following Sunday for a relaxing gathering at the ranch, with family and close friends.

"Are you moving to Rapid City?" Mitch asked Winona.

"I'm moving back to Cedar River," Grant supplied. "We'll look at getting a place on the north side of town to cut down my commute. But I'm doing so much interstate work at the moment, it's not imperative that I live in Rapid City."

"You'd be welcome to move back to the ranch," Mitch offered. "I suspect Red would love having you close by, Win."

"Thank you," she said and managed a smile, thinking that the last thing she wanted was for her relationship with Grant to be under some kind of Culhane sibling microscope, as much as she cared about them all. "But we really—"

"We appreciate the offer," Grant interjected, taking the heat off her in the process. "Thanks a lot. But I think we need our own space for the time being."

"Your brother is right," Winona said gently. "We have a lot to adjust to—and a lot to get ready for. And you guys know that better than anyone."

Mitch and Tess smiled at each other, then Mitch turned back to his brother. "I guess that's true enough."

They left shortly afterward, after hugs and handshakes and the promise to be in touch about the family catch-up on the following weekend. Once they were in the car, she spoke up.

"Ellie went all lioness," she said and actually managed a grin. "Thinking I've trapped you into marriage with another man's baby."

"My sister is a drama queen," Grant said as they drove through the gates. "Still, she knows me pretty well."

"What do you mean?"

"That if you needed someone to raise a child with, I would do it."

Winona sucked in a breath. Because, despite everything, of course she knew that about him. He would slay her dragons if need be. "But you *know* this baby is yours, right? I mean, I would never expect you to—"

"I know," he said and grasped her hand. "And I'm not unhappy about the baby, Winnie. I'm still in a kind of shock," he added and grinned, "but have accepted the idea."

"Resigned to it, you mean? And to your upcoming sixty days in purgatory?"

"You're the one who set the time frame, remember?"

"I need a plan," she said and pulled free, placing both hands in her lap. "And honestly, since you usually like things organized and in order, I'd imagine a workable plan with a time frame and parameters would be right up your ally."

"Ah," he said and turned off onto the highway. "Now come the terms and conditions."

Winona huffed. "What's gotten into you? Of course we need ground rules. Firstly, we need to promise to always be honest with each other."

"I thought we already did that," he said. "But if you're asking for assurances, then how about we talk about the marine."

"Dwight? What does he have to do with this?"

"You tell me," he shot back as they drove toward town. "A month ago he was the love of your life and all you ever wanted."

She wasn't sure she'd ever said that. And the truth was, she'd barely spared Dwight a thought over the last couple of weeks. "That was before he dumped me at the altar and I got married to someone else," she reminded him, hearing something off in his tone and not quite sure what to make of it. "I haven't heard from Dwight since that day and I don't expect to ever again."

His hands were tight on the steering wheel. "Okay, back to these ground rules—what's next?"

Winona stared straight ahead, seeing the town's welcome sign. "Well, I think we should *rent* a house first, in case things don't work out. And I don't think we should…you know…sleep together."

Grant pulled the car into a spot outside the Realtor's office. He didn't say a word as they headed inside and met with the owner, Leola Jurgens, who quickly detailed to them all the available rental listings. Grant was more interested in buying property, but he wasn't about to get into an argument with Winnie about it. She had her mind set firmly on renting a place. It seemed like she had her mind firmly set on a lot of things. Like not sharing a bed. Sure, he hadn't committed to this arrangement specifically with sex on the brain—but he hadn't bargained on *not* sleeping with his wife, either.

They made appointments to look at two homes the following day, after Winnie finished her morning shift at work. As they were leaving the Realtor's, she said she wanted to stop by the supermarket. They lingered in the store for a while and Grant added things to the shopping cart he knew she'd turn her nose up at—like alfalfa sprouts and avocado. Winnie was more a meat-and-potatoes kind of girl.

They were climbing the stairs to her apartment, his arms loaded with grocery bags, when his cell rang. He shuffled the bags into one hand and pulled his phone from his pocket. It was a number he now recognized.

Billie-Jack.

His gut rolled and he fought the urge to pick up.

Now wasn't the time or place to have his first conversation with his father in eighteen years.

"Something wrong?" Winnie asked, clearly picking up on his expression.

"Billie-Jack. Again."

"Oh," she said and sighed. "You haven't called him back yet?"

"No. Although I did speak to Joss about it."

"What did he say?" she asked.

"To keep the information to myself," he replied and offered a wry smile. "Joss hates Billie-Jack."

"Do you?"

"I'm not sure how I feel," he said and placed the bags on the kitchen counter.

"If you want to see him, then you should."

"It's complicated," he said and watched as she began unpacking the groceries.

"Most relationships are," she said and waved a hand between them. "But you know him, you remember him. You know what he's like and who he is. And yes, perhaps he has changed. Or maybe not. Either way, at least you can go into it without risking being disappointed."

"It would be easier if he hasn't changed," Grant admitted. "Then I could just tell him to go to hell and to leave the family alone."

"And what if he has?" she asked. "Then what do you do?"

"Then I have to make a decision that's not only mine to make—because I was younger than my brothers, I didn't see the worst of him. I think I saw what I wanted to see."

"You were, what, six or seven when your mom died?

It's natural that you would want to look to your father for stability and strength."

"Strength?" he echoed and gave a shallow laugh. "Yeah, I guess I did. Not that he showed any. He used to beat up on Joss and Hank and I remember how Jake would put himself in the middle of the fights to take the worst of it. But I still wanted his time, you know, I still wanted a father. By then the others had put up with so much of his crap that they were glad to see him go."

"But you weren't," she said, more statement than question. "But you were young, impressionable. Don't feel guilty because you wanted your dad to *be* a dad. That's a normal human need."

She had a point and he realized it was the first time they'd had a meaningful conversation about something *other* than the convoluted state of their own relationship for weeks.

"I'll do a better job than he did," Grant said and glanced at her belly. "I promise."

She nodded. "I know you will."

"It means a lot, you know," he said and rested on the counter, watching as she put the last of the items away. "That you think I can be a good dad. If I'm half the father that my brothers are, I'll get it right."

"Mitch is a good role model for fatherhood," she said quietly. "He was, what—eighteen when your dad left?"

"Yeah. And Joss got married straight out of high school because he and Lara were pregnant. If they can do it at eighteen, I figure I can do it at thirty."

She smiled, a deep, warm smile that caught his breath and made his stomach dive. It occurred to him that he hadn't seen her smile much lately. And he'd missed it. In fact, he missed their comradery, and the sense of companionship they'd always shared.

"It's good to see you smiling," he remarked and moved around the counter. "So, how about you get out of the kitchen and let me make us a sandwich of champions."

Her mouth curled at the edges. "Okay, but no avocado."

"Where's your sense of adventure," he teased, stupidly happy that they were talking like normal and there was zero tension hanging between them. Or at least they were pretending there wasn't. "One semisandwich of champions coming up."

She chuckled. "So, what's your plan for the next few days?" she asked, changing the subject.

"I'll stay in town for the rest of the week. I have to get back to the office Monday and fly out Tuesday to Duluth for a couple of days—a group of us from the office are working on a project for a food manufacturing company. But I'll be back by the Friday, you know, in case we find a place and start moving."

She didn't blink. "Ah, I have a rental agreement here, so I'll have to sort that out. And you said you were going to lease your apartment?"

Grant nodded and began preparing their food while she perched herself on a stool on the other side of the counter and entertained herself with her phone. It could have been any other day, he figured, with him in the kitchen and Winnie laughing at humorous memes she scrolled through on her social media accounts. She showed him a couple, laughing at a herd of baby goats wearing knitted pajamas and a meerkat lip-synching to a rap song.

"Promise me something," he said as he pushed a plate across the countertop.

She eyed the sandwich and then looked at him. "What?"

"That we'll always make each other laugh," he replied, feeling oddly serious.

She looked inside the sandwich, smiled when she saw he hadn't loaded it with ingredients she didn't like and nodded. "I promise. By the way, Leah's invited me to a party Saturday night. Would you like to come with me?"

Leah was his cousin and a good friend of Winnie's, too. Her mom, Sandra, was Billie-Jack's sister and had been killed in an airplane crash several years earlier, along with her daughter-in-law, Jayne. It had been a tough time for the family, but they had gotten through it with the help of many of their friends in town. Now, Leah was dating Sean O'Sullivan and they lived in a big house by the river. Grant liked Leah, and her brother, David, was a good friend as well as being his cousin.

"Sure," he said agreeably. "We should start socializing together."

"We've been socializing together for years," she reminded him.

"I meant as a married couple," he said. "Not just best friends."

She blinked and shrugged. "Sure…whatever."

They stayed in her apartment for the remainder of the day. Grant set up his laptop on the desk near the window and did some work, while Winnie did laundry. Later, Grant cooked pasta for dinner and afterward they watched television for a while. The whole evening was absurdly domestic…until Winnie dumped a pillow and blanket on the end of the sofa around ten o'clock and disappeared into her room with a vague good night.

He was irritated about being relegated to the couch—but bit his tongue. They had enough problems without adding fuel to any more.

As he tossed on the couch for the next hour or so, Grant figured he should have checked into the hotel again. Or gone to the ranch. Either would have meant he'd get some sleep. He was still awake by eleven-thirty and headed to the kitchen to make herbal tea. He was grabbing a mug from the cupboard when Winnie unexpectedly came out from her room.

"Sorry," he said. "Did I wake you?"

"Couldn't sleep," she replied and rubbed her eyes.

She wore a short white T-shirt that was almost translucent with the light shining from the hallway. He swallowed hard, averted his gaze and got back to his task. "Tea?"

"Sure," she replied and came into the kitchen.

Her feet were bare and her toenails painted some sparkly purple color. She had nice legs, he thought as he grabbed another mug. And cute feet. In fact, everything about Winnie was in perfect proportion.

"Why do you think we did it?" she asked, startling him back into looking at her face.

"What?"

"Got married. Had sex. Why do you think we did it?"

Grant stared at her. It was the first time she'd asked the question. Not the first time he'd thought it…but hell, he'd been thinking all kind of things lately. He'd been thinking things about Winnie that surprised him…shocked him actually. Like how perfectly smooth her skin was, or how her lips curled up at the edges when she smiled. And he remembered, too, that night in Vegas; even though they'd had way too much to drink, deep down the memories were acute. Polarizing. And, in a way, terrifying…because it forced him to regard her in ways he'd consciously avoided. As not just his best friend. But as a woman…vibrant, sexy, desirable—all the things he'd purposefully put out of his mind since they were teenagers because back then, of course, he'd had the usual lustful thoughts. Thinking about her like that now was confusing. But they were married with a baby on the way, so how could he *not* think about her?

"I'm not sure."

"I'm trying to figure it out in my mind, you know," she said, crossing her arms in a way that pushed her breasts upward and got him thinking that a white T-shirt was just about the sexiest thing he'd ever seen. "I know I was upset about Dwight and embarrassed by it all. I know we drank a lot…but we've been drinking together before and nothing has ever happened between us. Something changed that night."

"Does it matter so much?" he asked, tired of overthinking everything.

"Yes," she replied. "Because we're married and I'm sleeping in there and you're on the couch."

"Your ground rules," he reminded her. "Remember?"

"I know," she said and exhaled almost painfully. "But we need them, don't you think? Okay," she conceded, "*I* need them. And of course I know it's not logical for two people who are married, and are going to try and *be* married, to not sleep together."

"Then why suggest it?"

She shrugged. "I'm scared, I guess."

Grant stilled and looked at her. "Of me?"

"Of this," she said and waved a hand between them. "Of being…of having…of sex… I know that probably sounds crazy since we've already done it, but I don't have sex casually. And I know you, Grant. I know you only have casual relationships. And I don't want to be someone who is on a list of your casual hookups."

It was quite the accusation. And if it wasn't true, he might have been annoyed. But she was right. His list of hookups wasn't that long by some standards— but it was definitely casual. One, two, three dates was his usual style. A two-month involvement at the most. Commitment free. Danger free. But this was Winnie. His best friend.

His wife.

The woman carrying his child.

This was pure commitment.

"Being with you *is* different," he said quietly, not really sure why he said it but feeling the truth of it deep down.

Her brows rose up. "How do you know? How can we be sure?"

"Because I remember that night," he replied. "I remember kissing you, touching you. And yeah, maybe how it started is a little blurry, and we wouldn't have done it if not for that last batch of tequila shots, but we did…and it was really something."

"Was it?" she asked, her skin oddly pale beneath

the kitchen light. "What if it was just the alcohol and the—"

"What's this really about, Winnie?" he asked, ditching the tea making to stand in front of her, seeing uncertainty in her expression.

She shook her head, swallowing hard. "How can I know if you…if you really…you know, *feel* that way…"

"Feel what way?" he asked, seeing her expression look more pained with each passing second.

"You know what way," she replied quietly. "Attraction and desire. I don't want to be with someone who has to fake it."

Grant stepped forward and touched her shoulder. A simple gesture. One he'd done countless times. Meant to reassure and comfort. But her skin was warm beneath his fingers and touching her sent a fast message to that part of him he'd had under wraps around her. He quickly realized he wanted to kiss her. And more.

"There's nothing fake about this, Winnie."

She didn't look convinced. "You can say whatever you want, Grant, but it doesn't change the past. It doesn't change us. It doesn't change that we've never… that you've never looked at me as anything other than your best friend."

He touched her belly with the back of his hand— desperate, suddenly, to curve his hand over the safe place where their baby was growing. To feel their child. To feel Winnie.

"I'm pretty sure this disputes that idea," he said and everything he'd always thought—the rock-solid belief he'd held that he knew exactly who he was and what he wanted—had somehow become hazy. Because there was so much he didn't know…so much he couldn't be sure of. And it alarmed him down to the soles of his feet. Except for one thing—the undisputable fact that he was attracted to his wife.

"You want proof," he asked and took her hand, resting her palm against his chest. "That's my heart, beating like crazy because I'm this close to you. Because I do want you…very much."

CHAPTER EIGHT

WINONA KNEW WHAT she was asking him. For the truth. For assurances. To know that if they were going to try and make their marriage work, he had to at least be honest about his feelings.

About sex.

Because she'd been battling her insecurities for days, demanding ground rules, and knowing it was foolish to expect a sexless relationship. Because she didn't want that, either. But what she really didn't want was to think of Grant making love to her when he had no real feelings for her in that regard. Sure, his heart might be pounding…but was that enough? She knew him—although he didn't do commitment, he wasn't indiscriminate and didn't hook up simply because he could. Like Krystal, she thought—who'd been giving him the eye for months and who he'd turned down because he wasn't interested in her. That made him a good guy, right? Someone with integrity and character. Someone she could depend on to be faithful and loyal.

She knew he loved her. Oh, not the passionate, soul mate kind of love, but he cared and with the baby coming, she hoped that would be enough. But sex was different. Sex was about physical intimacy and desire and she had no reason to believe he thought of her in that way—other than their drunken romp in a Vegas hotel room.

His expression was unrelenting and she inhaled sharply, relaxing a fraction. He touched her face with his free hand, cupping her cheek for a moment before gently anchoring her head so he could look directly into her eyes.

Grant dipped his head and touched his mouth to hers and her lips instantly parted beneath the soft pressure. He moved closer and her hands climbed up his chest to his shoulders, her fingers holding on, her breasts pressed against him. Heat rushed up her legs and into her belly, startling her with its ferocity as he deepened the kiss, finding her tongue and touching it with his own. She pressed closer, deeper, hotter, and for a moment all she could feel was his mouth and her hands and the erotic roll of her tongue against his. She'd been kissed before. She liked kissing. But nothing prepared her for the onslaught of feelings cascading through her blood, her bones, her very soul.

When he pulled back, putting a little space between them, her breath was coming out sharp and erratic. He stared at her, scanning her face, his gaze blisteringly intense.

"See…not fake," he said softly and stepped back, releasing her. "About as real as it gets."

She wanted to believe it. She *longed* to believe it. "Okay, so you kiss nice—it's not exactly proof that you're suddenly attracted to me."

He laughed softly, deeply, and the sound rumbled through her like an orchestra playing an adagio behind her ribs. "Suddenly? Is that what you think? Or don't think?"

"I think," she said and moved away a little, "that this is something of a novelty and at some point you're going to realize it's too much effort."

"You're being a little ridiculous, you know," he said and leaned back against the counter.

"Because I want honesty?"

"Because you want absolutes," he said and sighed. "And frankly, Winnie, I'm all out. Did I just wake up one morning and realize I thought of you as more than a friend? Well, no. We did something we wouldn't normally have done, in circumstances that were unusual, and that has somehow shifted the dynamic between us. I don't want to waste time wondering why. The truth is, I could easily ask you the same thing."

"That's different," she said hotly.

"Why?" he shot back. "Because I'm a man and we think about sex differently? You're right, maybe we do. Maybe you and I are absolutely on different pages here. But believe me, making love to you would not be an effort. Get some sleep," he said, suddenly sounding impatient. "We have appointments to see a few houses tomorrow."

Winona didn't linger, even though she felt like she was being scolded. She returned to her bedroom and closed the door. Sleep, of course, wasn't on the agenda, and she only managed to sneak in a few restless hours.

When she got out of bed at half past six, the apartment was empty and she figured Grant had gone for a run.

He returned around 7:15—hot, sweaty and as sexy

as sin. By then, she'd already gone downstairs and grabbed a few things from the bakery for breakfast.

"Don't you ever cook breakfast?" he asked and looked at the strawberry cream-cheese bagel she'd placed on a plate.

"Not if I can help it," she replied. "I like to cook cakes and pies. You know that about me already."

"Well, it seems to matter more now that we're going to be living together. I gotta teach you how to eat something other than sweets," he said and shook his head.

She smiled übersweetly. "I suppose you'd prefer to raise our child on a vegetarian diet?"

"Would you object?" he asked.

Winona shrugged. "I can appreciate the benefits. But no kale juices, eggplant or avocado."

"Carnivore," he teased. "I'm going to take a shower."

"Don't use all the hot water," she warned, biting into her bagel.

"Join me, then?" he asked and pulled off his T-shirt. "For the sake of water consumption."

Winona rocked back on her heels and stared at his chest, almost choking on her mouthful of bagel. He really didn't have any right to look so good without clothes. It was too distracting. And all the talk about sex the night before had muddled her brain and she couldn't stop thinking about it. About him. About their future together as husband and wife.

"Is this flirting the new thing between us?" she asked, trying to keep her tone light.

"Why not," he replied and tossed the T-shirt over one shoulder. "Sure beats the tension and the arguing. We've always had fun together. I miss that. I miss us."

She missed *them*, too...so much she was aching inside.

"Me, too," she admitted.

He went to say something and then stopped, smiling instead. "Won't be long. I'll save you some water."

The rest of the morning had an odd tempo. Not their usual dynamic, but not the tightly strung, tense, almost borderline antagonism that had started seeping into the cracks of their relationship. After breakfast and taking turns showering, they returned to the Realtor's office and inspected two possible rental properties. Winona fell in love with the second one, a house on leafy Maple Street just out of town. It was a large, Colonial Revival style home, two-story, with a fabulously accentuated front door, wide porch with slender columns and windows with double-hung sashes.

"This was an estate sale and so has been empty for some time," the agent explained as they walked around the house. "I'm sure it will go on the market at some point, but the previous owner left it to her stepson and he's happy for it to be a rental for the moment. He lives in Yankton and has no interest in residing in Cedar River."

Winona looked around some more, going from room to room, seeing the beauty in the polished timber floors, hand-carved staircase and large stone fireplace in the living room. And the yard was huge with an array of shrubs and flowers and a large chokecherry tree in one corner. She wandered around the garden, spotting a bird feeder hanging from a tree branch. It would be a lovely house to raise a family in.

"I love it," she said to Grant as the Realtor walked

back inside, giving them some privacy. "It's probably out of my price range, though."

He frowned. "What?"

"Well, I have no intention of dodging my share of the rent."

He stopped walking and they both knew exactly what the conversation was about. "Are you going to be stubborn about everything?"

"No," she replied. "Just planning on paying my share."

He exhaled heavily. "It's my job to financially look after my wife and child."

"That's a little old-fashioned, don't you think? I have a job, Grant. I work and pay my bills, something I will continue to do."

He walked away, hands on hips, his shoulders tight. Winona remained where she was, watching him, feeling the tension between them grow as the seconds ticked by. Whenever he had something on his mind he always took a moment to reflect, to think, to consider his response. This was no different.

Finally, he turned, hands still on his lean hips. "Is everything going to be a battle? Can you at least meet me in the middle?"

"Of course," she replied. "The middle is me paying my share in everything."

"Look," he said, clearly exasperated. "I don't mean to come across old-fashioned, and I'll try harder to stop—I promise. But you and me and the baby are a family now. It's important to me to take care of my family. Despite you thinking I'm being bossy, I'm right here, doing this, *with* you. I'm honestly not trying to be demanding or last-century—just worthy of you both."

Winona stared at him, startled by the rawness of his admission, by the quiet intensity in his voice. And by the way his words made her feel. Feelings that suddenly had nowhere to go. Except into concession.

"Okay," she said softly, her heart banging so loudly behind her ribs she was sure he could hear it. "If you want to take care of the rent and the other things, then fine. But I will need to contribute something, understand? I have my pride and don't relish the idea of financially depending on anyone."

"I'm pretty sure we stopped being just *anyone* to one another a long time ago."

Of course he was right. And that was what made it so hard. If they were newly acquainted as well as being newly married, the situation would be very different. But they knew each other too well to negotiate.

"That's why it's so hard," she said, verbalizing her thoughts.

"Because we don't have any secrets from one another, you mean?"

I do have a secret...

And it twisted at her, churning her insides, making her mad with him but mostly with herself. Loving Grant had been her one constant for years. Being *in love* with him—silently acknowledging the resurgence of feelings she believed she'd tucked away forever—that made everything different between them. Because she was in love with him...had never stopped. She'd only buried her feelings away because she believed they were destined to be best friends forever. Not lovers.

And certainly not husband and wife.

"What if we bring more to this than we get back?"

she asked, wondering if he'd read between the lines of her words—if he'd know she was talking about her loving him.

But he didn't. He was only ever about the facts. "Everything I own, every penny I have, I would give to you in a heartbeat," he said quietly. "Before Vegas, after Vegas. It's only money, Winnie. And since you've called me short-arms-long-pockets for years, I would think you'd like seeing me dip into the stash. I've never been much of a spender."

She laughed. She had called him that many times over the years. Oh, he was generous in nature, but had never been someone to splash out on frivolous things. He bought quality over quantity. Everything he owned was a considered purchase, made to last and be functional. She may have laughed about it at times, but the truth was, she admired his ability to save and be sensible. He owned his apartment and his car and she was sure he had a sizable bank balance.

"Should we get a prenup?" she asked quickly. "Or postnup in our case? You bring way more financial security to this marriage than I do."

"Didn't you hear what I just said?" he asked, his voice ominously low. "About giving you everything I have? I don't care about money, Winnie. If I have it, it's yours."

She knew that, because he was a lot of things—and honest was at the top of the list. She conceded a little more for the sake of harmony. "So—this house? Let's do it."

He sighed and she heard an almost palpable relief in the gesture. A few minutes later they were back inside and discussing the lease agreement with the Realtor.

"I'll call the owner today so we can process your application quickly," the Realtor said and looked at Grant. "I manage a couple of your brother's rental properties, so I'm sure I can provide the owner with a reference on your behalf," she said and grinned.

"How many houses does Joss own?" Winnie asked once they were back in the car and heading into town.

"A few, I think," he replied. "Joss has got quite the property portfolio and is giving the O'Sullivans a run for their money."

Everyone knew the rich O'Sullivan family owed a substantial portion of the commercial real estate in town. "Since Leah's going to marry one of them, we should learn to like them, I guess."

"Old habits," he said and grinned. "And Sean's okay—he's not as stuffy and entitled as some of them," he said of Leah's boyfriend.

Once they returned to the Realtor's office, they quickly filled out the relevant application forms and Winona was suddenly put on the spot when she was filling in the section with her name.

Winona Culhane...

Could she do it? As a teenager she'd doodled the words countless times. She'd dreamed it. Fantasized about it. Cried over it the day he announced he had his first girlfriend. Cursed herself over it time and time again when she knew it was a pipe dream.

He was sitting beside her, waiting for her to finish signing the form, and she could feel the heat from his gaze searing through her skin. She noticed her hand was shaking as she wrote and she took a steadying breath. Looking at her new signature—which was both familiar and crazily unbelievable—the reality of their situation pressed down on her shoulders. They were married. Having a baby. Setting up house together. She was living her secret dream. Winona should have been singing her happiness from the rooftops. She wasn't because it didn't feel real.

They were on the street, walking toward the bakery, when he spoke again. "There's something I'd like you to do."

"What?"

"Wear your wedding ring."

Winona almost tripped up. "Ah…"

"Or rather, wear *a* ring," he clarified. "Honestly, I'd like us to get new ones."

Winona glanced at the ring on his finger, noticing how bare her own seemed. "Why?"

"Because this ring was bought for someone else," he reminded her and tapped the wedding band he wore.

With her emotions already stretched, Winona wasn't sure she wanted a battle, but she didn't want to simply comply, either. "Seems like a waste of money when we have perfectly good rings."

"Is everything about money to you?"

It was an odd thing for him to say. He knew she had certain beliefs about things, and wasting money was one of them. She'd spent her early years with a mother who lived week-to-week mostly on welfare, and by the time she began living with Red on the ranch, she'd already got into the habit of being careful with her pennies. It wasn't about being frugal—it was about pride, and her need to work for what she had and pay her way. She knew he was generous, but not wasteful, and usually it was one of the things she admired about Grant—even if she did tease him every now and then. But he'd never been poor…and Winona knew what poor was firsthand. She knew hand-me-down clothes, food stamps and going hungry as a child. Grant had lived on the ranch all his life, enjoying the comforts of family money, and even when his mom died and Billie-Jack was left to run the place for a couple of years, Mitch and his aunt Sandra had ensured the place stayed afloat.

"I don't think money is everything," she said quietly. "But our childhoods were a little different."

"I know that, okay. And I'm certainly not trying to blow off your concerns about money," he said and grabbed her hand when she realized they were outside Cedar River's only jewelry store. "You're right, our lives were very different growing up. I know the struggles you experienced before you came to live with Red. But I'm asking you, please, can we do this?"

His gentle tone undid all of her resentment and she gave in with a hesitant smile. "Sure. Okay, let's go look."

Winona had been into the shop many times over the years to buy gifts for her grandfather and some of her friends. The fob watch she'd bought Grant for his twenty-first birthday came from the small but well-stocked store.

Deep down, she wanted to protest. To refuse the suggestion because it seem pointless. But something held her back.

This ring was bought for someone else…

It hadn't occurred to her that *he* might have any insecurities. Maybe it was just plain old macho conditioning. She couldn't be sure. And since Grant wasn't renowned for expressing his feelings, she was left with questions rather than the answers she longed for.

Grant wasn't quite sure why he was making such a big deal about the rings. But it had been niggling at him for days. Weeks even. Distracting him when he should have been thinking about a dozen other things. But the last couple of days had solidified his belief that they were doing the right thing by staying married and trying to make it work for their baby. Their child needed both parents. And he certainly didn't want to be a part-time father. He didn't do anything in half measures. He was all or nothing. In or out. Black or white. It was how he'd always lived his life.

And yeah, his relationship with Winnie was strained, intense and at times downright awkward, but they cared enough about one another to push past the hard stuff—he was sure of it.

He watched her move around the store, her fingers trailing across the edge of the cabinets as she perused the displays. He knew she liked sparkly things and watched her expression lift into a smile as she walked around. The jeweler, a middle-aged man who'd taken over the store from his father, attended to them immediately.

"How about that one?" Grant suggested, looking at a large oval-shaped solitaire diamond.

She joined him at the cabinet. "That's an engagement ring."

"It's usually the custom to have one."

"These are not usual circumstances."

He shrugged. "Maybe not, but the less attention we draw to the fact, the better, don't you think?"

She didn't look impressed by that remark, either.

While she perused the cabinet, Grant looked at the wedding bands, found one he liked and tried it on. It fit and he nodded agreeably.

"They're all so expensive," she said, almost to herself.

He knew that look—knew she was deep in thought, imagining the worst, thinking about how wasteful it all was. But Grant wasn't about to bend on the issue. And he wasn't prepared to question why. "Just pick one that you like."

"If you insist on a rock, I like this one," she said and pointed to a baguette emerald surrounded by diamonds.

He admired the stone and waited while she tried it on. It fit perfectly and the jeweler remarked how it was unusual to find an exact fit the first time.

"A wedding band, too," Grant said and gestured to a selection of bands in the cabinet.

She took only a few seconds to find one she liked and the jeweler passed it to Grant. "I think that's your department," he said.

Grant took the ring and grasped Winona's hand, waiting until the other man moved away from the counter before he spoke. "So," he said and slipped the ring on her finger. "For better or worse? For richer or poorer? To honor and cherish?" He lingered over the words for a moment. "We know how the rest goes, right?"

Her eyes glistened so brilliantly he had to fight the lump thickening his throat. "Yes, I think we do."

"Here," he said and held out the band he'd chosen. "Your turn."

She placed the ring on his finger, curling her hand in his. "Tell me we're doing the right thing."

Grant cupped her cheek. "We are. You and me," he reminded her. "We always do what's right. That's just who we are."

She inhaled deeply and smiled. "Okay."

Half an hour later, the rings selected and paid for and the paperwork completed, they left the store and headed to the bakery.

"They feel a little weird," she said and shook her left hand. "And ridiculously expensive. I'm glad you opted in for the insurance, because I'm terrified I'll lose them."

"They fit perfectly," Grant said and grabbed her hand, linking their fingers. "So the risk of losing them is small. Stop worrying. There's a pawn shop in Rapid City we can take the old ones to, if you like."

She shrugged, and when they reached the bottom of the stairway leading up to her apartment, she turned to face him. "Thank you," she said and stood on her toes and kissed his cheek.

He flushed with pleasure. "It's been quite a day, hasn't it? What do you say we go to JoJo's for pizza tonight?"

She agreed and they spent a companionable evening hanging out together.

But Grant knew she was faking it. He could feel it right through to his bones. Because he was faking it, too, so much that his jaw actually ached from the tight smile he forced himself into presenting every time she looked his way.

Back in the apartment by nine that evening, they went their separate ways at bedtime. He stayed up and did some prep work on his laptop for a job in Duluth the following week, while she headed for her bedroom.

There was no late-night tea party, like there had been the night before. There was no repeat of the conversation about sex and definitely no kissing.

Which, as it turned out, was pretty much all he'd thought about for most of the day. Her perfume, for one thing, seemed to suddenly have a mind of its own and attacked his good sense at every opportunity, making him wonder about how much of the scent lingered on her skin by the end of the day. And her lips had been driving him crazy all afternoon—whether she was smiling, scowling or kissing his cheek. And her beautiful, sexy, memories-of-it-draped-over-his-chest hair wasn't doing his libido any favors, either.

The following day they headed to the ranch in the morning and endured Mitch, Tess and Ellie's scrutiny for a couple of hours. Hank was there for a visit and Grant dealt with a few minutes of query from his sensible, rock-solid brother while they were alone in the living room.

"Joss said last week you were getting a divorce?"

He nodded. "Things have changed. We're trying to work it out."

Hank chuckled. "Well, then, congratulations. You heading to Leah's tonight?"

"That was the plan," he replied.

"I'm on duty," Hank said. "I think Joss is going. The girls are with his in-laws this weekend and I think Leah is trying to set him up with the new museum curator."

"Well, you and Joss are the only single Culhanes left," Grant reminded him.

"And Ellie," Hank corrected.

"Don't kid yourself," Grant said and grinned. "She's half in love with Alvarez—she just won't admit it."

Hank's brows shot up. "I thought she despised him?"

"Same thing, really."

Hank laughed. "I guess. So, are you guys taking a honeymoon?"

He realized it wasn't something he and Winnie had talked about. "We haven't really discussed it. There's been a lot of other stuff going on."

"I suppose eloping and a baby on the way will do that," Hank remarked, still grinning. "I'm sure you'll be a good dad, though. Better than the one we had, that's for sure."

It was the perfect opening for Grant to mention Billie-Jack—but the words stuck in his throat for a few seconds. Of all the people their father's reckless-ness had impacted, Hank was the one who'd suffered the most. "Have you forgiven him?" he asked quietly, aware of the sudden stillness in the room.

Hank's expression flattened. "I try not to think about him."

"Yeah, me, too."

"You and Ellie were younger," Hank said evenly. "You needed him more. And the rest of us had Mom for longer and knew what a good parent was like."

"I miss her a lot," Grant admitted.

"Me, too," Hank said and sighed. "She had a way of making everything seem like it would work out. She was the glue that held us all together. Like Mitch is now. But, you know, forgiveness is a funny thing. It can creep up on a person over time. I don't hate Billie-Jack like I did. I don't wonder like I did. I guess I've put the memory of him from my mind. To me, that's better than hanging on to anger and resentment."

Grant admired his brother's resolve. But unlike

Hank, he *was* curious about Billie-Jack. And maybe his brother was right—he'd been younger and more impressionable when their father bailed and didn't have the maturity back then to compartmentalize his feelings like his older siblings had been able to.

One thing he did know—he wasn't about to burden anyone else with the knowledge that Billie-Jack had resurfaced after so many years. At least, not yet.

"Everything okay?"

They were on their way to the dinner party late that afternoon when Winona asked him the question. They'd barely spoken since arriving at the ranch and she knew him well enough to pick up on his mood.

"Just thinking about things."

She nodded and touched his arm. "You've been quiet the last few hours. Second thoughts?"

"About us?" he queried. "Of course not. I was wondering if you wanted to take a honeymoon. We haven't really talked about it."

"It's not necessary," she replied. "Everything about us is unorthodox. And with moving into the new place and the baby and everything else, I'm really not up for anything more."

"Okay," he said and shrugged as he turned the vehicle onto the bridge and headed down to the river. "Just trying to tick all the boxes."

"Well, stop it, will you," she snapped. "I don't need to be placated with sparkly rings and vacations. I agreed to do this and we're doing it."

"The rings were for me," he said. "The thought of wearing a wedding band you picked out for *him* bugged the hell out of me."

Her mouth opened. "You sound jealous."

"Well, of course I'm freakin' jealous," he said irritably. "A month ago you were rushing off to marry the guy."

Silence screeched between them. He'd said too much, admitted too much.

They reached the driveway of Leah's home and headed down it. There were several vehicles parked outside the big house and he recognized Joss's pickup and Jake's SUV. He wasn't usually restless about the idea of socializing but was pleased a couple of his brothers would be there.

She got out of the car and Grant was struck by how lovely she looked in a pale blue dress and sandals. It was a warm evening and there was a radiant hue on her cheeks. Was she glowing? Had pregnancy amplified her beauty? The notion struck him deep in the gut, and he experienced an acute sense of stupid male pride somewhere in the region that probably belonged in a museum. He'd never considered himself an alpha guy—more millennial than his tough, cowboy brothers.

"What are you thinking?" she asked as she came around the car.

"Actually, I was thinking how beautiful you look," he replied and hooked his arm through her elbow. "But I don't want to be accused of placating or ticking any more boxes."

Her brows shot up. "Or being a jerk, right?"

"Because I told my wife she's beautiful? Seems like that's my job." He led her toward the house. "Remember, I am new to the husband gig. Although forgiveness isn't something you're usually good at, try to overlook my rookie mistakes, will you."

She pulled her arm away as they reached the stairs. "Are you looking for an argument?" she asked.

"Maybe," he said and shrugged. "At least we're talking."

Her gaze was filled with unrelenting scrutiny. "What's gotten into you?"

His hair-trigger temper—something he usually kept under tight control—snapped. "I don't know. Maybe I'm tired of you looking for fault in everything I do."

Her skin visibly paled. "I don't do that."

"Sure you do," he shot back. "It's your *thing*, finding fault. Maybe if you'd found fault with your marine and realized he wasn't the one for you, we wouldn't be in this mess!"

The moment he said, he regretted it. Because Grant knew he sounded like a petulant, immature jerk. But he couldn't keep a plug on the thoughts—the *feelings*—churning through his system. It had been building for days, torturing him every now and then, threatening to break free and make him face exactly what he was—jealous. The bloodcurdling, stomach-dropping kind. He'd admitted it to her earlier in an off-the-cuff way, but since buying the rings he'd had hours to dwell, hours to consider his reasoning, hours to build a wall of defense around what he wasn't prepared to face.

He was jealous of the man she had been going to marry.

The man she had loved. Still loved, he suspected, because feelings didn't simply switch off, did they? And since he'd never been jealous before, the knowledge shocked Grant to his deepest core. It didn't make sense. She'd dated in the past, had a boyfriend—hell, she'd been seeing the marine for eighteen months—

and not once in that time had he faced the feelings suddenly tormenting him. And now, out of the blue, he was filled with a black, relentless rage that he couldn't shift, couldn't quell and couldn't understand.

Her eyes darkened for a moment and he suspected she wanted to tell him to go straight to hell. But she didn't. Because the door opened and his cousin Leah appeared. She greeted them both with a smile and a hug, making a cheerful comment about their marriage that fell flat between them as they headed inside.

But the tension remained. And Grant knew they were heading for a major confrontation.

The truth was, he didn't know how he was going to stop imagining that she wished she was married to someone else.

CHAPTER NINE

WINONA HAD SEEN many of Grant's moods over the years. But never this one. He spent the evening skulking like a caged animal, restless, on edge, as though he was looking for an escape the whole time they were there.

She'd always believed she knew everything about him, but this was new—this was unlike anything she'd experienced before. He'd always been so indifferent in relationships, so casual, she'd never had reason to think he was capable of, well...jealousy.

But clearly he was. He'd said as much. For whatever reason.

She tried to ignore him as much as she could, but it was impossible. Dinner was informal, more like a barbecue, and she was able to mingle, to show off her sparkly rings, to talk about the unexpected turn of events to friends and laugh and smile and act as though nothing was amiss. But she felt the friction building between them and every time she met his gaze it was filled with words unsaid.

It was weird seeing so many Culhanes and O'Sullivans in the same place, but since Leah and Sean had hooked up, the dynamic between the two families had changed. She hung around Jake and his wife, Abby, for a while, answering questions about their rushed marriage, and smiled appropriately when her sister-in-law said how it was all so romantic.

But it wasn't.

A mess.

That's what he'd called it.

And it was pretty close to the mark. Like they were playacting at being married.

Faking it.

God, what am I doing...?

It had only been a few days and already the tension between them was unbearable. What would happen when they were really living together? How could they possibly make it work? Would they have separate bedrooms? The Maple Street house had three bedrooms and a study—plenty of room for them to sleep apart *and* have a place for the baby.

She looked around and spotted Leah by the buffet table, chatting to Joss and Jake. She and Leah and Ellie had always been the firmest of friends, and even though the other two women were cousins, they'd never left her out of their circle. She cared about both women deeply and felt ashamed that she'd pulled away from their friendship in the past month or so. Perhaps if she hadn't rushed off to Vegas and asked only Grant to be there, if she'd included them, then her life wouldn't now be so upside down. They would have consoled her when Dwight proved to be a no-show. They would have drunk margaritas together, cried a little, called him a few names and then returned home.

But there would be no baby...

And that was the kicker.

Because, despite everything, despite the fact she

was deeply conflicted about her awkward relationship with Grant, she was over the moon about the prospect of having a baby. She'd always wanted a family of her own and couldn't stop the joy she felt every time she thought about the child she carried.

"So," Leah said as she sidled up beside her. "You're one for surprises."

Winona smiled. "Yeah…what can I say."

Leah was an artist, and with her long dark hair streaked with colors of pink and purple and in the flowing halter-style dress she wore, she looked unconventional. In her sensible blue outfit, Winona felt very ordinary beside her friend.

"Oh, I don't know," Leah said and smiled. "This kind of thing usually has a way of working itself out. It's kind of romantic when you think about it."

"That's probably a stretch, since we got drunk and ended up in bed together," Winona said and then felt bad. She didn't want anyone speculating about her relationship with Grant. "Well, anyway, we're trying to work it out as we go."

"That's all any of us can do," her friend said and placed a comforting arm around her shoulders. "And don't be a stranger, okay?"

Winona nodded. "I'll try harder."

Leah's expression softened. "You know, you've always been family to me and Ellie, and now that you're married to Grant, you really are family. So, don't take this the wrong way, but we never believed Dwight was the right guy for you."

"You didn't?"

"No," her friend replied. "And I'm pretty sure you didn't, either. Do you remember that time we played

Truth or Dare and you lost and I got to read a page out of your diary? I was about fifteen, you were fourteen?"

Memory rushed through her. She recalled the small, sparkly purple diary, the little notebook that held all her secrets. She still had it, tucked away in the back of the cupboard in her old bedroom at the ranch. "Yeah."

"Well, the page I read included these words, and I quote—'I want to marry him one day.' And I know you weren't talking about the latest pop star on MTV."

"Just teenage angst," Winona said, swallowing her embarrassment, recalling exactly the day and the moment she wrote the words about Grant in her diary. He was a senior in high school and was taking Missy Benson to prom, and Winona had cried on and off for days leading up to the event, knowing he'd be kissing Missy at the end of the evening, and maybe more. Also knowing that besides the soul-crushing fact they were friends, she was way too young for him back then. "It didn't mean anything."

"Maybe it does. Maybe it means everything worked out just as it was meant to. You know, it looks to me like you got what you asked for."

Winona stared at her friend, too stunned to speak. Because Leah was right. She did have what she'd wished for—all of it. Grant and a baby of her own. Maybe the way they came about wasn't exactly the stuff of fairy tales, but she had it all, nonetheless.

She looked across the room and spotted him near the wide door that opened onto the deck and he met her gaze instantly. She offered a tiny smile and he frowned, like he wasn't expecting a kind gesture, and it made her suck in a sharp breath.

I'm tired of you looking for fault in everything I do...

Was that really what she did? To everyone? Or to him alone?

She couldn't decide which option was the worst. Either way, she experienced a deep surge of shame that ripped through her like a tornado.

It took her a few minutes to summon the courage to walk over to him. He was talking to Joss and she moved up beside him, saying nothing. She simply grasped his hand and linked their fingers, feeling him stiffen. But after a couple of seconds, he relaxed a little and his fingers tightened around hers.

"You okay?" he asked quietly when there was a break in the conversation.

Winona moved closer to him and spoke so only he could hear. "Can you take me home?"

His brow furrowed. "Something wrong?"

"No," she replied. "Just tired."

He was still frowning, but he nodded, and ten minutes later they were heading back into town. Winona didn't say much, just a passing comment about how nice the evening had been and how happy Leah seemed. He didn't respond, didn't say anything, really, merely a sort of half grunt that was acknowledgment of her words.

Back at the apartment, she walked on ahead and dropped her tote on the hall table near the door. She looked at him, noticing that he was now standing by the window, staring out to the street.

"Grant?"

He turned. "Yeah...good night."

Winona swallowed hard, finding courage from deep down, knowing they were somehow at a crossroads. She wasn't sure how they got there. But she knew she had to do something to save what they had, even if she didn't know what that was—or she suspected they were doomed.

"I don't mean to find fault in you," she said quietly.

He held up a hand vaguely. "I'm really not up for another argument."

"Me, either. Actually," she said and moved forward a few steps, taking a breath, "I was hoping that you might…"

"Might what?" he asked when her words trailed off.

She took another step. "Well, that you might want to forgo the couch tonight," she said, coloring hotly. "I mean, it can't be comfortable and there's really no reason why we shouldn't sleep in the same bed. We are married, after all."

One brow cocked at a sharp angle. "Huh?"

A little frustration set in. "I'm asking if you want to sleep with me tonight."

He took a moment, like he was deciding something difficult. "Isn't that against your ground rules?"

"We both know it was a dumb rule," she said and shrugged. "But suit yourself. I'm going to have a shower and go to bed."

She did what she said she would, racing through a shower, slathering on body lotion, slipping into a shell-pink satin nightgown, and was back in the bedroom brushing her hair when she heard the shower going again. She flicked on the bedside lamps, switched off the main light, and she was just rubbing on hand cream when he appeared in the doorway, silhouetted by the light behind, dressed in a white tank shirt and a pair of cotton boxers, one shoulder leaning against the jamb.

Her breath caught in her throat, and for a moment

she was mesmerized by the image, catapulted back to those hours in Vegas when they had found passion in each other's arms. She wanted that again. Longed for it. Needed it like she needed air in her lungs.

"You know, Winnie," he said, his gaze slowly traveling over her. "If what you really want is for me to make love to you, you only have to ask."

She placed the brush on the dresser and straightened, sensing that they were in one of those pivotal moments. A moment there was no going back from. Only forward. Leah was right—she did have everything she ever wanted. And he'd tried, she knew, to make things as normal as possible. She knew it was up to her to reach out, to make a move, to set the rhythm of their relationship. To fix things, really, so they could have some kind of normal marriage. One that included intimacy.

She inhaled, finding strength from even deeper down than before. "Okay... I'm asking. Would you make love to me tonight?"

"Yes," he said and pushed himself off the jamb. "But I'd like you to answer a question first."

Her nerves rattled. "Sure."

"Why?" he asked. "What's changed?"

"Nothing," she replied, not really lying, because nothing had essentially changed. She'd simply gained some clarity and perspective about their relationship. About her role in their marriage and what she wanted. "I think I just needed some time, you know, to get things straight in my head. To adjust. Let's face it, the last month or so has been kind of overwhelming."

He nodded a little. "You're right, it's been surprising and...confusing."

"But I'm not confused about what I want," she said and took a few steps across the room, her toes digging into the carpet pile.

He met her by the bed, his gaze taking a leisurely trip down her body and back up as he stripped off his tank shirt and tossed it on the floor. She stared at his chest, his shoulders, his flat belly, the lines and contours of a physique that was perfectly proportioned and wholly masculine. She'd never tire of looking at him. Never find any other man as attractive, really, she realized as though she was suddenly in a kind of sexy dream with him in the starring role. Of course, he'd always played center stage in her dreams. Nothing had changed over the years. Only now, he was her husband and she could make her dreams a reality.

"So," he said softly, his voice deep and incredibly sexy. "What do you want?"

"You," she admitted, heat coursing through her veins. "This."

He smiled a little. "You wearing anything under that?" he asked, reaching out to touch her face.

"Not a thing," she replied, watching the pulse in his cheek.

His mouth was on hers within seconds and the kiss was hot, fierce and erotic. Winona wrapped her arms around him, touching his strong back, pushing herself closer, harder, tighter, wanting to feel all of him against her. He moaned low in his throat, deepening the kiss, taking her on a wild ride as their tongues met and withdrew over and over. His hands were in her hair, on her shoulders, on her hips, rubbing the silky fabric against her skin. When he cupped her behind and drew her hard against him, Winona was left with no doubt

of his arousal. Any insecurities she had about his desire or attraction for her were abruptly sent offstage.

He sat on the bed and gently pulled her toward him,
still kissing her, still tracing his fingertips across her
skin in an erotic pattern. She sighed against his mouth,
finding his tongue again and dueling with it, feeling
a hot rush of need pool down low. She'd longed for
passion like this, yearned for it. Dreamed of it. When
he eased her back, she went willingly, her fingers
threading through his hair as he kissed her mouth,
her cheek, her neck, trailing downward to her throat.
He pushed the nightgown straps down and trailed his
mouth along her rib cage, finding her breasts and the
nipples that ached for his caress. He circled one bud
with his tongue, then the other, and she arched her
back off the bed, experiencing pleasure so intense she
could barely draw in a breath. She said his name, holding his head against her, urging him to continue the
exquisite torture.

"Holy hell," he whispered raggedly against her flesh
and swiftly dispensed with her nightgown, openly ad-
miring her. "You're so beautiful, Winnie," he said as
one hand dipped between her thighs and he caressed
her intimately.

She wasn't sure how long they touched for—minutes, hours, eternity. But she came apart, once, twice,
feeling as though she was flying as the pleasure over-
whelmed her senses. Then all she knew was that she
needed to feel him, to run her fingers across his flesh
and touch every part of him. She pressed her hands
against his chest, feeling the muscles bunch, taking her
own erotic journey across skin and sinew. She tugged

at his boxers, dragging them over his hips, and reveled in the sheer beauty of his flesh.

Oddly, there was nothing shy or reserved about the way they made love. It wasn't awkward. It wasn't forced. It was hot, heady and arousing, like it had been in Vegas. He gave, she gave, he led and then she followed. But she took, too, touching him with her hands and mouth and with a confidence she hadn't known she possessed. He did that, she thought as pleasure overtook them, he taught her to take what she wanted, what she needed.

And finally, when they could take no more and craved release, he moved over her, resting his weight on his elbows, his green eyes never leaving hers as they joined together. She matched every move, every kiss, every thrust and erotic slide, and as the pressure built, so did the love that she felt through to the depths of her soul. She tumbled headlong into a vortex of pleasure so intense she couldn't get enough air in her lungs, holding him, grasping at him, as he tumbled with her in a white-hot rush of release.

Afterward, he rolled off her gently, grasping her hand and raising it to his lips. "Are you okay?" he asked, his voice low and raspy.

"Perfect," she said on a sigh.

"Yes," he said and exhaled, "you certainly are."

Grant knew that sex could addle a man's brain. Great sex, however, also did something else. It made him crave. Like he'd never quite craved before. In the past, sex was something enjoyable he did with someone he liked. Afterward, though, he would swiftly forget about the intimate connection and get on with his life.

But he didn't simply like Winnie. He loved her. And that changed sex.

The thing was, up until two hours ago, he hadn't quite believed that to be true.

But now, as he lay beside his wife, her lovely arm draped across his belly, her hair fanned over his chest, he was struck by how content and *happy* he was. The scent of her assailed him, reaching him on some sensory level he was unfamiliar with. Normally, after sex, he'd be asleep within twenty minutes, but for reasons he couldn't define, he didn't want to miss one moment of watching her, feeling her, experiencing her.

And it shocked him deeply.

She moved, moaning softly, and he soothed her with a gentle rocking motion. She was so beautiful, so uninhibited, so naturally sensual, that their lovemaking had taken him to another place. Another dimension. He felt ridiculous thinking it, but he couldn't dismiss the notion.

He kissed her forehead and she sighed, rolling a little, linking one of her legs around his. He could feel her belly pressed against his thigh, and wondered how long it would be before her pregnancy started showing. He wanted her to show, he wanted to splay his hand across her stomach and feel their child moving beneath his palm. The idea filled him with an excitement that he couldn't fathom. He'd never believed he was one of those people who felt deeply, too afraid of letting his guard down to allow anyone to get inside, but Winnie was well and truly in deep. So was their baby.

And somehow, instead of the normal anxiety he experienced thinking about it, as he lay with her in his arms, his pulse rate slowly winding down after such an intense physical release, Grant experienced an incredible sense of calm.

He slept, waking up around dawn to the lovely sensation of her hands stroking his chest. She lay on her side, the sheet tangled at their feet, her eyes closed, her fingertips touching him in a way that was both erotic and hypnotic.

"You keep doing that and I'm never going to get out of this bed," he said and grasped her hand, bringing her knuckles to his mouth and kissing her softly.

She didn't open her eyes. But she smiled. "That's my plan, Culhane," she whispered. "Although I can think of some other things I could also do."

Grant chuckled. "Be my guest."

Her eyes sprang open and she looked at him, all sexy and wanton and so hot he felt awareness creep back into his limbs and then move higher, because he was completely at her mercy. She didn't need another invitation and quickly moved over him, lying breast to chest, hip to hip, thigh to thigh, her hair cascading like a waterfall around them.

Within seconds he was inside her, and she straddled him, rising to her knees, gripping his hands and moving her hips in a way that almost sent him directly over the edge into that place that was a mix of both heaven and hell. She didn't speak, didn't do anything other than rotate her hips, creating an aching hunger in his blood that defied belief. When release came it was swift, sharp and soul-deep. He watched her through a daze of pleasure, feeling closer to her in that moment than he had ever felt to anyone else, ever.

She collapsed against him, breathing hard, her breasts pressed to his chest, her mouth quickly finding his in a kiss that was filled with passion and heat. He could barely breathe, but still kissed her, still took her tongue into his mouth, still gripped her hips to maintain the intensely intimate connection of their bodies.

"Now I'm definitely not getting out of this bed," he said on a strangled breath.

She laughed and the lovely sound reverberated in his chest. "Not even for your morning run?"

His brows shot up. "Seriously, do you think I have any energy left for running?"

She laughed again. "Dig deep, husband."

He liked the way she said the word and experienced a foolish sense of companionship and pride in that moment. He chuckled and rolled them both in one gentle movement, half pinning her beneath him. "Although, I gotta say, this isn't the most comfortable mattress in the world. We should go furniture shopping as soon as we know if we got the house."

"You're not planning on bringing your furniture from your apartment?" she asked, a little more seriously.

"Nah... I don't think all that chrome and glass would look any good in the Maple Street house. And I think we should get new stuff, you know, for a new start."

"Let's do the shopping together, as long as we split the bill," she said, clearly looking for a compromise. "It'll be fun. I can't wait to start buying baby things."

The look in her eyes when she spoke about the baby created an ache deep in his chest. "You're really happy about the baby, aren't you?" he asked, seeing pure joy in her expression.

She nodded. "I've always wanted kids, you know that. I guess it's because I had such a dysfunctional time growing up, before I moved in with Papa. And then I met you and saw what a real family was like. I want that for our children, Grant."

"Children?"

Her eyes shuttered for a moment. "I'd always planned to have two or three if I could."

"I guess I'm still reeling from the idea of one," he said, teasing her a little, "but I'll come around. Besides," he said and trailed a kiss from her ear to her mouth. "Making them is fun."

They stayed in bed for another half an hour, kissing, touching, talking about silly things. When he hauled himself up she seemed shy, covering herself with a duvet for a moment, and then she shrugged and dropped the cover, walking across the room naked before slipping into a cotton robe.

"Bit late for modesty, right?" she said.

"A little," he replied. "What would you like to do today?"

She glanced at the bed. "I'm sure we'll think of something."

They headed out to O'Sullivan's for breakfast a little later, and when they returned to her apartment, Grant did some work for a couple of hours. She interrupted him every now and then, offering coffee or a snack, sometimes more, which was incredibly tempting and distracting. It was far removed from the tense, almost distant dynamic of the previous days and he liked it…a lot.

"You know," he said and grabbed her hand when she walked past the small table where he was working, and gently pulled her onto his lap. "The more you distract me, the longer this is going to take and the less time I'll have to make love to you tonight."

"I know," she said and curled her arms around his neck, dipping her head to kiss his throat. "But I can't help myself. I wish you didn't have to leave tomorrow."

"Me, too," he said and rested his hands on her hips. "But I have some prep work I need to do and my flight for Duluth leaves early on Tuesday morning."

"When will you be back?" she said, kissing the spot just below his earlobe and making him crazy.

"Thursday," he replied raggedly. "Friday morning at the latest."

She pressed closer, distracting him even more. "How many of you are going?"

"Three," he replied. "Bill from tech support, Krystal and myself."

She pulled back immediately. "Krystal?"

"She's the training leader for this project," he said and saw the hesitation in her eyes. "Don't stress, she knows I'm married now."

"I'm not stressed. How'd she take it?"

"You know, I didn't wait around to ask. But I'm pretty sure she couldn't care less."

"What makes you so sure?"

"Because she's dating Bill from tech support," he said and grinned. "What are you planning on doing this week?" he asked, trying to shift his thoughts from X-rated to a more appropriate G-rated, and figured he'd have to settle on M-rated because she kept kissing his neck and it was mind-blowing.

"Start packing, I guess. And I need to talk to Regina about breaking my lease."

He nodded agreeably. "Have you given any more thought to her offer, you know, to go into a partnership?"

She sighed against his skin. "Yes. I need to think about my future. I need to do something with my life."

"You can do anything you want," he said, stroking her hips in a way that spiked his libido up another notch. "You're smart, beautiful, funny—"

"Broke," she reminded him.

"You know," he said as he grasped her chin and tilted her face to meet his, "we could go into the venture together. What's mine is yours, remember?"

Her brown eyes were warm and slumberous, filled with a kind of glazed desire that reached him deep down. "Together?"

"Business partners as well as husband and wife."

He hoped she'd make some concession and was pleased when she did.

"Okay, I'll think about it."

"Thank you," he said and kissed her softly.

"For what?"

"Not immediately putting a wall up," he replied. "For considering it. I heard the trick to a good marriage is compromise."

Her brows rose. "Did you just make that up?"

"Maybe," he conceded. "But it sounds about right. By the way, I'm gonna miss you this week."

She smiled, kissing him. "Me, too. Poor Krystal," she said, still smiling. "Doesn't know what she's missing."

He kissed her hotly and got to his feet, quickly forgetting about work, and carried her down the hall and into the bedroom. They made love in a leisurely way, ignoring the fact it was still light outside and that the lazy Sunday afternoon was doing its thing on the street below. Grant knew he'd never get enough of the taste of her lips, or the scent of her skin, or the touch of her hands.

And it floored him.

Of course he'd experienced desire before, and in varying degrees, but never with the burning intensity he felt for Winnie. The more he touched her, the more he wanted her. The more she gave, the more he wanted to give. It was jarring to his usual self-control. Because there was nothing controlled about the feelings coursing through him—feelings that were shifting and changing at an alarming rate.

No, he corrected, not changing…that wasn't it.

They were doing something else—they were intensifying. As though they'd lain dormant since eternity and were suddenly allowed to come to life. Now, he wondered how he'd even gotten through a day without kissing her, without thinking of her as more than just his friend.

Because this wasn't simple friendship, he thought as they held one another. It was deeper and more real than anything he'd experienced before.

It was high stakes.

And he realized, maybe for the first time in his life, what he had to lose.

Everything.

CHAPTER TEN

THEY GOT THE house on Maple Street, which was just as well because Winona had already started packing up her apartment. Grant called her Wednesday from Duluth and said the Realtor had contacted him that afternoon and would call her the following day to make arrangements for the key collection and some further documents to sign.

She was excited but couldn't quell the uneasiness that crept up on her every now and then. She couldn't quite define it. It wasn't overt. It wasn't grounded in anything substantial. They needed a bigger place, end of story. But still, she was rattled. She didn't say anything to Grant because she knew he would either dismiss her reservations—if that's even what they were—or placate her with assurances that they were doing the right thing. And yes, she agreed...mostly.

She'd believed, or at least hoped, that physical intimacy would bring them closer. But deep down she felt that being lovers had created an even wider divide. The sex was wonderful, and in his arms, she experienced pleasure and tenderness she hadn't known existed. But in her heart she knew it hadn't brought them closer—it only amplified how far apart they really were.

And made her lonelier than she ever imagined she could feel.

She longed to talk to him about it, but the words wouldn't come.

Winona worked morning shifts that week, and on Thursday she stopped by the ranch to see her grandfather. Of course, she spoke to him every day on the phone, but that wasn't the same as having a real visit.

She spotted Ellie hanging by the corral and figured as well as visiting Red she had some ground to make up with her friend. They'd hardly spoken in the past month or so, and Winona missed their friendship.

"Hey," she said when she approached. "You didn't make it to Leah's last Saturday night?"

Ellie pointed to the mare and young foal at foot that were prancing around the corral. "I was on foal watch," she explained. "This mare had trouble foaling last time, so Mitch and I didn't want to leave her in case anything went wrong."

"He's beautiful."

Ellie nodded. "One thing I gotta say about Alvarez— that champion stallion of his throws beautiful progeny. Speaking of which," Ellie said and glanced at her stomach. "How's my niece or nephew doing?"

Winona touched her belly. "Great. You know, we haven't had a chance to really talk about it."

Ellie shrugged. "What's to say. You married my brother and now you're having a baby. Once I got over the shock, I wasn't really surprised."

Winona suspected as much. In all the years they'd known one another, Ellie had never betrayed her. "You've never said anything…you know, about my feelings for Grant. To him, I mean. I know you've never come and asked, but I think you've always suspected."

"That you're madly in love with him?" Ellie said and grinned. "Of course I knew. I think the only person who was totally clueless was my brother. But he knows now and that's all that matters, right?"

She swallowed hard. Because he didn't know, did he? And how could she tell him when she knew he wouldn't say it in return. That would be devastating and humiliating. "Yeah, sure. We found a house—would you like to come by tomorrow and see it?"

"Love to," Ellie replied.

They made arrangements to meet up at Maple Street the following afternoon. "You can help me decorate."

Ellie smiled. "I'm really happy it all worked out for you both."

"Me, too," Winona said.

"You know what this means, don't you?" Ellie queried.

Winona's brows rose up. "What?"

"We're sisters now," her friend supplied. "Like we always wanted to be when we were kids."

Winona felt an incredible sense of inclusion and belonging in that moment, and quickly hugged her friend. She was still thinking about Ellie's words a little later when she was at the cottage with her grandfather sipping tea and talking about general things—the garden, the new chicken run he'd helped Mitch build. Then he changed the subject.

"How are things between you and Grant?"

"Ah…fine. Why?" she asked.

"Just making sure you're okay," he replied. "That's a grandfather's job."

"I'm fine," she insisted. "I promise. Papa, when we told you we were married and were having a baby, you didn't seem all that surprised."

"I wasn't," he said. "You and Grant go way back. I was probably surprised it hadn't happened sooner. But then you were dating that marine for a while."

Dwight? How long had it been since she'd even spared him a thought? As for thinking she was in love with him, just the notion made her twitch. So much of her life had changed in the past weeks.

"I never really loved Dwight."

"I know that," Red said. "I know you've been looking for love your whole life, Win. After your mother ran off and left you here, it left a little hole inside you, right?"

Emotion rose up and tightened her throat. "I suppose it did."

"Natural," he said gently, his eyes wrinkling at the corners. "And this old man wasn't much good at being both a mom and a dad."

"You were amazing," she assured him. "You still are. I've never been sorry Mom left me here, Papa. I know it was the best thing that could have happened to me."

His eyes glistened. "She's not a bad person, you know. But she was always spirited when she was young. Then she got mixed up in the wrong crowd and started getting into trouble."

Winona had heard the story before. "She was young and everyone makes mistakes when they're young."

"Not you," Red said with a sudden smile. "You were an angel. And now you're married to that fine young man and have a baby coming. I couldn't be prouder."

"You like Grant, don't you?"

He nodded. "Always had a sensible head on his shoulders, even as a little kid. He'll be a good husband and father."

"I know he will," she said, her chest tightening. "I love him very much."

Red nodded approvingly. "He loves you, too. I can see it when you're together."

Winona wanted to believe, wanted to imagine that the feelings he felt for her were more than friendship, more than duty for the child they had made. But self-preservation warned her that wishes were for romantic fools. And romantic fools inevitably ended up with a broken heart. Which was why, when he didn't return to Cedar River on Friday, like he'd promised he would, Winona was imagining all kinds of things.

The truth was, since they'd had such an incredible time together the previous weekend, she'd anticipated that he couldn't wait to get home quick enough—that he was as hungry for her as she was for him. When all she could do was think about being in his arms and feeling his hands all over her, it was clearly not the case for her husband. Sure, when he called Thursday evening and said he was delayed and wouldn't be home until Saturday, she longed to ask him what was so important. She knew he was committed to his work, but irrationally she expected him to put everything aside so he could keep his word. She wanted to start nesting and planning, not sit around pining because he was in another state. She knew she'd sounded tense on the call, and although he said he missed her, she longed for more. She wanted to say she loved him, like they used to do, before their relationship took a dive into something so complicated she didn't even have the words to describe it. She wanted him to reply with his usual *Ditto*. She wanted something. *Anything*. Just some assurance that she wasn't the greatest lovesick fool of all time.

Grant couldn't remember the last time he'd been so nervous. Maybe never. Maybe it wasn't really nerves. Perhaps it was plain and simple dread.

I'm seeing my father for the first time in eighteen years.

He wasn't sure what he expected. What he wanted. And over the past twenty-four hours he'd changed his mind about seeing Billie-Jack half a dozen times.

But now, here he was—sitting opposite the man who he hated and despite everything, still loved—and kept wondering what the hell he was doing.

Billie-Jack. Cancer. Chemo.

The three things were now etched in his brain. After weeks of avoiding it, Grant finally picked up when his father had called again and after several tense minutes, agreed to meet him.

For coffee, he'd first thought, and made arrangements to meet him at a café in Rapid City. Those first few minutes had been unbearably tense. There was no handshake, no hug, just an acknowledging nod. It also took Grant about thirty seconds to figure out that the old man was sick. Billie-Jack looked frail and like a shadow of the person he remembered.

"Yeah, the cancer's got me," his father said, clearly picking up on his observations. "I've been getting treatment. My doctor has arranged for me to continue at the hospital here."

Grant didn't know what to think...or feel. "Why did you call me?"

His father shrugged his bony shoulders. "I wanted to see you...to talk."

Grant's gut rolled over. "About what? The past? Your illness? Redemption?"

"Just to talk," his father said again. "I ain't expecting a miracle."

"Good," Grant replied. "Because I'm all out."

Billie-Jack cracked a smile and then motioned to Grant's left hand. "You're married?"

He nodded. "I didn't agree to come here today to talk about my life."

"Fair enough," his father said. "How are your brothers? Your sister?"

"I didn't agree to come here today to talk about them, either. What is it you want, Billie-Jack?"

He couldn't call him Dad—the word just wouldn't come. All he really wanted to do was bail. He wanted to get back to his real life—the one that was now centered around Winnie and the baby they had coming. The one that had nothing to do with Billie-Jack. All he could think about was how unhappy she'd sounded when they'd spoken on the phone. And how all he wanted was to take her into his arms and reassure her that everything would be okay. That *they* would be okay.

"I want to make amends, if I can."

Amends? That meant forgiveness. It was too much to ask. Too much to give.

"I can't do this," he said and got to his feet. "I have to go."

"Grant, please," Billie-Jack said and grasped his forearm. "I know this is hard. I know you're angry and you have every right to be—but I just want to spend some time with you...while I have time left."

Grant's insides tightened. He wasn't usually someone who ran from hard things—but he had so much going on in his life, he didn't know if he had the time or patience for anything else. But as he looked down at his father, he saw real regret in the other man's expression, and it twisted at something deep inside.

"I'll call you later," he said. "We'll talk some more."

Then he left the café as quickly as he could.

Friday morning, after a night of restless dreams, Winona headed to the new house and made a list of all the things they needed to purchase. The house was mostly clean but had been empty for some time and needed a good airing and the banisters needed a polish. She stopped by the hardware store and picked up some supplies after lunch and was unloading the parcels when Ellie arrived.

Her friend was dressed in jeans and an old shirt. "I'm here to help."

They spent the next few hours cleaning and laughing and reminiscing about their teenage years. Ellie ducked out to get coffee and donuts around three thirty and while she was gone Winona experienced a wrenching sense of melancholy. Sadness even. It should have been the happiest time of her life. She was hanging out with a friend and preparing rooms that would soon be filled with her own family. But all she felt was lost and alone.

"Win?" Ellie's voice cut through her thoughts. "Are you all right?"

She wiped her eyes, mortified that she was now crying, and continued hanging the living room curtains she'd ordered online. They were a little wrinkled, but Ellie assured her the creases would fall out quickly.

"I'm fine," she lied.

"You're upset?" her friend said and came across the room.

She shook her head. "Oh, this is my new thing… crying," she added and gave a self-deprecating laugh. "I'm sure it's just pregnancy hormones running riot."

Ellie draped an arm across her shoulders. "Are you sure? Is something bothering you? Is everything okay?"

She sucked in a breath and nodded, trying to ease the ache in her chest. "I don't know why I'm teary and emotional."

"Well, you've had a lot of change in your life recently, and that's a big upheaval."

"Is it?" she challenged, her voice higher than usual as she moved away, wrapped her arms around her waist and then turned to face her friend. "It shouldn't be. Because I have everything I ever wanted. I mean, I'm married to your brother and I'm having his baby and we're just about to move into this great house and I should be jumping up and down with happiness."

"But you're not, is that what you're saying?"

The emotions she'd been holding back for the past few weeks suddenly rushed to the surface and she couldn't stop the fresh tears that burned her eyes. Ellie was her friend, one of the best she'd ever had. But she was also Grant's sister and that meant loyalties could be strained. She certainly didn't want to cause any stress between the siblings, but in that moment, she needed a friend.

"I can't quite explain what I'm feeling… I'm confused," she admitted. "It's like I have this shadow hovering over me, and I hurt whenever I think about it."

"I'm not sure I understand," Ellie said, looking fraught. "Is this about my brother? Is your marriage in trouble?"

"I don't know," Winona said and sucked in a ragged breath. "You know how important you and your family are to me, right?"

"Of course. We care about you, too."

She nodded. "Grant and I have always had a strong friendship. Unbreakable. Unbendable. But now…"

"And now you don't, is that what you're saying?" Ellie frowned a little. "Even though you're married and—"

"It doesn't make sense, does it?" she said and sighed. "I know that. But I miss what we *had*. I miss the way things used to be, how *we* used to be, when we were just friends. How we would talk and laugh and confide in one another. We don't do that like we used to—we don't connect like we did before all this happened." The words tumbled out, each one hurting more than the last, and she took a moment to regather her composure, wiping the tears off her cheeks.

"Maybe you guys need to talk more," Ellie suggested. "Take a trip, spend some alone time together, have a honeymoon. A real one."

She shrugged. "Grant actually suggested it…but I thought we had too much going on—you know, trying to settle into a new situation—to add something else to the mix."

"Tell him you've changed your mind," Ellie said. "He'd go along with it in a heartbeat."

It sounded like a nice idea, Winona thought as she

went back to the window and fluffed out the curtains. And she was certain Grant would take her wherever she wanted to go. But a honeymoon vacation wasn't the cure for what ailed their relationship. That was the truth. And she wasn't sure she had the courage to face it.

She took a few long breaths and glanced at her friend. "Everything changed so fast and I… I miss *him*," she admitted. "I miss him *so* much."

"What are you going to do?" Ellie asked caringly. "Are you going to tell Grant how you feel?"

"I don't know. I know I can't go back. I know I have a baby on the way and I have to live my life in the present. But I feel…" Her voice trailed off for a moment and she struggled for the word. "Heartbroken."

She heard something, like footsteps, and was stunned to suddenly see Grant framed in the doorway. He wore suit pants and a blue shirt, sans the tie, like he'd come straight from the office. And he looked tired, she noticed.

She blinked and hoped the tears were gone from her eyes. "Hi," she said quickly. "What are you doing here? I thought you weren't coming back until tomorrow."

"I managed to change things around," he replied and moved into the room as he looked toward Ellie. "Hey, Brat."

"Hi," Ellie said as her gaze darted back and forth between them both. "It's good to see you. Well, I should probably get going. It's been fun hanging out," she said and quickly grabbed her bag. "Let me know if you guys need help moving."

She hugged them both and left.

Winona stayed where she was and stared at him,

taking in his tight-shouldered stance and five-o'clock shadow. "I'm surprised to see you."

"Clearly," he replied tersely.

Winona shook herself off, walked across the room and kissed his cheek, inhaling the familiar scent of his cologne, which wrapped around her like a cloak. "Surprised, but glad. How did you know I'd be here?"

"I didn't," he said. "I went to your apartment first. I bought you flowers, but they're also at the apartment."

"Flowers?"

He walked away, strolling around the room. "I thought it might cheer you up. Anyway, the place looks good. You should go furniture shopping in the morning."

She frowned. "Won't you be coming with me?"

"I have to get back to Rapid City in the morning for an appointment. I'll drive back in the afternoon if it's not too late."

Winona was confused. "So why did you come back today if you—"

"I came back for you."

Grant didn't know what to think…or what to make of what he had overheard, and his skin was burning so hot he could barely stand still. She missed her ex—is that what she was saying? She missed him and she was heartbroken.

"For me?"

He turned and looked at her. "You sounded unhappy on the phone last night. I thought perhaps I was needed here more than at…more than anywhere else."

More than seeing my father again…

But he didn't say that. Didn't want to burden her

with the truth. He was still reeling from having met with Billie-Jack the day before, still couldn't get the image out of his head of the thin, sickly looking man who barely resembled the father he'd once known.

And he clearly wanted to make amends. He wanted so much. And all Grant wanted to do was see Winnie.

Now he almost wished he'd stayed in Rapid City.

Anything was better than hearing she was heart-broken over another man.

He'd missed her so much over the last few days. He'd longed to see her, feel her, have her in his arms. He was feeling so many conflicting emotions. Desire, resentment, anger—all of it directed at the one person he'd always held closest to his heart. That was the killer—that she didn't know. Didn't see. *Couldn't see.* For days—no, weeks—he'd been walking around in a daze trying to figure out what he was feeling, why he felt different, why every part of him ached, even his skin.

"How was Duluth?"

He shrugged. "Just another job."

"And Krystal?" she asked, surprising him.

Grant scowled. "What? Since when have you been so paranoid about Krystal? Seriously? Give me a break, Winnie. I wasn't interested in her before we got married, and I'm even less interested now. What's this really about?"

But he knew. It was about the marine. It had to be, right? It was about her looking for an out…an escape clause, a way to end things because she was probably still in love with the jerk who'd abandoned her at the altar, and still missed him.

"I…don't know. I…can't. I'm so—"

"Unhappy?" he said, cutting her off. "Yeah, I can see that. You were talking to Ellie."

"I needed someone to talk to and she's my friend."

"Sure," he said, understanding completely. And he didn't have any problem with her confiding in his sister, other than the one obvious point—it meant she wasn't confiding in him. Like they used to do. "Are you finished here for the day?" he asked.

She nodded. "Yeah, I'm tired. I think I need to go home and lie down."

"Okay, I'll see you back at the apartment later on. I'm going to drop by Joss's place for a while."

"Is everything all right?"

Grant nodded. "Fine."

He waited for her to lock up, escorted her to her car and then they headed in separate directions. He didn't kiss her, didn't touch her. He drove directly to his brother's and Joss answered the door quickly.

"Why do you look like you haven't slept for two days?" his brother asked as he crossed the threshold.

Grant rubbed the back of his neck. "Because I haven't."

"Beer?"

"Coffee," he replied. "Strong."

They headed to the kitchen and Joss quickly made coffee, told him the girls were having a sleepover at the ranch because they were having a horse-riding lesson with Mitch the next morning.

"They like hanging out with Tess," he said and shrugged. "It's the mothering thing, I guess. And Sissy's at that age where she needs female advice. Dad just doesn't cut it when it comes to talking about bras and monthly cycles and stuff."

Grant managed a grin. "Do you think you'll get married again?"

"I don't know. I know the girls would like me to. But I don't mix my love life with the parenting thing, you know. Too complicated. I don't want them getting attached to someone and then find myself screwing it up. Let's face it, Lara was a saint and I'm not sure I'll ever find someone who could put up with me like she did—and someone who'll also love the girls unconditionally."

"Oh, I don't know," Grant said and drank some coffee. "You're a lovable guy. And an understandable one."

Joss stilled and regarded him curiously. "What's going on?"

"I saw Billie-Jack yesterday."

His brother's eyes bulged as he swore. "You did what?"

"For about ten minutes," he replied and sucked in a long breath. "He's sick."

Joss pushed back on his heels, taking in the information. "Sick?"

"Dying, is my guess," Grant replied. "He didn't say that, but I suspect it's terminal."

The flash of angry shock in his brother's eyes faded. "How did this come about?"

"He called again, I picked up," he answered evenly. "I thought there was little point in avoiding it forever."

"What does he want? Money?"

"Amends," Grant replied, suddenly weary from thinking and talking about it. "Money would be easier."

Joss sighed. "Have you told anyone else?"

"No."

"Not even your wife?"

"Winnie and I don't talk much these days. We've perfected the art of not saying what's on our minds."

"I thought you said she wanted a divorce?"

He shrugged. "We're trying this new sixty-day arrangement, you know, to see if we can figure it out." Although since neither of them had signed the divorce papers yet, the plan was already busted.

"Sounds complicated," Joss said and smiled ruefully. "And you know what, marriage shouldn't be complicated. It should be the smartest thing you've ever done. You should be the best version of yourself with that person."

He finished his coffee, ignoring the ache settled behind his ribs that seemed to be a permanent fixture. "So, about Billie-Jack, I thought I'd start with you—are you interested in reconnecting?"

Joss didn't hide his skepticism. "You're, what, the envoy now?"

"Looks like it. It was probably a stupid move to meet him, but I was curious."

"Is your curiosity now satisfied?" Joss asked. "Because it doesn't seem like it is."

"I don't think so," he replied candidly. "I have a lot of questions I'd like answered. About why he started drinking so heavily after mom died. About why he'd beat up on you and Hank the most. And about the day of the accident, when he knew he was drunk but drove, anyway, with two of his kids in the vehicle. I want to know why he didn't pull Hank free of the wreck. And I want to know why he hasn't made any contact until now."

"You want a lot. If I remember correctly, didn't he send you a postcard about five years ago?"

"Yes," Grant replied. "Just postmarked from Arizona and his initials on it."

"He must have thought we cared where he was," Joss said. "Let's face it, we were all grateful to see the back of him."

Grant didn't respond. Because back then, at twelve years old, he *wasn't* happy to see his father go. He'd raced after him that day, begging him to stay, and then begging Billie-Jack to take him with him. No one knew that. Afterward, he'd been too ashamed to admit as much to his brothers.

"Does that mean you don't want to see him?" he asked.

"I don't think so," Joss replied. "I need to think about it."

"Are you pissed because I did?" he asked flatly.

"A little," his brother admitted honestly. "But I understand. Let me talk to Hank—since we're twins, he'll probably prefer to hear this from me."

Grant agreed. "Sure. I'll tell the others over the weekend."

"Don't forget the party on Sunday," Joss reminded him. "It's in your honor, remember?"

He remembered. But he wasn't looking forward to being center stage at a celebration for a marriage that was becoming more strained every day. He stayed at his brother's place for a while longer, heading back to Winnie's apartment around seven thirty. The kitchen light was on, but that was all, and he noticed she was lying on her side on the sofa, wearing a bathrobe, fast asleep. He spotted a plate and mug on the kitchen counter and a candy wrapper on the coffee table in front of the sofa. At least she'd eaten something and was resting.

He settled himself in the love seat opposite and saw her eyes spring open. "Hey, did I wake you?"

She pushed herself up onto one elbow. "No, I wasn't really sleeping, just dozing. Thank you for the flowers," she said as her mouth curved a little. "They're lovely. Unexpected, since flowers are generally not your style."

"I've given you flowers before."

"Once," she corrected. "When I was sixteen."

It was meaningless talk, the kind he knew was said to fill the silences between them. "I wanted to assure you that absolutely nothing happened with Krystal while I was in Duluth. I was there to work, and actually I hardly saw her."

"You don't need to—"

"Well, clearly I do," he said, cutting her off, "since you asked about her. I wouldn't do that to anyone," he added. "And I certainly wouldn't do that to you. Know that whatever happens between us, I would never dishonor you like that."

"I know. I overreacted. But I am committed to this marriage."

Grant dropped his gaze for a second. Because he couldn't—wouldn't—look in her eyes and see the lie in them. "I'm going to take a shower and make it an early night," he said and got to his feet.

Twenty minutes later he was showered, shaved, and he walked into Winnie's bedroom. She was in bed, sitting up against the pillows, wearing a long college T-shirt, her dark hair tumbling around her shoulders.

"I really am sorry about before," she said and pulled back the covers on his side, clearly inviting him into the bed. "About Krystal. My emotions have been seesawing all over the place lately."

Grant hovered in the doorway. He saw the gleam in her eye and wondered if she knew how sexy she looked with her tumbling hair and lips so naturally red she looked like she had already been kissed thoroughly. But he hadn't kissed her. He didn't dare. Because the way he was feeling, the way his heart was pounding, he knew he would betray and humiliate himself. He'd beg her to forget about the marine and think only of them…of *him*.

"Forget about it," he said and slipped into bed beside her, trying not to touch her.

But as he flicked off the bedside light, she curled up against him. It would have been easy to take up the invitation he knew she was offering…to roll her over and kiss her luscious mouth, to slide his tongue around her tightly budded nipples, to touch her intimately and hear her come apart at the gentle rhythm he knew she liked. Perhaps her acquiescence was a peace offering, an olive branch, a way of making amends for almost accusing him of doing whatever with another woman. The invisible wall he'd heard her talk about to his sister seemed higher than ever. She was going to try, obviously, despite their marriage feeling like something she had to endure.

Her hand slipped beneath the tank shirt he wore and rested in between his pecs, her fingers twirling through his chest hair. It was erotic and at the same time hypnotic, and his breathing quickly changed from rapid to restful.

"What time are you leaving in the morning?" she asked softly.

"Early. I said I'd be at the hos—" He stopped, holding on to the truth. "At the appointment at nine."

"What kind of appointment?"

He hesitated for a moment. "Just...work."

Grant had called Billie-Jack a couple of hours after their meeting at the café and said he would see him the following day at the hospital where he was receiving treatment. There were still things unsaid between them. And he wanted answers. He *needed* answers before he spoke to the rest of his siblings.

Lethargy climbed over his limbs and his mind wandered. Before his relationship with Winnie had gotten so complicated, he wouldn't have hesitated in confiding in her. They would have talked it through. She would have made him see the situation from all angles, not just his own. That's what pained him— that he didn't trust their *new* relationship enough to share what he was feeling.

And he wondered if he ever would.

CHAPTER ELEVEN

GRANT LEFT EARLY the following morning and Winona heaved a sigh of relief the moment he walked out the door. He seemed so far away, so distant and cold. Not the man she was used to. But the man he'd become since Vegas.

And she was sadder than she had ever imagined she could be.

He'd rejected her in bed. Sure, he hadn't pushed her away, but there was a remoteness in his response to her touch, an indifference that hurt soul-deep. Is that what they'd become? She'd been kidding herself the weekend before, playing the role of wife and lover and setting herself up for the biggest fall of her life. It was simply sex. Physical release. It didn't mean closeness. Sure, it felt like it at the time, when the mind was hazy in the afterglow of pleasure and everything seemed right in the world. But reality quickly set in.

Sex was not love.

Love was not sex.

All she had to do was learn to compartmentalize her feelings. Accept what she had and learn to live with the crumbs of a friendship and a marriage based on obligation and loyalty. Because she would have that, she was sure. He would play the role of her husband because he was honorable to the core and a good person. Grant wouldn't cheat. He would be generous and faithful. He would also be a considerate and passionate lover. But there would be a huge divide. A permanent line in the sand with their roles clearly laid out. Wife and mother. Husband and father. And a busted friendship lying in ruins at their feet.

But still, she wanted to try. She wanted the chance to get him to open up. She longed to show him how much they could have if he met her halfway.

Winona headed downstairs to pack a few boxes into her car to take to the Maple Street house when she spotted Grant's car still parked beside hers. And Grant perched on the end of the hood. He still looked so tired and she suspected he had gotten as little sleep as she had.

"I thought you had a secret appointment in Rapid City?" she asked, verbalizing her curiosity for the first time. Of course she'd considered all kinds of possible scenarios, none of which made any sense. A wedding ring didn't give her carte blanche on his movements and he was entitled to his privacy.

"I do," he said, his pallor oddly ashen. "Would you like to come with me?"

He looked directly at her as he spoke and Winona saw raw vulnerability in his expression and it quickly sliced right through her. He wanted her with him. Needed her, by the look on his face. It was enough to make her nod. "Okay, sure."

He nodded and within minutes her car was locked, and they were on their way.

"Where are we going?" she asked.

He exhaled heavily. "To see my father."

Winona gasped. Of all the things she might have expected him to say, seeing Billie-Jack was not one of them. She was about to ask another question when he explained that his father was in the hospital receiving treatment.

"I saw him on Thursday when I got back to Rapid City," he said. "We talked for a while. I was planning on seeing him again yesterday."

"Until I had an emotional breakdown and made you come home, right?"

"You didn't make me do anything," he said quietly. "But I still have some questions for him."

"How did you feel seeing him after so long?"

He glanced at her. "Like I was in a movie of someone else's life. Weird, detached, but drawn into it at the same time. And about twelve years old all over again."

"Have you told your family?"

"Only Joss."

"That's why you went there last night? What did he say?"

"Not much," he replied.

Unsaid words hung in the air and she pushed a little more. "Grant? Please. You can talk to me."

He exhaled. "The thing is, I feel guilty for wanting to know why he left, because I know the rest of my family don't care. They've moved on, forgotten about him, I guess."

"Well, you're younger and perhaps not as jaded," she suggested. "I know what it did to you when he left."

Winona didn't ask him why he'd turned the car around and come back to get her. He had his reasons. Moral support, perhaps. And really, as his wife, it was her job to be that support when he needed it. They did the rest of the trip in uneasy silence and she was relieved when they finally arrived in Rapid City. The hospital was in the center of town and he found a parking space easily. He held her elbow as they walked into the ward and down a long corridor. She felt the tension emanating from him and grasped his elbow reassuringly.

Winona had seen a lot of pictures of Billie-Jack Culhane, but he'd certainly changed over the years. He greeted them politely and Grant quickly introduced her.

"This is my wife, Winona," he said, and the older man nodded.

"You're Red's granddaughter," Billie-Jack said, his eyes wrinkled in the corners. "My son told me you'd recently married, congratulations."

It was strange, making small talk with someone who she knew had wreaked absolute havoc on his family nearly two decades ago. Now, Billie-Jack looked small and old and without any kind of power. There was medication being transfused into his arm and a water jug on the side table. There were a couple of cards next to the jug and a small bouquet of flowers. Whatever had transpired in his life since he left Cedar River, he'd obviously maintained a connection with someone.

"The cards are from my girlfriend, Mindy," the old man explained. "She doesn't live here—she's in Arkansas. I told her I was coming back to try and see my kids and she understood. I'm sure she'd rather I was back there continuing treatment, but this hospital is a good one."

He kept talking and she noticed how tightly coiled

Grant was beside her, like a wound-up top ready to spin. Finally, he spoke.

"Why did you do it? Why did you drive that day? And why the hell did you leave Hank in the truck?"

Billie-Jack's faded green eyes shadowed over. "The truth is, I can't remember much about it. I remember driving, I remember you and Hank being in the truck, I remember Jake being on his motorbike behind me, but I don't remember much about the accident. I know I was drinking that day," he admitted and looked at them both. "I drank every day. After your mom died, I lost part of myself. I couldn't handle the pain day to day. Couldn't handle anything."

"You didn't try," Grant said flatly.

He took a sip of water. "Look, I ain't makin' excuses. I was no good back then. I was a drunk. I was a bad husband, and after she died, I beat up on my kids." He made the acknowledgment without any expectation of forgiveness. "I was weak and a crap father. But that day, I just remember being out of the car and hearing yelling. Jake was there, racing around the truck as it was on fire, and I remember seeing you on the ground, sitting on the grass," he said and looked at Grant. "In my head I knew Hank was still in the truck, but I kinda blacked out, and couldn't think straight. The booze, I suppose."

He gazed out the window for a moment, the years seeming to weigh on him heavily for a moment. Then he turned back to them, shaking his head. "Anyway, like I said, it's no excuse. I should have given my own life to get him out of the there—or at least died tryin'," he admitted sadly. "But I wasn't a good man back then.

And a violent drunk isn't the kind of person who should be raisin' kids."

"And that's why you left?" Grant said, his voice so tight she knew each word was hard for him. "Because it was best for everyone?"

"I had to," Billie-Jack said. "And I knew Mitch would look after you, because he had your mom's strength. I was no good for you all. I used to take the strap to the twins and Jake would get in the middle of it, trying to get me riled into hitting him instead. And I did most times. Sometimes I hit you, too. Do you remember that?"

Grant nodded. "I remember."

"You wanted me to take you with me," Billie-Jack said dully. "I know that. I saw you runnin' after me that day. But where I was going was no place for a kid. You were better off with your brothers and sister." He sighed. "Look, I didn't come here expecting that forgiveness was going to be easy to get. I know I screwed up. You all have every reason to hate me and I'd understand. But I wanted to try," Billie-Jack said, his voice cracking. "I've got a whole bunch of regrets behind me, but for the last ten years I've managed to live a decent life. I met Mindy, got a job working at a timber mill and made peace with the guy upstairs. I've also come to realize that it's the things in life I haven't done that I regret the most. That's why I'm here."

Winona felt Grant's hand reach for hers, his fingers tight. "You want forgiveness? It's not only mine to give," he said, and she could feel the intense pain vibrating through him.

Billie-Jack nodded. "I know...but it's a start."

Winona wasn't sure what she expected Grant to

say. He looked somewhere within the past, perhaps somewhere within himself. And she recognized the polarized expression on his face. She'd witnessed it before—the morning she'd told him she was pregnant. Shock. Disbelief. Lack of control. Things that undid him. And she knew, in that moment, that she needed to hold on tight, to lead him to where she believed he wanted to go.

"Grant," she whispered, leaning close to him, speaking so only he could hear. "Do what feels right for *you*."

He met her gaze, his glittering green eyes boring through her with burning intensity. And he nodded, clutching her fingers, taking all the strength he needed. He backed up, making his way to the door, and she followed in his wake. If he didn't want closure, she would understand and support his decision. But when they reached the door, he turned, half shielding her, his focus suddenly and completely on the old man in the hospital bed.

"Okay," he said quietly. "You want forgiveness. Here you go—I forgive you for falling apart after mom died. I forgive you for beating up on us when you were drunk. I forgive you for failing to protect my brother when the truck was on fire. I forgive you for walking away and leaving us. And I forgive you for not taking me with you."

Each word was like a rock hitting the ground with a resounding thud.

"And now," Grant said, "it's over. Good luck to you. We're done."

The adrenaline, mixed with a dose of relief that was coursing through his body, was palpable, and as they headed to his apartment in Rapid City, Grant was so exhausted he felt as though he'd scaled a mountain. It was Winnie's suggestion they go to his apartment for a while instead of driving directly to Cedar River and he quickly agreed. He wanted a shower and a change of clothes; he wanted to wash away the tarnish of the last hour that seemed to be clinging to his skin.

But he was glad she was with him. He wasn't sure what had motivated him to turn the car around and return to Cedar River. He only knew he needed her like he needed air in his lungs.

"It feels hollow in here," she said when they walked into the place. She'd been in his apartment countless times, and had never much liked the smooth chrome, black and glass decor.

"Well, it hasn't been lived in much lately."

She jerked her gaze to his. "I wasn't being critical," she explained. "Just, you know, being me…finding fault in everything."

Grant looked at her. "That cut deep, did it?"

She shrugged loosely. "I know I'm not perfect. And I didn't mean to say something so hurtful."

"I guess we all say hurtful things sometimes."

"Not you," she said and gave a humorless laugh. "You don't say anything."

Grant's chest tightened. "I've always thought actions speak louder than words," he said, suddenly so weary he could barely stand up. "I'm gonna take a shower and get changed. Make yourself at home."

He disappeared upstairs and wandered around the master bedroom for a while, opening drawers, looking at all the things he needed to pack to transition to the Maple Street house. Maybe he should simply leave the apartment as it was, so he had a place to crash that was close to work.

Or maybe I know my marriage isn't going to make it...

The notion banged around in his head like a chant. Because he knew, deep down, what that meant. Part-time fatherhood. Seeing his child on the weekends. Exactly what he wanted to avoid when he'd insisted that they stay married. Instead, Winnie had suggested they go ahead with the divorce, before then putting a time frame on their marriage to see if they could fumble through and make it work. They were a couple of weeks down and already he felt the strain and knew she did, too.

Because she's probably still in love with someone else...

And what was worse? Being together out of some old-fashioned sense of doing the right thing? Sleeping in the same bed, reaching for one another in the dark to feed a physical hunger, out of little more than duty and guilt? How long would it be before the cracks started to show? Wouldn't it be better to raise their child apart, with respect and friendship? It seemed like the healthier alternative.

Perhaps that's what they should have planned all along. His ideals about having some kind of happily-ever-after seemed like a foolish pipe dream. What did he have to compare it to? Seeing Billie-Jack had galvanized something inside him. That it was okay to fail at something. He'd felt guilty most of his life because he hadn't experienced the same loathing his siblings did for their father. Grant was the one who'd wanted to go with him. Another pipe dream, as it turned out, but one he could finally live with.

He stripped off and headed for the shower. The steaming water felt good, cathartic, as it beat down, and he rested a forearm against the tiles, exhaling heavily.

"Do you want some company?"

Her jerked around and saw Winnie standing outside the shower cubicle, completely naked.

"Ah—what?"

She slid open the door and the steam escaped. "I figured you might need me," she said as she stepped into the shower, the water hitting her shoulders and running down her breasts. "To wash your back, maybe?"

"Is that all?"

"Whatever you want," she replied, the provocation in her voice unmissable.

He wanted to believe her. He *ached* to believe her. But the thought of making love to her when she was thinking about someone else cut through him like a shiny blade. "Sex doesn't fix things, you know?" He said the words more to himself than to her.

"I know," she said, water now plastering her hair to her head. "But for whatever reason, you asked me to come with you today to do something that was incredibly difficult. You needed me. And right now, I think you still need me."

He inhaled sharply. "That's the damnable thing about you and me, Winnie. We've been friends so long I think it's blurred what we need from each other."

She pressed a hand to his chest. "Like last night when we were in bed? You were thinking about today, about Billie-Jack, about your family."

"I was thinking about a lot of things last night."

"You didn't want to make love to me," she said hollowly.

I did, so much... But he didn't say it. Instead, he looked at her, his body quickly responding to her skin, her hair, her hard nipples. He couldn't deny it, couldn't halt the primal reaction she evoked in him. Grant groaned and reached for her instinctively, wrapping his arms around her and finding her hot, wet mouth, which was so clearly eager for his kiss that his knees almost buckled. They kissed deeply, tongues and teeth clashing, like they were starved of one another. And her hands were everywhere—over his back, his thighs, his chest—her fingers hot and seeking. He wasn't sure how, but he lifted her up to his hips, one arm bracing them against the tiles, the other anchored around her waist, and slowly entered her. She clung to him, kissing his mouth, his neck, any place she could find as they settled into a fierce rhythm that quickly had them both free-falling into an abyss of pleasure so intense Grant wasn't sure his legs would hold out.

When it was over, he supported himself against the wall and gently set her back down, their labored breath mingled and testament to the passion they had just shared. So much for his earlier thoughts about respect and friendship. He was kidding himself. His libido had suddenly begun to rule him—one touch, one smile, and he couldn't control himself.

He wanted to resent her so much in that moment he could taste it. But instead, he turned the resentment into self-disgust at his own stupid male weakness.

"I'm not sure I can walk after that," he breathed into her hair, drifting down to nuzzle the tender spot at the base of her throat.

Her arms were still around his waist. "I wish we could stay like this forever," she said against his chest.

"We'd get all pruned after a while," he said, running his hands down her hips, loving the feel of the water cascading over her skin. "Thank you for coming with me today."

She smiled. "I'd do anything for you."

Except think of me as the man you really love...

He had no idea where that thought came from and it had nowhere to go but remain banging around in his head. He switched off the faucets and then they were quickly out of the shower. They dried off and got back in their clothes soon after.

"What do you plan on telling your brothers and sister about Billie-Jack?" she asked as they dressed.

"The truth," he replied. "And they can make whatever decision they choose."

"Did you mean what you said? About being done with him?"

Grant's hands stilled on his belt buckle. "I think so. I needed to hear it from him, you know, the admission that he screwed up. Hearing him say it switched off something inside—something I've been hanging on to for years."

"What's that?"

"Fear," he admitted. "Of screwing up. Of checking out when things get difficult. Of making the easy choice instead of the hard one."

"That doesn't sound like you."

"Doesn't it?" he shot back and slipped on his shoes. "I was the one who insisted we stay married because of the baby. If I remember correctly, you believed we could successfully co-parent our child without the wedding ring."

"I know, but I—"

"What if you were right?" he asked, tired of the pretense, tired of her *trying* so hard. "And maybe I said we should stay married because it was the easy option and it would mean we weren't as screwed up as our parents."

"We'll never know, I guess."

"I'd rather not leave it to chance," he said quietly. "I don't want to make the wrong the decision now, and risk hurting my kid down the track."

Grant sighed, seeing her building distress and knowing he could do nothing for her. He wanted to hold her and protect her from the world and everyone in it. He wanted to be the kind of husband and father he witnessed his brothers Mitch, Jake and Joss being. But he couldn't because of one indisputable fact—Winnie was still in love with someone else. She might make love with him as though they were the only two people in the world, but beneath that facade was the truth he knew she couldn't fake—her heart was broken and there was no room in it for anything other than sex, obligation and duty.

"I think it's time we both accepted the truth. This marriage is never going to work."

Winona stared at him, fighting the heat suddenly burning behind her eyes. They'd just shared the most intense and erotic lovemaking of her life and now he was saying they were done?

"I don't understand," she said rawly. "I thought you wanted us to—"

"At this point I don't think it matters what I want," he said, cutting her off. "Let's face it, Winnie, this situation isn't one either of us ever imagined we'd be in."

I did, she cried to herself. *I dreamed it. I longed for it.*

"But we just…" Her words trailed off as she gestured toward the bathroom. "You know."

"Didn't we establish that sex doesn't fix things?"

Pain seared through her. "I guess I imagined it would be enough."

"For how long? Six months? A year or two? Until the novelty wears off and we realize that's *all* we've become—two people who are great in bed together. Do you really think that's enough? And when it's not, do you think that's fair on our child, Winnie?"

Nothing was fair. Particularly not the cold, uncompromising way he was looking at her. Half an hour ago they were in the middle of something so intimate, so erotic, it defied belief. Now he regarded her as though they were nothing to each other.

"I'm not sure I know anything anymore."

He sighed with a kind of heavy resignation. "I'm tired of pretending we can make this work. Whatever you think we have here…it's not enough. I want… more."

He strode to the dressing table, pulled open the drawer and extracted a large envelope. He pulled out the contents, grabbed a pen from the bedside table and quickly scribbled his name on the appropriate page.

"There," he said and dropped the pages onto the bed. "Our divorce papers. All you have to do is sign and it can be finalized. I know it's what you want, Winnie."

He left the room and, once he was out of sight,

Winona dropped onto the bed and picked up the papers with a shaking hand. And then, in the quiet of the room, sadness overtook her. She felt about fifteen all over again. Like the girl who'd pined over him for years, dreaming about having his love but never quite believing she would ever get it.

Confusion settled in her chest and she splayed a hand across her belly. Maybe in time the hurt would lessen. Perhaps she'd find someone else to love, who would love her. But it didn't seem likely. He said he wanted more—but what did that mean? Had he come to realize that he wanted a relationship...or even love? Did he believe he'd be *settling* if they gave their marriage a chance?

Her sense of rejection was consuming and soul-crushing, but the tears she wanted to shed wouldn't come. Her throat ached, her fingers were numb, and she could barely catch her breath...but she *wouldn't* fall apart. Not here, in the cold bedroom of his soulless apartment.

She tucked the papers into her tote and headed downstairs, spotting him by the front door.

"We should get going," she said quietly, too hurt to say much else.

He nodded and, once the apartment was locked up, they headed back to Cedar River. The silence between them was thick, tense and worse than she could have imagined. When they arrived outside the bakery he moved to get out of the car, but she put up a hand.

"No, don't," she said dismissively. "You should stay somewhere else tonight. Maybe Joss's. Or the hotel. Just not here."

"Of course," he said, his fingers tight on the steering wheel. "We have that thing at the ranch tomorrow, remember?"

Oh, God, the party. Winona had forgotten all about it. She remembered the two missed calls she had on her cell from Ellie and guilt immediately pressed down on her shoulders. "We need to cancel. I can't possibly go."

"It's a little late to cancel, don't you think? Look, I don't want to be a part of it any more than you do, but Ellie and Tess have gone to a lot of trouble, so we should probably fake it a little longer and try to make out like everything is okay. We can wait a week or so to tell everyone anything different."

"Lie, you mean?"

He glanced at her, his green eyes icy cold. "All right, I'll call Tess and tell her we're—"

"No," she said quickly, cutting him off. "You're right. We'll get through tomorrow like it's business as usual. I do think we should talk about the house, though, since we've just signed a lease."

"The house is yours to live in, Winnie. Once the baby is born, I'll drive down as often as I can and bunk at the ranch or stay with one of the twins."

He had it all figured out—clearly.

"Great, I'll see you at the ranch at three o'clock tomorrow."

"I'll pick you up," he said quietly.

"I'll drive myself," Winona insisted as she opened the door.

His hand touched her arm, gently holding her. "Winnie, I don't want us to hurt each other."

She stilled, shrugging off his touch. "Too late."

Then she headed up to her apartment, dropped onto the sofa and cried until she was all out of tears.

CHAPTER TWELVE

"You're what?"

Grant glanced at his brother. "Getting a divorce."

He was sitting on the couch in Joss's living room later that night, after calling each of his siblings to explain about Billie-Jack. Considering everything that had happened, they all took the news reasonably well. Grant didn't offer any suggestions, or try to negotiate a meeting with their father; he simply relayed the facts. He didn't expect any of them to see the old man, and frankly, he didn't much care. He couldn't control how they dealt with it and it wasn't his job to make amends on Billie-Jack's behalf. That settled, now he was sipping a beer he didn't really want, watching a baseball game he had little interest in. And he really didn't want to get into the details of his failed marriage. But since over the last hour they'd exhausted the topic of Billie-Jack, Grant knew his brother would want to have a discussion about Winnie.

"Ah, didn't we have the marriage-shouldn't-be-complicated talk yesterday?"

"Yeah. Things change."

"This is kind of a record speed," Joss said, brows up. "What happened?"

"Good sense prevailed," he said and stared at the television. When his brother didn't respond, he looked up. "Six weeks ago, she was going to marry someone else."

"And?"

"And we got drunk, got married and got laid. It's not supposed to happen like that."

"Oh, there's a set plan for marriage, is there?" Joss inquired, clearly amused.

"There should be."

Joss chuckled. "Like me getting my high school girlfriend pregnant at eighteen and then getting married as a teenager, and then being a widower at twenty-three?"

"You loved Lara."

"I did," Joss agreed. "I still do. That doesn't mean we didn't make mistakes along the way. So, this idea about what relationships should be—enlighten me."

Grant scowled. "I don't know...just not like this."

Joss's brows shot up. "Maybe like Mitch and Tess—get married, have a series of tragic miscarriages, get divorced, hook up randomly a few years later, get pregnant and get married again?" Joss offered, grinning a little. "Or Jake and Abby—date in high school, he joins the military while she marries his best friend, best friend dies, he comes back to town, knocks her up and finds out he has a son six years later? Yeah," Joss said and grinned. "I see what you mean—your situation is way more convoluted. Do you love her?"

"That's a stupid question," he said and scowled some more. "It's Winnie, of course I love her."

His brother tutted. "I mean, are you *in love* with her?"

Grant averted his gaze from the television and looked at Joss. "There's a difference?"

"Of course there's a freakin' difference. I love her, too," he said impatiently. "We all love her. But *you're* the one who married her and got her pregnant."

Grant ignored the twitch in his gut and the bluntness of his brother's words. He knew exactly what he had done. "She still loves the marine."

"You know that for sure?"

"Yes," he replied dully.

"You didn't answer the question," Joss said quietly. "About being in love with her."

Grant's temple throbbed. He didn't want to answer the question. He didn't want to think about Winnie and the desolate look on her face as she raced from his car. He wasn't sure he'd ever get that look out of his mind.

"I'm not sure I know what that even means."

Joss shook his head. "Man, you really are screwed up, aren't you?"

"Just because I'm not falling in and out of love on a regular basis, it doesn't make me a screwup. I care about Winnie," he said and got to his feet, striding back and forth. "So yeah, I love her, okay. Of course I do. She's my best friend."

"That's all?" Joss asked.

He stilled. "That's everything."

And then, suddenly, as he said the words, it all made sense. His rage, his resentment, his never thinking any man was good enough for her; the bone-aching jealousy he experienced every time he thought about the man she'd almost married. And the other things—the pleasure of her touch, her kiss, the way making love to her transcended all rational thought. The way he couldn't talk to anyone the way he could talk to her.

Not even his brothers, even though he'd never admit it to them.

"I feel like I have this great weight pressing in my chest," he admitted, running a hand through his hair. "Almost like it's twisting inside my rib cage. Is that…" His voice trailed off and he shrugged. "Is that it?"

Joss grinned. "You mean being in love? You feel like crap, you can't eat, you can't sleep. Yeah, that would be it."

Grant's shoulders dropped. He'd loved Winnie since they were kids…and somehow, in the last few tumultuous weeks, something incredible had happened—he'd fallen in love with his best friend. It was like a light had been switched on inside him. He also remembered what he'd done just a few hours earlier. He'd said they shouldn't hurt one another, and she replied that it was too late. Was she hurting like he was?

"I signed the divorce papers today," he said.

"Nothing that can't be undone," Joss remarked.

"Maybe…but…the marine…"

"Is she still in contact with him?" Joss asked, all big-brotherly.

Grant shook his head, feeling about twelve years old. "I don't think so. Except in here," he added and tapped his chest.

Joss stood and slapped him affectionately on the shoulder. "Get some sleep. And tomorrow, do yourself a favor and go and talk to your wife."

Sleep would have been great. He couldn't quite remember the last time he'd slept through the night. Was it really only a week ago? When he'd had her arms wrapped around him.

Grant tossed and turned most of the night and woke up early. He went for a run, ate breakfast with his brother and nieces and tried to act normal around his family. But what he really wanted to do was tap on Winnie's door at 8:00 a.m. and beg for her to give them another chance—even though he was the one who'd signed the divorce papers.

He waited until ten and drove to her apartment. However, she wasn't there. He asked at the bakery and Regina informed him she hadn't seen Winnie that morning. He tried her cell and it went to messages. He sent a text and didn't get a return message. He held out for about twenty minutes, pacing the street outside the bakery. Still nothing. He took a chance and drove to the house on Maple Street, but there was no sign she'd been there that morning.

Grant lingered outside for a few minutes, thinking how warm and welcoming the place looked. In a flash of a few seconds, he saw his life so clearly—his car parked in the driveway, Winnie greeting him on the porch with a gentle smile, a couple of kids racing around the yard, a shaggy dog playing chase with a stick. It seemed so real it rendered him breathless. If he inhaled he'd pick up the scent of her perfume mixed with the aroma of the cookies she loved to bake. He could almost hear their kids laughing, calling him Daddy, clearly delighted he was home. And Winnie— her beautiful eyes meeting his with the promise of what was to come when they were finally alone after dinnertime was done and their children were asleep. The image polarized him; the memory of things that hadn't even happened yet struck him with such force he could barely breathe.

He pushed some life into his legs, got back into his car and drove to the ranch.

And the first thing he saw when he arrived was her orange VW parked outside her grandfather's cottage. He pulled up in front of the main house and walked up the path between the dwellings. She was on the small porch, hands on hips, wearing jeans and a bright pink T-shirt, her beautiful hair hanging around her shoulders, before he made it to the bottom step.

"The party isn't until three," she said, her cheeks flushed with color.

"I know," he replied and kicked absently at a rock on the ground. "I thought we should talk."

"I haven't signed the divorce papers yet," she hissed. "If that's what you're wondering. But I will. The quicker we finish this, the better."

He could see the hurt in her expression. "Is that what you really want?"

"It's what *you* want," she reminded him. "You were the one who tossed them in my face right after we made love, remember? Nice going, by the way, very considerate."

Guilt, and a good dose of shame, pushed down squarely on his shoulders. "I'm sorry... I wasn't thinking straight. I was—"

"And why did you do this?" she asked brittlely, cutting him off as she shook her left hand. "Why did you insist we buy new wedding rings if this was the plan all along?"

"It wasn't the plan," he replied. "But you—"

"Why did you say we should get a house? Make me believe we were going to, I don't know, *try*? Why did you kiss me? Touch me? Make love to me?" She fired out the questions so fast he didn't have a chance to reply. "Why did you pretend that you wanted me?"

Grant rocked back on his heels. "I wasn't pretending."

"No," she said with a tight, disbelieving laugh. "Then what changed? Last weekend everything seemed so right...like we were happy. And then yesterday, you asked me to go with you to see your father and I thought that meant something."

"It did," he assured her. "I needed you."

"You needed me?" she echoed, her eyes glittering. "For what? One last hookup? I know I was the one who initiated our little shower scene, but you didn't exactly take a lot of convincing. Any *body* would have done, I guess."

"Don't say that," he said, hating the way she made it sound so casual. "It's just that I was... I don't know... pissed, okay. I was mad at you for what you said the other day."

"What I said?" she repeated. "I don't understand."

"That you missed *him*," he said, each word clawed from his throat. "The marine. I heard you when you were talking to my sister. You said you missed him, and you were heartbroken."

She shook her head, searing him with an incredulous expression. "That's what you heard? That's *all* you heard?"

"I heard enough."

She laughed humorlessly. "I wasn't talking about Dwight," she said, the sound of the other man's name making him twitch. "I was talking about *us*. I was talking about you!"

"Me?" he echoed in disbelief.

"Are you that wrapped up in yourself that you can't figure it out?" she demanded, tears falling from her eyes. "You really are unbelievable, Grant. Do me a favor and go straight to hell," she said before she walked back inside and slammed the door.

He stayed where he was for a few minutes, feeling like a heel, a fool and a coward.

"Give her some time to calm down, son."

Grant saw Red to his left and realized the older man had heard most, if not all, of the entire exchange. He took a long breath. "I am in love with her, you know. For real."

Red nodded. "I know. Just let her cool down for a while—you know she's got a quick temper."

He knew that. He did, too. But he was better at keeping it under wraps. Grant managed a tight smile and walked back to the main house. Tess was there, and Ellie, and they were busy in the kitchen with Mrs. B, making preparations for the small gathering they were having that afternoon. Only family and a couple of close friends, thank goodness, because Grant wasn't sure he could stand anything more. But there were gifts and a cake set up on a long sideboard in the main dining room. Mitch tried to talk to him in the hallway about something and he brushed off his brother's conversation because his head, heart and insides hurt so much he couldn't concentrate on anything other than the thought of being miserable because Winnie had told him to take a hike.

He looked out of the window, noticing things about the ranch he hadn't spared much time to look at over the years. Like the flower beds. And the garden ornaments he figured his brother had bought for Tess because he knew she liked that kind of thing. He'd never been one to envy others, but in that moment, he did. He envied how easy Mitch and Tess made it look. He envied that Joss could still talk about Lara, even though he obviously missed her, and that Jake was so open about how much his wife and son meant to him. He envied emotional honesty because he'd always been too afraid to allow himself to feel it.

"I said I was heartbroken because I've lost the most important thing in my life."

Grant turned on his heel and saw Winnie standing in the doorway, clutching a small, faded and well-worn purple book. She was breathing hard, like every word caused her pain.

"Winnie, I—"

"Our friendship," she explained quietly. "Which has always meant more to me than anything else. But since Vegas, we've lost that, and I feel that loss so deeply I almost can't bear thinking about it. That's what's killing me, knowing we've lost what we had."

He swallowed the emotion burning in his throat. "It's not lost. I'm right here."

"No, you're not," she refuted. "Oh, you've been trying at times, like I have, but nothing is the same as it used to be. And the thing is, a part of me is glad. Because I'm really happy about the baby and I can't wait to be a mom—but I know it's come at a huge price."

"What price?"

"You and me. Our incredible friendship," she replied. "Which I've always treasured. Because I've always treasured you."

The way she said the words made him draw in a sharp breath. He wanted to believe her...so much. "But the marine...six weeks ago he was the love of your life."

"I never said that," she replied softly.

"Then why were you going to marry him?"

Her eyes glistened. "Because you never asked me."

Stunned, he stood still, unable to move if he tried.

"This is my diary," she said, her voice so raw it cracked. "I started writing in it when I was thirteen. I stopped writing in it when I finished high school. In this book I poured all of my heart, my thoughts and deepest feelings. Read it," she instructed. "And you'll see how there's only one man that I've ever loved."

She dropped the book on the sofa and left the room.

Grant wasn't sure how long he stood there for—minutes. Long enough for him to see Winnie's VW career down the driveway in a cloud of dust and grit through the window. He looked at the book, almost too afraid to pick it up. But he did. He held it in shaking hands, sat down and started reading.

Dear Diary,
I can't stop thinking about him. I know I'm dreaming. I know Grant will never look at me as anything more than a friend. But I love him so much. I want to marry him one day.

His heart raced. But he kept reading. Kept absorbing every word.

Dear Diary,
Grant came back from college this weekend and bought me flowers for my birthday. I'm going to

press the roses into a book and carry them in my
wedding bouquet when we get married.

All this time. Emotion lodged firmly in his throat
and he flicked the page, and then another. The pain, the
angst, the tortured teenage yearning of a girl clearly in
love—it tugged at him so profoundly he blinked back
the burning in his eyes.

Dear Diary,
Grant brought a girl to the ranch today. She was
pretty and smiled a lot and I think he likes her.
I wanted to die. I wish I had the courage to tell
him to wait for me to grow up. Diary, I love him
so much. I'll always love him. I just hope that one
day he realizes that he loves me, too.

Grant felt the wetness on his cheeks well before he
realized he was crying. Damn. He wiped at his face
as he read some more, the ache in his chest so intense
he could barely draw a breath.

Dear Diary
Callum kissed me today. But he's not who I
wanted to kiss. I was thinking about Grant the
whole time. I don't think I'll ever love anyone
else the way I love him. I dream about him all
the time. I dream about getting married and having babies with him one day. I want three kids,
two boys and a girl. I know I have to forget my
silly dreams, because he's never going to think
about me that way, but I honestly don't know if
I can.

He closed the book and sucked in a long breath. All this time. Years. She'd loved him. *Him*. And he'd been too foolish to see it. Too blinded by old fears of abandonment that he'd tried to deep-freeze his feelings. Grant got to his feet, pushed back his shoulders and exhaled.

"Is everything all right?"

He looked around and saw Ellie and Mitch in the door. "Everything's going to be fine."

Neither sibling looked convinced. "Isn't that Win's old diary?" Ellie asked curiously.

Grant nodded and tucked the book under his arm. "Yeah."

"She let you read it?" his sister asked, eyes bulging.

It was obvious Ellie knew exactly what was written in the tattered notebook. "You knew?"

"Of course I knew. Everybody knew...and knows. Except you, I'm guessing," she added. "Where *is* Win?"

"I'm not sure. But wherever she is, she's mad as hell at me." He pulled his car keys from his pocket. "I'll be back. Don't start the party without us."

"Where are you going?" Ellie asked as he strode out of the room.

"To go find my wife and beg her to forgive me for being an idiot," Grant said as he passed them.

Winona wasn't sure why she fled to the Maple Street house. She should have gone home to her apartment. But the big house drew her, and she wanted to see it one last time. Because she absolutely would not be living in the place without her husband. She'd stay at her apartment. Or go and live with her grandfather. Or find somewhere else where every room wouldn't be sure to remind her of her broken dreams. Because the big house with the chokecherry tree in the yard and perfect window seat in the living room was not going to be where she spent her days and nights pining after a man who was obviously determined to divorce her and raise their child separately.

Well, if that's what he wanted, that's what he'd get.

Because she could do it. She felt strong and resilient and empowered by the truth of her own words. Admitting her feelings to Grant had switched on something inside her—resolve. And the determination to raise her child as a single mom. She didn't have to screw it up like her own mother had. She had a job and a support network of family and friends. She wasn't her mother. She didn't need to be married. And she knew Grant would be a good father to their child. He just sucked at being a husband.

Winona walked around the house for over half an hour, going from room to room, memorizing the wallpaper and the architraves, the intricately detailed ceiling that rose in the main stairwell and the ornate fireplace in the living room. She lingered in the kitchen, and then again upstairs, forging images in her mind of a nursery she knew she wouldn't have, but it still gave her comfort to dream a little. Finally, when her emotions were spent and she'd had enough wallowing in what-ifs, she headed back downstairs to collect her tote.

And saw Grant standing by the window seat in the empty room.

He met her startled gaze and she noticed her diary in his hand. "I worked out why I can't sleep these days."

Winona held her breath, her heart thundering. "Why?"

"Because talking to you at night, right before I go to bed, has always been like a kind of tonic. The kind that makes me forget any troubles, any stresses. I miss hearing you say that you love me," he said raggedly, swallowing hard. "Turns out, I need that because it's the only thing that soothes my soul."

"Is it really?" she dared ask, shocked by his admission. It was the closest he'd ever come to truly admitting anything.

He nodded. "And I worked out why I hate the marine, and that jerk from high school, and any other guy you've dated."

"You have?"

"Because I was crazy jealous," he admitted. "I didn't know what it was at the time. That's because I'm afraid of real intimacy, which I'm sure you know."

"That's quite a confession," she said softly, her emotions hanging all over the place.

His mouth pressed into a tight line. "Do you want more?"

"I want it all," she replied.

He nodded fractionally, then let out a long and weary breath. "I love you, Winnie."

She gasped and then steeled herself. "I know you do. But—"

"And not that thoughtless *ditto* thing I've been saying to you for years," he said and dropped the diary on the window seat. "I know now that my actions, my responses, were never enough. Never what you deserved. Because despite my stupid behavior, despite acting as foolish as I have for so long, I promise you that with all my heart I'm absolutely and completely in love with you."

And then, without warning, he dropped to one knee and looked up at her.

"Grant, I—"

"This is how I should have done it," he said rawly. "Long before now. Winnie, will you marry me?"

Stunned, she stared at him for a moment, and then stated the obvious, her heart beating an erratic tattoo. "We're already married."

"I mean, marry me again, at the ranch, or in the chapel in town, or even at the courthouse if you like," he said quickly, urgently, like he couldn't get the words out fast enough. "I just know I want to do it again, with our family and friends around. A real wedding and a honeymoon and all the beauty and joy that you deserve."

Winona's heart was racing so hard she was sure he could hear it. He looked so raw, so vulnerable, and she quickly melted. She walked across the room and stood in front of him and he wrapped his arms around her, burying his face into her belly. Winona touched his head, threading fingers through his hair, feeling him tremble against her.

"Yes, I'll marry you," she whispered. "Again."

He kissed her stomach over and over, splaying his hands across her belly. "Thank you. God, I love that we've made a baby together."

He couldn't have said a more beautiful thing if he tried. Winona tugged on his shoulder and urged him to his feet. "That was kind of romantic, you know," she said and pressed against him. "On one knee and everything."

"I can be romantic," he assured her. "I promise to try harder."

"You don't have to," she replied and led him to the window seat. "Just be yourself."

"You mean, overcautious, commitment phobic and borderline predictable."

"Yes," she said and smiled, happiness tightening her chest. "I love all those things about you."

He glanced at the diary between them and grasped her chin. "Yeah, I kind of figured that."

"Silly schoolgirl dreams," she whispered.

"It was very sweet," he assured her again, holding her gently. "Made me cry actually."

Winona's throat burned and her brows shot up. She knew what that admission would have cost him. "Really? You never cry."

"I know," he admitted. "But I've decided I'm not going to be one of those fathers who tells his sons to stop blubbering and man-up."

"Like your father did?"

He nodded. "Yeah. I think that's part of the reason I hold back from admitting how I feel about things. Well, the way I *used* to hold back. From now on, I promise I will always be honest about what I'm feeling."

"Grant," Winona said, reaching up to hold his face in her hands. "I know that about you. You're my best friend…and best friends know that stuff."

"So, I have no secrets?" he teased.

She shook her head. "None, I'm afraid. I know that you say *Gladiator* is your favorite movie, but it's actually *The Blues Brothers*. I know you became a vegetarian after one Thanksgiving when you saw my grandfather prepare the turkey from scratch," she said with a grimace. "I know that you have a quick temper but you're such a control freak you always manage to keep it under wraps."

"Except when I think about you almost marrying that marine," he admitted.

Then he kissed her—a loving and tender kiss that literally made her insides sing. Winona kissed him back with every ounce of love she had been holding in her heart.

"Grant," she said in between kisses, "about Dwight..."

"I'd rather not talk about him, you know."

"Just for a moment, and then we'll forget all about it, I promise. I suspect you're curious about why I accepted his proposal?"

"You told me," he replied, "because I didn't ask you."

She smiled, loving him so much she had trouble drawing in a breath. "It wasn't only that. I think I just wanted to belong, you know, to something or someone. And the long-distance relationship thing suited me, because I could be a part of something but still hang on to what I really wanted. Which was you, of course."

"I'm an idiot," he muttered.

She smiled. "And anyway, I guess it's a good thing in the end that he did leave me at the altar," she said and laughed softly. "Or otherwise we wouldn't be here right now."

He grasped her chin again, holding her steady, his touch gentle and loving. "Do you really think I would have stood by and let that happen?"

Winona's eyes widened. "What would you have done?"

"I don't know," he replied, kissing her cheek, her

neck, the tender spot below her ear. All the places she loved to be kissed. "But I'd have figured something out. Because when I think about it, I realize that even then, I always knew he wasn't the guy for you."

"You did?"

"Sure," he said, still kissing her neck. "The thought of losing you made me realize how much I needed you. Because I love you," he said, now against her lips. "So much."

"Ditto," she breathed and then smiled.

He pulled back a little, meeting her gaze. "Yeah... I'm not going to be saying that anymore, okay?"

Winona grinned. "Just every now and then," she teased. "And for the record, when we were in Vegas at the chapel, I was secretly hoping you wouldn't let me go ahead and marry him."

His gaze softened. "Why didn't you ever say anything?"

"Say what? And when—some opening in between your casual dating life?"

"Ouch," he said and smiled. "I am that predictable?"

"A little," she said. "But I understood. I know you didn't want to get too close to anyone. I know losing your mom, and then Billic-Jack leaving, closed off something inside. I guess I knew that because I understood loss—I understood what it meant to be left. So most of the time I tried not to think about what I really wanted because I didn't want to lose what we had. It's a lot, really. There were times when I thought it was enough."

"You know, even though we have all this...you'll always be the dearest friend I've ever had."

Happiness radiated through her. "I love you, Grant.

So before, when you admitted you were a big crybaby," she teased again, "you said *sons*... Are you planning on more than our little peanut here?" she asked, touching her stomach.

Grant's large hand covered hers. "Well, I have read your diary, and I know all *your* secrets."

She sighed happily. "I'm so looking forward to being a mom. To having a family. To sharing that with my grandfather and your brothers and sister...and with you," she added.

"Me, too," he said, kissing her again. "And about this house...you really like it, don't you?"

She nodded. "So much. How did you know I'd be here?"

He shrugged. "I just knew. I drove by this morning looking for you, and realized you were right—this is the perfect place to raise our family."

"Do you think we could—"

"Absolutely," he said, gently cutting her off. "We'll talk to the Realtor and see if the owner is interested in selling sooner rather than later. We'll make an offer and go from there. I'll put my apartment on the market, and I also have a lot of money saved," he said, looking faintly embarrassed. "Enough for a generous deposit and some renovations and anything else you want. Like, we should probably buy a big SUV for all the kids."

"That would be sensible thing to do. We can put my VW in storage as a graduation gift for our firstborn," she said and grinned. "And there is something else I've been thinking about."

"What's that?" he asked.

"The bakery," she replied. "I know Regina would

love me to take up her partnership offer, and I thought that with the baby coming that I wouldn't be able to fit something else in, you know. But I think I can," she said, feeling strength seep through her bones. "I think I'm ready to live my real life. To stop being afraid of failure and do what I know will make me happy."

His arms tightened around her. "Of course you are. I'm so proud of you."

"I'm proud of *us*," she said and swooned a little.

He kissed her again, sighing against her mouth. "I can't believe I've missed out on kissing you and making love to you for all these years. I have a lot of time to make up."

She chuckled. "Yes, you do, Culhane."

"Ah, one thing," he said, pulling back a little. "Those…ah…papers I gave you yesterday. Do you have them?"

She nodded and grabbed her tote, extracting the documents with shaking hands. "I didn't sign them."

His jaw tightened. "I'm ashamed that I did," he said and gently took them from her. "I can't even begin to think how much that must have hurt you, and I'm sorry. Hurting you is the last thing I ever want to do. I have no excuse other than I was stupidly jealous and didn't think you wanted or loved…me."

"I've loved you since that first day I arrived at the ranch and you talked me down from the hayloft when we were kids," she admitted. "I've loved only you for most of my life."

He visibly shuddered. "I promise you, Winnie, with all my heart, that I will love you and cherish you for the rest of my life. I will always honor you and be faithful to you," he said and quietly tore up the paper in his hands and tossed it in the fireplace. "I'll be the kind of husband you deserve and a much better father than my own."

Winona looked at her husband—strong-willed, proud, stubborn, sometimes infuriating—and saw only the tender love in his expression. For her. For them. For their future. And she believed him to the depths of her heart.

"Grant, have you reconciled your feelings for Billie-Jack?" she asked gently.

"I'm not sure," he replied. "Some, probably not all. That will take time, I guess."

"I'll support whatever decision you make. I mean, if you do want to see him again, I'll go with you, be there and help you through it."

"I know. It was weird telling everyone about him— but also kind of like lancing this painful wound, almost cathartic. They can make their own minds up about what they want to do. It's not my job or place to tell anyone how to feel about things. When he first contacted me, I thought I was protecting them by keeping quiet. Turns out, I was only protecting myself because I felt guilty that I didn't quite hate him as much as everyone else."

Winona knew how much that statement cost him. Knew how achingly vulnerable the words made him feel. "You're allowed to love your father—even if it hurts."

He swallowed hard. "I know. But honestly, I'm tired of looking back. I only want to look forward from now on—and to our life together. We should get going," he suggested and held out his hand.

Winona touched his fingertips and was gently pulled into his embrace. "Where to?"

"The ranch," he replied. "We have a party to get to."

She smiled. In the midst of all she was feeling, Winona had forgotten about the get-together at the ranch. "They must all think I'm a lunatic racing off like that."

He chuckled. "You needed to give me a chance to come to my senses."

She didn't disagree. And she loved that he'd risked his heart and pride to come after her. "What shall we tell everyone?"

"The truth," he said and kissed her. "That we love each other very much. That we'll be together until we're old and gray. That we're gonna have a bunch of babies and live happily-ever-after."

She smiled. "I like the sound of that."

"Me, too," Grant said as he kissed her.

Winona kissed him back, knowing she had his love and commitment, knowing she had all she'd ever longed for.

And so much more.

EPILOGUE

A year later...

"YOU KNOW, YOU can put her in her crib."

Grant cradled his daughter, Rorie, in the crook of his arm. "I know."

Winnie's beaming smile made his belly leap. "We'll never get everything done tonight."

"Sure we will," he assured her. "I've mastered the art of decorating those little cupcake things with one hand."

"Sweetie," she said and laughed, "our three-month-old daughter is better at cake decorating than you are."

He placed his free hand to his chest and touched the spot above his heart. "That's harsh."

"But true," she replied. "Anyhow, you have other talents."

Grant caught the gleam in her eyes and grinned. "Is that right?"

"Yes," she said and moved toward him, gently easing their sleeping child from his arm. "I need that shelf put up by the water cooler."

"Boss lady," he said and watched her for a moment as she placed Rorie in her crib. Grant never got tired of watching them, of seeing the love in Winnie's eyes for the baby who'd brought them together in a way he'd never imagined possible.

There were other things, too, that had made their relationship stronger over the past year. Like having a proper wedding surrounded by their family and friends. Like buying the house on Maple Street and making it their own, and Grant pulling back from traveling on business too much so he could spend more time with his family. And the bakery—which had been known as the Muffin Box for years and was now re-branded simply as Winnie's. As it turned out, Regina was happier to sell the place rather than take on a business partner, since she wanted to go on the road with her drummer boyfriend. And a couple of months earlier, after much consultation with an accountant, a lawyer and the bank, Winnie had made the decision to purchase the place for a fair price. After a week of being closed for renovations, the bakery was ready to reopen.

"The place looks amazing, by the way," he said. "Are you excited about reopening tomorrow?"

"Over the moon." She propped her hands on her hips. "Do you think the renovations work? It's not too much?"

The walls were mounted with framed pictures of Cedar River from past to present. Winnie had decorated the shop with old-fashioned baking utensils and mixers, and she'd even set up the pastry case to have a whole new look, all styled to pay homage to the town's rich history. He admired his wife's commitment to the project and was so proud that she'd realized her dream.

"It's perfect," he replied and moved toward her. "Like you."

She laughed and pressed against him. "Are you drunk?"

Grant grasped her chin gently. "Not a chance. Remember the trouble I got into the last time we had too much champagne?"

"But then we wouldn't have all this," she said, waving a hand between them and gesturing to their sleeping child.

"Oh, I don't know," Grant said and brought her closer. "I'd like to think we would have ended up here eventually."

She met his gaze. "Oh, no, I know that mushy look."

He smiled warmly, his heart rolling over. "Better get used to it, Mrs. Culhane."

"I am," she assured him. "I love that you're so sentimental these days."

Grant chuckled, because most days that's exactly how he felt. "Do you know what I love?" he asked, holding her close, kissing the soft spot below her ear. "You. Rorie. Our life together."

"No regrets?" she asked.

"Not one," he replied and felt the truth of his words seep through him. Some days, he couldn't believe he'd gotten so lucky. Being a husband and father had profoundly changed him. Loving Winnie made everything so right in his world and had also given him the courage to truly let go of his resentment toward Billie-Jack. "One day I'm gonna thank that marine for standing you up at the altar."

She smiled against his mouth, kissing him softly. "Me, too."

"I love you, Winnie."

Her lips curved. "Ditto."

And that, he thought as he kissed her, was all he needed to know.

* * * * *

THE SERGEANT'S MATCHMAKING DOG

CARRIE NICHOLS

This book is dedicated to the wonderful vets and
staff at Banfield Pet Hospital Hixson.
They have not only taken wonderful care of my beloved
furbabies but helped with my fictional one.

CHAPTER ONE

"C'MON, WHAT'S WRONG with that one? Looks like a perfectly good bush to me." Former marine staff sergeant Gabe Bishop sighed as he glanced at what seemed like an endless row of forsythia bushes. Their bright yellow blooms created a natural fence between the still-dormant grass of someone's lawn and the cracked concrete of the sidewalk where he stood.

"Just pick one…any one…" He rubbed a hand over the scratchy stubble peppering his chin. "Please."

Suspending his search for the perfect spot to relieve himself, Radar lifted his head to give Gabe a long-suffering look. As if his human companion should understand the protocols by now.

"I should be training you—" Gabe yawned "—not the other way around."

He still had to lug in all those storage boxes crowded in the back of his Jeep Sahara. But what he longed for most was a hot shower after being on the road for close to twenty hours, fueled by truck-stop coffee and a quick nap at a rest area.

The animal went back to examining the bushes and Gabe sighed again. "You can bet marine dogs perform on command."

Radar whined his displeasure and Gabe regretted the disparaging remark. The dog might bear an uncanny resemblance to the Belgian Malinois the military favored, but Radar had been only the camp mutt, a mascot of sorts. Despite the circumstances, Gabe considered Radar's contribution to their squad every bit as valuable as sniffing for explosives. Radar's mere presence had boosted the morale of those men and women stationed so far from home, family and everything familiar.

Gabe might have told himself he'd been honoring a promise while he fought bureaucratic red tape to get the dog stateside, but that was simply an excuse.

The truth was he hated to think of what Radar's fate might have been if he'd been abandoned after command had ordered the evacuation of their forlorn desert outpost. Yeah, like he wouldn't have done his damnedest—promise or no—to get Radar to safety.

Radar had never been an active marine, and since his honorable discharge last Friday, neither was he. Even if he was no longer addressed as SSgt. Bishop in daily life, that identity would always be a part of him. A rank he was proud to have attained. Once a marine, always a marine. *Oo-rah!*

The irony didn't escape him that civilian Gabe was a lot like Radar—searching for a perfect bush. Huh. "Sorry, buddy. I—"

A drilling clatter had him tensing and scanning his surroundings for anomalies. Same blue-collar neighborhood lined mostly with single-family brick ranches and a few duplexes like his rental unit. Nothing had changed from five minutes ago. So, what—?

The noise sounded again. Spotting a red-bellied

woodpecker drumming an aluminum rain gutter, Gabe relaxed his guard and snorted a laugh. Looked like Radar wasn't the only one intent on marking his territory this sunny April afternoon.

He shook his head. Such vigilance. What had he been expecting? This was Loon Lake, a place that travel brochures had dubbed quintessential New England. It boasted of a grass-covered town square and the ubiquitous eighteenth-century white clapboard church with a soaring steeple. Brick-fronted small businesses with colorful awnings and antique-looking streetlights crowded along Main Street. Despite appearances, the awnings and white-globed lamps were new.

Gabe grinned. How much squabbling had taken place before the town council voted to approve those lamps? He may have been barely twenty when he'd left for basic, but he knew residents enjoyed nothing better than arguing over mundane details. Pa had come home from those meetings grumbling about—

Radar pulled on the lead, jerking Gabe out of his thoughts and back to practical matters, like getting back to the rented duplex to finish unpacking so he could settle in and begin his new life. Whatever that might look like. With his pa gone, he had no relatives in Loon Lake, but the town was still home.

He tried to turn them around, but Radar dropped down on his belly in the middle of the sidewalk. Gabe tugged again on the leash, but the dog wouldn't budge.

"What have I told you about mission creep?" he asked, referring to a shift in objectives that resulted in further commitment and time. The dog whined and Gabe shook his head. "Fine, a couple more blocks, but that's it. I can haul your seventy-five-pound butt home if I have to. Don't think I won't."

Radar rose and did a full-body shake, his tags jingling merrily. Gabe narrowed his eyes at the dog's actions—looked like this human needed to practice his alpha-dog skills. They continued to the end of the street and turned to follow the sidewalk along a wider, busier road.

Sure, they didn't have to worry about snipers or improvised explosive devices, but being so exposed made his scalp prickle. He disliked that feeling of being watched, even benignly, and he'd already pegged the woman across the street as a curtain twitcher.

At least no one had shown up on his doorstep with casseroles or baked goods—yet. And with any luck, they wouldn't. He'd had enough handouts in his childhood to last a lifetime.

"Yeah, I know what you're thinking, dog. Why come home if I wanted to avoid attention?" Truth was he'd been yearning for something familiar, and his memories of growing up in Loon Lake weren't all bad. And frankly, after being away for a decade, he assumed the residents' memories of the kid with the free lunches and hand-me-down clothes would have dimmed. Even if the legacy of the teen who'd learned to cover embarrassment by acting tough and getting into trouble hadn't been erased.

After Radar had marked a tree, a lamppost and an azalea bush—apparently those were acceptable—Gabe succeeded in coaxing him to head toward home. As they approached their street, a school bus stopped with a squeal of the air brakes and a hiss as the pneumatic door swung open. Hoping to get away before any kids got off, he pulled on the leash, but Radar sat on his haunches, once again refusing to move. Damn, but he was going to have to establish who was in charge in this relationship.

The dog stared intently at the bus, his ears thrust forward. When he whined, Gabe gave him a pat on the head. "I guess this is your first time seeing one of those, huh?"

A bespectacled boy wearing a gray T-shirt, jeans and black Chuck Taylor high-tops bounded off the steps. The kid's mouth formed a giant O and he made a beeline toward them, his backpack bouncing around his thin shoulders. Gabe zeroed in on that backpack and tensed, but Radar whimpered and pressed against him, grounding him, bringing him back to the moment and their surroundings.

"What a cool dog, mister." The boy, who appeared to be around six or seven, dropped to his knees and thrust out a hand to pet Radar on the head. "Is it a he or a she? What's his name? Is he yours? What kind is it?"

As Gabe was trying to decide which question to answer first, running footsteps pounded on the pavement behind them. Reacting to the threat, he spun around. A woman sprinted toward them, a blond ponytail tied high on her head bouncing along behind her. He assumed a protective crouch and unconsciously reached for his hip—for the weapon that had been his constant companion for the past decade.

Radar whined and once again broke the spell. Although the dog hadn't acted in any official capacity, he'd alerted them to enemy advances on the compound, saving them from surprise attacks. But no hostiles or suicide bombers looking to kill them here. Trying to get his heart out of his throat, he swallowed and straightened up.

"Theodore Andrew Miller, what do you think you're doing?" The woman skidded to a stop, her pink-and-purple sneakers scattering pebbles. She gulped in air. "What have I told you about approaching strange animals?"

"But it's not a strange animal. It's a dog." The boy scrunched up his face, and the tops of his brown-framed eyeglasses shot past his eyebrows. "See?"

Gabe coughed to disguise the laugh that had bubbled up, and the woman threw an angry scowl in his direction. She had pale blue eyes, a small turned-up nose and freckles sprinkled high across her cheeks. And, oh yeah, she was spitting mad. And kind of young to be this kid's mother. But who was he to judge? Especially considering his past.

"Teddy, I saw you rushing up to him with your hand out," she said. "That dog could've bitten your fingers off."

Her scolding may have been directed at the boy, but Gabe bristled as if those words had been tossed his way. People could think what they wanted about him, but he wasn't about to allow anyone to label Radar a menace. "Ma'am, my dog wouldn't hurt anybody."

She dismissed his words with a wave of her hand. "How was Teddy supposed to know that?"

Okay, so she had a point. He scratched the scruff on his cheek, debating how best to proceed. "If it helps, I'm not a complete stranger to—"

"You're a stranger to us," she said, critically eyeing him up and down as if he and his dog didn't belong on this well-tended street.

"Excuse me, ma'am, but my dog is leashed as required by law. *Your* boy approached us, not the other way around. So, if anyone's to blame, it's him." Heat crept up his neck and settled in his cheeks. Could he get any lower, shifting fault to a kid? Even if it was the truth.

The boy held up a hand, turning it over several times, and Gabe winced at the burn scars on both sides.

"See," he said. "The dog didn't bite me."

"This time," the woman said.

"Will your dog be happy to see me from now on, just like today, mister?" The boy plunged his fingers into the thick fur on Radar's neck.

Gabe nodded, but there wouldn't be a "from now on" if he could help it. He planned on a hassle-free civilian life. His immediate future would consist of finding a job and maybe catching up with a few friends from school.

"See? It's okay because the doggy's going to be nice to me the next time too," the boy said, sounding like that settled the matter. Radar drummed his tail on the sidewalk, and the kid gave him a hug.

The woman closed her eyes, and her lips moved as if she were counting or praying for patience at the child's literal directness. Gabe cleared his throat, and her eyes flew open.

"Teddy, you know better than to talk to strangers. Especially ones with—" she threw another mistrustful glance at Radar "—dogs."

Gabe tightened his fingers around the leash. Okay, now he was pissed. He may have found her appealing in a fresh-faced, wholesome sort of way, but her attitude was sticking in his craw. "Look, lady, I don't know what you have against dogs, but—"

"I have nothing against dogs," she rushed to supply. "But, as I've explained to Teddy, some predators use them to lure unsuspecting children. It, uh, it was nothing personal," she said, a slight blush spreading across her cheeks, highlighting all those tiny freckles. "I apologize if it came across as an insult."

He clamped his mouth shut on the stinging retort that had sprung to his lips. Huh. Her reasoning made sense. How could he argue against child safety? He wouldn't, because he was leaving, getting away from her, her strangely alluring freckles and her kid. He'd go home and take that shower and clean up as he'd planned before Radar had hijacked the mission.

Aside from moving and opening the rest of those storage boxes, the most drama scheduled for today was plopping on the couch and watching some spring baseball, maybe sipping a cold brew. Whether that cold brew would be coffee or beer had yet to be determined. His gaze roamed over the woman and those blue eyes shooting fire at him.

Beer was in the lead.

"You weren't even at the stop when the bus came," the kid said, as if sensing a weakness he could exploit.

"You're right—that's my fault. That last batch of cupcakes took longer to bake than I anticipated." She grimaced. "And, of course, this is the first time in a month that damn bus has been on time."

Gasping, the boy unfolded and sprang up like a marionette whose strings had been pulled taut. "Uh-oh, you have to put a quarter in the jar for using that word. You made me last week, so it's only fair that you do too."

"I have a feeling I owe more than a quarter after nearly suffering a heart attack. C'mon, Teddy, we need to get home." She held out her hand, her gaze darting between the boy and Radar.

The kid scowled. "But I didn't even get to find out the dog's name or nothin'."

"His name's Radar," Gabe told him. Maybe that would pacify the child and he'd allow her to lead him away.

"There. You know his name. Let's go." She had a death grip on the boy's hand and began marching away but threw a cautious glance over her shoulder.

Teddy twisted around and raised his free hand. "Bye, Radar. Bye, mister."

"What happened to the jacket you had on this morning?" the woman asked as they walked away.

"I dunno… Musta left it at school." The response drifted back to them, and Radar gave a low woof, then whined.

"Listen to you." Gabe rubbed the soft fur behind the dog's ears. "You'd think you were losing your best friend in the world."

The woman was saying something, but they were too far away to make out the words, and Radar whined again.

"Forget it, dog," Gabe muttered. "We don't need any part of whatever they've got going on. From now on, we're in a no-drama zone."

Radar looked to the pair and then back, tilting his head. Gabe clucked his tongue. "What makes you think I'm even interested?"

Wagging his tail and panting, Radar pressed against Gabe's leg.

"Okay, sure, she's cute and I didn't see a wedding ring." Yeah, okay, he might've checked. He noisily blew out air between his lips. Why did he do something as silly as scan for a sign that she was off-limits? He wasn't even looking for any sort of relationship.

Radar made a nonmenacing growling noise deep in his throat.

"Look, even if she's single, she can't be more than early twenties. That's too young." *Are you sure?* his inner voice taunted. Because the way that heart-shaped butt filled out those jeans and those hips swayed as she walked away didn't look too young.

Radar started forward as the pair put more distance between them, and Gabe tightened his grip on the leash. Glancing up, Radar tried out his forlorn life-is-so-unfair whimper. How was a guy supposed to hold out against that oh-so-expressive head tilt and impressive vocal range?

"Forget it. I'm not in the market. Even if I was— which I'm not—my thirty going on fifty is definitely too old for all that fresh-faced innocence." He snorted. Was this what his life had come to? From maintaining the discipline and efficiency of the men under his command with field training exercises to arguing with a dog over a woman?

Radar auditioned a different sound, but Gabe stood firm. "What do you know? You're a dog. My guess is she had your undying devotion when she mentioned she baked cupcakes."

He patted Radar on the head and exhaled. "Temptation, thy name is woman."

Radar looked up at him and Gabe shook his head. "Yeah, I have no idea where that came from either."

But he did know the blonde walking away was temptation, and in his experience, that path generally ended with trouble.

Thankfully, those scrapes were nothing more than teenage antics, like the time he'd tried to hijack a rival school's stuffed mascot. Those shenanigans could be traced back to his desire to impress a certain cheerleader. Tracy Harris. Yeah, he'd impressed himself right into a shotgun wedding upon graduation.

He knew better now, and this woman, with that sweet face, had to be the kind of woman who was all in…marriage, kids and forever. So he was going to avoid her—and temptation. Getting the rest of his life on a good track was his first—and last—priority.

He had enough old mistakes on his conscience. He didn't want any new ones.

Been there. Done that.

Even though Teddy was unharmed, Addie Miller's heart continued its staccato rhythm as they headed toward home. Seeing her brother running up to that humongous dog and being too far away to do anything had scared the holy— Oops! She owed the swear jar enough quarters for one day. Nothing like feeling helpless to bring out her potty mouth. She may have needed that tough exterior as protection in the past, but now that she was responsible for Teddy, she needed to set a good example.

Inappropriate language aside, she'd had to acknowledge the sickening truth. If something had happened to Teddy today, the blame would've been hers and hers alone. How could she have allowed baking cupcakes—or anything at all—to distract her?

Queasiness roiled her stomach. Were her promises meaningless too? Was this how she made up for not being there for Teddy in the past?

If he'd gotten mauled by a dog or snatched by a stranger, that would make her no better than their mother, Michelle. And she'd owe an apology to those social workers who'd warned her she'd been ill-equipped to take on such an enormous responsibility, caring for her much younger half brother at her age. She couldn't magically change how many years she'd been on this earth, but she could step up and do what was necessary.

She glanced at Teddy's hand in hers and, seeing the burn scars marring his hand and wrist, choked back a sob. Although she'd been away at college when he'd plunged his hands into scalding hot water, she blamed herself for not being there to prevent it. The fact her brother's care had been her mother's responsibility, and not hers, never mattered one whit to Addie's conscience.

"Addie?" Teddy squeezed her hand and frowned. "It's okay. Radar didn't hurt me. He was a really, really nice doggy," he added in a wistful tone.

Addie blinked against the burn in her eyes. "I'm sure he was, but—"

"—dogs are expensive," he finished for her and kicked a pebble across the sidewalk until it disappeared into a thicket of forsythia bushes. "Joey Johnson said people give puppies away for free when they don't want them. Maybe we could get one like that."

"Even if we did, veterinary care costs lots of money." Her conscience was a hot poker, jabbing her for using the trite excuse. "It wasn't just about the dog, sweetie. That man you spoke to was a stranger. Do you remember how I've asked you not to talk to strangers?"

Teddy's chin hiked up. "You talked to him."

"Yes, I did, but I'm an adult and—"

He pulled his hand from her grip, crossed his arms over his chest and stuck them under his armpits. "But you're my sister. How come you get to act all adult? Make rules for me and stuff like that? Jocy's older sister doesn't do that."

Because you deserve a responsible adult in your life. Tag, she was it. "I was lucky enough to be born first, and you know how much I like having you live with me. You know that, don't you?"

He nodded but stuck out his lower lip. "But it's still not fair."

Life rarely is. She ruffled his hair, a gesture Teddy said was for babies, but even as he ducked to get away, she saw his lips twitch as he fought a smile.

"If you like having me live with you so much, why won't you let me walk home from the bus stop alone?" His expression turned calculating. "I'm big enough, and besides, all the kids on the bus laugh because they know you're my sister."

Her stomach flip-flopped. She understood that he might find her presence embarrassing. How many times had Michelle embarrassed her by showing up at school functions high, inappropriately dressed or hanging off the arm of some guy who was most likely her dealer? Oh, how she'd longed for a mom who volunteered to bake cupcakes for school parties or chaperoned field trips.

She sighed. Was it too much to ask that Teddy

wait until after the hearing for permanent custody to go through a rebellious phase? She didn't trust their mother to keep her word about not fighting it. The family counselor she'd spoken with had assured her that Teddy's actions were a good thing. Testing boundaries meant he felt safe living with her. "I understand how you feel, sweetie, but maybe we—"

"Hey, look! Radar is following us."

She whipped around, and sure enough, the man and his dog had closed the distance between them. This time she concentrated on the owner. He was at least two, maybe three, inches over six feet, with thick brown hair that spiked on top but was cut shorter on the sides. He had straight dark eyebrows above a hawk nose and generous lips surrounded by a thick sprinkling of dark stubble. How had she not noticed he had the most amazing hazel eyes? Or that despite the dusty and torn clothing, he didn't look as disreputable as she'd first assumed. How had she not noticed any of those details before now?

Maybe because the dog had scared the crap out of you. Still does.

She turned back to her brother. "Teddy, why don't you run on ahead? I frosted a cupcake for you and set it aside. And you can play some *Mario Kart*."

"Why?" Teddy's eyes narrowed behind his glasses. "What's going on that you don't want me to know about?"

"Nothing is going on." She pressed a hand to her stomach. To think she'd been thankful when Teddy had started coming out of his shell, had started feeling comfortable enough to question her. "You're the one always begging me for more video-game time."

"But I want to see where Radar is going."

So did she. She'd resided here long enough to know everyone on the street at least well enough to wave when they drove by.

And she'd definitely remember both of them.

CHAPTER TWO

MAN AND DOG caught up to them before she could order Teddy inside. The animal sat at the man's feet when he stopped. Obedient, but excited shivers coursed through its body.

Was it possible for a dog to yearn? If so, this one did it every time he glanced at Teddy. Her heart constricted. She was still fearful, but maybe it was time— past time—to face this fear straight on and put it behind her.

If only... She reached out blindly for Teddy's hand because fears weren't wished away.

"Are you lost, or did you need something?" she asked, trying to sound polite, but it came out as more of an accusation than an inquiry.

The man held his hands up, palms out, the leash threaded through the fingers of one hand. "Neither one. We're just minding our own business and going home."

He had large, calloused hands with blunt-tipped— Wait... What? "Home?"

He nodded and pointed. "This is us, the duplex up there on the left."

He was indicating the house with brick on the bottom, blue clapboards on the upper half and black shutters. One of only two multifamily dwellings on the street, it was well cared for, and like the other homes, it was set back to allow for a decent-sized front yard. Despite being only a renter, she felt a sense of pride being able to offer her brother such a stable—

"Oh boy! Did you hear that?" Teddy tugged on her hand, bringing her back to the current situation. "Radar's moving in with us."

Teddy did a little dance and the dog's plumy tail waved in an arc as if he too was celebrating this happy news. The dog who was invading her space.

Clearing his throat, the stranger rubbed a hand across his mouth and met her gaze. Those mesmerizing eyes seemed to both mock and challenge her. As if he had read her mind.

"Did you know only 5 percent of the population have hazel eyes?" she asked.

"What?" He blinked and frowned, furrowing the skin between his brows.

Her face flamed. Damn her encyclopedic brain that collected trivia. Her thirst for knowledge came in handy at her job as a library assistant, but not so much when the information she retained spewed back up at the most inopportune times. "Nothing. I— "

"She was talking about eye color and—"

"Teddy, why don't you go inside...? Now."

"But—but—"

"You may as well listen to her." He pinned her with his gaze. "Radar and I are heading to the previously *unoccupied* side, if that makes you feel any better."

No, it didn't make her feel any better because that enormous dog would be living... Right. Next. Door.

Teddy scrunched his nose. "What does un—unoccupied mean?"

"Empty," she answered automatically, her mind still processing the fact they were her new neighbors. She shook her head. "But—but I spoke with Natalie a few days ago and she didn't tell me anyone was moving in."

He lifted a broad shoulder in a negligible shrug. "You'll have to take that up with the person who actually owns the house."

"Sam's mom owns the house," Teddy said, the man's sarcasm going over his head. "Are you and Radar new in town? We used to be new, didn't we, Addie?"

"Actually, I grew up in Loon Lake, but I've been away for over ten years," the man said.

"Wow, that's a long time." Teddy's eyes widened. "Were you in jail, like—?"

"Teddy! You're being rude." She squeezed his shoulder but felt like a hypocrite because he was asking the questions she was too polite to voice. Exactly who was this new neighbor and where had he been for ten years? Her curiosity was justified because she had social workers combing through her life, checking Teddy's living arrangements. Really? Like that justified being nosy or judgmental about a stranger?

And underneath all that justification was the fact that Teddy's life experiences—like her own—had him making the leap from *absence* to *jail*.

Teddy hung his head. "Sorry for being rude."

"I'm sure your mother will be relieved to know I wasn't incarcerated. I—"

"Addie's not my mother." Teddy's head popped up. "Even if she acts like it and I live with her. She's just my sister."

She winced at his use of the qualifier *just*. Despite what anyone said, she didn't need him testing her authority. Not now. Could he say something like that to a social worker or judge?

"Then your sister will be happy to know I've been in the marines, not jail." He quirked an eyebrow at her as if to say he'd known she'd been as curious as her brother.

Teddy's eyes lit up. "The marines! Was Radar with you too?"

She tried to disguise her relief and... "The marines? That means you must be Gabriel Bishop, the war hero everyone has been—"

Oh God, Addie, just shut up. Running your mouth isn't helping.

"I see gossip is still the number one sport in Loon Lake," he said with a cynical twist of his lips.

Before Addie could form a response, Teddy rambled on. "Is Radar a war hero too? Did he wear all the cool stuff like I seen in that movie about the military dog? Remember that movie we saw, Addie?" Teddy leaned closer to the dog, trying to drag her with him. "The one in the movie had a vest and goggles just like the soldiers, but they were all dog-sized. Does Radar have all that 'quipment'?"

"No. He didn't have any of that. He was—" The dog woofed and tilted his head to look up at his owner, who reached down and scratched him behind the ears. "But he was every bit a member of our squad. He was one of us."

That canine mouth pulled back into a giant, goofy smile, and for the first time in fifteen years, she felt something other than petrified of a dog.

"Wait till I tell the other kids I live next door to a war hero and a marine dog." Teddy bounced on his toes. "Does Radar—?"

"Teddy, why don't you go inside?" she suggested again. "You can have that cupcake now and play some *Mario Kart* before setting the table for supper."

"But—but—"

"The offer of video-game time can be rescinded at any time." She gave her brother a warning look.

Radar whined as if he too was objecting. Gabriel Bishop shook his head at the dog. "Don't you start."

Despite the uncomfortable situation, Addie grinned at the dog's expression of dismay. She glanced up and her gaze met her neighbor's. Swallowing, she said, "Kids, huh?"

Gabriel's gaze held hers, and his mouth slowly curved upward until he was smiling at her. That simple gesture sent tingles skittering across her skin until he broke eye contact with a frown. But that smile... Talk about panty-melting.

Huh, maybe the dog wasn't the biggest threat to her peace of mind after all. But still, she'd feel a lot better if he owned one of those purse-sized pups instead of a big mean-looking one.

No, that wasn't fair. She spared a look at the dog. Yes, he was big, and that size alone was scary, but the way he was looking at Teddy bordered on adoration. How could she argue against that?

"Like I said, Radar and I are going inside, so you might want to listen to your sister."

The dog whined but trotted up the sidewalk to follow his master into the house, but not before giving Teddy one last doleful glance before the door shut.

Teddy heaved a put-upon sigh. "Can I have two cupcakes and play for two hours?"

Had Michelle even considered limiting Teddy's time watching television or playing video games? She should put her foot down, order him into the house. Letting him take advantage of her guilt wasn't healthy. "One cupcake now and another after supper."

A speculative gleam shone in his pale blue eyes. "What about *Mario Kart*? I don't have any homework."

"An hour and a half. And I don't want any arguments when I ask you to dry the dishes after supper."

He did a fist pump and ran ahead into the house. She glanced at the previously unoccupied side of the duplex—the one where that big dog now lived—and sighed. She'd work on setting stricter rules with Teddy. But first, she needed to get tough with herself and work on getting over her fear of dogs.

She would be doing it because overcoming it would be a step toward being the person Teddy needed her to be. All that self-improvement had nothing to do with those eyes flecked with brown, green and blue.

"Believe that and you'll be buying beachfront property in Arizona," she muttered and went into the house.

Once inside, she headed into the kitchen. Teddy had devoured a cupcake and left the plate on the counter, leaving not so much as a crumb behind. She set the dish in the sink and checked on him in his bedroom, where he was already playing his game. Shutting his door against the electronic noises, she pulled out her cell phone and made a call.

"I know why you're calling," Natalie said by way of greeting when she answered and added, "And I'm so sorry for not letting you know," before Addie could even speak.

Addie didn't pretend to misunderstand what Natalie was talking about. They had been friends ever since Addie had moved to Loon Lake. They'd bonded over single parenthood and formed their own supportive network of friends and single parents. "No apologies necessary. It's your place and I don't have any business putting my two cents in."

This wasn't about making Natalie feel guilty, so she injected lightness she wasn't feeling into her voice. "I was just surprised to learn I had a new neighbor."

"When I saw your name pop up on the caller ID, I realized I should have given you a heads-up. But since you're not upset, then I guess that means you've seen Gabriel Bishop."

"Oh, I've seen him." Not some of her finest moments. First, casting the new neighbor—an honest-to-goodness war hero, according to absolutely everyone who'd come into the library this past week—in the role of potential child snatcher. Then, instead of apologizing for her mistake, she'd stood there and spouted eye-color trivia at him. "But I meant no apologies necessary because it's your property and you can do what you want, rent to whomever you want."

What had gotten into her? She was usually more astute at reading people, but seeing Teddy with that big dog had flustered her, and all reasoning and logic had fled. She may feel justified in her reaction to seeing Teddy talking with a strange man, but letting it turn her into a shrew was unacceptable.

Natalie chuckled. "And the fact he's a hunk—and single, I might add—doesn't hurt, huh?"

Addie rolled her eyes even though her friend couldn't see her. She'd had it up to here with match-making. Her Harlequin ladies—the nickname she'd given the women who frequented the library and left with stacks of paperback romances—were on a mission to get her fixed up. Would they still feel the same if they knew her secret or would they redouble their efforts? She hadn't even confessed to Natalie that she was still a virgin at the ripe old age of twenty-two. It was nothing to be ashamed of, so she wasn't even sure herself why she hadn't told anyone.

Every week the ladies presented her with another choice. Loon Lake might be a small town, but its supply of single guys under the age of forty was starting to feel inexhaustible. Not that she didn't sometimes yearn for the closeness of having someone special to share her life with, but she wasn't going to be like their mother and bring a parade of unsuitable men into Teddy's life. She knew from childhood experience how confusing that could be. Of course, there'd been times when she'd been grateful that they'd disappeared because—

"Hey? You still there? I'm sorry if—"

"Stop apologizing!" Addie shook her head to clear the lingering thoughts from her past. "I'm not upset. Just…"

"Distracted by thoughts of a certain mouthwatering marine?" Natalie sighed. "If you weren't such a good friend, you'd have to fight me."

"Oh please." Addie tsk-tsked. "You are so in love with your husband you glow."

"Don't they say that about all pregnant women? I have a feeling Gabe could—"

"Will you cut that out?" Addie interrupted huffily

but softened it with a laugh. Natalie and Des Gallagher were one of the happiest couples she knew, so all of this was Natalie's attempt at matchmaking. All the bliss-fully married couples she knew were as bad as those ladies at Colleen's Cut and Caboodle.

As if all those speculative glances cast in her direc-tion by the library patrons each time Gabriel Bishop's name was mentioned weren't enough, now she had her good friend trying to matchmake. She needed to steer the conversation back toward her original pur-pose. Much safer territory. "I was surprised you rented it now, because you said you planned to get repairs and renovations done first. You mentioned talking to Ben McNamara about doing them."

"Oh, I did, and, hmm, you know Ben's hot and he's—"

"Stop it," Addie said before her friend could get carried away.

"Okay. Okay. I did ask Ben, but he's super busy with those Victorians on the other side of town. He gave me some names, but before I had a chance to talk to anyone else, I bumped into Brody and Mary at the Pic-N-Save."

Brody and Mary Wilson had transformed their farm on the outskirts of town into Camp Life Launch, a summer program mainly for children being raised in the foster care system. Although Addie's own time in the system had been brief, it had changed her, and she volunteered at the camp whenever she could. To repay her, the Wilsons allowed Teddy to attend some of the camp sessions to help Addie with childcare during the summer break from school.

"Anyway," Natalie continued, "Brody told me that

Riley Cooper had told him that Gabe was looking for a place. The one Gabe was supposed to rent fell through when the owner's niece had a quickie wedding and decided she wanted it."

Addie snickered. "The Loon Lake grapevine in action."

"You got that right. Anyway, when I told Des, we decided to offer the place to Gabe. He was relieved to find another place, especially one that was partially furnished. He was so grateful, he agreed to do some of the renovation work along with any other issues that pop up. You'll have a maintenance person living on the premises."

"That's a good deal for both of you." Addie paced the kitchen, straightening the napkin holder and salt and pepper shakers on the small maple kitchen table before moving on to the living room.

"And not a bad deal for you since he's   Oh, I don't know—" Natalie heaved an exaggerated sigh before continuing, "Mr. Sex-on-a-Stick."

Good grief. Did everyone think she couldn't attract a man on her own? "I meant it's a good deal because it shortens Des's honey-do list."

"Which is why I am grateful for Gabe's willingness to take on the repairs and renovations. Ever since that national magazine did a feature on glass artists, Des has had more work than he can handle."

Natalie's husband was a gifted glass sculptor and had been a onetime, self-proclaimed scrooge until Natalie and her young son, Sam, burst into his life. Now he was a dedicated family man. Addie bent down and picked up a stray LEGO, placing it on the coffee table.

At least she hadn't stepped on it. "But that's good, right? He deserves to have his talent recognized."

"Yes, it's very good. I'm just sorry I didn't warn you ahead of time Gabe was arriving. I meant to call you yesterday but fell asleep right after supper. I'd forgotten how tiring this first trimester is."

"Well, you just take care of yourself." Addie knew how excited her friends were about the pregnancy. And she was elated for them, but she couldn't help feeling envious and wondering if it would ever be her turn.

Natalie snorted. "No need to worry about that. Des is worse than a mother hen, and even Sam is waiting on me. I feel like a queen."

"As well you should," Addie told her, happy that Natalie had found love with a former naval aviator, whose career had been cut short when he'd received life-altering injuries. Her friend had lost her first husband in a tragic accident, which had also left her young son with a traumatic brain injury that had resulted in the boy being nonverbal.

They talked a few more minutes before ending with a promise of getting Teddy and Sam together soon. Natalie and Sam had lived on the other side of the duplex before she married Des, and the two boys had bonded over their love of LEGO bricks.

Back in the kitchen, she rooted around in a cupboard next to the refrigerator until she found a plastic storage container. She began frosting the cupcakes she'd left to cool while she picked up Teddy from the bus stop. She'd save some for her and Teddy, with the rest going to the monthly library meeting. The laminated sign Addie put on the door read Coffee & Conversation, but everyone in town referred to the meetings as Drinks & Drama. Small-town life's double-edged sword. People had your back in times of trouble but loved nothing more than to argue over mundane details of how to enact those plans.

As she frosted the cupcakes, her thoughts kept going back to her new neighbor. From what she could recall from the library patrons, Gabe had been awarded medals or ribbons or whatever it was that marines got for bravery on the battlefield. He'd said the dog wasn't military, but that didn't mean he hadn't done something heroic too. Maybe saved his life or something. Was that why he'd been so offended on the dog's behalf?

Great. She'd insulted two of America's finest in one day. *Nice going.* More snatches of this past week's gossip floated around in her head. She frowned. Not all of it had been flattering. Several ladies had lowered their voices and spoke of rowdy behavior and police involvement, but obviously nothing serious enough to keep him out of the military.

Retired schoolteacher Trudy Canterbury had clucked her tongue when recalling that Gabe had gotten married like "five minutes after graduating high school." Shaking her head, Trudy had added his wife had divorced him about "five minutes after he'd deployed."

Having your wife divorce you while you were off fighting for your country couldn't have been easy. And now, thanks to her and her big mouth, she'd verified that he'd been the subject of town gossip.

Instead of putting the cover over the cupcakes, she set it aside and reached into one of the overhead cabinets and took down a plate. It was inexpensive melamine but one of her favorites. He probably wouldn't notice or care about the sunflowers or goldfinches, but using it made her feel better. Like an apology inside another apology.

She took out three cupcakes and arranged them on the plate. Did she even want to see Gabe Bishop again this soon? As if not seeing him was an option, considering he lived next door. It wasn't as if she could avoid him forever. And, knowing he nor the dog were a danger to Teddy, talking to him again wouldn't exactly be a hardship. Except that would also mean seeing Radar. But nothing in this life ever came without cost.

"Think of it as exposure therapy." Yeah, because that had worked so well in the past. She snorted. Maybe if she'd actually, really exposed herself...

Before she could change her mind, she grabbed her peace offering and went out the front door to the rectangular cement stoop the side-by-side duplexes shared. Throwing her shoulders back, she crossed the oh-so-short distance separating her from the dog.

Thankfully Teddy was in his room playing video games. Groveling would be embarrassing enough; she didn't need an audience. She could set an example about taking responsibility by apologizing for her mistakes some other day. No doubt another teaching moment would arise in the next dozen or so years.

Her new neighbor's wooden door stood open, so she knocked on the glass of the storm door. Repairing or replacing the broken doorbell had been on Natalie's to-do list, so she didn't even bother with it. As she waited, she turned her head and glanced toward the house across the street in time to see the lace curtain in the front window fluttering. *Are you getting all this, Mrs. O?*

A widow in her eighties, Maureen O'Malley was

one of the ladies who congregated weekly at Colleen's Cut and Caboodle. Come Thursday, you could bet Addie's visit to the new neighbor would be discussed as the regulars had their hair washed, styled and sprayed. Maureen was also the street's unofficial neighborhood watch. Nothing got past Mrs. O. What she didn't observe personally, she got from plying the gregarious mail carrier with her ricotta cheese cookies. Not many were strong enough to hold out against those frosted morsels of heaven.

Grinning, she turned back and— Yikes! The dog— Radar—was on the other side of the glass. He didn't bark or growl, just stood there watching her with an intenseness she found jarring. How long had he been there eyeing her? He seemed to be looking directly into her. Hey, at least he wasn't smacking his lips. Did he know how frightened she was? Heck, Mrs. O could probably see her knees knocking without the aid of her trusty binoculars.

The dog's nose began to twitch. Gulping, she did her best to control her reptilian brain reaction. Definitely flight—fight wasn't even on the menu.

Calm down. The dog was probably more interested in getting at the cupcakes than doing anything to her. Right? If she was lucky, the scent of the treats would mask the smell of her fear. Not that it mattered since dogs were also masters at reading body language. She groaned inwardly. Sometimes she hated her penchant for retaining bits of trivia.

"Did you know your sense of smell is around forty times greater than mine? Heck, you can probably pick out the individual ingredients even through this door. Red velvet cake batter has cocoa powder, vinegar or buttermilk, and it's the chemical reaction between them that—"

"Did you want something?"

Addie startled at the deep male voice and nearly dropped the plate. The cupcakes bounced and she clutched the dish tighter. She raised her gaze to Gabriel Bishop, who now stood behind his dog. He'd not only changed his clothes but shaved, and if his damp hair was any indication, he'd showered too. Whoa. He cleaned up nice. Maybe Natalie and the library ladies knew what they were talking about. *Down, girl.* She bit her lower lip to contain the nervous laughter that bubbled up. "I... I..."

He scowled. "Did you need something, or did you come to give my dog a baking lesson?"

"Actually, we were talking about his sense of smell. Like I was telling him, dogs have up to three hundred million olfactory receptors in their noses and— Uh, well, never mind." Oh yeah, this wasn't embarrassing or anything. Her face hot enough to melt the cream cheese frosting on the cupcakes, she thrust out the plate. "Here, I came to give you these."

An emotion flickered across his face and disappeared before she could interpret it. The glower that replaced it was all too easy to read. Why couldn't she prevent trivia from dribbling out when she opened her mouth?

"Why?" he demanded, his straight brows clashing together.

"Why?" she echoed. Okay, embarrassment had tainted her presentation, but his reaction seemed out of proportion to her lack of grace. She shuffled her feet. "I wanted to apologize for my—" she swallowed "—earlier behavior. I—"

"Apology accepted. Was there anything else?" The dog whimpered and he gave Radar a pat on the head.

"You, uh, you don't want the cupcakes?" They weren't Maureen's coveted cookies, but they weren't bad. Teddy loved her red velvet cupcakes, and her little brother wasn't one to spare her feelings with spurious praise.

"I don't need chari— Uh, I mean, that's not necessary." He curled his palm around the edge of the inner wooden door and started to push. "The apology was sufficient."

"Oh. Well, um…" She took a step back as the door swung shut with a firm *thunk*. "Ohh-kaay."

She stood for a moment staring at the closed door. She stuck out her tongue, then called him a name that had her owing the swear jar another quarter— Ha! Considering Teddy had had to give up a quarter for saying "damn" while playing a game, she probably owed it some serious folding cash. A few more encounters like this with her new neighbor and she'd go broke. Of course, that wasn't exactly a long ride.

CHAPTER THREE

GABE STOOD IN the center of the room and shifted his weight from one foot to the other, his gaze trained on the front window. She—what had the kid called her? Addie?—was crossing the street with her plate of cupcakes. Probably going to visit the curtain twitcher to report his rude behavior.

Radar made his I'm-not-happy-with-you noise, a cross between a woof and a growl, before ambling over to the window, his nails clicking on the hardwood floor. He stood panting, his breath fogging the glass, and watched their neighbor—or more likely those cupcakes she was carrying—sashay across the street.

"Yeah, I get it. I acted like an ass." Gabe sighed and rubbed the back of his neck.

"Bed," he ordered the dog.

Taking out your bad behavior on an innocent dog is beneath you.

Radar went to his dog bed and threw himself down. He lowered his head to his paws and breathed out a canine sigh. Gabe snort-laughed. That dog belonged in Hollywood.

"I don't know what you're complaining about. She can call them red velvet if she likes, but I could plainly see those cupcakes were chocolate. Dogs can't have chocolate."

Radar lifted his head, gave a low woof and lowered it again.

"Hey, I didn't make the rules."

No, but he could have been polite and accepted her offering. Instead, seeing her had slammed him back nearly two decades.

Back to that day when he'd opened the door of their trailer to his classmate Alan and Alan's mom. She'd been clutching a covered casserole dish, offered presumably because his pa had been injured on the job and unable to work.

He may have forgotten what food was in that dish, but branded on his brain was the woman's appalled expression as she'd glanced around the dilapidated trailer and junk-strewn yard. Her expression had morphed into pity when her gaze met Gabe's. What ten-year-old boy wanted to be pitied in front of his peers? That was the first time he'd experienced feeling ashamed of his circumstances, but not the last.

Seeing his new neighbor standing at his door with an offering had not only thrown him into his past but had him thinking serving his country hadn't changed a damn thing. As if she were saying he didn't belong on this neatly tended street. Of course, she'd been making a simple neighborly gesture.

Yeah, she looked like the do-gooder type. He rubbed a hand over his face. Closing the door on her hadn't been his finest moment. About on par with placing blame on the kid earlier. And ordering Radar into his dog bed. What was it about that woman that had him acting like a first-class jerk?

He knew the difference between apologizing or being neighborly and charity.

Shoving both hands into his back pockets, he watched as the curtain twitcher answered her door. The elderly woman smiled and nodded her head, obviously pleased to accept the cupcakes he'd refused. Damn, but he was a fool. The question was, what was he going to do to make up for his behavior? It wasn't this woman's fault he had issues—apparently unresolved ones—from his childhood.

"Got any ideas, dog? Short of only going out under cover of darkness to avoid her, what can I do? I signed a year's lease on this place." His financial situation wasn't dire. He still had a good chunk of combat pay squirreled away, but forfeiting a year's worth of rent wasn't possible. Not after all the dough he'd shelled out getting Radar here. Not that he begrudged a penny of that money.

The cupcakes disappeared inside the house along with the humans. Radar glanced up and woofed in response.

"Yeah, yeah, easy for you to say. You didn't hurt her feelings. You were happy enough to see her and her cupcakes."

He picked up one of the boxes he'd dragged in earlier and set it on the coffee table. Like the initial rental that had slipped through his fingers at the last minute, this apartment had come partially furnished. Loon Lake might celebrate him as a supposed war hero, but when it came to renting a furnished place to a guy with a seventy-five-pound dog, his status wasn't all that impressive.

* * *

Two days later, Gabe flattened the last cardboard storage box, glad the task was done at last. Unpacking had taken much longer than he'd expected. Mostly because he hadn't anticipated the flood of memories that had been in storage for so long. Those things included a few keepsakes from his mother, who had passed away from cancer when Gabe was six. After his pa's death during his second deployment to Afghanistan, he'd disposed of or donated most of the contents of their mobile home, except for small items he'd boxed up and put into storage. At that time, he'd vowed to deal with them in the future.

"Welcome to the future," he muttered, glancing over at a dozing Radar.

Surrounded by a bevy of new toys, the dog had supervised the proceedings from the comfort of his bed. Gabe shook his head at the sight. Looked like he needed to avoid the animal aisle at Pic-N-Save unless he was shopping for pet food.

Maybe he should stay out of local businesses entirely. He'd run into Sheriff Grayson Granger at the Pic-N-Save despite going first thing in the morning to avoid as many customers as possible. The sheriff had recognized him. No surprise there. The surprise was that the man had been genuinely pleased to see him, offering his hand.

Gabe had half expected the sheriff to slap on a pair of cuffs when he'd stuck out his own to shake. But Granger had pumped Gabe's hand and clapped him on the shoulder to welcome him home and thank him for such meritorious service.

While he appreciated the sheriff's forgiveness for youthful transgressions like underage drinking and some graffiti tagging, both of which he'd paid for. One with getting sick from drinking bourbon straight from the bottle and the other with having to clean up what he'd spray-painted. Looking back, he had to say he'd gotten off light. Not sure if it was a small-town thing or if his pa making him apologize to the sheriff had helped. But he hated all the war-hero nonsense. Since when did doing what he'd been trained to do count as heroism? He threw himself onto the sofa. If he'd been a true hero, he would have saved more than his own life. Radar would be with Tom and—

A wet nose nudged his hand. Radar whimpered and rested his head on Gabe's knee. The dog looked up at him with adoration, not a hint of reproach. Sighing, he rubbed Radar's ears. Why was everyone so willing to forgive him? What had he done in his life to deserve such magnanimous absolution? He'd escaped a teen-age marriage by joining the marines and he'd literally escaped death in Afghanistan by winning a coin toss.

Radar's ears twitched and he broke away. Trotting to the door, he sniffed around the bottom. Gabe may not be able to rattle off numbers regarding the dog's olfactory receptors, but he did know Radar recognized the person on the other side, because his tail was working like a metronome. Radar sat and stared at the door in anticipation. Finally someone knocked.

Sighing again, he dropped the flattened cardboard on the pile and went to check. With careful timing, he'd managed to avoid his neighbors since shutting the door in the woman's lovely face. Several times he'd thought about going over to apologize, but he hadn't gotten past the thinking stage.

Maybe this would be his opportunity. Drawing a deep breath, he pulled open the door, vowing to use the manners he'd been taught.

Teddy stood on the other side of the glass. Okay, he wasn't disappointed. Nope. He'd only hoped it was her so he could apologize for his boorish behavior. Yup, that explained it.

As soon as he unlatched the storm door, Radar pushed his nose out. Gabe made a grab for his collar, but the dog was faster and wriggled through the space, showering the kid with sloppy kisses.

"It's so good to see you again. I missed you so much," Teddy told the slobbering dog.

"Yeah, it's been a whole two days," Gabe said. You'd think by the way they greeted one another that the pair had been cruelly separated for months instead of days. What had gotten into Radar?

Teddy lifted his head. "Huh?"

"Nothing. Forget it," Gabe said. It wasn't the kid's fault he was in a bad mood. He'd regretted acting like such an ass to his pretty neighbor. He didn't want to subject her brother to the same treatment. What harm would it have caused to have taken her cupcakes? Instead, he'd been petty.

Teddy hugged Radar, who hadn't stopped squirming and nearly knocked the giggling kid onto his butt on the cement steps outside the door.

Great. The last thing he needed was to have to explain scrapes or injuries to the boy's sister. No telling how she'd react. Especially if Radar was to blame.

And it would be his fault for repaying her apology with rudeness.

"Sit," he ordered Radar before dealing with the boy.

Teddy scrunched up his face and glanced down. "Here? But…"

Gabe bit the inside of his cheek. "I was talking to Radar."

Radar obeyed, but ripples of excitement continued to course through his entire body.

"Wow. He listens real good. I'll be sure and tell Addie." The boy dropped to his knees and put his arms around the dog. "She keeps saying dogs are too expensive. I said we just won't take it to the vet, but she says that's not the way good parents should behave," the boy parroted his sister.

Gabe rubbed a hand across his mouth. The kid did a pretty good imitation of Addie.

Teddy rested his cheek against Radar's fur. "I think she just doesn't like dogs too much."

The movement caused the sweatshirt sleeve to pull up and expose those scars marring the child's hands and wrists. Yeah, definitely burn scars. Gabe grimaced. Not fresh, but the kid couldn't be more than six or seven. How did—? He pushed those thoughts aside. Not his business. And he wasn't making it his business either. He needed to get his own life in order, not get involved in someone else's.

Gabe glanced down at the boy. He really shouldn't be encouraging drop-in visits. "Was there a reason why you came?"

"Oh yeah…" The kid sprang up and straightened his shoulders. "Hello, Mr. Bishop. I'm Teddy from next door. I tol' Addie you already know that, but she said

I needed to be polite and that maybe it will rub off on you. Uh—" He scratched his scalp. "But I think I wasn't s'pose to say that last part, because she said it real low and I'll bet she doesn't know I heard her. You won't tell her I tol' you, will you?"

Gabe coughed into his hand. He didn't want to hurt the kid's feelings by openly laughing. Something about this kid made his chest tighten, like the time he'd had pneumonia. The past couldn't be changed, so he had tried hard not to dwell on all that emotional stuff over the years. But if he'd survived, his own son would have been only a year or two older than Teddy, so comparisons were inevitable. Would he have been a chatterbox? Or a dog lover? Would he and Tracy still be together?

"...to ask if you had a wrench we could borrow. She also said to just come back if you said no or shut the door in my face. But I said you wouldn't do that. You wouldn't, would you?"

Gabe rubbed a hand over his chest. To be honest, closing the door on the kid had been his first instinct. Something about Teddy and Addie set off alarm bells. Like getting involved with either would drag him further than he wanted to go. Not only was she young, but responsible for a kid. He doubted she was out for a good time.

"For starters, you can call me Gabe." *Yeah, that's a big step toward not getting involved.* "Now, did your sister say why she needs a wrench?"

"She's trying to get the water turned off under the kitchen sink."

The boy was busy petting Radar and telling his newfound friend how much he'd missed him, so Gabe prompted him. "Why is she doing that?"

"Because the handle thing on top broke." Teddy buried his fingers in Radar's fur. "It was real cool. I heard Addie yell a bad word, so I paused my game and ran into the kitchen. I was gonna make sure she put money in the jar, but water was spraying up and…" The boy paused to draw in a breath. "Addie was getting wet trying to stop it, so instead I got the bucket she uses to wash the floor, and she put it over the water. It didn't stop it, but now it's going into the sink instead of into the air."

Gabe scooped his keys off the small table in the hall. That sounded urgent and like something he could help with. That was even better than a simple apology. "I have a toolbox in my Jeep. I'll get it."

"Addie was so mad I didn't even tell her she owed the swear jar. Good thing the clipboard lady wasn't there today. I heard Addie tell Sam's mom that the lady scares her, and she has to be careful what she says in front of her."

Gabe had no idea what the kid was talking about but nodded as if he did. He stood at the open door and pressed the key fob to unlock his Jeep sitting in the driveway.

Teddy looked up at him. His light blue eyes seemed to be searching for reassurance. "I thought being an adult meant you didn't have to be afraid of stuff like that anymore. What about you? Were you afraid when you were in the war?"

Oh kid, don't look to me for answers. Any answers to anything. Gabe clenched his jaw. How had their simple conversation morphed into this? Yeah, he needed to put some distance between him and the child. And his sister. She was obviously responsible for her brother and needed someone she could rely on. His divorce proved he wasn't reliable. "Why don't we save this discussion for another time?"

"Why are people always saying that?"

"Because right now your sister needs help getting the water shut off."

He definitely didn't want to get involved in their family drama, but he could take a look at her leak. It was part of his agreement with the landlord and had nothing to do with his neighbor's bright blue eyes or those freckles begging to be kissed.

"Can Radar come with us?"

"Did you say there's water on your kitchen floor?"

"Just a little from before we got the bucket over it."

"Even so. I don't think we need Radar adding to your sister's troubles by having a dog tramp through wet floors." Gabe pointed to Radar. "Radar, bed."

The water was a good excuse, but he also agreed with Teddy that his sister didn't like dogs much. Or maybe just his pet. Or him. But that was okay because he wasn't getting involved.

Teddy stuck his bottom lip out in a serious pout and Radar began to whine. Damn, but those two were killin' him. How had he gone from being the sergeant dubbed tough as a woodpecker's lips to pushover in record time? And what happened to keeping his distance and not getting involved?

"How about you two play outside? I have a tennis ball you can throw. Radar likes to play fetch."

"Really?" The boy's face lit up. "Hear that, Radar? We can play ball."

Radar woofed his agreement.

Gabe shook his head. You would've thought he'd

promised to take the kid to a theme park, but it felt strangely satisfying to make the kid happy with such a simple gesture. The strange tightness in his chest had eased and he couldn't help grinning when he retrieved one of Radar's tennis balls.

"Um…" Teddy made a face. "Maybe I should tell Addie first."

"I'll let her know," Gabe said and handed Teddy a ball. "You'll just be here in the front yard."

"Yeah, she forgets I'm not a baby anymore." He ran down the steps but Radar stayed in the same spot, looking at Gabe as if seeking permission to follow.

"At ease," he said, and the dog tore off after Teddy and the ball. That had been one of the commands Tom had taught Radar. Gabe smiled, but the memory was bittersweet.

He watched for a moment while Teddy threw the ball. The kid could use some pitching lessons. Did he not have anyone to toss the ball with and give him pointers on holding it? Maybe he could— No. None of his business. He opened the back of his gray Jeep, then grabbed his tool chest and the cardboard box of assorted fixtures Natalie had given him.

He'd find out what was wrong with his neighbor's faucet and fix or replace it because that was the neighborly thing to do. After that, he'd stick to his side of the duplex and mind his own business.

Gabe let himself into Teddy's side of the duplex and glanced around. The living room was the same size as his and had similar-looking, hand-me-down furniture. Had he ever lived in a place with brand-new pieces?

He didn't know Teddy and Addie's family situation,

but taking responsibility for a younger sibling couldn't be easy. As the product of a single-parent household from the age of six himself, he knew it could be a struggle.

Unsure of his welcome after their last encounter, he shifted the box under his arm, gripped his tool chest tighter and headed for the kitchen. He hefted both onto the scarred wood of the table and opened his mouth to announce his presence, but nothing came out. He forgot why he was here. His attention was riveted on the heart-shaped butt sticking out from the open cabinet under the sink as she knelt on her hands and knees.

"Well? Did he have a wrench?" she inquired and started to shimmy backward. "Teddy?"

Gabe swallowed and found his voice. "He did, but if the shut-off valve is stuck, you need Channellock pliers, not a wrench."

She made a startled noise and got up before clearing the cabinet. He winced at the noise her head made when making contact with the wood but couldn't prevent a grin at the curse words she uttered.

"Better not let your brother hear you use that language. He seems pretty keen on that swear jar."

"It's on the honor system," she muttered distractedly and scooted out the rest of the way and scrambled to her feet, facing away from him as she grabbed a towel and wiped her face.

Good thing she had her back to him. He figured it was best not to let her see him grinning. He was probably in enough hot water with his attractive neighbor as it was.

He wiped off the grin and cleared his throat. "What exactly happened?"

"The faucet has been dripping, and when I tried to turn it off a bit tighter, the handle snapped off. It was like the Old Faithful geyser in here."

Opening the tool chest, he lifted the tray out and set it aside. The pliers would be on the bottom along with a small can of WD-40. His pa might not have noticed what a mess their yard was, but he'd kept his tools in pristine condition. "That's what Teddy said. Did the shut-off valve break too, or is it just stuck?"

She folded the towel and put it on the counter. "Stuck. After what had just happened, I was careful not to force it too much."

"Good. It should just be a case of loosening it. I'll spray it first with some, um…" He glanced up as she turned around and had to clamp his mouth shut around what would most likely be an embarrassing sound.

Her T-shirt was soaked and plastered to her chest, giving him a peek at what appeared to be a pink lace bra. Pink was suddenly his new favorite color.

As an officer and a gentleman, he should look away, turn his back, something. Except he was no longer an officer.

And obviously not a gentleman either.

Yeah, he should look away. He really, really should. He should be ashamed of himself. He really, really should.

"Some what?" she asked, using her fingers to explore the back of her head and pulling the shirt even tighter across her chest.

Her puzzled gaze met his while he was still doing the whole fish thing of opening and closing his mouth.

"You—you, uh…" He swallowed and waved a hand in her general direction.

She glanced down at herself and turned beet red. "Yes, well, if you, uh, if you'll excuse me, I'll just go and dry off."

He nodded like a bobblehead doll and called himself all kinds of jerk as she turned and fled. Damn. His teenage self had had smoother moves. And look what that had gotten him. He and Tracy Harris couldn't keep their hands off one another. So much so he found himself married and anticipating fatherhood at eighteen. He cursed and reached for the pliers. Turning back toward the sink, he spotted a clear glass jar with a white screw-on lid. It held an impressive array of coins and a few bills. *It's on the honor system.* He patted his front pocket for loose change and dropped it in. With a snorted laugh, he hunkered down to get under her sink.

CHAPTER FOUR

ON HER WAY to her bedroom, Addie stopped to grab a towel. Safely alone, she peeled off her wet clothes and draped them over the hamper in the corner. The loose change she'd shoved into her jeans' pocket at the Pic-N-Save fell out and hit the floor with a jingle.

She stooped to retrieve the coins. Those belonged in Teddy's jar. Despite referring to it as Teddy's, she'd instituted the whole thing as much for herself as for him. As if to prove a point, most of the money in it had come from her.

Even though she no longer needed that tough outer shell since she'd left her mother's world behind, some habits were hard to break. The swear jar was christened the day she'd gotten called to the school for Teddy's own inappropriate language.

Setting the coins on the dresser, she used the towel to dry off and put on a more sedate white bra. Not that it mattered now. She'd already given the sexy new neighbor a show. Why had she let Natalie talk her into buying such racy underwear that time they'd taken a girls-only shopping trip a few months ago? It wasn't as if there was anyone but her to see it. At least, no one until today. She hurriedly finished dressing in dry clothes.

Catching her reflection in the mirror above the dresser, she frowned. It was her day off from the library, so she hadn't bothered with any makeup. Maybe that was a good thing since she'd just taken an unexpected shower at the kitchen sink. Still... What was the harm in a little lip gloss?

Plenty. After the show you put on, do you really want to go back in there looking like some femme fatale? What sort of message would that send?

Her? A femme fatale for wearing lip gloss? Shaking her head at her silliness, she hurried back to the kitchen before she gave in to the urge to drag out her neglected stash of makeup. She was supposed to be concentrating on the upcoming hearing in family court, not on the hot former marine next door. Growing up, she'd never been anyone's priority, and she didn't want that for Teddy.

The men in her mother's life always came before her children. Eventually, getting high came even before the men, unless they were keeping her supplied. So her children were ranking a distant third.

She stopped short in the doorway when she saw legs and scuffed tan boots sticking out from under the sink. It took her a moment to realize the water was no longer gushing from the broken faucet. "Ooh, you fixed it."

As a distraction from thinking about what was attached to those long limbs, she dropped her Pic-N-Save change into the jar. There was a jingle as the coins dropped.

He scooted out from under the sink and stood, wiping his hands on the dish towel she'd left on the counter. "I got the water turned off. The fixing part comes next."

"At least you stopped Old Faithful."

He hitched his chin toward the empty bucket she'd overturned onto the spurting faucet handle. It had been redirecting the water into the sink. She'd even placed a can of beans on top of the bottom of the bucket to keep it in place. "Inventive solution."

"Actually, Teddy suggested it. Probably saw it on television." She grinned. "Who says watching cartoons is a waste of time?"

"Not me." He chuckled and folded the towel.

Her stomach flip-flopped at the way his eyes crinkled in the corners when he laughed. Afraid her reaction to him might show in her voice, she cleared her throat before speaking. "Thank you for coming to my rescue."

"It was my pl—" he started and stopped. Swallowing, he continued, "Uh, just keeping up part of the bargain."

Her face grew warm. Like shutting the door in her face, was he deliberately shutting down any friendly overtures? He couldn't think she'd staged the wet T-shirt incident, could he? "Well, I still appreciate it. I guess I'll need to pick up some new faucet handles."

"That won't be necessary."

"You're not going to tell me you walk around with replacement faucet handles."

"Okay, I won't tell you." Laughing, he opened the box on the table.

"But—but…" she sputtered. His deep laugh had sent ripples straight to her tummy, leaving her incapable of coherent speech.

He poked around in the box. "Actually, Natalie gave me a box of supplies she had for her planned upgrades of this place. So, I can exchange them right now, if that works for you."

"It does, and Teddy will be relieved. He had a fit one time when I filled a water bottle from the faucet in the bathroom." Good Lord. What was wrong with her? Why did she just say something so inane? It wasn't as if they shared anything more than an address.

Good grief, what must he think of her?

"You made him drink bathroom water?" He glanced up and stared at her, eyes wide. He shook his head. "How could you?"

"Not you too! It comes out of the faucet just like—" His laughter interrupted her and she shook her head. "I almost fell for that."

"Sorry. I couldn't resist." He pulled some items from the box and went back to the sink.

She fiddled with the neck of her sweatshirt. Maybe she should have been more receptive to those ladies' matchmaking attempts—then she'd have had more practice with flirting. Was that even what they were doing? Flirting? Or was she misreading what had just happened?

She dropped her hand. "Speaking of Teddy, I should go check on him. He must've gone straight back to his video game. Now that Sam has moved, he doesn't have anyone to play outside with."

He turned back toward her. "Then you'll be pleased to know he's in the yard playing fetch with Radar."

Some guardian she made. She was in here flirting, thinking of only herself, and hadn't given a thought to Teddy's whereabouts. "You left him outside—all alone—with that dog?"

"That dog's name is Radar and he's mine." He scowled at her.

Heat flared in her cheeks. She opened her mouth, but he continued before she could form an apology.

"Like I said before. Radar isn't a threat to Teddy… God knows why, but they seem to have developed a sudden and deep connection."

She had trouble getting enough air into her lungs. In her rational mind, she knew he spoke the truth. Just because the dog scared the wits out of *her*, that didn't mean he was a menace. She could probably be confronted with Lassie and be just as afraid. "I can see that but—"

"In case you hadn't noticed, your brother is not a toddler needing constant supervision while playing in the front yard."

He had no idea what could happen when a child was left unsupervised. Unfortunately, she knew all too well. She pointed toward the window over the sink. "And in case *you* hadn't noticed, there's all sorts of things out there that could hurt him."

He glanced out the window, then back to her. "Like what? Grass stains? Sorry. I'm not seeing it. It's a peaceful street."

"You have no idea how unsafe the world can…" Her voice trailed off when he raised an eyebrow. Her shoulders drooped. Well, didn't she look like a shallow fool? How many tours had he served in a war zone? *Good going, Addie.* "Right. Afghanistan."

He ripped open the seal on a small box. "You have every right to be concerned for his safety. I've seen his scars."

"I should have been there." The words were out before she could stop them. Her mind whirring, she studied her feet. What was she doing? Why would she admit such a painful feeling to a virtual stranger?

Because their mother had been clean since Teddy's birth, Addie had accepted a college scholarship and moved away. Unfortunately, without Addie's help, Michelle couldn't cope and fell back into old habits. Addie should never have trusted her enough to leave. But she had, and Michelle had left a pan of boiling hot water in the sink and Teddy had tried to sail his toy boat in it when their mother left the room.

He cleared his throat. "Even when we are, sometimes we can't prevent the bad stuff from happening."

Her head popped up at his quietly spoken words, and her gaze collided with his and held. She saw what was probably reflected in her own eyes. Guilt. Regret. Sadness. No other words were spoken. They weren't needed, but she did wonder what memory had caused those emotions to appear in his eyes.

Although they were almost strangers, she sensed something meaningful had passed between them. As if they were letting the other see a piece of themselves they didn't normally show the rest of the world.

The refrigerator's ice maker dropped cubes into the bin in the freezer, breaking the silence.

"I didn't mean to—"

"I shouldn't have—"

"How about this?" He held out his hand. "Hi, my name is Gabe Bishop, and I'm your new neighbor."

She looked at his hand for a second, then grabbed it and shook. "Nice to meet you, Gabe. I'm Addie Miller, and I live here with—"

"Addie! Hey, Addie." A door banged, followed by sneakers slapping on the floor. Teddy appeared in the kitchen, wide-eyed, disheveled and panting. "Radar just saved my life."

"What? What are you talking about?" She rushed to her brother and hunkered down in front of him, checking him for signs of fresh injury. "Are you okay?"

"I threw the ball and it went into the street and—"

"Oh, Teddy, you didn't." She couldn't shut down the gut-churning thoughts of what might have happened. He was standing in front of her—unharmed—and yet her mind insisted on playing scenarios that would have sent Teddy to the ER.

"Someone want to tell me what's going on?" Gabe asked, glancing between them.

"Radar ran right in front and tripped me," Teddy finished.

Gabe set the new faucet handle next to the sink. "I'm going to venture a guess and say you attempted to run into the street after the ball."

She was her mother's daughter, responsibilities forgotten whenever a man was on the scene. She tugged Teddy closer. "Twelve percent of all traffic deaths in this country involve pedestrians," she stated by rote but gave a squirming Teddy a fierce hug.

"Yuck, Addie," Teddy protested. "I'm too old for PDA."

Addie wasn't sure if she should laugh or cry. "How do you even know what that means?"

"I get around," Teddy said as he took a step back and shrugged. "I know stuff."

Gabe snickered, covering it with a cough. Addie glanced toward the sounds, but instead of seeing him, Radar filled her field of vision. The dog sat patiently next to his owner. Her heart began beating against her chest as if trying to escape her rib cage. Thoughts crashed inside her head. The dog. In her kitchen. In her space.

She inhaled. *That dog* had protected Teddy, she argued with herself. Determined, she swallowed back her fear and forced herself to look Radar in the eyes. "Thank you, Radar, for protecting Teddy."

The dog thumped his tail and looked up at Gabe, who rubbed the fur between the large ears. "Good job."

She turned her attention to Gabe, not easy with the animal in the room. Gabe seemed to be studying her. Had he guessed her secret? Yeah, it wasn't exactly a big mystery. She wasn't sure if it was embarrassment or guilt that made her guard her secret. Embarrassment because she was an adult afraid of a dog. Yes, in certain circumstances she might be justified in being afraid of a dog like Radar, but this wasn't one of those. And guilt because her fear prevented Teddy from getting a fervently wished-for pet of his own.

Her fear stemmed from being bitten as a child. But she was now an adult and should be able to conquer her phobias. An incident from her youth shouldn't be ruling her life as a grown woman. Even the physical scars had begun to fade with time.

Gabe raised an eyebrow in inquiry. Oh yeah, he knew, but he also seemed to be asking her if she was okay. She nodded and managed a bit of bravado with a thin smile. Satisfied, he turned his attention back to attaching the new faucet handle. He wasn't going to out her in front of Teddy.

"Can Radar and I go back out and play? I promise I won't run into the road," Teddy said, reaching out to give Radar a pat on the head. "And besides, it was old Mr. Peterson driving. Even you say turtles could beat him down the street. And you never say anything bad about anyone."

Good thing, or it would be all over Loon Lake in a heartbeat. She made a mental note to not only curb her swearing but not to engage in any gossip. At least around her little brother.

A tingling sensation swept up the back of her neck. How was it that Teddy heard all the stuff he wasn't meant to and yet appeared to be tone deaf to the things she told him directly? Like not to talk to strangers or dart into the street. How was she supposed to keep him safe if her cautions went in one ear and out the other?

"I shouldn't have said that about sweet Mr. Peterson. Don't repeat it to anyone. Please." What sort of things did he spill to the social worker? Or the court-appointed advocate? As if she didn't have enough to worry about. "How can you play without a ball?"

"Oh yeah, I forgot." His shoulders slumped and he patted Radar. "I'm sorry for losing your ball."

"Maybe you should also apologize to Mr. Gabe."

Gabe shook his head. "That's not necessary."

"I didn't mean to lose the ball. Honest." Teddy pushed his lower lip out. "I can go right now and—"

"No, you can't. You stay out of the road. Next time it might be a less sedate driver." She shuddered to think what could have happened. She glanced at Radar and silently thanked him again.

"Don't worry about the ball. There's plenty more where that came from." Gabe gathered up his tools. "I'm going to test turning on the water. Then Radar and I are going home."

"Ooh, can I watch?" Teddy stopped petting Radar to

gaze up at Gabe. "It was really cool before, with water squirting everywhere."

"Yeah, real cool." Addie rolled her eyes, but secretly she had to admit it had all turned out okay in the end.

Yeah, you can say that because you got to see Gabe at work.

Teddy puffed out his chest. "I was the one who came up with using a bucket on the water."

"That's what your sister said. Very clever. Put her there, sport." Gabe fist-bumped with a beaming Teddy. "Do you want to test the faucet?"

Teddy did a little bounce. "Can I? Really? Did you hear that, Addie?"

Seeing the excitement and admiration on her brother's face at such a mundane task gave her a fleeting moment of anxiety. Lots of boys grew up to be well-adjusted, successful men in female-only households. Plus, he had Des Gallagher and Brody Wilson in his life. True, her friends' husbands were busy with their own growing families, but they definitely made excellent role models.

Teddy grunted as he leaned over the sink to turn the water on. "It works. Look. It works."

She nodded. "I see that. We need to thank Mr. Gabe."

"Thanks, Mr. Gabe. Maybe now you could show me how to fix stuff so I can help too."

Gabe was at a loss for words. The earnest pleading in Teddy's expression as he looked up tugged at something Gabe had kept buried deep inside. And it stung. This kid shouldn't be looking up to him, and yet the admiration in his gaze filled a spot he hadn't even known was empty.

He'd been about Teddy's age when his pa had allowed him to help around their home. He could almost taste the pride he'd felt when Pa had put that flat-head screwdriver into his open palm. He could still feel the smooth wood of the handle, the indentations where his father's initials had been carved into the wood.

"Mr. Gabe?"

Gabe blinked as he came back to the present.

"Teddy, why don't you go to your room? You can finish playing your game before supper."

"But…"

Radar leaned against his leg and Gabe winced. Obviously, his silence had spoken volumes, and it probably said something he hadn't meant to relay. Hurting the boy's feelings was the last thing he'd intended. He inhaled deeply, hoping his voice didn't betray his riotous feelings. "Next time I do a job that requires an extra set of hands, you'll be the first person I think of."

"Really?"

Radar snuffled and Gabe laughed. "You're right, Radar. Teddy will make a great helper."

Addie smiled, but it didn't reach her eyes. Did she think he was just placating her brother? More important, was that what he was doing? Saying something to make the kid happy, then not intending to follow through? He made a mental note to find something he could ask Teddy to help with. "Here. We'll shake on it. How's that? Radar, shake hands with Teddy."

Radar offered his paw to Teddy, who was beaming as he took it. "Wow. That's so cool. Radar shook hands with me. Did you see that, Addie?"

"I saw. That was really cool," she said, her tone infused with a sense of wonder.

How many times a day did Teddy say that? He'd barely spent any time with the boy, but he'd bet this was a pattern with him. And yet she was able to react without spoiling his enthusiasm.

He needed to remember he wasn't in a position to get involved with anyone, and especially not a woman who was responsible for a child. But it was that dedication to her brother that drew him to her. He swallowed. He was finding way too many things to admire about Addie Miller.

"Did you teach him to shake hands?"

Teddy's question broke into Gabe's musings, and he shook his head. "Wish I could take credit. A good buddy of mine, Tom, taught him just about everything he knows."

"If your friend taught Radar all that stuff, how come Radar lives with you? Did he teach him for you? Like at school? Why doesn't Radar live with him?"

Because life and death came down to a flip of a coin and a moment in time. I'd give my life to go back and change.

"Tom died, so now I take care of Radar." He hoped that would satisfy the boy.

Radar whined as if he'd understood the reference to Tom.

Oh man, why had he mentioned Tom? He should've taken credit and left it at that. He suspected a simpler approach with Teddy worked best.

Judging by his scars and how his earlier questions alluded to fear, Teddy must've experienced some of life's ugliness. He had no idea what Teddy's mother suffered from, but the kid hadn't had an easy life. And he suspected neither had his sister. Was that why, even in a town like Loon Lake, the woman was so protective?

Teddy bent down to hug Radar. "I'm sorry the man who taught you all that cool stuff died. Our mom didn't die, but she kept getting sick, so I live with Addie now. Just like you live with Mr. Gabe now. It's gonna be okay. You'll see."

Damn, but that kid, whom he barely knew, had the ability to scrape him raw emotionally. If he wasn't careful, these two would be drawing him in, and he sure as hell had no business going there. Even if she didn't have responsibility for her brother, Addie definitely looked like the forever type. And he was obviously missing the gene that made him a good bet for the long haul. Just ask the Marine Corps. When he'd joined, he'd intended on being a lifer but got burned out after a dozen and didn't reenlist. He'd promised his ex-wife a lifetime too and that promise had ended in less than two.

"Mr. Gabe?"

Gabe blinked and refocused his attention. He couldn't help but smile at the expectant expressions not only on the boy but Radar too. "Yes?"

"Can Radar and me play again sometime?"

"I think Radar would like that," Gabe said, and Radar woofed his agreement. "But we have to make sure it's okay with your sister."

Teddy balanced on his toes and gave his sister a pleading look. "Can I, Addie? Can I?"

Radar's attention was fixed on Addie too, as if understanding his stake in the conversation. But that wasn't possible, was it? And what the hell happened to not getting involved? Between the boy and Radar, he was being sucked in.

She sighed. "As long as Gabe doesn't mind."

Ah, so she'd caught how he'd said Radar would like it and left himself out of the equation. What was wrong with him when he was around her? Why did she bring out his inner rudeness?

Feeling everyone's gaze on him, he said, "I don't mind."

Teddy scuffed his toe on the vinyl flooring. "And, uh, maybe I could, like, help you again next time you work on something?"

"Teddy, why don't you go finish your video game? I'm sure we've wasted enough of Mr. Gabe's time."

Yeah, she'd caught his less-than-enthusiastic response to Teddy playing with Radar. Snapping his fingers at the dog, he opened the door to the backyard. "Patrol."

Radar hesitated and Gabe nudged him out the door. "You can play with Teddy tomorrow."

Teddy hadn't said a word, but his shoulders were hunched forward as he started to leave the room.

Gabe heaved a sigh. "Teddy, wait."

The marines had taught him better. So had his pa. He had to remedy the situation, needed to figure out how to live next door to Addie. He was a grown-ass man and a former marine, so why was it so hard to keep his reaction to his new neighbor under control?

CHAPTER FIVE

GABE SCRATCHED HIS chin. Did he want to do this? Not really, but his reluctance to get involved faded away when confronted with the hopeful expression on the boy's face.

"I may have something tomorrow, if Addie says it's fine. Come over when you get home from school. Okay?"

"Really?" The boy's eyes widened, and he turned to his sister. "Can I, Addie? Can I?"

Addie nodded and the boy grinned from ear to ear. "Gee, thanks, Mr. Gabe. What about maybe tonight? I—"

"You have Cub Scouts tonight. Remember?"

The boy's shoulders drooped again. "Oh yeah."

"You like Cub Scouts, and Mr. Gabe already invited you for after school tomorrow," Addie said.

The boy gave him an assessing look. "You won't forget by then? Sometimes grown-ups forget so they don't have to do stuff."

"I won't forget." In his peripheral vision, he saw Addie move closer to Teddy. Gabe put a hand to his chest. "You have my word on it."

That seemed to satisfy the boy and he loped off to his room.

"Sorry about that," she said after Teddy had left. "That was sweet of you, but I'll understand if you don't want him getting in your way. I can make some excuses if—"

"I'll keep my word." Did she think he'd string the kid along? Why not? He hadn't exactly been Mr. Congeniality around her. She opened her mouth and he rushed in before she could say anything. "As long as you don't think I'm taking advantage of him if I let him help me wash my Jeep."

"That sounds perfect," she said with a nod. "He can't get into too much trouble with that."

He huffed out a laugh. "Obviously you've never seen a preadolescent boy wash a car."

"You may have a point." She grinned, carving deep dimples into her cheeks. "But thank you anyway."

Trying not to embarrass himself over those dimples, he shrugged. Where was all this cool resolve he'd promised himself a few minutes ago? Talk about running hot and cold. No wonder she expected him to weasel out of a promise to Teddy. "Hey. I'm the one getting the free labor."

Her blue eyes softened as she continued to smile. Gabe swallowed a groan, starting a mental list why getting involved with Addie was a bad idea. Over a decade had passed, but except for the more stable financial standing, he wasn't in a much better place than when he'd married Tracy. He was approaching thirty now, and yet here he was, back to figuring out what to do with his life, picturing the community-college brochure waiting for him on the kitchen counter. He still wasn't convinced his decision not to reenlist after Tom's death had been the right one. Maybe cutting and running was his MO when things got tough. If so, then he had no business in a relationship. With anyone.

"And, just so you know, I wasn't doubting your word. It's just that Teddy has not always been able to rely on the things people have said to him."

Her words broke into his musings. A sudden urge to know more about her came over him. After all, he wanted them to be friendly neighbors. Yep, that was it. "And what about you?"

"Me?" Her head snapped back. "I have always tried to—"

"No! I said it wrong." *Way to go, Gabe.* "What I meant was, do people break their promises to you?"

He began packing up his tools before he could ask more stupid questions and get in deeper with the lovely neighbor, his lack of control being what it was.

"I'm not seven."

His head snapped up. "No, you're not."

Was that his voice? It sounded more like a rusty rasp, thanks to his memory of exactly how adult she was playing in his head. In vivid detail and bright saturated colors on a continuous loop.

She blushed, making her freckles stand out in contrast. He had never thought he'd be attracted to freckles. Or dimples. Or women who blushed.

"Well, I don't know how to thank you for coming to my rescue." She cleared her throat. "I baked another batch of red velvet cupcakes, if I can tempt you."

She was tempting all right, but he ordered himself not to go there. *Concentrate on the cupcakes.*

"Red velvet? Are those the ones with chocolate and—" he tried not to make a face "—vinegar?"

A flash of humor crossed her features. "Don't say it like that. The acidity of the vinegar or buttermilk is what causes a chemical reaction with the cocoa powder and gives the cake a reddish color. But you have to be sure the pH balance hasn't been neutralized like with Dutch-processed cocoa powder or the reaction won't occur. Anyway, I used buttermilk instead of vinegar because I like the tangy taste paired with the mild chocolate and vanilla and..."

Her voice had trailed off.

"Gotcha." Someone throw him a life preserver! He was drowning in those dimples.

"Sorry. I'm a librarian." Now she looked more embarrassed than amused. "Information is my game."

He wiggled his eyebrows, hoping to put her at ease again. "So, conversations with you will be like auditioning for *Jeopardy!*?"

"Look at you, putting your answer in the form of a question," she said.

"And you're a fountain of information." He was rewarded with another blushing smile. A sense of humor. He liked that. *Are you sure you want to find out even more things about her?* chided an inner voice.

"More like a babbling brook of useless trivia." She laughed.

Gabe's gut wasn't the only part of his anatomy that reacted to her expression and the sound of her clear, sweet laughter.

"So, would you like some?"

A breathless "Oh yeah" slipped out before he could

prevent it. But judging from her puzzled reaction, they were on totally different wavelengths.

Now it was his turn to blush. At least, judging from the warmth rising up his neck to his cheeks, he figured he was. What was he? Seventeen again? Hell, he— Oops.

He hitched his chin at the swear jar. "You said that was honor system?"

"'Fraid so."

He dug into his pocket for some coins, found none and pulled out his wallet. "You were talking cupcakes, right?"

"Of course. What did you think I meant?"

"Cupcakes," he said but opened his wallet and stuck a bill in the jar. "And, yes, please. I want to apologize for not accepting them the first time."

"I thought maybe you didn't like cupcakes. Of course, you could have given them to the dog after I left, except they have chocolate in them, and—"

"—chocolate is toxic to dogs," he finished. "See? You're not the only one capable of trivia."

"But that one isn't so trivial."

"Not to a dog owner. No." He shut his tool chest and secured it with a snick. "I heard the microbrewery on the town square sponsors trivia nights. Maybe we could put all that knowledge to work sometime."

You call that noninvolvement?

Maybe she'd refuse and—

"They do, but it's on Tuesdays."

She moved past him and he caught the scent of grapefruit. "You don't like Tuesdays?"

She pulled a plastic container and cover out of a cupboard. "It's a school night."

Ah, yes. Teddy. She was responsible for her brother. And he was steering clear of that sort of commitment. "Summer's coming."

"You're right—it is. That will give me time to brush up." She arranged cupcakes in the container and put the cover on with a *snap* sound. "I'm weak when it comes to sports knowledge, though."

"That's where I come in," he said and accepted the cupcakes, setting them on top of the cardboard box. "I'll be the strong one when it comes to those categories."

Do you even know what noninvolvement means?

Once in his own kitchen, Gabe set Addie's cupcakes on the counter and took off the cover to grab one. They smelled delicious. Thank goodness she'd renewed her offer.

Radar stood at his feet and watched, unblinking, while he peeled off the paper surrounding the cake part. The dog crowded closer and pressed against Gabe's leg as if to remind him of his presence.

"Sorry, bud, but these are for me. You can't have chocolate in any form whatsoever." He walked across the small kitchen and ran the flat of his hand over the motion-activated cover on the trash can, tossed the paper in and waited for it to close. His life would get more complicated if that dog ever figured out how to get the lid to open. A feat that wouldn't surprise him. Radar was uncannily smart—he'd had to be to survive life on the streets in Kabul—but he was still a dog and not above rooting through the trash.

Just like no matter how much he warned himself

about his appealing neighbor, he hadn't been able to stop his reaction to seeing her lacy bra.

And now he had to go buy supplies to wash his Jeep with her brother. But the kid wasn't so bad, and it was obvious he was thirsty for some male bonding. His father had always made time for him. Even when he'd probably been dead tired from working two low-paying jobs.

Although he hadn't gotten the chance, he liked to think he'd have been as good a father to his own son as his pa had been to him. He sighed and pulled open the refrigerator. It had been easy to block out thoughts of the past while trying to stay alive in some war-torn hellhole.

He tried to imagine what his life would've been like if his son had lived, if he and Tracy had stayed together, if he hadn't joined the marines. Would they have been on a street like this, tossing the ball around in the front yard? Would he have been able to provide for his family?

When the economy had taken a downturn and construction work dried up, they'd moved in with his pa. He'd already been contemplating the military when Tracy lost the baby at almost eight months. That plan had then gotten shelved, at least temporarily.

He shook his head. What was he doing standing here with the refrigerator door open?

Grabbing a longneck, he ambled into the living room with Radar on his heels. He sank onto the couch, put his socked feet on the coffee table and grabbed the remote for the new television he'd splurged on. Maybe some baseball in high-def would help occupy his thoughts, keep him from playing what-if.

* * *

Addie deposited items on the polished wood counter of Loon Lake General Store. She'd run in to grab a couple of things while Teddy was at his Scout meeting.

"I hear Gabe Bishop moved into the other side of your duplex," Tavie Whatley, the seventysomething owner of the store, commented as she rang up the items.

"Yes, he did." Last thing she needed was another person trying to matchmake her with Gabe. And the elderly shopkeeper was anything but subtle. The woman had her hand on the pulse of practically everything in town. She was the person you called when you wanted results. Many referred to the woman as a benevolent dictator. Her heart was in the right place, but her methods could be a bit heavy-handed.

"Is it true he's got a military-type dog with him? I hear tell he dragged that dog with him all the way from Afghanistan."

"Yeah, the dog is from Afghanistan," Addie answered cautiously, wondering where this was heading. She glanced at her watch. Pic-N-Save was farther away from the church where the Scouts were meeting, but it may have been faster after all. The Pic-N-Save cashiers were friendly, but most didn't give her the third degree.

"Since he's your new neighbor and everything, I was thinking we should get him to help get Pets for Vets off the ground."

Addie bit her lip. Pets for Vets was the most ambitious project ever discussed at Coffee & Conversation. Not only would the program be expensive, but it would require more expertise than anyone who attended the meetings had. The purpose would have been to provide pets to veterans wanting companionship and the comfort animals could provide. "I didn't realize we were going ahead with that. I thought we'd decided it might be more than our little group could handle."

"*Harrumph*. Now that Gabe is back and has his own dog, it's the perfect time to revive this." Tavie patted her sprayed helmet of gray hair.

"I get that a program like that would be a great help to some of our local veterans, but I only mentioned it in passing because of that television segment. I thought I was making conversation about a charity that provided comfort animals to veterans. I certainly wasn't championing doing anything like that with our little group." She needed to learn to keep her big mouth shut. She should know by now that nothing was ever just conversation if it was said within earshot of Tavie.

"But it's a perfect idea. Give yourself some credit, Addie." She bagged up the purchases.

"I really can't take credit for this." She held up her hand. Really and truly she couldn't. She wouldn't.

"Sure you can." She reached out, her gnarled fingers covering Addie's. "Tell Gabe to come to the next community meeting and we'll take it from there."

She picked up her bags but paused at the door. "Well, I—"

"Sorry to rush you, sweetie, but I gotta be closing up. Ogle will be wanting his supper." Tavie came from behind the counter and opened the door, making the old-fashioned bell jingle merrily.

Five minutes later, Addie found herself banished and standing in the parking lot as the older woman shut off the lights inside the store. How exactly had she gotten railroaded into asking—excuse me, *telling*—Gabe to come to the community meeting at the library?

She swore as she opened her car door. "And I'm not putting any money in the stupid swear jar. So there," she told the universe as she got behind the wheel and started the engine.

Yeah, who was she kidding? She'd meant what she said about using the honor system.

She made a mental note to check up on that charity. Maybe she could contact them and find out more about it.

Her new neighbor hadn't said Radar was a trained comfort canine, but she couldn't help noticing that the dog appeared to have sensed his master's moods and reacted. She may not have thought about it at the time—too busy being frightened of the dog—but she'd observed the animal leaning against Gabe's leg. Was that some sort of signal?

She pulled into the parking lot of the historic white church just as the kids were coming out of the side door that led to the meeting area in the basement. Teddy came out with one of the leaders and she rolled down the window and waved. Her brother spotted her and ran to the car.

"What's in the bag?" she asked after he'd climbed onto the booster seat. She didn't pull out of the parking spot until she heard the click of the seat belt.

"A stupid block of wood."

Oh dear, sounded like Scouts hadn't gone well. Thinking that he could make friends and build some normal childhood memories, she'd encouraged him to join. This wasn't the first time she'd worried about a decision. Nowadays, she questioned her choices a lot.

"They must've given you a block of wood for a reason." She glanced in the rearview mirror. Teddy stared out the window, arms crossed. And, oh my God, he looked like he might start crying. *Addie, what have you done?*

"They said it's to make a miniature race car for the Pinewood Derby. But it's just a stupid block of wood. I asked if I could make one outta LEGO bricks 'cause I know how to do that, but Joey's dad said no. Then Joey tol' Brandon that I didn't have a mom or dad... just a sister."

She had trouble dragging air into her tight chest. Why did kids have to be so cruel? "Where was Mr. Johnson when Joey said this?"

"He was on the other side of the room, helping Timmy tie a square knot."

Yeah, a kid like Joey knew enough not to say mean stuff in front of adults. "Who's Brandon?"

"A new kid. Now he probably thinks there's something wrong with me," he said and sniffed.

"There's nothing wrong with you. Don't ever think that. There's lots of kids who don't have parents to live with."

"None at my school."

Her throat began to clog and she tightened her grip on the steering wheel. What was she supposed to say? She had a feeling telling him he was special was the wrong thing.

In the end, she simply told him she was sorry. What else could she say? She'd talk with the family counselor again for some advice. The fact she had lots of people in her life she could turn to didn't alleviate the sadness of not having parents to turn to for advice.

She pulled onto their street and slowed as they got near their home. "Maybe I could help you make a pine-wood racer."

"Do you know how?" His question sounded like an accusation.

"Not yet. We'll look it up. I'm sure we can find a video to show us how—"

"Look, Addie, look. Mr. Gabe and Radar are outside in the yard. Do you see them?"

"Yes, sweetie, I see them."

She pulled into the driveway on her side of the building with a sigh of relief. At least Teddy was temporarily distracted from his problems. For the moment, anyway.

He undid his seat belt. "Hurry, Addie, hurry. Before they go back inside."

She gathered up her bags and exited to let him out. Teddy was off like a shot as soon as she opened his door.

Radar looked to Gabe, who nodded. Evidently that was all the signal he needed, because Radar ran to Teddy, and they greeted one another with barks and giggles.

"You found it," Teddy shouted, holding up a tennis ball.

Gabe motioned to the dog. "He did."

"Did he look both ways before crossing the street?" Teddy asked as he picked up the ball.

Gabe nodded. "We did."

"You remember that yourself next time," she cautioned and shook her head. "Sometimes I think it goes in one ear and out the other."

"I'm sure my pa thought that about me at his age."

Gabe chuckled. Sobering, he shook his head. "And a decade later, for sure."

Was he referring to his early marriage and divorce? She wanted to ask, but there wasn't any way she could dress up pure curiosity as concern.

He pointed to her bags. "Do you need some help with those?"

"No, there's nothing that can't keep." She set them on the stoop.

"Look, Addie, look. We're playing ball," Teddy called and threw the ball for the dog.

"I see that." She lowered herself to the top step and heaved out a sigh. "One of these days, I'm going to change my name and not tell anyone what the new one is."

Gabe threw his head back and let out a brawny burst of laughter before sitting next to her. "You're very good with him."

She pulled her knees up and rested her arms across them. "You wouldn't be saying that if you'd been with us on the drive over here."

"Want to talk about it?"

"Some of the kids were making fun because he lives with his sister."

"Do you have permanent custody of him or something?"

Normally she wouldn't be discussing this with a virtual stranger, but there was something about sitting on the steps in the fading light of an unseasonably warm spring night. "You heard him tell Radar that his—I should say *our*—mom was sick. She's been in rehab. Not for the first time. Which is why I've filed for permanent custody. We're waiting for the hearing in family court."

He blew his breath noisily between his lips. "That's a lot to take on at your age."

"I'm older than I look." She fisted her hand. Maybe telling him wasn't such a good idea.

He reached over and took her curled hand in his. "I didn't mean it as an insult. You're what? Twenty-one? Most people your age are trying to figure out what they want to be when they grow up."

"I'm almost twenty-three," she said but found it hard to concentrate with her hand in his warm, calloused one. She fought the urge to lean against him.

"You're using the prefix *almost* and adding time to your age."

"Maybe I ought to start counting my age in dog years. I'd be what? One hundred and fifty-four." She rubbed her temple. "No. Wait. That would make me three and a half."

He barked out a sharp laugh. "Whoa. That's way too young."

"Yeah, well, I guess everyone seems young when you're ancient," she shot back without any real rancor. "Exactly how old are *you*?"

"Almost thirty-one," he said with a cheeky grin.

"See? Ancient," she said, but she wasn't sure he'd even heard her. His attention seemed to be on her lips.

He leaned closer, and instead of pulling back, she moved toward him, her hand still in his. Saliva flooded her mouth at the thought that he might kiss her. Would he? How would those full lips feel on hers? Would the stubble on his face be soft or—?

"Addie? Hey, Addie."

She jumped back at the sound of Teddy's voice. Folding her hands, she rested them on her lap where they couldn't get her into any trouble. She swallowed, twice. "What is it, Teddy?"

"Can I ask Mr. Gabe if he knows how to make pine-wood racers?"

"Do you want him to ask?" she said out of the side of her mouth.

"What are they?" he whispered back.

"I haven't had a chance to look up to see how it's done, but it's a small block of wood that gets turned into a race car."

"Wood? I can probably work with that."

She turned toward Teddy. "You may ask."

Addie yawned after tucking Teddy in bed and switching off his light.

After the Scout meeting, Teddy had been sullen, but Gabe had quickly changed that when he'd used his phone to look up pinewood racers. He showed Teddy pictures of finished miniature cars and they discussed which ones appealed to him.

What a difference that thirty minutes in Gabe's company had made. By the time they'd come into the house, Teddy had been excited for the derby.

Time had nothing to do with the difference in Teddy's attitude.

"Give credit where credit is due. It was Gabe and Radar," she reminded herself as she pulled Teddy's door shut.

She hoped she wasn't making a mistake getting involved. And not just for Teddy's sake. He wasn't the only one whose heart could be broken.

CHAPTER SIX

THE NEXT MORNING, after a brief stop at the local vet, Addie drove out to Brody Wilson's farm. Her passenger, safely secured in a cat carrier, was vocalizing her displeasure at her predicament.

"I don't like this any better than you," she told the feral cat and sneezed twice.

So much for the meds she'd taken before this outing. At least her cat allergy was merely annoying, not life-threatening. Despite what might be an allergy to cats, she hadn't minded capturing the scrawny creature when it started hanging around the dumpster in the library parking lot. They'd set out the trap so they could have the cat checked by the local vet. That had been nearly two months ago. The feral feline had been reasonably healthy for a stray. But also very pregnant.

Since the weather had still been cold, Dr. Greer had agreed to board the cat until she gave birth and nursed her kittens. The vet and her staff had made sure the babies were socialized with people so they could be adopted. Unfortunately, the mama cat, which Addie had named Agatha, was too feral to be adopted out.

After reading an online article, Addie felt as though she'd found a solution. The item had talked about such cats being rehomed on farms. When she brought it up at a library meeting, Trudy Canterbury had suggested taking the cat to Brody Wilson. Everyone agreed, saying Brody's farm was virtually an animal sanctuary.

Several people had relayed to her a story about the time Bill Pratt, a local farmer, had brought a calf to Brody in hopes that he'd take her. The mama cow had rejected her offspring, and so it would need to be bottle-fed in order for it to survive. It seemed Bill's young granddaughter was very concerned about the animal's future. Bill had assured the youngster he'd find the calf a good home. Someone had suggested Brody because he'd taken in a pair of abandoned alpacas and nursed them back to health. Bill Pratt told everyone that Brody had assumed responsibility for the young cow in order to impress Mary. Evidently it had worked, because Brody and Mary were now husband and wife. Brody had adopted Mary's young son, Elliott, and was raising the boy as his own.

Addie glanced at the cat carrier and frowned. Tavie had assured her that she'd cleared it with Brody. Maybe she should've called him too, but she'd been running late and didn't want to keep the vet waiting.

"How did I get into this, anyway? Me and my big mouth," she said as her ancient Toyota rumbled over the cattle guard at the end of Brody's driveway.

Everyone had stepped forward with helpful advice and monetary donations, but when it came to taking the cat to Brody, they were all suddenly too busy. They said they thought she was just the right person to take the cat out there, since she'd made the suggestion in the first place. So here she was, with a scrappy cat and a batch of cupcakes to sweeten the deal.

"A spoonful of sugar, right?" she said to Agatha.

Her answer was an angry yowl from the cat carrier.

"Now, don't be like that. Brody has a heated barn, and if the town scuttlebutt is correct, he also has a soft spot for strays. He and Mary both. As a matter of fact, I think all his animals were homeless at one time."

She parked next to the two-story white farmhouse, its shiny red metal roof gleaming in the morning sunshine. A covered porch with wind chimes hung from the rafters ran across the front of the home and wrapped around one side. A cedar play set with a swing sat in the side yard, evidence that this was a family home as well as a business.

Brody and Mary Wilson ran summer camps for children being raised in the foster care system. Although Addie's own time in the system had been short, she, like Teddy, had been forever changed by the experience. So she admired Mary's vision and Brody's hard work transforming his farm and setting up a nonprofit to make Mary's dreams come true. She also admired Brody's relationship with his adopted son. It was plain to see he doted on the little boy, and Elliott worshipped his dad.

"You wait here," she told the cat as she opened the driver's door. The cat hissed in response. "Yeah, I know, silly me. Where else are you going to go?"

Good grief, she was beginning to sound like Gabe with Radar, the way she was chattering away to the cat.

She started up the sidewalk toward the house and glanced over to the barn and the gray Jeep parked there. Was that Gabe's? What was he doing here? Not that it was any of her business where her neighbor spent his time.

As a former Army Delta Force sergeant who'd served in Afghanistan, Brody probably had a lot in common with Gabe. It wouldn't be surprising for them to form a friendship.

"And it's none of your business," she reminded herself. Gabe was her neighbor. The fact he'd been helping, first with her leaking faucet and then with Teddy's race car, didn't give her the right to keep tabs on him.

The wooden screen door opened with a creak and drew her attention away from the Jeep and back to the house. A tall, broad-shouldered man wearing a chambray work shirt and faded denim stepped onto the wide porch. Before the door shut, a young boy with a mop of dark curls and wearing footed dinosaur pajamas scurried out and went to stand next to Brody.

"I'm *El-ee-ot*," the boy said, turning to her and holding up three fingers. "I'm this many olds now."

"Hello, Elliott. Wow, three years old. You know what that means?" She smiled at the winsome little boy, who shook his head. "It means you're old enough to come to story hour at the library. We read stories and do crafts. Doesn't that sound like fun?"

"Mama says no." The boy tilted his chin down and frowned. "Mama says I gotta use the potty first."

Brody ran his hand over the riot of curls in a tender gesture. "But we're working on that, aren't we, big guy?"

"Alice don't got to," Elliott said in a put-upon voice and scowled up at his dad. "How come I gots to?"

Brody sighed as if that was an old argument. "Your sister is just a baby. She doesn't know better and you're a big boy now."

Crossing his arms over his chest, Elliott pouted. "No fair."

Addie rubbed a hand across her mouth to wipe the smile off her face. She loved seeing the two of them together. It told her that there were men in the world who made wonderful dads to children who were not theirs biologically. Could she hope for something like that for Teddy? *And myself*, she thought as her mind went straight to Gabe.

Don't go there, she warned herself. Weaving possibilities around her sexy neighbor could lead to disappointment, and she was responsible for protecting Teddy's tender heart.

She smiled at Elliott. "Well, the crafts and stories will be there whenever you're ready. There's no rush."

She recalled her mother's impatience when Teddy had been potty training. Addie had taken over. That should have been a warning sign of their mother's instability, but she'd ignored it.

Brody patted his son on the shoulder. "It's okay, bud. Go in and get dressed."

"Okay, Daddy." Elliott gave her a heart-melting smile and a wave. "Bye-bye, liberry lady."

"Bye, Elliott."

Brody watched him go back inside. Shaking his head, he turned back to her. "It will happen eventually, right?"

"The average age for boys to master toilet training is thirty-one months." Brody raised an eyebrow and she continued, "Sorry. It's the librarian in me. All this trivia roiling around in my head. Sometimes it overflows and comes out through my mouth. Yuck, that sounded gross, didn't it?"

"Considering what we were talking about…" Brody took a toothpick out of the pocket on the front of his shirt. He unwrapped it and put it in his mouth. "So, what brings you all the way out here this morning?"

Hadn't Tavie called or was Brody giving her a hard time for the pure enjoyment of it? If so, she could play along. "I'm here to talk about a fantastic employment opportunity."

"What? How did you even hear about it?" He scratched his head. "Anyway, I'm sorry to say you're a couple hours too late. It's been filled."

"What?" Had someone else from the group sneaked out here before her to rehome a feral cat as a barn cat?

He shifted the toothpick from one side of his mouth to the other. "Forgive me for saying this, Addie, but he was more what I was looking for."

Her throat tightened as she glanced over her shoulder at her car. What was she going to do now? The cat was totally feral. No one would adopt her. "Are you sure you couldn't use another one?"

"Another one? I'd love to help you out but…" Brody frowned. "What happened to your job at the library? I would have thought that—"

"Oh no! I think there's been some sort of miscommunication." She exhaled and chuckled. "The job isn't for me. It's for Agatha."

"Agatha?"

"She's been hanging around the library and—"

He held up his hands, palms out. "Hold on. What exactly are we talking about here?"

"The feral mama cat we rescued. I thought Tavie was going to call and explain it to you." Addie huffed out an annoyed breath. "She said she was going to reach out."

"Yeah, it's never good when Tavie calls me." He shrugged sheepishly. "I may not have returned her message yet."

"Great." Her shoulders slumped. "If you didn't talk to her, then that means I've shown up here—out of the blue—trying to dump a stray cat on you."

He moved the toothpick around his mouth. "Pretty much, yeah."

"I'm sorry." What was she going to do? After telling Teddy all this time that they couldn't afford a dog, it wasn't as if she could take the cat back home with her.

"Addie?" He held up his hand. "Just explain what's going on."

"I promise this isn't so bad. We all chipped in and had Agatha spayed after her kittens were weaned," she said, wanting to make sure he didn't think he was going to be responsible for placing kittens.

Brody pulled another toothpick from his pocket, touched the one in his mouth, grimaced and put the wrapped one back into his pocket. "Exactly how many kittens am I expected to house?"

"Oh no, I'm not asking you to take kittens. They've all been weaned and placed in good homes, so that just leaves the mama. Agatha's recovered from her spaying, but she's totally feral, so placing her with a normal family is out of the question."

He gave her an affronted look. "Are you calling my family—?"

"Absolutely not." Good Lord, talk about messing this up in every way possible.

Note to self: never let anyone volunteer you for any-thing again.

Maybe she should have asked for Gabe's opinion. After all, he'd gone to Afghanistan and had returned with a dog. She didn't know the specifics, but even with her fear, she could see that Radar was devoted to Gabe and he to the canine.

What was she thinking? Yes, he'd helped out with Teddy last night, but she couldn't start running to Gabe every time she had a problem, expecting him to help solve it.

Brody quirked an eyebrow. "So, what are you ask-ing me to do?"

She needed to quit mooning over Gabe and get this back on track. "Well, considering you have a nice barn and outbuildings, we were hoping you could use a good mouser. We thought she'd make a great farm cat. She could live in the barn and be out of the elements in winter and be fed regular meals. We also chipped in and bought cat food so—"

"Okay. Okay. You've sold me. We were meant for one another. Any more convincing, and I'll need wad-ers." He rolled the toothpick in his mouth and narrowed his eyes. "What I want to know is, who is this *we* you keep talking about?"

"Mostly the attendees of the Coffee & Conversation meetings at the library and a few generous patrons who heard about what we were doing." A donation box at a few key locations in town hadn't hurt either.

"I see." He lowered his eyebrows at her. "Miss a few meetings, and suddenly there's a Brody'll-do-it list, is that how it works? I'm not the only one in Loon Lake with a barn. What about Bill Pratt of Hilltop Farm? Why couldn't he—?"

"He already has several barn cats," she said and swallowed her laugh. Bill had been gleeful while relaying the story of the calf to her.

"Is that what he told you?" He pointed the toothpick at her. "Let me guess. He was at the meeting."

She nodded and he shoved the toothpick back into his mouth.

"He was, and you weren't there to object when your name came up." Relief unfurled the knot in her stomach. Brody might grumble and complain, but it went against his nature not to help. Just like Gabe jumping in to help Teddy turn his block of wood into a race car.

He tsk-tsked. "I guess I assumed you'd have my back, Addie."

"What can I say? I'm only one person."

"No wonder your meetings are so popular," he said but moved off the steps. "People go to protect themselves."

"That, and Natalie's baked goods." Her red velvet cupcakes were good, but the disappointment in the room was palpable anytime attendees discovered Natalie—and, more important, her treats—wasn't going to be at the meeting. The red velvet cupcakes—the ones she'd risked missing Teddy at the bus stop for—couldn't hold up against anything her friend chose to bake.

"Yeah, as soon as poor Des tasted those, he was well and truly captured. Poor guy was— What?" he asked, all innocence when she shot him a glare.

"He wasn't captured. That's a terrible thing to say," she told him but ruined her scolding by laughing. "They fell in love. Just like you and Mary."

"Not the same at all." He shook his head. "I can't imagine what Natalie sees in a grump like Des. As for me, Mary and Elliott couldn't resist my charming personality."

He held up a finger when she opened her mouth to respond. "Ah, now, Addie, don't forget I'm the one you're asking to do a favor."

"Got it. Charming personality." She smothered another laugh.

They might be teasing and joking around, but the forever families both Des and Brody had created gave her hope that someday she might find that. Once again, Gabe came into her mind's eye and she shoved him away. She and Teddy were a package deal.

"Speaking of Des, why didn't you take the cat to him? He has a barn."

"True, but as you said yourself, he's such a grump. Whereas *you*, with your charming personality…"

"I'm going to have a moat and a drawbridge installed at the end of that driveway," he muttered but followed her to her car.

She used her key fob to unlock the trunk.

His mouth dropped open. "You brought the cat in your trunk?"

She rolled her eyes at him. "The cat is in a carrier on the front seat. The food is in the trunk. You can carry the food and I'll get Agatha."

With a grunt, he removed the humongous bag of dry kibble and the carton of canned food from the trunk. "Remind me again—what's wrong with this cat? Other than its name."

She opened the passenger door and grabbed the carrier. "There's nothing wrong with her or her name.

She was never socialized, so she's skittish around people."

"Only because she hasn't met my Mary yet. She'll have that cat eating out of her hand in no time."

"And here I thought you were the charming one in the family." She raised an eyebrow at him.

"Thin ice, Addie, thin ice." He shifted his bundle and thrust his chin at her, but ruined the gesture with a huffed-out laugh. "If this cat's not into people, how do you know she'll stay long enough to eat all this food?"

"Well, if your charismatic personality doesn't win her over, I'm sure a dry barn on rainy days or long winter nights and a consistent food source might. That should go a long way to convincing her to make this her new home." Maybe she should try again to convince Teddy to settle for a cat. She sneezed. She'd put up with what appeared to be an allergy if it would make Teddy happy. Except the last time she'd mentioned it, he'd said he'd be happy with a cat if he also had a dog.

"Tell me she's not going to be a threat to Serenity."

"What?" She set the carrier down while she sneezed several more times.

"Mary's crow, Serenity."

"And you're giving *me* grief over a name?"

Brody grunted. "Mary named it."

Chuckling, she picked up the carrier and resumed following Brody toward the barn. "That's right—I forgot she rescued one and earned its undying gratitude. Crows have the intelligence of a seven-year-old, so they're probably smarter than the cat. I don't see it as a problem." *Let's hope.* "Hear that, Agatha. No messing with the crow."

At the barn, Brody set the bag and box on the ground

to roll open one of the giant double doors, releasing the scent of hay, horses and sawdust. Addie blinked to adjust her eyesight from the bright sunshine to the dim interior. Hooks holding things like bridles, halters, shovels, a pitchfork and numerous tools lined much of the rough wood walls. Although she hadn't had a lot of experience in barns, she figured this one was scrupulously clean.

Brody picked up the cat food and hefted his burden higher. He pointed toward a partitioned room with an open door in one corner of the vast barn. "Let's get everything set up in the office. I'll get a metal trash can to keep the food safe from critters."

"I hadn't thought of that," she confessed.

"Well, if Agatha—we may have to revisit that name—does her job, then there shouldn't be any critters to get into the feed."

"I guess you have a point." At least he was being good-natured about her essentially showing up and dumping a cat on him. She didn't know the full story of Gabe and Radar, but it couldn't have been easy getting the dog to this country. Another admirable quality. As if she didn't already have enough to admire about him.

"And there's nothing wrong with Agatha's name," she felt compelled to add.

"Uh-huh. I have a wooden box we can put an old blanket in to make a bed," he said as he led her into the office and placed the bag just inside.

He closed the door with his foot and set the canned food on a large metal desk cluttered with paperwork. "I figured we could put out some food and leave her in here for a bit so she knows this is where it is."

"Good idea. I'd hate for her to bolt before she gets to know the place." Addie set the cat carrier on the floor.

Brody opened a desk drawer and pulled out a ceramic ashtray. "Don't worry. It's clean. Been clean for a few years now."

He dumped the contents of one of the cans into the makeshift dish and set it down. "I'll open the cage and let her come out when she's ready."

"She'll probably wait for us to leave." She unzipped the opening to the carrier and stepped back, but the cat, for all her vocal complaints, huddled in the corner.

Yeah, she could relate. After her experiences, she found trusting people difficult—especially when it came to Teddy. She saw her friends together, Brody with Mary and Natalie with Des, and yearned for a close, loving relationship of her own. Of course, that would mean learning to trust again. If she couldn't open up, she might end up in a solitary life like Agatha.

"So, you can call me with any questions or if you have any problems. She's been to the vet recently, so she's up to date on that. If you have any issues with, um, with—"

"We can afford to take care of it." His brow pulled into an affronted frown. "If that's what you were trying to say."

You and your big mouth. First, she insulted Gabe and let him know the local gossip had been about him, something she deeply regretted. She hadn't meant to hurt or insult anyone. "Sorry. I only meant—"

He held up a hand. "It's okay. Getting the camps up and running wasn't easy, but even with the expansion, we're on solid footing with them now. Mary makes sure to keep us afloat. She leaves no stone unturned when it comes to finding grant opportunities."

"That's right. You do some weeks for kids with cancer."

"Yeah. Liam and Ellie McBride help out a lot with that." They left the office and he started to shut the door behind them but paused and looked to her for confirmation.

She nodded. "Keep it closed for a short while."

"Gotcha. She needs to get her bearings." He eyed the surrounding area. "I could put in a cat door. That might help."

Addie smiled. No wonder everyone had suggested bringing the cat here. Did Gabe have a soft underbelly like Brody? Was that how he'd ended up rescuing Radar and doing what was necessary to bring him to this country? He'd certainly been offended on the dog's behalf when she'd suggested that Teddy could have been bitten.

"You can wipe that Cheshire-cat grin off your face right now, Addie Miller. This is not an animal sanctuary and I am not a pushover."

Still grinning, she made an X over her heart. "The thought never crossed my mind."

He scowled, but his eyes held more amusement than annoyance. "So, when is the next meeting?"

"Meeting? I— Oh, you mean at the library. Next Tuesday at noon."

"I guess I'd better make a note of that."

She shrugged. "You could always send Mary."

"Ha! She'd have me signed up for everything."

"And you wouldn't be able to say no to her."

He heaved an exasperated sigh, but his face turned all soft. "I haven't figured out a way yet."

As they stepped from the barn, a dog bounded around the corner in a blur. Heart pounding and adrenaline coursing through her veins, Addie darted behind Brody so he was between her and the animal. She went rigid with fear.

"Halt," came a sharp order from somewhere on the other side of the building, and the dog immediately obeyed and went down on all fours.

Breathe, damn it, breathe.

Brody frowned and glanced over his shoulder at her. "Relax. That's just Radar. He won't hurt you."

It took a moment for the information to implant itself in her brain. Yes, it was Radar.

She relaxed slightly when she recognized both dog and owner's voice. She might not have conquered her fear of dogs, but instinct told her Radar wouldn't hurt her.

"Gabe is here?" Which was a stupid question because not only had she recognized his Jeep earlier, but she'd just heard his voice.

Her breathing still shallow and her legs wobbly, she fought to regain control over her apprehension.

Despite their short acquaintance, she found the thought that Gabe was nearby comforting.

CHAPTER SEVEN

GABE SWORE AS he slammed the cover on the clipboard he'd been using to make notes in the expanded bunkhouse. Radar surely couldn't get into any trouble on Brody's farm, but Gabe figured he'd better check to see what had attracted the dog's attention.

Radar had been entertaining himself chewing on a Kong chew bone while Gabe worked. The dog's ears had perked up, and he'd dropped the toy, dashing off.

He'd yelled for the dog to stop but couldn't be sure Radar would obey the command. If he wasn't going to behave, bringing him along in the future would be out of the question. This morning all he'd been doing was working up an estimate. Brody had wanted to hire him for some finish work on the bunkhouse expansion. He wasn't sure if working construction was what he wanted long-term, but for now, it would get him out of the house. Maybe even prevent all those extreme thoughts of his tempting neighbor.

As he came around the side of the barn, he understood Radar's enthusiasm. At least the dog had obeyed his command and was lying with his belly on the ground. But his tail was brushing the dirt, kicking up little dust plumes.

"Sit," he said, and the dog sat up, but he didn't release him. Addie's fear was plain, despite what he assumed were attempts to conceal it.

He vowed then and there to help her overcome her fear. If she let him. Some instinct told him she didn't trust easily, but he'd give it his best shot.

Because it was the right thing to do and not because he couldn't stop thinking about those dimples when she graced him with a genuine smile. Or how much he wanted to kiss those freckles.

Yeah, he was a real humanitarian.

"He must've heard your voice and took off. Probably hoping Teddy was with you."

She shook her head. "He's in school. I was just dropping off a homeless cat."

"Dropping off a homeless cat?"

"It had been hanging around the library, and I was worried about it. Unfortunately, it's feral, so it needed a special placement. Brody has agreed to let it stay in his barn. It will make a good mouser. I couldn't stand the thought of it languishing in a shelter or—" she shivered "—having to be put down. At least this way I'll know it's safe, warm and fed."

"So, you *do* like animals…just not dogs." He'd suspected that fear was the motivation for her reactions to Radar.

Her head snapped up. "I never said I didn't like dogs."

"So, it's not dogs in general…just mine," Gabe said, and Radar whined as if in agreement.

"Now you're making assumptions. Both of you," she said, straightening her shoulders.

He scowled. The fact she was including Radar when

she spoke made his stupid heart pump a bit faster. Just like when she'd thanked him for preventing Teddy from running into the street.

"Sorry, guys. As fascinating as this is—" Brody cupped a hand around his ear "—I hear my Mary calling me."

"Sorry. I—"

"I didn't mean to—"

They looked at Brody as if he'd appeared out of thin air.

Removing the toothpick from his mouth, Brody guffawed and shook his head. "Just what I thought. Love to stay and referee—I mean, *chat*—with you two kids, but duty calls."

Gabe narrowed his eyes and glowered, not appreciating Brody's smug expression. As if he saw something Gabe couldn't. Or didn't want to. Working construction and getting involved with a woman he had no business getting involved with. Talk about déjà vu.

All the guys had been enamored with Tracy back in high school, and he, the boy from the wrong side of the tracks, had won her attention. Dating Tracy had fed his ego.

And we know where allowing the little brain to think for the big brain ends up.

He tensed when Addie gave Brody a hug. Radar whined and gave him an accusing look, as if telling Gabe it was his fault she was hugging someone other than him. He included the dog in his sour thoughts.

Yeah, because he'd been thinking the same thing. He wanted her hugging him, not another man. Was that his ego talking again?

"Thanks so much for taking the cat," she said and pulled away from Brody.

"Yeah, yeah. I'm a regular saint," Brody replied and turned to Gabe. "I'm sure you can testify to that."

Gabe cupped his ear. "Is that Mary I hear?"

Brody made a face. "Point taken. Got what you needed?"

Gabe nodded. "I'll get some figures written up and give you a call."

Brody nodded and turned his attention to Addie. "And don't worry. I'll check on your cat in a bit."

She raised her brow. "*My* cat?"

Brody harrumphed. "Agatha, you say? Sounds like a maiden aunt."

"Or the greatest mystery writer that ever lived," Gabe said.

Her eyes widened and he did his best not to preen when she rewarded him with a dimpled smile. Score one for those hours spent in his bunk reading mysteries to escape from his reality. Both during his time in school and again in Afghanistan.

"And that's my cue to leave. Play nice, you two." Chuckling, Brody headed toward the house with a backward wave. The side door to the farmhouse opened and closed, but Gabe only had eyes for the woman in front of him.

She motioned with her hand in the direction of her car. "Well… I guess I'd better get going too."

He fought the urge to reach out and physically stop her from leaving. "I don't want to keep you if you're on your way to work."

"I'm not. I had some personal time coming, so I took

today off. I wasn't sure how long this would take me."
She took a step toward her car.

Radar looked up at him and whined.

Say something. He cleared his throat. "I haven't been
to Aunt Polly's since returning home. Are the pancakes
still as good?"

She gave him a quizzical glance. Which he totally got because he wasn't sure where this was going.
Served him right for giving voice to the outlandish
thoughts in his head when she was near. He glared at
the poor dog as if this was all his fault.

"I don't know what they were like before you left,
so I may not be the best judge," she said. "But Teddy
and I love them. My favorite are the buckwheat ones
with warm maple syrup."

His gaze zeroed in when she licked her lips, and he
swallowed a groan. "I was always partial to ginger-
bread with whipped cream."

"Teddy always wants whipped cream on his. He
doesn't like maple syrup."

Gabe clutched his chest. "What? That's practically
sacrilegious in these parts."

"Tell me about it. We've been accused of being flat-
landers because of it," she said, using Vermonters' term
for non-natives.

He laughed along with her. He quite liked that laugh,
especially if he was the one making her do it.

He'd been six years old when his mom died, but he
recalled Pa saying over the years how much he missed
her laugh. "Your ma would've laughed at that," Pa
would say with a sad smile. He hadn't really appreciated his father's sentiment...until now. It wasn't simply

the sound of Addie's chuckle but the way her blue eyes sparkled and the way her cheeks dimpled.

This wasn't simple ego. He had a deep longing to connect with Addie the way he imagined his father had with his mother. If his mom had lived, would he find it easier to connect with a woman now?

Radar pressed his cold wet nose against Gabe's hand, jerking him out of his head. She had taken a few steps toward her car.

"Um…" he began.

She stopped and glanced back with an air of expectation. Yeah, what was he doing?

He cleared his throat. "Would you like to go for pancakes? Well, I mean, you don't have to have pancakes. I just thought you, uh, might like to go to Aunt Polly's."

Radar looked up at him. *Okay, dog, you're right.* That was a bit pitiful, but it had been a while since he'd asked a pretty girl on a date. Date? No, this wasn't a date…exactly. More like two neighbors going for coffee. It wasn't even noon, for crying out loud.

She studied him for a few seconds. He wasn't holding his breath. Nope. Not at all.

"Okay. I'd like that." She gave a decisive nod. Glancing at her car, she said, "I'll meet you there?"

His breath whooshed out. "Sounds good."

See, it's not a date. It wasn't even noon and they were going in separate cars. The fact it wouldn't make sense to leave either vehicle here at Brody's farm was beside the point.

"Retrieve your bone," he said to Radar and pointed in the direction they'd come.

Radar tore off that way, his tail wagging wildly. Gabe had barely gotten the passenger door open when

the dog came loping back, jumped in and dropped his
bone on the passenger seat. He settled himself next
to the black rubber chew. Inching forward, he fogged
the windshield with his whining and panting as Addie
drove her Toyota down the driveway.

Gabe slipped into the driver's side and started the
car. Radar divided his attention between watching Addie's Corolla and giving Gabe what were clearly accusing looks.

"Cut me some slack, will ya? I know it wasn't my
smoothest delivery, but she agreed to meet me at Aunt
Polly's. So it's all good."

He couldn't be sure, but the dog seemed to understand, because he finally settled back to enjoy the ride.
Gabe also enjoyed it. He found the countryside with
its rolling hills and grazing cattle soothing after having been in dusty brown, war-torn areas for so long.
Once in town, he admired the tidy, brick-fronted businesses and their bright awnings. Several buildings,
including the church, dated back to the Revolutionary
War, he knew.

Did the town still go all out decorating for Christmas and Independence Day? Main Street in Christ-
mases past had always been awash with lights and
wreaths with giant bows. His memories of Christmas
were surprisingly pleasant. His pa had done his best to
see that Gabe had received at least one frivolous gift,
or, as he'd called it, a not-socks gift. Flags and bunting
replaced the wreaths on the Fourth of July. His father
had taken him to see the town's fireworks display. He
recalled holding tight to Pa's hand, trying not to flinch
at the loud explosions and failing. If his son had sur-

vived, would they have done the same? He liked to think he'd have held his son's hand in reassurance too.

He slowed as soon as he spotted Addie waiting at the entrance to the popular café.

"I told you she'd be here," he said to the dog as he pulled into a diagonal parking spot in front of the town's popular eatery.

"Sorry to disappoint you, but you'll have to wait outside."

The dog made his life-isn't-fair whine and hung his head.

Gabe jumped out of his Jeep and fed the parking meter before he looped the leash handle over the meter. Reaching back into the vehicle, he pulled out the new gadget he'd bought online. It was a portable water bottle with attached dish. He set it down in front of Radar and promised to sit by the window to keep an eye on him just in case. Although, he wasn't overly worried because this was Loon Lake and not many people would want to mess with a dog of Radar's size. Yeah, he did a good imitation of a guard dog, but the pup was a big softy.

Radar had no choice in his appearance, but Gabe had, by choice, taken on a disguise. First as a trouble-making teen and later as a badass marine.

Yeah, they were two of a kind.

Addie couldn't help the little shiver of anticipation as Gabe tended to Radar. When was the last time she'd had a real honest-to-goodness date?

Slow down, girl. This isn't exactly a date.

It might not be, but she'd worn a silly smile on her face the entire drive to town from Brody's place. When

Gabe had first mentioned Aunt Polly's, her pulse had increased and her head had filled with will-he-or-won't-he? thoughts. You'd think she was some teenager wondering if the cute boy in class would ask her to the prom.

Her appreciation of his qualities had increased when he'd picked up on her naming of the cat, and he hadn't laughed. Or at least not so anyone would notice.

And when he had asked if she wanted to go for pancakes, she'd had to take a moment to compose herself. She hadn't wanted to embarrass herself by appearing too eager.

Whatever you do, don't refer to this as a date, she cautioned herself as he approached. "Radar looks so disappointed at not being able to join us for—" *not a date, Addie!* "—uh, for pancakes."

Gabe glanced back at the Jeep. "I guess he'll be okay. I promised to bring him a treat if he behaved."

"We can sit by the window," she said, and her insides melted at the way Gabe's hazel eyes softened when he looked at the dog.

This man really had a good heart. And if she wasn't careful, he'd be stealing hers. And maybe the dog too, because he no longer seemed as scary as he had that first day. "Did that satisfy him?" He shrugged and she continued, "Even if he's only of average intelligence, he's capable of learning approximately one hundred and sixty-five words." She groaned inwardly. Why was she quoting trivia again? This might not be a date, but it already had developed all the awkwardness of one.

"What if he's above average? I've never owned a dog before, but I'm pretty sure this one is exception-

ally smart," he said and winced. "Of course, I probably
sound just like your typical proud pet owner."

"If he's extra-smart, he probably knows two hundred and fifty or so." Of course, she had no idea how
much Radar might have picked up or how long Gabe
had had him. "What about you?"

His lips twitched. "I guess I'd have to say I'm about
average intelligence."

Warmth rushed into her cheeks. "I meant, do you
think he understood?"

"Whew." He swiped a hand across his forehead.
"For a minute there, I was afraid you were going to
make me recite which one hundred and sixty-five
words I've learned."

She laughed as he opened the door to the café. She
hadn't had much experience with a man teasing her,
but she liked it. Sure, her male friends liked to kid,
but that was different. This was definitely different.
As was her reaction.

Between trying to keep her mother clean and Teddy
taken care of, she hadn't dated in high school. However,
once on her own in college, she'd intended to explore
guys the way most girls had in high school, maybe
even shed her innocence. But her college career hadn't
lasted long enough to do either.

She passed him as he held the door for her and was
hit with a variety of familiar smells emanating from
the restaurant. Coffee, cinnamon and vanilla.

Since it was the slow time between breakfast and
lunch, the half-dozen stools in front of the long counter held only two customers. The tables in the middle
of the dining area were empty, and only a few of the
booths along the front were occupied.

A trim gray-haired waitress greeted them with a cheery "good morning." Her hands full with a coffeepot in one and two plates stacked with pancakes in the other, she inclined her head toward a vacant booth near the windows facing the street. "Have a seat and I'll be over in a jiff."

Although he didn't actually touch her, Addie noticed Gabe raised his hand so it hovered behind her back as they made their way to the booth. He dropped it as she slid onto the bench seat. He sat opposite her and pulled out the plastic-covered menus that nested between the napkin holder and condiment bottles.

She accepted the one he offered and set it on the table in front of her. "I don't know why I'm looking at this. I always end up ordering the same thing."

He nodded. "It's been a while for me, but these items look familiar."

"Did you miss Loon Lake while you were gone?"

He tilted his head from side to side. "Yes and no. I was glad to leave when I joined the marines, but once I decided to muster out, this was where I wanted to come. That probably makes no sense."

"I can certainly understand it. I had never lived here, and yet I was homesick for a place just like Loon Lake. I'd say I was nuts, except the Welsh have a word for it. They call it *hiraeth*."

He gave her a quizzical frown. "What's that?"

"I can't roll my *R*s, so I know I'm not pronouncing it correctly, but it's something like *hye-ree*. Anyway, it's translated as *nostalgia* or *homesickness*, but it can also apply to yearning for a place that never existed or that you've never experienced personally. I found what I'd been longing for when I moved here."

"Sorry for the wait," the waitress said as she set two ruby-red, pebbled-plastic tumblers filled with water on the table. "Good to see you, Addie, and welcome back to you, young man."

"Nice to see you, Vera," Addie responded. *And thank you for rescuing me before I made a fool of myself.* She mentally kicked herself. What was she thinking, talking about an esoteric concept like *hiraeth* with a hot guy, a former marine at that? Not that he wouldn't understand, but she bet he wasn't as interested as he pretended. "How are you enjoying those cozy mysteries?" she asked the waitress.

"Very much. Thanks for tracking them down for me." Vera leaned closer to Gabe. "I love Addie and our library, but if I want anything racy, I travel over to Burlington or St. Johnsbury, where no one knows me."

"Vera, you know I don't check out books and tell," Addie joked.

"I know, but people here have long memories. I still blush whenever I see Pastor Cook's wife." Vera lowered her voice as she leaned over the table. "She asked what I thought of a certain sexy book when it was hot outside. Ha! Get it? Hot. Sometimes I kill myself. You've read it, haven't you, Addie? I thought—"

"Hey, Vera, quit horning in on Addie's date and get over here and refill my coffee," an elderly man in overalls and a flannel shirt called from across the café.

"Quit your yapping and wait your turn," Vera shot back. She pulled her pad and pencil from her apron pocket. "Have you decided yet?"

They gave their order and Vera scurried away to give the grumbling customer a piece of her mind along with his coffee refill.

"I'd forgotten how entertaining small-town places like this could be," Gabe said and shook his head at the goings-on.

Should she bring up the fact someone had called this a date? Or should she just ignore it? Like that time he'd almost kissed her. She might be ignoring it, but she certainly hadn't forgotten it. Nor had she stopped imagining it.

CHAPTER EIGHT

ADDIE UNWRAPPED HER straw. What the heck—she may as well clear the air. "Just so you know, I don't consider this a date."

His head snapped back. "You don't? What activities do you think constitute a date?"

Buzz. Wrong choice, Addie. "Well...no. I just meant..."

He reached over and captured her flailing hand. "We don't have to label this. How about we just enjoy our pancakes, hmm?"

She exhaled. He was holding her hand, so perhaps she hadn't spoiled whatever this was after all. "Deal."

He gently squeezed her fingers before releasing her. "Tell me how long you've suffered from cynophobia."

She inhaled sharply. Why was she surprised? She shouldn't be, because Gabe was an intelligent guy, a battle-tested marine, so he was observant and capable of assessing situations he was in. "You know that I'm afraid of dogs?"

He lifted one shoulder. "I guessed as much, and you've just confirmed it."

She gazed out the window at the activity on Main Street, aware of his intent gaze on her. After getting her thoughts in order, she turned back to him. "I was around Teddy's age when I was bitten. I still have the scars on my stomach and thigh."

His expression grew serious. "What happened?"

"We lived in a duplex—not as nice as ours, but that's beside the point. I was playing by myself in the yard and a neighbor's dog had been roaming freely. I liked dogs and approached it, and it bit me...twice."

He touched his mouth. "Were they serious bites?"

"I was treated in the ER. It was my own fault. I shouldn't have—" She broke off and shook her head. Angry that even after all this time she was ready to parrot Michelle's words. She was no longer seven years old and she was no longer a dutiful daughter. She couldn't be if she was to save Teddy. "No. It wasn't my fault. I was just a kid, but I swear I didn't do anything to the dog to create such a reaction."

He watched her intently. "What made you think it was your fault?"

"I didn't, but my mother made me say it was my fault."

"Why would she do such a thing?"

She inhaled in an attempt to get her riotous emotions under control. "Because she was off getting high when it happened, and when the authorities opened a case file, she didn't want to be charged with neglect. She made me tell the social worker that I had disobeyed her and went over and teased the dog. I—"

"Here you go." The waitress was back with two plates stacked high with pancakes. She set the plates in front of them, frowned, then switched them. "If you need anything else, just holler."

"Thanks," they said in unison.

Vera gave them a sly smile as she wiped her hands down the front of her apron. "Enjoy," she said and left.

Addie buttered her pancakes, then made a small pool of syrup next to the food on the plate. She sliced off a piece and dipped it in the puddle. Sensing his gaze on her, she paused with the fork partway to her mouth and smiled. "That way, I can get a consistent amount of syrup in each bite."

He nodded his head in salute. "Ingenious."

"Or an unquenchable sweet tooth."

"I'll remember that," he said and began to eat.

Her heart tripped up at his words. What did he mean by that? Why would he want to remember that about her? Maybe he was collecting information about her the way she was about him.

"Getting back to what we were discussing, I'm sorry you had such a terrible experience." He took a sip of water. "No wonder you're afraid of dogs."

"She had me convinced it was my fault." Was this why he'd invited her? So they could discuss her fear? "Not only that, but my anger about what happened and the way my mother forced me to accept blame are wrapped up in how I feel about dogs. And I've felt that way about them ever since."

He finished his pancakes and pushed the empty plate aside. "I won't let Radar invade your space, if that will make you feel better."

"No, don't do that, please." She reached across the table and touched his hand as it rested in the empty spot left by his plate. "I hate that I'm afraid. I've wanted to overcome it for a while now. Especially since Teddy loves dogs so much."

"He doesn't know you're afraid?"

She made a face. "Having to confess something like that to my baby brother isn't something I relish. Especially since I'm trying to establish my authority over him."

He flicked his wrist so her hand now rested under his, and his thumb stroked over her knuckles. "You may not want to hear this, but I think it would be best to come clean with him. However, in the meantime, I'd be willing to help you overcome your phobia."

"Do you know what to do?"

"I've been studying up on it."

"You have?" Embarrassment disappeared as quickly as it had appeared, and an unexpected warmth surged through her at the tenderness in his touch. Her heart expanded at the thought that he would go to all that trouble for her. He could have said her fear was her problem and she needed to solve it, which had been her mother's attitude.

Color rose on his cheeks. "A little bit. It's amazing what you find on YouTube."

"Thank you. I'd like that."

"So, what happened with the neighbor's dog and your mother?"

"I never went near the dog or the neighbor ever again. As for my mother, she eventually went into detox. Not that it took. Well, I shouldn't say that. It took for a while. Until it didn't."

"I'm sorry for what you've been through. Both of you," he said, releasing her hand when Vera appeared at their booth with the check.

Addie started to reach for the bill, but he was faster.

"I invited you, so it's my treat," he told her.

"Then let me leave the tip," she said as she dug into her purse for her wallet.

"Deal," he said and went to the register by the door to pay.

As they left, she couldn't help feeling hopeful over Gabe's willingness to assist her. She'd thought he'd laugh at her predicament, but he'd seemed genuinely interested in working with her to overcome her fear.

The entire time Gabe was interacting with the cashier, he was acutely aware of Addie. After setting some bills on the table for the tip, she went and stood by the door to wait. He smiled at the thought of her waiting for him. As if this were a date. Yeah, he'd told himself it wasn't, but as soon as she'd denied it, he'd balked like a rookie pitcher. Date or no, spending time with her was something he enjoyed.

Returning his wallet to his back pocket, he met her at the door. "Would you like to work with Radar after we get home? I'm assuming you might not want Teddy distracting us. He's in school, right?"

"Yes, he is." She smiled and nodded. "That would be great. And, yes, I think it will be easier without an audience."

"So, the backyard, then?" He followed her to her car.

Laughing, she said, "Yeah. I don't need Mrs. O'Malley watching me."

He raised an eyebrow. "The curtain twitcher?"

"She's really sweet, but also very..." Addie pulled on her bottom lip.

A pleasant hum sang through his blood at the sight. What he wouldn't give to be tugging gently on that full lip. He reached past her to open her door for her and cleared his throat. "…observant?"

"Exactly." She slipped into the driver's seat. "See you in a few?"

"Sure thing," he said and closed her door. Who knew such a simple act of courtesy could feel so satisfying?

Flexing his fingers, he watched as she backed out of the parking spot. He had yearned to touch her again before she left, wanted to feel her warm, soft skin under his fingers. Would she be that way all over?

He shook his head in an attempt to shake loose those thoughts. He had no business getting involved with her. She was too young, too caught up in trying to raise her brother. He'd help her with her fear of dogs and then step back.

"Excuse me."

A voice broke into his thoughts. He'd been standing inert in the middle of the sidewalk, and a mother with a baby stroller was trying to get past him.

"Sorry," he mumbled and went toward his car.

Radar, who'd been sitting patiently next to the parking meter, greeted him enthusiastically. Gabe pulled a crumpled napkin from his pocket and uncovered a small piece of bacon.

"Now remember…" Gabe glanced around. "This never happened. Bacon probably isn't any healthier for you than it is for me, but I won't tell if you won't."

Radar practically inhaled the treat.

"Did you even taste it?" Gabe laughed as he opened the driver's door. "And sit on your own side."

The dog whined but jumped in and moved to the passenger seat. After putting the portable watering dish away, Gabe slipped behind the wheel and started the Jeep.

"We're going to help Addie overcome her fear of dogs, so I'm going to need your cooperation." He checked traffic and pulled out of the parking spot. "You'll have to remain calm and submissive. Be on your best behavior. Got that?"

Radar gave a low woof as if in agreement with the plan, and Gabe laughed. He'd taken on the task of getting the pup stateside and assuming ownership to honor a fallen friend, but he hadn't honestly anticipated how much he'd come to care for him. Gabe had considered Tom one of his closest friends, but Radar was also becoming an integral part of his life.

Just like your new neighbors.

Because he automatically included Teddy. And wasn't that something.

Addie stopped her pacing long enough to glance out the window for the familiar dark gray Jeep.

"You can do this," she told herself. It would be worth it to spend time with Gabe, right?

The Jeep drove past and she inhaled deeply to calm her nerves. A knock sounded at her front door several minutes later.

She swung it open and gave them both a somewhat shaky smile. "C'mon in. We can go through the kitchen to the backyard."

"Radar, heel," he said as he stepped inside. "If you're uncomfortable at any point, be sure to let me know."

"Did you study up on this too?"

His amused gaze met hers. "Why? Do I sound like a YouTube video?"

One of the videos she'd watched about overcoming phobias had talked about replacing bad memories with good. Looking into his eyes, she decided she was halfway there already.

"Maybe I'm just listening like I'm watching one," she said as she led the way through the house and out the back door.

Once outside, Gabe touched her arm. "I'm serious. We'll take this as slow as you want. I want you to be comfortable."

"Thanks. I hate that I have this fear. All my life when I've seen people with their dogs, I've always felt as though I was missing out." She disliked being allergic to cats and afraid of dogs. There were a lot of things in her life that she'd been unable to control, but this fear felt like something she could, should be able to manage.

He had Radar come and sit near her.

"I'm told that the best way is for you to act like a human but to think like a dog," he said.

"How does that work?"

"I'm not totally sure, but it sounded good when the Dog Whisperer said it." He winked.

By the end of an hour, Addie was convinced Radar was the most patient, chill dog she'd ever encountered. *Calm* and *submissive* had been Gabe's words to describe him, and she had to agree.

Although she was quaking inside, she reached over and stroked the velvety fur between Radar's ears.

Of course, she realized that not all dogs were like Radar, but she didn't have plans to interact with every one she met.

As a reward for being so cooperative, Gabe gave the

dog his favorite chew toy and released him to go and play with the bone.

"I did it. I was able to pet Radar without suffering a heart attack." As happy as Radar, she threw her arms around Gabe without conscious thought. What was she doing? She felt heat creep up her neck into her face. Even her ears were warm. She would have pulled away, but his arms went around her before she could.

Pulling her close, he fitted her body to his. "I have thought about this ever since Teddy interrupted us."

"Me too," she admitted, his words giving her courage to admit her feelings. She wasn't in this alone. "Why do you think I suggested the backyard instead of in full view of the street?"

"I like the way you think," he said and lowered his head until his lips were inches from hers.

"Like a dog?" she asked.

He laughed, and his breath blew warm on her face. She put her hands on his chest and over his heart until his lips finally brushed across hers. His lips were firm but gentle. She opened her mouth, and his tongue swept in to brush against hers. More, she wanted more.

Not a total innocent, she'd been kissed before, but those had felt more like adolescent fumbling compared to this.

He lifted his mouth and whispered, "I think you're vibrating."

"What?" She pulled herself out of her haze, reluctantly moving away so she could look up at him. "Oh, it's the alarm on my phone. I set it so I wouldn't forget to meet Teddy at the bus stop."

"I guess I was a bit premature with my self-congratulations, huh?"

* * *

She laughed, which was the response Gabe had been going for. It helped lighten the mood, and he loved the sound of it.

He couldn't decide if the interruption of this intimate moment was a good thing or not. After his disastrous first marriage, he'd promised himself he wouldn't let anything like that happen again. Sure, he'd married Tracy after getting her pregnant, but he hadn't stuck around; he had failed her. Worse still, with the clarity of hindsight, he could see that most of his feelings regarding Tracy had involved teen hormones. And the fact that the homecoming queen had shown interest in the kid from the wrong side of the tracks.

In contrast, Addie seemed like the type of woman who would expect him to be a stand-up guy, and he knew his past actions proved he was anything but. He'd just have to explain about his track record and she'd probably run a mile. But he sure liked kissing her. Her kisses were like a drug, one he could become easily addicted to.

Sure, his attraction involved hormones, that was a fact of life, but his feelings toward her went much deeper than that.

He kissed her again, a light peck on the lips, because he couldn't help himself from tasting her one more time. "Would you mind some company on the way to the end of the street?" he asked.

Gabe stepped away from her before he was tempted to deepen the kiss. Tempted? He already was that. And not just tempted to keep on kissing her. Was she wearing another lacy bra today? he wondered.

He shouldn't be doing this at all. Never mind again.

"More exposure therapy?"

She's speaking. Pay attention. "Hmm?"

She grinned as if she'd known his thoughts had been elsewhere. Of course, if she'd known exactly where his thoughts had been, she might not be smiling like that. Or maybe she—

Radar woofed and forced Gabe out of his head. "If you don't want him to come with us to pick up Teddy, I can put him inside."

The dog whined as if he understood he might be left out. He looked to Addie as if he also understood the decision was up to her.

She reached over, gently stroked his head and stepped back, inhaling deeply to calm herself as they'd practiced. "It's okay. He can come."

Gabe put Radar's leash on him, and they walked through the side yard to the front of the house. He couldn't help but notice that, across the street, Mrs. O'Malley's curtain was moving.

"We have an audience," he said in a stage whisper.

Her hands flew to her mouth and he burst out laughing. "That gesture's not gonna help us look innocent."

She elbowed him but grinned. They fell into a companionable silence for the first part of the walk, but every so often their shoulders would bump. The occasional contact thrilled him, but it went deeper. He felt close to her, a kinship he hadn't felt with anyone since leaving the marines. Like they were linked by common goals and shared objectives. "How did Teddy get the burn scars on his hands and arms?" Acid filled his throat and entered the back of his mouth. Oh man, why in the world had he asked that? Of all subjects to pick, why that? "Forget it. I know it's none of my—"

"It's okay. It's not a big secret or anything. It happened when I was away at college. Michelle—our biological mother—had left him unattended. He pushed a chair over to the sink to sail a toy boat I'd sent him. She'd left a pan of hot water there and he received severe burns when he plunged his hands in to retrieve the toy. The neighbors heard his cries and called the police. They couldn't find Michelle, so of course child services were called in."

Wanting to lend her whatever strength he could, he took her hand. "Child services contacted you?" he prompted.

"No. One of the neighbors had my cell number and called me right after 9-1-1." She sighed. "I just wish she'd contacted me sooner. I would have come home so I could've prevented Teddy from getting burned in the first place. It's all my fault for sending the boat. But he'd kept talking about one when I called, so I found one and mailed it. I figured he'd get a kick out of it."

He winced and swore under his breath. "That doesn't make it your fault."

"I believed her when she said I could trust her. She was done with that stuff for good. Clean and sober. So, I went off to college, left Teddy in her care and—"

"Hold up right there." He stopped and turned to face her. "How old were you?"

"Eighteen."

"You did what millions of people your age do. Going off to college is like a rite of passage for so many high school graduates."

She sighed. "I know, but one of the times I called her, she mentioned how she'd met someone…" She shook her head, her pretty eyes clouded. "I should have come straight home, checked him and the situation out. I knew what happened when she got involved with the wrong guys. I was selfish."

Gabe put his finger across her lips. "She was the mother. You were his sister…practically a kid yourself. Why did you feel it was your job to protect him?"

She shrugged. "It's what I'd always done when I was home and what I could have done once again, had I been there."

He thought about Tom and that stupid coin toss that had changed everything. They'd argued good-naturedly about whose turn it had been to go into the convenience store. The toss of a coin made Gabe the winner and Tom had to go inside to pay for their drinks. He paid all right, but with his life. Yeah, he knew about guilt, irrational or not.

For the first time since returning home, he had the urge to tell someone about it, but before he could say anything, the school bus arrived.

Just as he had on that first day, Teddy scrambled off the bus and raced over to his sister and Gabe. He once again threw his arms around Radar.

Gabe glanced at Addie, who winced, so he hunkered down so he was eye level with the boy. He touched Teddy's shoulder to be sure he had his attention. "It's good that you and Radar get along so well, but you need to know that not all dogs are as happy to see you as he is."

"Whaddaya mean?"

"I'm just saying that you should find out if the dog is friendly before you reach out."

"But you said Radar wouldn't bite me," Teddy said, and Radar woofed in agreement. "You even tol' that to Addie."

"And that's true, but not all dogs are like Radar, so make sure you ask the owner if it's okay first." Gabe lifted his fist. "Deal?"

Teddy did a fist bump. "Deal."

Gabe's heart lurched. Most people might consider this an inconsequential moment, but to him it was anything but. He'd never considered himself a sentimental guy, but he might have to revisit that opinion since meeting his new neighbors.

Gabe glanced at Addie, who mouthed a thank-you and seemed to relax a little. He grinned to himself. Yeah, this was a special moment. Small in the scheme of things, but special to him.

"I'm so glad you're here," Teddy said. "The other kids on the bus didn't believe me that I live next door to a hero dog and that he likes me. Now they *have* to believe me."

"It doesn't matter if the other kids believe it or not," Addie said. "As long as you know it's true."

Teddy thought about it for a minute, then shrugged. "But it's better when they know it too."

"You're right. I guess it is." She laughed and reached out her hand. "Want me to take your backpack for you?"

He handed it to her. "Mr. Gabe? Can I hold Radar's leash?"

Gabe glanced at Addie, and after she nodded, he handed over the leash. He fell into step beside her as the dog and the boy led the way along the sidewalk.

"Addie, look, I'm walking Radar."

"I see that, sweetie."

Gabe leaned closer. "Thought of a new name for yourself yet?" he asked, referring to her earlier wish for anonymity when Teddy kept using her name.

She thought for a moment, then laughed as if she was recalling her comment too. His stomach did a little somersault.

Another little moment, but monumental in the way it made him feel. Like maybe he hadn't lost everything when he'd lost his son. Maybe second chances were real.

Teddy turned back. "What're you guys laughing at?"

"I'm just happy that you're getting to walk Radar," she told him.

"Mr. Gabe, did you find something for me to help you with today? You said you wouldn't forget. Remember?"

"You're right. I had planned to wash the Jeep today, but it's still kinda chilly outside." The kid looked so dejected, though, that it broke his heart. "I haven't played ball with Radar yet. Maybe you could help with that."

The kid lowered his chin. "Is that *really* like helping you? It doesn't sound much like it."

Busted. He looked to Addie for guidance.

"As much as you love dogs, you should know they require lots of exercise," his sister told him.

"Oh yeah, I forgot."

He waited until Teddy was chattering away to Radar about how they were going to play ball before saying quietly to Addie, "He might have those physical scars, but he seems happy and very well-adjusted."

"Thanks. I still wish I'd been there to prevent the accident." She slowed her steps, letting her brother get even farther ahead with the pup. "What did you mean when you said even when we're there, sometimes we can't prevent the bad stuff from happening?"

"Oh, that." He'd been referring to his being outside the store, only feet away, when Tom was killed. He'd been close enough that he could still smell the cordite, feel the shock waves that had blown him off his feet, taste the soot that had rained down. Did he want to give her an answer? It would mean explaining what had happened, how he'd escaped with his life by winning a stupid coin toss. Just because she'd opened up to him didn't mean he needed to bare his soul. Not yet, anyway—not unless he was going to become a permanent part of her and Teddy's lives. And that wasn't going to happen.

CHAPTER NINE

ADDIE MENTALLY KICKED herself for spoiling the otherwise touching moment with her probing. His resulting silence told her he didn't want to share. "It's okay. I didn't mean to pry."

"Remember I mentioned my buddy who taught Radar all those commands? He was actually the one who first rescued Radar too. His name was Tom." She nodded and he continued, "We were out on routine patrol through town—"

"In Afghanistan?"

"Yeah. Whenever we were in that part of town, we stopped at this little family-owned store. They had those slushy drink machines. We couldn't get those in camp, so we'd stop, but we couldn't both go in. Someone had to stay with the vehicle. The person going in would pay. This one day, we stopped and argued over whose turn it was to pay."

He winced as if the memory was painful. Inhaling, he continued, "We flipped a coin. Tom lost, so he went into the store. I was waiting outside, standing by the vehicle, when the whole world exploded. I was knocked off my feet by the blast."

Emotion rose in her chest, clogging her throat. Her

mother might not have died, but Addie had lost her to the drugs, so she understood that helpless feeling.

"It was a suicide bomber. Everyone inside the store died." He shook his head. "I was how many feet away from Tom? And I couldn't do anything about it."

She wanted to hug him to her, console him, but settled for placing her hand on his arm as they arrived at the duplex. "I'm so sorry. That must've been terrible. Were you badly hurt?"

"I survived."

She squeezed his arm. "Teddy and I are glad you did, and I'm sure Radar is too."

"If I'd lost that coin toss, Radar would be with Tom now."

"And I'd still be afraid of dogs," she reasoned. "You may not think what you did—rescuing Radar like that and bringing him back to America, then starting to help me get over my phobia—is that big of a deal, but believe me, it is, and I—"

"Mr. Gabe?" Teddy interrupted, distracting Addie from her concern over Gabe. "Do you have Radar's ball?"

"Sure. Let me get it," he said and slipped into the house.

"Are you gonna watch me play ball?" Teddy asked.

"Of course. Let me get a couple chairs from the carport." She retrieved two canvas seats. There was just enough room for the both of them on the cement pad in front of the two doors.

Gabe came back out, raising an eyebrow. "Are we the bleachers?"

"Yup."

He tossed the ball to Teddy, who made a running

grab for it, but tripped, and the ball went over his head. He started giggling when Radar trotted over and dropped the ball on him.

For the past year, she'd envied her friends for the families they'd formed, but now she was experiencing some of that happiness.

Watching Teddy laughing and playing relieved some of the burden she'd been dragging around like an old suitcase, and she blurted out, "I can't thank you enough for bringing Radar into his life."

He shifted in his seat. "Look, if you're saying that because—because of what I told you before, I wasn't looking for sympathy, reassurance or anything at all when I said it."

"What? No." His reaction shouldn't have surprised her because she knew a lot of veterans wanted to put things behind them. "I'm saying it because I can't help second-guessing everything I do with regards to Teddy."

"Why?"

"I want to keep him safe, but I also want him to have a normal, happy childhood."

"He's a bright, inquisitive boy. I would say you're doing a wonderful job."

"But I'm not his mother...even you said that. What if I'm damaging him?" Okay, so maybe she was having trouble letting go of some of that guilt. After all, she'd had it for a long time. If she'd been able to prevent her mother from relapsing, Teddy's life would be so different now.

"Are you asking me if you're damaging him by keeping him safe, giving him a secure environment to grow up in?"

"Well, if you're going to put it like that…" she said.

Unwilling to explore the feelings he'd churned up, she abruptly changed the subject. "Have you lived your whole life in Loon Lake?"

"Before I joined up, yeah. But I didn't grow up on a street like this." He glanced around the neighborhood. "And it wasn't across town in one of those big Victorians either, if that's what you were wondering."

She hadn't thought that, but he was starting to sound defensive, so she kept silent. She had a feeling her probing earlier had forced a confidence he now regretted. Plus, she didn't want him to stop talking about himself, about his life. Why she wanted to know as much as she could about him was something she was trying not to examine too closely. For all her talk about resisting the town's matchmaking efforts, she realized she was taking an avid interest in All Things Gabe. After that kiss and the time he was spending with Teddy, she could admit to herself her interest in him was swiftly becoming *more* than avid.

"We lived over on the east side on that road that leads to the secluded end of the lake."

"Isn't that the area where someone built that gorgeous log home?" She'd checked out the apartment above the garage after Ellie Harding had moved out, but the place wasn't big enough for both her and Teddy.

He nodded. "Yeah, but it's changed a lot in the past few years. There weren't any houses that impressive back then. The trailer is gone now, but Pa and I lived in a single-wide on an empty lot. No manicured lawns or ornamental bushes, just lots of dirt."

She turned her head toward him and took a moment

to admire his profile. God, but he was gorgeous. Not pretty-boy handsome but… Natalie's words popped into her head. He seemed to be lost in the past, staring straight ahead, but not as if he was actually seeing the street or the trees in front of them.

"We moved around a lot, sometimes in the middle of the night when rent was due. Your place may not have been glamorous, but it sure beats a cheap motel," she said, imagining their trailer was a lot better than many of the places she'd lived in when Michelle was using.

"Maybe, but the front yard was nothing but a graveyard for dead lawn mowers and snowblowers. Pa never gave up hope of getting those rusted castoffs running again. He called them 'precious metals waiting to be mined.'" He shook his head. "Precious, my ass. It was all junk, plain and simple. And if he did manage to get one running, instead of selling it, more often than not, someone had a sob story and he'd end up giving it away, or practically free."

"Sounds like he was caring and compassionate." She laid her hand on his arm.

"Yeah. Too bad his only son was such a disappointment," Gabe said bitterly.

She squeezed his arm. "I find that hard to believe."

"Believe it. His dream was for me to go to college. He didn't get a chance to go himself and really wanted that for me. Make something of myself. He hoped I'd get a baseball scholarship. I might have had a chance… not for the major leagues, though. I wasn't that good."

"What happened?"

"I got the homecoming queen pregnant. Instead of going off to college, I got married and found a job working construction." He huffed out a bitter laugh. "Listen to me. I sound like a Bruce Springsteen song."

"You a Springsteen fan?" He might think of what he did as a cliché, but she knew not all men took responsibility for their actions. She knew two who hadn't. She and Teddy might not share the same biological father, but both men had one thing in common. They'd skipped out. As an eighteen-year-old, Gabe must have been scared by marriage and pending fatherhood, and yet he'd acted with honor. That earned him her respect, even if the marriage hadn't worked out.

He shrugged. "My pa was, so I grew up listening. You?"

"Oh yeah…"

"What? I would have thought he was before your time." He gave her a puzzled glance.

"Remember, I'm one hundred and something in dog years." She couldn't contain her laughter any longer and he joined her.

She was relieved that he wasn't still upset over having confided in her earlier. Her conversation with Tavie Whatley last night, about inviting Gabe to their community meeting, popped into her mind. And not for the reasons the other woman had suggested. Ogle, Tavie's husband and a Vietnam vet, had managed to get a lot of the local veterans to open up to him. And Gabe could use someone to talk to, someone who understood what he'd gone through, someone who could provide advice on transitioning back to civilian life. They probably said things to Ogle they wouldn't to others. Maybe Gabe could come to terms with what had happened to him in Afghanistan, as well as the circumstances of his childhood and failed marriage.

"Has anyone invited you to our Coffee & Conversation meetings yet?"

He frowned. "Not that I know of."

"Well, now I'm inviting you." She smiled. A spoonful of sugar, right?

"Why?" he asked, giving her a side-eye look.

Maybe she should have bribed him with a real sugar treat. "Why not? Wouldn't you like to get involved in the community? I think it's a great opportunity to get to know people and help out those less fortunate."

"I'm really not interested."

"Oh," she said, because she didn't know what else to say. Until he'd refused, she hadn't realized how much she'd been counting on him agreeing.

She had to ask herself why it meant so much to her for him to integrate into the community. Had she wanted it for him or for herself? If he was invested in the town, he'd stay, maybe take another chance at creating a family.

Gabe stood up. "You two about done? I hate to break it up, but I have to work up some figures for Brody."

"Of course. I have to see if Teddy has homework before supper." And she wanted to think this over in private.

Even as a child, she'd never been one for fairy tales. So why was she suddenly letting herself act as if her life could be one? Teddy needed to be her top priority, and her dream of having a happy family like her friends needed to stay just that—a fantasy and nothing more. Giving her brother a stable foundation in a safe neighborhood was what she needed to concentrate on, along with finishing her degree and becoming a full-fledged librarian.

* * *

Once inside, Gabe called himself all sorts of names. Why had he acted like that? He hated that he'd put that look of hurt on her pretty face. But when she'd talked about people getting together to help the needy, he imagined they'd be looking at him. He had nothing against the good people of Loon Lake, but he could only think how they would be remembering him as one of those less fortunate. His childhood was over. He had no wish to dredge up all those old memories and the way they made him feel.

Looked like Radar wasn't happy with him either and made his displeasure known by grumbling low in his throat. The dog probably knew he'd acted like a jerk, but after talking about what had happened to Tom, Gabe felt off-kilter. What was it about Addie that made him want to share bits of himself he'd always kept hidden?

Then she'd talked about those community meetings, and it had gotten under his skin.

He went into the kitchen, took two pieces of leftover pizza and a soda from the fridge and threw the food on a plate. After putting the plate in the microwave, he dumped some dry kibble in Radar's bowl and re-filled the water dish.

Was she getting supper too? Would she be sitting down to help Teddy with homework? He imagined she would be the type to check over the boy's lessons.

The dog plunked himself down in front of the water dish and noisily lapped up water. The microwave dinged and Gabe took the pizza out. He grabbed the clipboard he'd used at Brody's to take notes and went to the small desk he'd set up in the living room for his laptop.

He'd told Addie he was going to work on figures for Brody, and that was what he'd do. He wasn't going to think about that kiss. Or how much he'd like to do it again. Or how he should go and apologize for his behavior. He had nothing to apologize for. He was under no obligation to go to her meeting just because she'd invited him. So why did he regret refusing?

He ate the pizza without tasting it while working up an invoice for Brody. Laughter drifted to him from the apartment next door. What were they laughing at? He shook his head. None of his business. And he wasn't feeling left out. Nope. Not at all.

His phone dinged with an incoming text and he jumped on it.

The text was from an old school friend he'd bumped into when he'd picked up his pizza yesterday. He was at the courts and asking if he'd like to play some basketball. Normally, he'd say no, but maybe this was just what he needed to get out of his own head.

Radar wasn't too happy that Gabe was leaving without him, but his owner didn't want to have to worry about his dog while playing hoops.

He'd jumped on the distraction and initially it had felt good to connect with old friends. But he'd been gone too long, seen too much to pick up where they'd left off. He realized he had more in common with new acquaintances like Brody Wilson and Des Gallagher than the guys he'd hung out with in school. The fact Brody and Des had both seen action was responsible for their instant brotherhood.

But he'd joked around and shot some hoops. He might even have gone with them for beers after the game if he hadn't twisted his knee.

He'd laughed off falling on his butt when the knee gave out but still used it as an excuse to skip extending the evening. He pulled his Jeep back into his driveway, cut the engine and grimaced. Opening the driver's door, he inhaled and swung his legs out of the vehicle. He tested his left knee by putting weight on it and swore when pain shot through the entire leg. His knee felt similar to the time he'd sprained his ACL. He didn't think— No, make that he *hoped* that wasn't the problem. Although it hurt like hell, it wasn't quite that bad.

He slowly made his way into the house, hoping the old lady across the street wasn't watching. He didn't need the whole town knowing how stupid he was for playing in a pickup game and getting injured at his age. Huh, maybe that had put up the weird invisible barrier between him and his old friends. Was it his experiences that made him feel so much older than those guys?

Radar greeted him at the door and whined when he shut it. Great. The dog probably needed to go out and relieve himself.

"My stupidity isn't your fault. I'll let you into the backyard, but don't go far."

He laboriously limped through the house and into the kitchen. If he hadn't been rude to Addie, maybe he would have spent the evening with her and Teddy.

"Make it quick," Gabe told the dog as he opened the back door and switched on the spotlight that was supposed to illuminate the area. Nothing happened. He groaned and said a few words that would have had him filling Teddy's swear jar.

Fixing that light was one of the things on his list of repairs. Unfortunately, it involved climbing the ladder to reach the bulb attached to the highest peak on the corner of the building. About all he was able to do at the moment was shuffle around. He was hardly the role model that someone like Addie and Teddy deserved in their lives.

Radar bounded out the door, his nose to the ground. Then he raced to the edge of the yard near the trees that backed up to the property line.

"Great." Gabe leaned against the doorjamb, trying to keep his weight off his now-throbbing leg. Story of his life. He had no one to blame but himself. It was his responsibility to change the light. He'd been responsible for Tracy's pregnancy. Same with Tom. He'd been the senior officer and could have ordered Tom to stay with the vehicle. He'd been blaming the flip of a coin, but it was ultimately his fault.

Sighing, he called for the dog and received an answering bark. He whistled a few moments later with no response. What was causing Radar to ignore his commands? He couldn't handle a misbehaving dog. What made him think he would be a good influence on an impressionable boy like Teddy?

"Addie, did you hear that?" Teddy asked, getting up and going to the back door to look out.

"What, sweetie?" She finished loading the dishwasher, added detergent and latched it shut.

"I think I heard Radar barking. Out in the backyard."

She went to stand next to him and put her arms on his shoulders. "It's possible. He lives here. Gabe might have let him out to relieve himself."

"You mean, to take a whiz?" he asked, giving her a mischievous look.

"Where in the world did you hear that?" She pushed his shoulder.

He grinned and ducked his head. "At school. A lot of the kids say it."

"Well, it's not very nice."

"What do you want me to say? Take a—"

"Don't you dare." She shook her head. Was this what she had to look forward to, raising a boy? Would Gabe have known how to handle this? And why was she thinking in terms of his help? He might enjoy kissing her—and she believed he did—but that was a far cry from wanting to step up and take responsibility for a seven-year-old boy. "Let's not talk about going to the toilet at all right now."

"But you said I could ask you anything."

"And you can. And you did, and I answered." She sighed and pushed him toward the table. "Finish your homework if you want to watch TV before bed."

"But you didn't say what I could say."

"You can say he's using the bathroom."

"But Radar is outside, not—"

A knock at the back door interrupted him. "Maybe it's Mr. Gabe and Radar."

Teddy had the door open before she could react.

It was indeed Gabe and he looked a little worse for wear. His pallor was a bit gray and he had deep grooves around his mouth. She started to reach out but pulled back. If he was in pain, and she believed he was or had been, she wanted to comfort him, but would he accept it or push her away? He'd pushed her away once tonight; she wasn't sure if she had the strength to put herself out there again.

"Come in. Is Radar with you?" Teddy stuck his head out the door.

Gabe nodded and limped in holding on to the door-jamb.

Unable to help it, she rushed to his side. "What happened? Are you okay?"

He nodded. "A reminder that I'm getting too old to play pickup basketball."

"Do you need anything? What can I do?" She realized she'd been trying to herd him inside and he was resisting, albeit shakily. She had to remind herself she was not responsible for taking care of Gabe, no matter how much she felt the urge to do so.

He sucked in a breath. "I'm not here about me. It's Radar. I don't suppose there's any twenty-four-hour emergency vets in town."

"Why? What happened to him?"

Teddy pulled his head back in. "Is Radar okay?"

Gabe massaged the back of his neck. "He got into something he should've left alone."

Her mind filled with all sorts of horrors, just like it had the time Teddy said he'd almost run into the street. She hated the thought of anything happening to the dog. Being afraid was not the same as not liking the animals, though. She didn't want to see Radar *or* Gabe come to harm.

Gabe put his palm against the wall, obviously needing the support. "Come."

Radar came to the open doorway. For a moment, she didn't register what she was seeing. The dog's snout was full of porcupine quills. He slowly swung his head back and forth trying to dislodge them.

"The poor thing," she said, her stomach tightening in sympathy for the poor creature.

"Do they hurt?" Teddy asked.

Gabe nodded. "I'm sure they do. Don't touch him. I don't want those quills getting worked in any farther."

"Are you gonna pull them out?" Teddy asked, and Radar whined.

Gabe shook his head. "I think that's a job best left to a professional. I understand it's not as straightforward as it seems."

"Oh my God, he looks so pitiful." Addie cupped her palm over her mouth and shivered. "I think he's going to need sedation."

"Why?" Teddy asked.

"Because if he jerks while they're trying to remove them, he might break the quills. The quills are actually designed to work their way in deeper, so they need to be taken out in one smooth pull with pliers. They can migrate to other parts of the body." Sometimes she hated her encyclopedic brain.

"Who designed them?" Teddy scrunched up his face.

"Mother Nature, I guess," she said.

"What happens if they do break?"

"The vet will need to switch to sanitized tweezers to…" Her voice trailed off and she glanced up.

Gabe shifted his stance. "This is all my fault. I trusted Radar to come straight back, but he's still a dog and dogs chase porcupines. Damn. I spent so much time concentrating on keeping him safe from snipers and IEDs that I forgot to take into consideration the more mundane dangers lurking here at home."

"To what?" Teddy demanded.

She frowned at her brother. "To *what* what?"

Gabe cleared his throat and winced as he looked at a pathetic Radar, his snout full of quills. "I think your sister was talking about using tweezers to dig the pieces out."

"Ew," Teddy said, and he made a face. "That sounds—"

"I don't think we need to discuss this right now, Teddy." She glanced at Gabe. The poor guy looked positively queasy. Her earlier annoyance at his dismissive behavior after their kiss evaporated.

"But it's happening now," Teddy whined.

Despite the circumstances, Gabe laughed at his comment. Her gaze met Gabe's in a common understanding that they were protecting Teddy from the gory details. This silent communication passed between them as they stared at one another over his head. Was this what it was like to be intimately close to someone? Sharing moments without the need for words?

"I think your sister is getting grossed out, so maybe we can talk about it later."

"Hey, I..." Addie started to object, but Gabe winked at her and she understood what he was doing. She smirked at him and said, "I guess we'll both have something to discuss later."

"Agreed, but first I need to find emergency veterinary care."

"We don't have a twenty-four-hour— Wait. I do have Dr. Greer's personal cell number. We were on a committee together last year for the annual Independence Day celebration. I'm sure she'd be happy to help an animal in distress." She grabbed her phone off the counter and scrolled through her contacts.

"I hate to put you on the spot, but do you think you could call her?" He gave her a pleading look. "Radar didn't get into this mess by himself. I should have gone outside with him, called him back immediately when he darted off."

Radar sat, watching patiently while Addie tried to reach the vet. Her heart went out to both man and animal.

Teddy hunkered down in front of Radar, his hands between his knees, avoiding touching the dog. "Learning lessons is no fun, huh?"

Addie drew in a sharp breath. Was that what Michelle had told that little boy, a sweet child in pain, when he'd gotten burned? Oh, she had no doubt that was where that sentiment had come from. Their mother had been quick to tell her that she hoped she'd learned her lesson after she'd gotten bitten by the neighbor's dog. It was her responsibility now to undo the damage Michelle had done to Teddy—*and* to her.

CHAPTER TEN

GABE SHIFTED HIS WEIGHT, easing off the sore knee as much as possible to relieve the pain. Whatever his discomfort, he was pretty sure Radar was in a heck of a lot more, and that was on him for getting them into this mess. But none of that mattered now because Addie was there and willing to help, despite his earlier treatment of her.

Evidently the call had gone through, because she was speaking with someone, explaining the situation. The tension he'd been carrying in his shoulders drained away. He hoped to have the chance to make this up to her.

"Uh-huh," she said and gave him a thumbs-up.

His heart did that stumble thing he associated with Addie and he sagged against the wall. He might not be seeing his bed or even his couch as he'd planned, but at least Radar would receive the necessary treatment. He'd been fooling himself when he'd said he was honoring a promise when he brought the dog home. Truth was, Radar had burrowed deep into his heart and he'd walk to the ends of the earth to see that he was taken care of. How many times had Radar brought him out of his dark thoughts? Retrieved him from the nightmare of war and brought him back to reality without any formal training?

Addie set her phone on the counter. "She says she'll meet us at her office. She's going to try to contact her vet tech too. She mentioned he might need anesthesia when they go to get all of the quills out."

He straightened up and away from the wall, pulling out his own phone to call up the GPS. "Where is her office?"

"I know exactly where it is. Teddy, go get our jackets from the closet by the front door."

The boy sprang up, his expression hopeful. "We're going with Mr. Gabe and Radar?"

She glanced over at Gabe, her chin at a determined angle. "You don't look like you're in any state to drive yourself."

He opened his mouth to argue but closed it again. As much as he wanted to protest, she was absolutely right, so he nodded. "Okay, but we should take my Jeep. I have a crate for Radar in the rear."

She bit her lip. "Is it a stick?"

"The car?" He shook his head. "No."

"So, I get to ride in Mr. Gabe's Jeep?" Teddy asked, as if it were some sort of treat.

"I thought I told you to go get the jackets," she said and picked up her purse from the kitchen table. "Unless you prefer I call Mrs. O to see if…"

"I figured that would get him moving," she said as Teddy ran from the room.

He marveled at how she'd kept a cool head and did what was necessary. Sure, he'd helped her with her phobia, but she wasn't miraculously cured, and yet she wasn't letting it prevent her from helping them.

"I can't thank you enough," he said, and Radar whined. Even the dog recognized how special this woman was. "Make that *we* can't thank you enough."

She waved her hand. "It's what neighbors do."

"I also owe you an apology."

"For what?"

"For earlier. I was rude when you invited me to your meeting."

"It's not *my* meeting. It happens to be held at the library and—"

"Here, Addie." Teddy came back with two jackets and handed her one. "Mr. Gabe? Will it cost a lot of money to get Radar fixed?"

Radar whined as if the question had been weighing on him too.

"Teddy." Addie's tone held a note of warning.

"I was gonna say that maybe we should take the swear jar with us, just in case. You know, if Mr. Gabe needs extra money to help pay. If that's okay with you, Addie. You're always saying how much money it costs when you take a dog to the doctor."

Addie gave Gabe an apologetic look and opened her mouth, but before she spoke, he said, "I don't think that will be necessary, but I appreciate your generous offer." He glanced at the dog. "And I'm sure Radar appreciates it too."

"Well, we'd better go. We don't want to keep Emily waiting," Addie said and handed her car keys to Teddy. "Get your booster seat from our car so we can put it in Gabe's."

He felt a bit disoriented sitting in the passenger seat of his own vehicle, but it did feel good, being off his knee.

"Is everyone buckled in?" Addie asked before starting the Jeep.

"Yes, ma'am," Gabe said.

"Yup," came Teddy's response.

A whine from the crate in the back was Radar's reply.

Teddy giggled. "Radar answered too. Did you hear that, Mr. Gabe?"

"I certainly did." Gabe chuckled and glanced at Addie, who met his gaze before she backed out of the driveway. The gloom and doom he'd been feeling earlier had lifted; it had eased the moment Addie had asked what she could do to help.

All rational thought fled when he got lost in her sparkling eyes, which looked as if the sun were shining through them. He felt warmth flood his face. Where the heck had that corny thought come from? And at a time like this, no less?

"Mr. Gabe?"

"Yes?"

"Do you like Addie?"

"*Teddy,*" she groaned.

"What? Last year, when I tol' you I liked Ashley Cook from my school, you said I should tell her."

"Yes, but…" She stopped at the end of their street and waited for traffic before pulling out.

What was he supposed to say to a seven-year-old? "Yes, I have feelings for your sister, but they're not exactly appropriate, at least not enough to admit to a young boy about his sister"?

"Well, to answer your question. Yes, Teddy, I like your sister," he said and paused before adding, "Very much, in fact."

Now he'd gone and done it. Home less than a month and admitting to having feelings for a woman. And not just any woman, but one who was responsible for an impressionable boy. Returning to Loon Lake, he hadn't intended to live a celibate life, but this was definitely not what he'd planned either.

"That's good 'cause Addie likes you."

"Teddy," she said in a pained tone.

Gabe arched an eyebrow and looked over at her. "Is that true?"

She briefly took her eyes from the road to look at him. "Yes," she said shortly and shifted her concentration back to her driving.

"See?" Teddy leaned back in his seat. "It worked. Just like with Ashley Cook."

"Yes, it, uh, did," Gabe said and bit the inside of his cheek to keep from laughing. When he could talk without chuckling, he said, *"And a little child shall lead them."*

"Huh?" came from the back seat.

"Nothing," they both responded at the same time.

He had a feeling Teddy's definition of liking was a bit different from his. His encompassed a whole range, from lustful thoughts to enjoying sitting on the front stoop with her and talking about everything and nothing.

Addie switched on the blinker and pulled into the turn lane.

"We're here," she said, sounding relieved as she drove into the parking lot.

The veterinarian's office was located in a newer one-story, detached building with a brick facade and white-painted trim. Addie parked the car next to the door.

A petite woman wearing a white lab coat over light green scrubs met them at the entrance. Her long blond hair was pulled back into a ponytail. The pin under the front pocket said Dr. Emily Greer, DVM.

"Thank you so much for meeting us," Addie said as they embraced.

"I'm glad I was able to come," the vet replied.

Teddy ran up to her. "Hi! Remember me?"

Dr. Greer gave him a hug too. "Of course I remember you, Teddy. You came last year with your sister to the July Fourth celebration and helped me set up my booth."

"Radar came all the way from Afghanistan," Teddy told her.

The vet grinned. "My, my, he came a long way."

"Oh, he didn't come today." He shook his head. "He came a long time ago. At least two weeks, huh, Mr. Gabe?"

"At least two weeks," Gabe said, grateful Teddy had distracted them while he practically crawled out of the car. Not good for his manly image.

Addie introduced Gabe to the vet, and they exchanged pleasantries.

"I guess I'd better meet the patient."

Gabe switched off the ball game on TV when Radar abandoned his post on the couch to run to the front door. It had been three days since their injuries, and both were healing nicely. Radar more so than him, since Gabe was still limping a bit—like now as he followed the dog to the door.

Dr. Greer had removed all the quills without any

breaking, so she hadn't had to resort to digging any out with tweezers.

Gabe was using the RICE method of rest, ice, compression and elevation to take care of his knee, and it was responding.

"You'd tell me if it was someone other than Teddy, wouldn't you, boy?" he said to the dog as he reached for the knob.

Gabe laughed when Radar gave him a look that said he knew his job. Sure enough, Teddy was on the other side, his hand poised to knock. Gabe's chest swelled at the sight. He looked forward to the boy's company as much as he enjoyed Addie's.

So why had he done little to encourage seeing her except in passing in the days following their emergency trip to the vet? Sure, he'd been staying off his feet to heal his knee, but that was only part of it. Had it been because he'd admitted liking her? Or worse yet, her admitting she liked him? Which was scarier?

Oh man, thoughts like that just illustrated how deep his feelings went.

"How did you know I was here?" the boy asked as Gabe opened up.

"Radar told me."

"He did?" The boy giggled and hugged Radar. "How'd he do that? He can't talk."

Wanna bet? Gabe grinned and replied, "He came to the door to let me know you were here."

Teddy scrunched up his face. "But I didn't even get to knock before you opened it."

"True, but dogs hear better than we do," he told Teddy. "They hear sounds four times farther away than we do, so he must've heard you coming."

Teddy slowly shook his head. "Now you sound like Addie."

Gabe laughed. "I'll take that as a compliment."

"Huh?"

"Nothing. I— What have you got in your pocket? Radar keeps trying to stick his nose in it."

The boy put his hand in his hoodie and held up a clear sandwich bag with cookies shaped like bones. "Look what I made."

"You baked those?" Gabe smiled but wasn't sure where this was heading.

"Yup. Well, Addie helped. Can I give one to Radar?"

Radar threw Gabe a hopeful look and whined.

"I don't normally let him have human food, but I guess one won't hurt. They don't have chocolate or raisins, do they?" Did Addie even know Teddy had brought the cookies over? She knew chocolate was toxic for dogs and would never willingly feed it to Radar. She might be afraid of dogs, but she would never harm one.

"No. Addie looked up a bunch of dog recipes and used the best one."

"Dog recipes? You mean those are dog cookies?"

"Yeah, but Addie says it's okay for people to eat them too. I tried one and it was kinda yucky." He made a face. "I told her they were pretty bad, but she said it won't kill me. And she said dogs' taste buds are different than ours."

"These aren't really cookies but dog biscuits?"

The boy held the bag up. Radar sat at Teddy's feet, his eyes on the bag. "You can try one if you want. I did."

"So you say, but I think I'll pass." Gabe chuckled, but Addie's gesture made all sorts of mushy stuff happen in his chest. Truth was, he'd missed their company and was through avoiding spending quality time with them. "Why did you and your sister make these?"

"I asked if we could buy some for Radar, and she said making them would be more special. She said it's like when I make stuff during art at school or when the library has arts and crafts. She says she likes those cards better than store-bought." Teddy paused for breath and opened the bag. "Do you think that means they're more special? Do you think Radar will think they're more special?"

"I'm sure Radar will enjoy the ones you baked for him." And Gabe wouldn't be rude enough to refuse them as he had with the cupcakes. He'd sooner eat a dog biscuit than hurt the kid's feelings. And he'd do anything to protect the boy. It didn't matter that he wasn't his own flesh and blood. This bond went deeper than duty.

"Addie says if Radar likes them, we'll fix more for her library thing."

"She's going to feed dog biscuits to the library patrons?"

"Well…they are homemade."

"But—"

Teddy burst out laughing. "Gotcha!"

It seemed the kid had a sense of humor. "Very clever."

"Not really. I said the same thing you did to Addie, and that's what she said. I didn't make it up myself. Can I give one to Radar?"

"Sure. Hold it on your open palm and let him take it."

Teddy did as he was told, and Radar looked to Gabe,

his tongue hanging out of the side of his mouth. He put the dog out of his misery and nodded. Radar gently removed the treat from Teddy's hand and wolfed it down in two bites.

"He liked it." Teddy held up the bag. "Addie said not to give him too many. She said that was for you to decide. You will let him have more, won't you, Mr. Gabe?"

"I will." He nodded solemnly and accepted the bag. "What is your sister doing today?"

"She's cleaning up the mess we made in the kitchen baking the dog biscuits." Teddy hunkered down to pet Radar. "Did you watch any videos about making a race car for Cub Scouts?"

Teddy was looking at him as expectantly as Radar had the bag of homemade dog treats. Although he'd never been a Scout himself, he now knew about all there was to know about the Pinewood Derby. It was a toss-up who was more excited, him or Teddy.

"I did. And I need to be sure I have all the things we'll need before we start building it."

"You mean it? You'll really help me?" Teddy asked, and Gabe nodded. "It's spring break, so I don't have school next week. Do you think we could do it then?"

"I think that can be arranged. Will you be home every day?"

He nodded enthusiastically. "Addie says she's taking vacation days so I don't have to go to the library with her or stay with that Mrs. O'Malley. I told Addie I was old enough to stay by myself, but she says no. What do you think, Mr. Gabe?"

Knowing better than to get in the middle of that, he held up his hands. "I think your sister knows best."

"My mom used to leave me alone, and I was just a little kid then."

Gabe was at a loss for words. What could he say to the boy? That his mother had been irresponsible and Addie was anything but?

"My mom says if I go back to live with her, she promises not to do that again, but she breaks her promises. You won't tell Addie I said that, will you?"

"Well, I—"

"I think our mom likes to break her promises, 'cause she does it all the time."

Gabe shifted in discomfort. "Have you talked to your sister about that?"

He shook his head. "I think Addie believes her because she says Mom can't help it because she's sick. But I'm not a baby. I know she does bad things."

"I think you need to talk to your sister about this."

"I can't."

"Why not?" Gabe asked.

"'Cause it's like when a little kid believes in the Easter Bunny or the tooth fairy. I'm not supposed to tell the adults I know something's a lie."

"Well, I'm not sure it's exactly the same thing. Your sister is an adult," he reminded Teddy.

"I'll think about it, but I don't want to ruin anything for her. Can Radar and I play ball now? Addie says if I do, she'll come and sit on the steps to watch us."

"Sure." And he could sit on the steps with Addie. God, he must have it bad, when lounging on the front stoop with a woman sounded like fun. Huh, it must've been longer than he'd realized since he'd been with someone.

In between deployments, after his pa had died, he'd

stayed on base, hung out with other marines. He'd gone out with women, but those few times could be best described as hookups, nothing resembling a proper relationship.

"Mr. Gabe?"

"I'll put the biscuits away for now. I bought Radar a Frisbee. Would you like to play with that instead of the ball?"

"Okay. Can you show me how to throw it?"

"Sure thing, bud." If someone had told him that he would enjoy showing a seven-year-old how best to throw a Frisbee, he would have thought they were nuts. But being able to share things with Teddy gave him a good feeling. It was not the same as serving his country but important nonetheless.

He may not have appreciated it enough, but his pa had always been there for him, even when he'd messed up and gotten into trouble as a teen. Sure, the old man hadn't lectured, but he'd taken the time to set him straight. He might not have had all the newest gadgets or expensive clothes like the other boys, but his pa had given him what mattered. And now he found he wanted to do that for Teddy. Give him the gift of time, listen to him and let the boy know he was important.

He'd just finished giving Frisbee-throwing pointers when Addie came onto the front stoop. He limped over to the chairs she'd already set up. Radar and Teddy both paused in their game of fetch. Radar's tongue lolled out of the side of his mouth, and Gabe swore the dog wore a smug expression. *Oh man, Bishop, you are losing it.*

"Addie, look. We're playing Frisbee. Mr. Gabe taught us."

"I see that, sweetie."

Addie looked at Gabe and her heart melted. He'd been so patient with Teddy. She needed to be careful or she'd be falling for her neighbor. If it wasn't already too late. Which did not make sense, because she barely knew him.

She noticed he made a face as he lowered himself into the chair.

"How's the knee?"

"Getting better," Gabe replied, adding, "I made a pact with Radar. He's to stay away from porcupines, and I'll refrain from playing basketball."

She loved his sense of humor. "How about a game of trivia instead?"

He raised an eyebrow. "Right now?"

"Unless you can't handle it."

"Bring it."

"You ready?" She rubbed her fingers on her chest and blew on them.

"What two countries share the longest international border?"

"The US and Canada. *Pfft*. You can do better than that." He puffed up his chest and motioned toward his pecs with his open hands. "Get rough. I can take it."

But could she? She remembered those calluses on his hands and wondered what they would feel like in certain other places on her body. *Get back into the game*, she ordered herself. "Who wrote *The Silence of the Lambs*?"

"Look at you. Going all librarian on me." He narrowed his eyes and studied her. "Thomas Harris. Now, how about I quiz you? I like to know exactly what *I'm* getting into."

"Bring it, Marine." She lifted her chin.

"When does the Marine Corps celebrate its birthday?"

"November tenth." She blew on her fingertips.

After playing several more rounds and calling it a draw, Gabe said, "Teddy tells me he's off school next week."

"He is."

"Maybe the three of us could do something. Go for pizza, maybe take Teddy to indoor miniature golf. I think he'd like that."

And so would I. That sounded just fine to her—in fact, more than fine. It sounded like a plan.

The next day was unseasonably warm, so when Teddy dropped by to see if he could help with anything, Gabe suggested they wash the Jeep together. He sensed that Teddy wanted to talk about something.

Although he hadn't thought about it at the time, washing his pa's old heap with him hadn't done a thing to improve its appearance. Washing it had been an excuse to spend time together and for Pa to impart wisdom without appearing to lecture.

"Everyone says you got medals and stuff for bravery in Afghanistan," the boy muttered.

"It's true I was awarded a distinguished service medal, but I was just doing what the marines taught me." Gabe increased pressure as he rubbed the soapy sponge over the hood and side panels. What was he supposed to say to the kid? The last thing he wanted was to glorify war, but neither did he want to lie. "I'm not sure I'd call doing my job being brave, though."

"Oh." Teddy's shoulders slumped, and he scuffed the ground with the toe of his sneaker.

"Why did you ask, bud?"

Teddy lifted his bony shoulders and let them drop. "I thought maybe you could teach me."

"To be brave?"

The kid nodded.

"What makes you think you're not already?"

Gabe thought about the burn scars on the boy's hands and arms but didn't want to call attention to them. Did the other kids pick on him for that? Gabe knew firsthand how cruel other children could be. He recalled the first time someone teased him because he didn't have a mother. As if he were to blame for her death when he was six. Teddy was staring at his feet. Did he get teased for living with his sister? "Have kids been bullying you for something?"

"Not me but my friend Sam. Some bigger kids called him 'dummy' because he can't talk." Teddy shrugged again. "It's not his fault. He got hit by a car when he was really little, and that's how come he can't talk. But he's a real good LEGO builder."

Gabe nodded, proud of Teddy for befriending Des and Natalie's son, Sam. Before spending time with Teddy, he wouldn't have thought it possible to feel like this about a boy who wasn't his biological son. He had to swallow to dislodge the lump in his throat before he could speak. "You don't need to talk to assemble LEGO bricks, huh?"

Teddy's face brightened. "Yeah. He put together an airport set all by hisself, and he's real good at finding the pieces we need in the big bucket."

"Did you tell your teacher about the other boys?"

He shook his head vigorously. "They said if I snitched, they'd know it. Addie says that if you stand up to bullies, they will back down. But girls sure are different, ya know what I mean?"

Gabe cleared his throat to stop the laugh that threatened to emerge. "I think I do, bud. Can you get the hose and hand it to me?" Gabe pointed to where he'd left the implement. He felt as though he were tiptoeing his way through a minefield. He was honored Teddy had come to him, but he worried about saying the wrong thing. What did he know about giving advice to a kid, really? Would he have automatically known what to say if his own son had lived? Would having raised him from infancy given him special insight, or would he have the same fear of messing up, saying the wrong thing?

Teddy ran over to the hose and picked it up by the nozzle and handed it over. "Girls say mean things and pull each other's hair and stuff, but us guys don't do that, do we?"

"Sometimes, bud. But I don't think your sister wants you to get in trouble for fighting either. I could give you tips on how to defend yourself if someone tries to start a fight with you."

Teddy shrugged. "I learned to do that pretty good in one of the places I went to before I came to live with Addie."

Gabe winced at Teddy's matter-of-fact tone. They had a lot in common, because circumstances had made both of them vulnerable as children. In very different ways, of course. He had never been in any physical danger, just suffering dented pride at having to accept charity. Teddy, however, had suffered much worse and had the scars to prove it. What else had the boy been through in his relatively short life? No wonder

Addie was so protective. "Okay. Then what are you asking me?"

"Teach me how to be brave. Whenever I stand up to those bigger kids, I feel... I feel..." He glanced around as if afraid someone would hear him. "I'm scared."

"Being brave doesn't mean you're not scared. Hel—" He cut himself off before he swore, adding, "*Heck*, I was scared most of the time in Afghanistan."

The boy's eyes grew larger behind the lenses of his glasses. "You were?"

Gabe nodded and adjusted the nozzle. "Being scared has nothing to do with bravery, Teddy. Sounds like you were being courageous when you stood up for your friend Sam."

"How was I brave if I was scared the whole time?" Teddy shook his head and hunched his shoulders forward.

"Facing your fears and not giving in to them is what being brave is about."

Teddy scowled. "How can that be true, if you're afraid at all?"

Gabe waved the hose back and forth to rinse the soapsuds off the side of the Jeep. "You said you were afraid, but you still stood up to the boys picking on your friend. I tell you, Teddy, that's the definition of bravery."

Teddy thought for a moment, then smiled. "For real?"

"For real."

Gabe was glad he could help the kid. It gave him a good feeling.

Except what he felt was a heck of a lot more complicated. *Good* didn't even begin to describe his feelings for Teddy and his sister. *Complicated* with a big *C* was more like it.

He was wading into deep water and couldn't be sure of keeping his head above it. If he drowned, he could take Addie and Teddy with him.

Hurting either of them was the last thing he wanted.

CHAPTER ELEVEN

ADDIE PUT UP the Tea & Talk sign she'd laminated on the door of the community room. The meeting was held at the library on a monthly basis, although the name alternated. The vote to name the group had been deadlocked, with no one wanting to give an inch. She laughed. It was nice to think that was one of the most controversial things in her life. She'd been the one who'd come up with the compromise. Every once in a while, she'd put up the wrong sign to see if anyone noticed. Someone always did and called her out on it. She'd act like it had been an honest mistake and correct her error, secretly chuckling to herself.

Despite the hot tempers over the name, good things were accomplished by the group. They discussed projects that benefited the residents of the town. At Christmas, they decorated an "angel tree" at the library, where children were allowed to hang holiday wishes. Then benefactors would select a paper angel and fulfill what was written on it. The majority of the messages were from underprivileged children or from parents who couldn't afford to give presents that year to their youngsters. But the library also partnered with adult social services to grant the wishes of elderly people with limited means or no close relatives.

With the porcupine incident and school break behind her, she'd given up trying to interest Gabe in today's meeting. They'd been getting along so well she didn't want any controversies to threaten their budding friendship. She had to admit, at least to herself in the dead of the night when she couldn't sleep, how much she'd grown to care about Gabe in such a short time.

What if he didn't share her growing feelings? Or panicked and pushed her away? She needed to protect Teddy from getting hurt if he grew too attached to Gabe. The children always suffered when the adults mismanaged their relationships. She didn't want her brother to become collateral damage.

She'd just set a stack of the minutes she'd printed out from last month's gathering on a small table by the door when someone bumped into her. It was her friend Natalie.

"You were deep in thought." Natalie grinned. "Does it have anything to do with what's been happening with you and our war hero?"

Addie tried to act innocent. "What do you mean?"

"I heard you and Teddy were seen with Gabe at the pizza parlor. And that he and Teddy were playing video games."

Addie cursed her light complexion. She didn't need to see a mirror to know she was blushing like some schoolgirl. "Well, he does live next door to me, so our being seen together isn't exactly notable."

Except it was more than that and she was worried. What if Gabe didn't share her growing feelings? Was she strong enough to protect her and Teddy from heartbreak? Teddy wasn't the only one who'd fallen in love. She drew in a sharp breath. Oh my God, she'd fallen in love with Gabe. It was too late for both of them and she—

"Earth to Addie. Are you even listening to me?" Natalie bumped her again. "I said that's not what I heard."

"What? What have you heard?"

"You were seen playing mini golf, and I also heard something about you and him at the vet. For someone who doesn't like dogs, you going with him to Dr. Greer seems like something."

"I told you I don't dislike dogs… I just exercise a healthy dose of caution around them." But not even she believed that statement at this point.

"Uh-huh," Natalie said and made a noise in her throat.

Addie sighed. "Gabe's dog and Teddy have bonded." And she and Gabe had bonded, too…like she never had with a man before.

"Considering how hot Gabe is, I'd say that's fantastic. Gives you an excuse to hang out. Or am I missing something?"

"You're not missing anything. It's a good thing, Teddy spending time with a guy like Gabe and a dog like Radar."

"So?"

"I'm not sure getting involved with someone right now is in our best interest." That was her go-to excuse. Like telling Teddy they couldn't afford a dog. She could count the number of dates, let alone actual relationships, she'd had on one hand.

Probably accounts for the reason you're still a virgin.

"Because of the upcoming custody hearing?"

"Yeah." Not to mention the whole I'm-still-a-virgin thing. Admitting her fear of dogs was one thing. Admitting she was like some old maid from one of those historical romances her Harlequin ladies were always checking out was another matter. She wasn't even quite sure how she'd gotten to be twenty-three and not done it. Maybe thinking in euphemistic terms like *done it* would explain it. She felt like some sort of throwback, and she didn't even have the threat of being labeled with a scarlet letter as an excuse.

Admitting her cynophobia to Gabe was hard enough... Imagine admitting this! What would he think of her? Would he finally see her as too young and put an end to their growing friendship? How would that affect Teddy? Her little brother would hate to be cut off from Radar and Gabe.

"Maybe you being in a relationship would help you relax and open up a bit," Natalie suggested.

"Being married or engaged might, but shacking up with my neighbor, not so much."

Natalie clucked her tongue. "Well, sure, when you put it like that..."

"How else would I put it? Besides, my first responsibility is to Teddy." She refused to have boyfriends or even father figures coming in and out of his life. She didn't want him growing up thinking that was how men behaved around women. Sure, not all relationships succeeded, but having revolving-door ones wasn't what she wanted to teach him either.

"Not to the extent that you should forgo having a life for yourself. We all make sacrifices for our children, but self-martyrdom isn't going to help anyone."

"I know, but not all of us can easily find a great guy like Des." How hard had she actually looked? Even when their mom wasn't using, a lot of the care for Teddy had fallen on her. Or had Addie simply used their mother's addiction as an excuse after seeing so many unhealthy attachments? She had to admit that going on a few casual dates would hardly harm Teddy or give him the wrong idea.

Natalie hooked her arm through Addie's and sighed. "He is pretty wonderful."

Addie laughed and nodded. Her friend was definitely smitten with the former naval lieutenant. Somehow Natalie and Sam had managed to turn the town scrooge into a family man. They even ran a successful hippotherapy business on their farm on the edge of town.

Natalie pulled out a covered container from the tote bag she had and opened the cover.

Addie looked up from measuring grounds into the coffeepot, her mouth already watering. "Ooh, what did you bring this month?"

"I baked some cranberry bars."

"And Des didn't eat them all?" Addie knew Natalie's husband had a sweet tooth.

"Ha! I had to make a double batch or he wouldn't have let me out of the house."

"He isn't coming?" She set the coffee to brew.

"No. He's still swamped with orders for his crushed glass ornaments." Natalie pulled out a seat. "What's on the agenda for today?"

"Expansion of our shut-in meals program." Addie sat next to her friend.

"Are there people we've missed?"

"Not people but pets. What if we expanded it to include their animals too?"

People started filing into the meeting. After greetings were exchanged and everyone sat, Addie began explaining the suggested program revisions.

"You want to bring meals for dogs?" someone asked.

Addie grinned. "Not meals. Dog and cat food. We could bring dry and canned."

"What made you think of this?"

Addie shook her head. "I didn't really think of it myself... I read an article about it and thought it was a good idea. The piece I saw was about dogs, but I think we should include cats. I know some of our seniors have both." In reality, though, she knew what had sparked the idea. *Gabe and Radar*.

Marian Benedetti, an avid cozy-mystery reader, with a preference for the ones having covers featuring cats, lifted her eyebrows at Addie, a smile playing about her mouth. "So, this has nothing to do with a certain hunky hero being seen around town with a dog?"

"Absolutely not." Uh-oh. She may as well have announced to these meddling ladies that she had the hots for Gabe. Yeah, the skepticism around the table was palpable now. "Gabe isn't a senior citizen, nor does he need anyone's help to feed his dog."

"Oh, on a first-name basis, are we?"

Of course we are. We're both adults and this isn't a Jane Austen novel. The sarcastic reply came bubbling up, but she clamped her lips around it. She didn't want to alienate any of these people, even though she did wish they'd mind their own business.

She drew in a calming breath. "As I was saying, I know Ogle helps deliver meals to people who can't make it to the weekly luncheons at the church. I'm sure he wouldn't mind taking dog or cat food too."

A few people asked questions and Addie made some notes. "We'll talk to him. We should check with Pastor Cook. We might be missing some seniors, or there may be some who feed themselves but could benefit from the extra help with pet food. I've noticed some people boxing up some of their meal at the weekly luncheons at the church. I always thought it was so they could have the leftovers for supper or the next day, but I sometimes wonder how many save some of it for their pets."

"See what you started? And I thought you didn't like dogs." Natalie playfully bumped shoulders with Addie.

Addie felt heat rise in her face. "It's not that."

Since confessing to Gabe about her fear of dogs, she didn't feel as embarrassed to admit it aloud. Gabe didn't laugh or pity her. Instead, he helped her. Like they were comrades in arms—or partners in life. When Natalie gave her a questioning look, Addie shrugged. "I was bitten as a kid and have carried a fear of dogs ever since."

Natalie nodded, her expression understanding. "That's understandable."

It was, wasn't it? Why had she always tried to keep her phobia a secret? Maybe it had more to do with what had happened *after*—her mother's response to her injury—than the actual dog bite. The attack had made her afraid of canines, but what had happened as a result had made her afraid to admit the weakness. Because of her injuries, social services had been called. Addie had felt the need to take on the burden of responsibility for having her and her mom come under such scrutiny.

As if admitting things or asking for help was wrong. Maybe it was time to place the guilt where it belonged. With Michelle, who was the parent.

Addie shook her head to clear her thoughts and listened as Ellie McBride talked about helping the seniors at the skilled nursing facility feel more involved in town activities.

"Maybe we can have a weekly activity session at the library. Addie?"

"You mean like the story hour we have for the kids?" She began making notes as Ellie explained her ideas.

A disturbance caused Addie to glance up from her note taking. Gabe hovered in the doorway, looking around hesitantly at everyone. The pencil in her hand snapped in half as their eyes met across the room. Did she possess the ability to hide her newly acknowledged feelings of love, or was it written all over her face?

Natalie leaned closer. "I thought you said he wasn't coming."

"That's what he told me," Addie whispered back.

Gabe paused before entering the room. Did he really want to join them? He was doing this because, as much as he'd hated being the object of charity as a kid, the people of Loon Lake were kind, generous people, and ignoring them now that he didn't need their help would be rude. But he'd considered staying home because he didn't want the attention or the exposure.

Yeah, okay, Addie had wanted him to get involved. Coming to the meeting had nothing to do with the disappointment that had briefly shadowed her eyes when he'd refused her invitation. He'd remembered she'd worn the same expression when he'd turned away the cupcakes.

What was it about her and her expressive blue eyes that made him want to avoid disappointing her? It wasn't as if he owed her anything. But he had to admit to himself that something about being with her and Teddy had softened his heart. He wanted to spend as much time with them as possible, even if that meant getting more involved with the town and their nosy neighbors.

Before he could retreat, Ogle Whatley had spotted him and was heading across the room toward him. Too late to turn back now. As well as owning Loon Lake General Store with his wife, Tavie, Ogle owned the local towing and repair garage.

"So good to see you back safe and sound, son." Ogle grabbed him in one of those guy hugs. Letting go and stepping back, the older man said, "Glad you could make it to the meeting. Our Addie didn't think you were going to be here. She mentioned that you've been busy with repairs and upgrades to Grace Pierce's place."

Gabe frowned, trying to place the name.

"Grace was Natalie's grandmother. She left the place to Natalie when she passed away," Addie said as she came to stand next to him, bringing her fresh scent with her. He still hadn't quite figured out how she always smelled like grapefruit. Shampoo, maybe? Whatever it was, it had him spellbound.

"Sorry I haven't gotten over to see you since you've been back," Ogle was saying.

"That's okay. I wouldn't have expected you to go out of your way."

"As much as your dad helped me, coming to see you was the least I could do. Of course, I may have ulterior motives."

"My pa helped you out?" Why didn't he know about this?

"I like to keep my eye on some of our vets and offer up what I can whenever necessary. Your dad started by repairing a snowblower for one of my Korean vets. Then when a case of gout curtailed some of my activities, he took over my route."

"Route?" He tried to recall his pa mentioning any of this and couldn't. Guilt burned in his gut that he hadn't made the effort to get home more often before his father had passed away. He owed his pa for trying his best as a single parent. It was too late to repay his father, but maybe he could pay it forward in another way.

"Not everyone can make it to the weekly luncheons for one reason or another, and I make it a point to deliver a meal. Not to mention the missions Tavie sends me on. Your dad took over those missions too."

"He did?"

Ogle nodded. "He was the first person she called to help when she needed it."

Gabe straightened his shoulders. Knowing his pa had been someone people turned to for help filled him with pride. "I didn't realize how involved he was."

"Yeah, he said how proud he was of what you were doing and wanted to help out our veterans. I sure do miss him."

"So do I."

Ogle clapped him on the shoulder. "Like I said, he preened like a peacock over your service and all that you did."

Despite the sudden thickening in his throat, the tightness in his chest eased. Maybe he hadn't disappointed his pa after all.

"Too bad your dad won't be here for the parade, but I know how proud he was of you."

Gabe swallowed. Ogle's expression was open and honest. Had his pa gotten over his initial disappointment at his son picking the military over—? Wait. "What parade?"

Ogle chuckled, his Santa Claus–like belly jiggling. "We still have a parade for Memorial Day, and of course you're going to be our grand marshal."

"I am?" He groaned.

This was exactly why he hadn't wanted to come to this meeting. Nor did he want to get involved. All this hero talk made him uncomfortable. Anything he'd done was far from heroic. He couldn't even take credit for Radar. Tom was the one who'd rescued the dog and had even devised the plan to bring him to the US. All Gabe had done was honor his friend's dying wish.

Guilt ate at him to think he was enjoying the companionship and comfort from Radar when it was Tom who should be doing it. And he'd left his wife for the military after they'd lost their child. Was that the behavior of a hero?

Addie and Teddy should watch out; he was bound to let them down too. No matter how much he was coming to care for them both.

Gabe stayed to help Addie clean up after the meeting. She appreciated his presence and the fact he'd stuck around.

"I have to admit I was shocked when you showed up," she said as she locked the room.

He shrugged. "I gave it some thought and decided you had a point. If I'm going to be around for a while, I should try and assimilate."

"I'm glad you came."

He smiled, warmth flooding his body at her words. "I got to see your official librarian persona."

"I guess I need to confess that I'm only a library assistant, since I haven't graduated yet. I quit after my first year. But I'm taking online classes."

"What made you want to be a librarian?"

"I always considered the library to be my sanctuary when I was a kid. And I wanted to be able to give other kids, and everyone else in the community, that type of positive experience."

Gabe felt the sting of guilt at how he'd grown up, not regarding his home as a sanctuary but instead feeling ashamed of where they'd lived. That front yard full of dirt, weeds and rusting hulks. At least his home, as embarrassing as it might have been for him, had never been a place to fear or feel unsafe, like theirs was for Addie and Teddy. His pa may have struggled with low-paying jobs, but he had never raised his hand in anger at his son or abandoned him to use drugs. As a matter of fact, since his return, Gabe realized he was seeing his father in a whole new light. Instead of being an object of scorn or pity as Gabe had always feared, his dad had been genuinely liked and admired by the residents of Loon Lake. And rather than just accepting charity, his father had worked hard to give back to the community and veterans. Gabe now felt ashamed of his feelings back then. But even though he couldn't change his past, he knew he could change his future—maybe be like his pa, going from taking help in the past to giving back now.

"Were…?" He cleared his throat and started again. "Were things always so bad for you as a kid?"

"Only when she was using. There were times when she'd get clean, and things would be good for a while. But she always had trouble finding a job that paid enough, so we tended to live in sketchy areas."

"You didn't grow up in Loon Lake?"

"No. Nothing like this. I used to pass by streets like this one and wish I could live there."

Welcome to the club, he thought, but said, "You must be proud that you can bring Teddy up in a place like this."

"Yes, I was so relieved to get the job here. Everyone said I could make more money working at a bigger library, but for me, it wouldn't be worth it. Despite what I sometimes say, I consider Loon Lake a wonderful place." She glanced at him, her cheeks dusted with pink. "Although, I guess if you're looking for trouble, you can find it, even in a place like this."

"Ah, I see some of my youthful transgressions have been discussed."

"They didn't keep you out of the marines, so I have to assume they weren't that bad. Or you simply didn't get caught."

He grinned. "Maybe a little of both."

"Is that supposed to make me feel better?" she said.

"It doesn't?"

She sighed. "I know you're not a bad influence on Teddy—far from it—but I need to keep a close eye on him. I want him to grow up without getting into trouble. I know I have a tendency to smother him, but I can't help it. Maybe once the judge rules on permanent custody, I'll be able to relax a little." He raised an eyebrow at her, and she laughed before sobering. "Or maybe not."

"Is it because of those scars?" he asked.

"I can't help feeling that if I had been there, I might have prevented it."

"What made you comfortable enough to leave?" As soon as the words were out of his mouth, he regretted them. Although she was obviously trying to hide it, she'd been hurt by his question. Those words probably sounded more like an accusation than a simple question. Time for damage control. "Addie, I didn't mean that the way it—"

She held up a hand. "You're right. I never should have left."

He grabbed the hand she was holding up. "No. I need you to listen to me before you get it in your head that I was accusing you of anything. I'm not. You're Teddy's sister. None of what happened to him was your fault. It wasn't your responsibility to protect him. It was your mother's."

"But I knew what she could be like. I should have—"

"Didn't you say that she'd been clean for a long time?"

"She had been. At that point, anyway. I honestly don't know what happened after I left." She shook her head. "Well, I do," she muttered, bitterness lacing her tone. "She met some guy and he was a recreational user. My mother doesn't seem to understand that she's not a recreational user. Just like an alcoholic can't have just one drink. From what I can gather, he dumped her when she started using again, which only compounded the situation." She choked back a sob. "I should have stayed."

"Why? What could you have done? Honestly?"

She gave him an are-you-nuts look. "I could have prevented him from getting scalded."

"Are you saying I should have known that Tom was going to be killed that day he walked into that store?" he retorted.

"No, of course not."

He put his arm around her and held her close. "See? It doesn't mean we should stop ourselves or other people from living their lives."

"He's been wanting to walk home from the bus stop alone, and I can't quite work up to that," Addie said. "I keep thinking of all the bad things that could happen."

"Bad things happen in this world, and we can't prevent them all."

"I do the best I can to prepare him for them."

"True, but you might want to let him make some mistakes on his own," he said softly. He didn't add that it might help the boy cope in the future when the mistakes got bigger. No matter what that doctor had told him about Tracy losing the baby, he'd always wonder if he could have done something to prevent it.

She sighed. "You're right, but the thought of him walking home all alone from the bus stop..."

"Maybe we can work something out," Gabe suggested. He had an idea.

"Like what?"

"Well, I know the old lady across the street keeps a pretty keen eye out for the goings-on in our duplex.

Are there any other people who could, say, be on the lookout at the time he's due to walk home?"

"There's a retired widower between here and the bus stop."

Gabe nodded. "We could check with him... Maybe he'd be willing to take a look out his window too. Would that make you feel a little more secure?"

"That might just work."

CHAPTER TWELVE

"Do you know what kind of dates your sister likes to go on? Or if she ever has any?" Gabe asked Teddy and winced. Huh, that question had sounded a bit more subtle when he'd practiced it in his head. Not that he'd had much experience discussing dating with a seven-year-old. After setting up a tool bench in the carport, he and Teddy were working on his wooden car for the Pinewood Derby, turning the block into something that resembled a race car. He'd helped the boy make a paper pattern so they could cut the block into the shape Teddy wanted.

For the past week, Teddy had been walking home by himself from the bus stop on the days that Addie was home. When she worked, the school bus dropped him off at the library, where he did his homework, read or helped the younger kids on craft days.

Teddy scrunched up his face as he cut the paper. "Whaddaya mean dates?"

Yeah, what did he mean? He demonstrated how to put the pattern against the wood and trace. "I was just wondering if there's anything you think your sister would consider special."

"Special?" Teddy's tongue sneaked out between his

lips as he concentrated on using the pencil to draw around the pattern onto the wood.

After Teddy finished tracing, Gabe clamped the wood to the table they were using. He got out safety goggles and a child-sized pair of work gloves.

Teddy looked askance at the safety items. "What's that for?"

"For you. I made sure my marines were properly equipped before sending them on a mission."

"You mean I'm like one of your marines?" the boy asked. Gabe nodded and Teddy grinned from ear to ear.

Gabe used the coping saw to get the cuts started before handing the little saw to Teddy. "Here. You take over and finish the cutting."

He helped Teddy keep the blade straight as the boy sawed through the wood. It took a while, but the block eventually turned into a wedge shape. "Now we need to sand the rough edges."

Gabe demonstrated how to rub the sandpaper over the edges.

"It sure takes lots of sanding, huh?" Teddy held up the sanded piece and turned it over in his hands. "This is really cool. Tell me again why we need to put those weight thingies in it?"

"Because a heavier car will run faster. Do you know what inertia is?"

"Uh-uh."

Gabe scratched the stubble on his cheek. "Your car needs to build up speed going downhill to sustain it along the flat part. It will eventually slow down on the flat part, but if it's going really fast, it should make it to the finish line before it stops."

"So, we can put lots of weight on it?"

Gabe shook his head. "Sorry, bud, but your car can't weigh more than five ounces total, so we'll get as close as we can without going over."

He felt frustrated at not being able to get any information out of Teddy, even though he knew it wasn't realistic or fair to be pumping the kid for it. He supposed he could approach her friend Natalie, but that sounded embarrassing.

More embarrassing than begging a child for the details of his big sister's love life?

He'd discovered Addie's birthday was coming up, and he wanted to take her on an honest-to-goodness date. What he and Addie had been doing so far on their own could be classified only as hanging out. They'd done a lot of that lately. When Teddy was in school or off with friends, they worked more on getting her increasingly comfortable with Radar. When Teddy was there, they tossed the ball around, watched movies, ordered pizza.

As much as he enjoyed time spent with Teddy, he wanted some alone time with Addie. He wanted to explore what had started growing between them, maybe take it to the next level. Only way to accomplish that was with adult time.

"...for me, Mr. Gabe?"

Gabe glanced up from the package of decorative derby-car accessories he was attempting to open. "I'm sorry, bud—what?"

Teddy pointed to the package. "You got that 'specially for my car?"

"Sure. We want it to look cool while it's going fast."

The boy made an inarticulate sound and jumped off

the stool he'd been perched on. Reaching out, he threw his arms around Gabe.

"Thank you," the boy said, his words muffled in Gabe's midsection.

Gabe blinked and swallowed against the clog in his throat. He patted Teddy on the back awkwardly. "You're entirely welcome."

Radar wandered over and whined, refusing to be left out.

The boy pulled back, surreptitiously rubbing his nose on his sleeve. Giving the dog a hug too, Teddy giggled when Radar repaid him with sloppy kisses. He wiped his face and went back to his stool, then bent his head over his wooden car as he continued to sand it. Gabe blinked a few more times, and once the package came into focus, he finished opening the accessories. They worked in silence for a few minutes.

"Why was you asking about Addie?" Teddy asked suddenly.

"Oh, I was just wondering if anyone has taken her somewhere that she really liked. You know, it's her birthday coming up, and I thought I should know what she enjoys doing." He should be ashamed of himself, grilling Teddy about Addie's dates.

"You mean like the time she went with Mr. Ogle to that petting zoo? She said they were going to see about getting animals for the live nativity. She said that was a lot of fun, but they ended up using Brody Wilson's cow and his alpacas. I don't know if that counts."

Gabe barely restrained a chuckle. He should have realized that—

"Oh wait. I know. I know. She said she'd like someone to take her to the opera."

Opera? Attending the opera was about the last thing Gabe wanted to do. *Is this really about you? Or about giving Addie what she wants?* She'd sacrificed so much for her brother that she deserved something special for herself. "Well...if you're sure."

Teddy's head bobbed up and down. "Yup! I heard her say so herself."

"Thanks." He nodded, but his response lacked the enthusiasm of Teddy's.

After Teddy had gone home, Gabe opened up his laptop and checked. Looked like the Boston Lyric Opera was the closest to Loon Lake. He checked on dates and times. He hesitated a moment, staring at the Purchase Tickets button. Addie's sweet face appeared before him and he hit the selection. He'd survived basic training, numerous combat deployments and a bomb blast. How bad could a few hours at the opera be?

Addie made sure she oohed and aahed over Teddy's car. He and Gabe had worked on it for two days. Although the little racer was impressive, she could tell Gabe had allowed her brother to do much of the work himself. Just one more reason she was falling in love with Gabe. And she was. She might still be coming to terms with her feelings, but she couldn't deny the truth any longer.

Teddy ran to his room to put his car on his bookshelf.

"Thank you for helping him," she told Gabe.

He shrugged. "I enjoyed it as much as he did. I came back with him because I have something to ask you."

"Me?"

"I know your birthday is coming up and I wanted

to do something special. Since you will soon be officially twenty-three. No more *almost* about it," he said and chuckled.

She shivered as the sexy sound made the hairs on the back of her neck stand at attention. "I've given up on the dog-years thing. So, what did you have in mind?"

He licked his lips and shifted slightly. "It, ah, would just be the two of us. If that's okay with you."

"Absolutely," she said, then felt a twinge of guilt over how quickly she'd forsaken Teddy. "I mean, I—"

"No guilt. You deserve to be spoiled a little." He reached out and cupped her cheek.

She leaned into his touch. "Thanks. Do I get a hint at what this surprise is?"

"I can tell you a little bit about it, and if you're still interested, we can finalize plans."

"O-okay." Still interested? What could he have planned? Her heart sped up. Did his plans involve taking things to the next level? Because hers did.

"It will involve going to Boston."

"I like Boston." Maybe they were on the same wavelength.

"Enough to stay overnight?" He raised an eyebrow and she nodded. "I can book a suite…separate bedrooms if…if, ah—"

"That won't be necessary." She shook her head.

His Adam's apple bobbled as he swallowed. "Okay. We can come back that night. It will be late but—"

"No, no. I meant one room is fine." Good grief. She was making a mess of this. Well, wasn't every day that a woman lost her virginity, so some nervousness was expected. Right? At least, that was the plan. "For both of us, that is."

Relief suffused his features, and he gave her a seductive lopsided grin. He leaned down and—

"Addie! Hey, Addie," Teddy called from the other room.

He touched her nose with his. "I'll go and make the hotel reservation."

"And I'll call Natalie to see if Teddy can stay with them."

"Good idea." His gaze met hers and he hesitated.

"Addie?" Teddy called again.

She watched him go and couldn't stop grinning as she went to see what Teddy wanted. She didn't know what Gabe's surprise was, but she knew how the evening would end. Even knowing she would have to confess her secret to him didn't diminish her excitement.

"Where are we going?" Addie asked for the umpteenth time after dropping Teddy off at the Gallaghers' to spend the night with Des, Natalie and Sam.

"To Boston," Gabe replied for the umpteenth time.

The stars must be in alignment because her birthday and the opera fell on the same day. Plus, she'd been granted the day off from work. A sure sign their friendship was evolving into something more.

"I know *that*, but you said later tonight was a surprise." She shifted in the passenger seat to face him. "How will I know how I'm supposed to dress if I don't know where we're going?"

He headed toward the interstate, wondering if he should have come out and told her, but the thought of surprising her had appealed to him. "You said you packed a nice dress."

"I did." She sank back into the seat. "You know you

didn't have to splurge on a suite in the city. You could have booked something in one of those budget places by the highway on the outskirts."

He shrugged. Part of his reasoning had been to avoid being presumptuous. A suite with separate sleeping arrangements seemed a safer bet. He still wasn't sure if they'd be utilizing the second bedroom. Either way, he intended for this time to be special. It was about Addie, not him. "It's your birthday."

After he'd driven through town and picked up the interstate, he reached over and took her hand and interlocked their fingers.

"Thank you." She squeezed his hand. "No one has ever done anything special like this for me."

Her words reminded him of Teddy's, and he smiled, happy he could make her feel as special as she was.

Gabe negotiated the heavy Boston traffic acutely aware of the woman seated beside him. He had trouble swallowing, as if his mouth was full of sand kicked up by rotor wash in the desert.

He couldn't remember feeling this nervous about being with a woman, even in high school. Was it because ignorance had been bliss back then? Or was it because his feelings for Addie outstripped anything he'd previously felt, including those for Tracy?

He pulled into the parking garage for the hotel, glancing over at Addie before he reached for the ticket. She smiled but her lips trembled ever so slightly. Was she nervous as well?

After parking the Jeep and helping her out of the car, he shouldered their overnight bags and rested his hand on the small of her back as they headed for the elevator.

This was either going to be epic or a giant flop, he thought as he pressed the button for the lobby and the doors slid shut.

"Good afternoon," the hotel clerk greeted them as they stepped forward in the line. "Sorry for the wait."

"Looks like you're having a busy weekend," Gabe said and pulled out his wallet.

The clerk nodded. "There's a lot of people in town for *La Bohème*. They're only doing several performances this season."

Addie nodded. "Most critics consider it his best."

Gabe handed his charge card to the desk clerk and turned to Addie. "Who?"

"Puccini."

Damn, but he was in over his head with all this opera stuff. Ask him batting averages of this year's starting lineup for the Red Sox and he'd sound knowledgeable. But this? He signed the papers the clerk handed over.

"He's the one who composed it," Addie said. "It's not just an opera but a symphony too."

Huh, maybe this was a good thing after all. He took her hand as they made their way across the lobby to the bank of elevators. "So, you really enjoy this opera stuff?"

She shrugged. "I've never been. Never gave much thought to it. Why?"

"But you enjoy listening to it?" he asked as they stepped into the elevator.

"Can't say that I do."

The elevator doors slid shut, and he narrowed his eyes, suspicion thumping in his chest. Why had Teddy told him this was what she'd wanted more than anything for her birthday? Had he been had by Teddy, or had the boy made an honest mistake?

"You seemed to know a lot about this Puccini guy."

Grinning, she tucked her hand around his arm. "Haven't you learned by now that I know a little bit about a lot of things?"

The elevator glided to a stop and the doors opened. "Are you saying you're *not* into opera?"

"Sorry to disappoint you, but the only opera I knew before was from watching an old *Seinfeld* episode." She squeezed his arm before letting go. "Is this my surprise? Are you a closet opera fan?"

He inserted the key card into the lock. The electronic mechanism whirred and clicked. He pushed open the door and indicated for her to go before him.

"What a gorgeous room," she said and twirled around, arms held wide.

"About this opera thing…" He shut the door and set their bags down. May as well come clean. "I've already bought tickets."

She dropped her arms and went to him. "I admit I am surprised by your choice. I'd have figured you more for baseball and hot dogs. But it'll be great."

Yeah, great. What he wouldn't give for the crack of a bat and a cold beer. He groaned and rubbed a hand over his face. Served him right for taking dating advice from a seven-year-old.

"Teddy," he muttered sotto voce.

She tilted her head. "What's he got to do with all this?"

"He's the reason we have opera tickets." He sighed. "I asked for his advice, and that is what he suggested."

She burst out laughing. "I'm sorry, but—"

"Yeah." He nodded.

She threw her arms around him. "This is the best thing anyone has done for me. I feel like Cinderella."

His arms held her close when she would have pulled back. "But—"

She cut off his protests with her lips on his.

"Best birthday ever," she said against his lips.

Not about to let a chance to kiss Addie pass him by, he pressed his lips to hers and coaxed her mouth open. Their tongues dueled and sent his pulse surging through his veins.

He hated to pull away, but blood was starting to leave his brain and he wanted her to enjoy every bit of the evening before things got out of hand.

"I made dinner reservations at an Italian restaurant nearby," he told her and rested his forehead against hers.

"Then I'd better get dressed." She started for one of the bedrooms but turned before entering. "I thought you were going to get us a regular room."

He shrugged. "They were booked up, so I kept the suite."

Dimples scored her cheeks. "Okay. Just checking."

That smile made him weak in the knees.

Later that evening when he was sitting listening to music he didn't understand in shoes that pinched, he thought about that kiss and how the evening would end.

He reached for Addie's hand. Maybe Teddy's advice wasn't such a disaster after all. Making a mental note to tell her again how beautiful she looked tonight, he squeezed her hand and she turned to him and smiled.

* * *

Although she'd enjoyed her very first opera, during the stirring performances, Addie's thoughts kept straying to how this evening might end. He'd kept the suite, but she didn't think there'd be a need for the second bedroom.

The entire evening was overshadowed by what would be coming at the end of it. At least, she hoped it was coming. Should she tell Gabe? If he changed his mind, then what?

Stop being such a drama queen, she cautioned herself. People didn't actually die of embarrassment.

If she didn't tell him, would he be able to figure it out? Were normal guys—not those larger-than-life heroes in books—able to tell?

What was she even thinking? Of course she had to tell him.

And now that they were making their way back to the hotel, one thought kept racing through her mind. *Tell him.* That insistent voice in her head wouldn't be quieted.

But all her good intentions vanished when they entered the common area of their suite and he shut the door, reaching for her.

He brought his mouth down on hers, and she opened immediately for him, her tongue meeting his. Without lifting his mouth from hers, he began walking her backward to the bedroom he'd used to get ready.

Once there, he frowned at her dress. "How does this work?"

Feeling giddy from his kisses, she giggled. "It's a wraparound. See?"

She undid the garment and let it fall open, then

tossed it onto a chair by the bed with much more bravado than she was feeling. Maybe fake-it-till-you-make-it wasn't such a good idea here.

"Mmm, very user-friendly," he said, his eyes widening.

"You can thank Diane von Furstenberg." She waved her hand. "Don't ask."

"Okay." He laughed, shucked his jacket and toed off his leather dress shoes with a deep sigh.

"What?"

"Those pinched," he said and undid his belt.

Oh dear, things were progressing at a faster pace than she'd anticipated. She really needed to confess.

He pulled down his pants while unbuttoning his shirt. He tossed aside the shirt and removed his socks. Clothed in nothing but navy blue boxer briefs, he took her into his arms.

She could feel how ready he was. Physically she was because her panties were soaked from just watching his haste to undress. But the fact she was still thinking about it made her wonder if she was mentally ready. "You're wearing the pink lace bra," he groaned, "I have been having dreams about it."

They fell silent for several minutes as they explored one another's bodies. Addie reveled in being able to run her hands over his impressive chest. She lightly traced several angry-looking scars, her heart aching for him.

She looked up at him. "The blast?"

He nodded, and when he opened his mouth, she put her fingers over it and began kissing each scar.

Groaning, he laid her on the bed. "My turn," he whispered and removed her bra. He sucked on one nipple, then the other. He slowly worked his way down her stomach and circled her belly button with his tongue. His fingers dipped under the waistband of her lace thong, and she shivered with unexpected sensation. But she jerked her head up and out of the delicious delirium...

"Gabe..."

He lifted his head, his pupils flared and dilated. "What is it?"

"There's, uh, something I should probably tell you."

He scooted up so his gaze was even with hers.

When he frowned, she drew in a deep breath, fear coiling in her gut. "I've never...you know..."

She motioned her hand back and forth between them. Talk about embarrassing. She shouldn't have even brought it up. Would he have been able to tell? Did guys even notice those things? It wasn't as if this were one of those Victorian romances where women knew next to nothing. She understood the difference between fantasy and real life. And considering her age, she was a virgin because she'd never had sex, but it had nothing to do with a certain belief. She'd been ready years ago. She'd wanted her first time to be with someone special, and that special someone hadn't come until now.

"Uh, Addie?" he interrupted her musings. "Could you be a little more specific?"

Her face on fire as much from what she'd been thinking as from the situation, she blew out her breath. "I haven't...had sex before. Ever."

He sat up. "You're telling me that you're a virgin?" Shock was written all over his features, and she cringed.

"Yeah. That."

"But you're twenty-three."

"That's why it's a bit embarrassing," she admitted.

"I knew you were too young for me," he muttered and swung his legs over the side of the bed. *No!*

"Now, hold on." She grabbed his arm. "Are you saying you've changed your mind? Is that what's going on here? And how the hell am I too young for you? How do you figure that? I'm twenty-three, no more *almost* about it, and you're thirty. Seven years is nothing."

"I was thinking more in terms of—"

"No," she interrupted, swatting his arm. She knew where this was going and wasn't going to let him get away with it. "You don't get to pull that life-experiences card. I'm sure you suffered a lot of horrific, life-changing things in Afghanistan, but my childhood was not all about Mom, apple pie and family togetherness."

"You're right about your experiences being different from mine, but—" He pressed a finger over her mouth when she opened it. "Let me finish. Yes, I was going to say different, but no less traumatic."

"Okay, but I'm confused. If you agree I'm not some clueless kid, does that mean you want to continue?"

"I definitely want to continue." His gaze met hers, and he made what sounded like a groan deep in his throat. "But I have to be sure. This is a big step for you...bigger than I had imagined when I planned this."

"Well, I need to get rid of my status at some point," she muttered. "I certainly don't want to die a...virgin."

He raised an eyebrow. "Are librarians allowed to use that sort of language? Not to mention all the money you'll be owing the swear jar."

She frowned. "You mean *virgin*?"

"I was referring to that verb you were *thinking* of using as an adjective."

She shook her head. How did…? "But I didn't say it out loud."

His sudden, deep-throated chuckle sent tingles down her spine, and she shivered.

"You didn't have to say the word. It was on your face." He placed his fingertip on her cheek and lightly traced the freckles.

"Don't you want to," she joked, changing the pitch of her voice, "boldly go where no man has gone before?" She wanted him badly, but she wasn't sure how to proceed. It wasn't as if she'd done any of this before.

He burst out laughing. "I'm not sure about the *boldly* part." He frowned. "But you do know your status has nothing to do with how I feel about you and this, right? Whether or not you were a virgin, I'd still want to be with you. I care about you."

"I would hope so."

"You're special, no matter what," he said and lowered his head.

Taking his time, he used his tongue all over her body, licking and teasing parts she had no idea were so erogenous. Who knew the backs of her knees were so sensitive? Or that spot where her neck met her shoulder? His tongue was magic, and he knew how to use it.

"Gabe," she begged. Was that hoarse whisper hers?

"Tell me what you want."

"I don't know what…" She squirmed. "…to ask for."

Evidently he knew, because his fingers found that spot that craved his touch. "Is this it?"

"Yes. Please." She wasn't above begging. "Gabe…"

"Let it happen, Addie."

And she did. She understood the reference to fireworks in those books.

He removed his boxer briefs and scooted up. "Are you ready for me?"

"Yes."

He reached over her to the bedside table and grabbed the condom he'd left there earlier. "These are pre-lubricated, but I don't think we need it. Still, I don't want to hurt you."

"This is the twenty-first century. I know to expect some discomfort the first time."

He rolled the condom on and slowly entered, filling her, but then stopped. Was something wrong? Why had he stopped? Despite the discomfort, she liked the fact he was filling her. She knew physically the act would be similar with someone else, but the fact it was Gabe stretching her made her heart do a little flip-flop.

"Uh, Gabe? I know this is my first time and all, but aren't you supposed to be moving or something?" Why was she expecting him to do it all? "Is it my fault? Am I supposed...? I mean, am I not...?"

"It's me." He groaned. "If I don't do box scores in my head to slow this down, it's gonna be over soon."

"Oh. But that's okay. We've got all night. I mean, in all those books—"

He made a noise that was a cross between a groan and a laugh. "Exactly what books have you been reading?"

"The good ones?"

He laughed and started to move. It ached a bit at first, but then delightful sensations soon began to rocket through her body. "Tell me if anything hurts."

"Want me to raise my left hand like at the dentist?" she gasped. "Sorry—am I killing the mood?"

He grabbed her left hand and brought it to his lips

and kissed her palm. "What happens here is between us, and we can be any way we want."

"Was that a yes or a no to raising my hand?" she teased.

"You tell me to stop and I will."

"Oh no. Please don't stop now that it's getting good."

He lifted up on his elbow to look into her eyes. "Just getting good?"

She smiled dreamily. "It was all good before…very good…excellent."

"And now?"

She ran her fingers through his hair. "What's better than excellent? Transcendental?"

He hooted a laugh.

"Don't stop. I'll keep quiet."

"But, sweetness, if you're quiet, how will I know if I'm being transcendental or not?"

She lifted up and kissed him.

He used his finger to bring her to the brink again and waited until she'd tumbled over before he thrust one last time and cried out her name.

CHAPTER THIRTEEN

AFTERWARD, HE PULLED her into his arms and brushed the hair back from her face. He'd done his best to make it as good for her as it had been for him. But he also knew that was impossible, because no matter how gentle he'd been, she'd experienced discomfort.

She'd thrown him for a loop when she'd admitted this was her first time. He'd been scared but concentrated on making it good for her. In doing so, he'd made it ground shaking for him. For the first time, he'd not only experienced physical satisfaction, but the tenderness of the moment shifted something inside him. So, in essence, it was a first for him too.

An idea occurred to him and he got out of bed. "Be right back. Stay there."

She laughed. "I have no plans to go anywhere."

In the bathroom, he ran warm water onto a washcloth. Back in the bedroom, he showed it to her and gently ran it over her body, kissing and caressing as he went. "This may help if you have some discomfort."

He threw it into the sink after they were done. Crawling back into bed with her, he pulled the covers over them and held her. "Sorry if my surprise was a bit off the mark."

She rubbed her cheek against his chest as she curled into him. "Considering I had a surprise for you too, it's okay. I actually enjoyed it. What about you?"

"Oh, I *definitely* enjoyed it."

She lifted her head to look at his face. "You may well turn into an opera buff."

"Oh. You were talking about the opera."

She laughed and he kissed her nose. A feeling that defied description rose in his chest. He didn't know what to do with all the tender feelings rising up. It was like when Teddy had thrown his arms around him but even more indescribable.

She threw one of her legs over his. "Tell me about your dad. You mentioned a few things but not much. I overheard what Ogle said about him at the meeting."

He kissed the top of her head. "I forgot to thank you for making me go."

She lifted her head. "I did not *make* you go."

He chuckled. "Ah, but you did, because it was either show up or have you disappointed in me."

"Really?"

"Yup. But I'm glad you invited me. Ogle told me things I didn't know about Pa, things I wouldn't have realized on my own."

"What do you mean? You must've known your dad was pretty special."

He wasn't proud of his feelings from back then, but he wanted her to know him, even if it meant telling her things he'd have preferred not to. She meant too much to him now. "I wasn't a very good son."

"I don't believe that for one minute."

"It's true. I was ashamed of where we lived. All

that junk in the front yard and the fact he always had low-paying jobs. What kind of son did that make me?"

"A normal kid. Want to talk about being ashamed…? My mother was an addict who exchanged sex for drugs. As for you and your father, I would say you were embarrassed. I think there's a big difference between that and being ashamed. You said he did the best he could after your mom died, and I heard the caring in your voice and saw it in your eyes."

"I disappointed him." He shook his head, flooded with memories. "His greatest wish for me was to go to college so I could do better than him. Instead, I got a girl pregnant, had to get married and joined the marines. Never made it to college."

"Well, no matter what you say, I heard Ogle saying how proud your dad was. Quit blaming yourself for acting like a teenager when you were eighteen."

"Maybe you should take your own advice," he told her.

"What's that supposed to mean?"

"It means you should quit blaming yourself for what happened to Teddy. If anyone was at fault, and I'm still not sure about that, it would be your mother."

"But if I had been there—"

"Don't." He took both her hands in his and squeezed. "You were a kid yourself."

She made noises with her tongue on the roof of her mouth. "I was eighteen."

"Exactly."

"You were in the marines, taking responsibility, when you were eighteen."

"Actually, I was nineteen when I joined the Corps."

"Because you wanted to provide for yourself and your wife."

He snorted, unable to give himself a break, even if he'd been confronting someone else in the same situation. He'd said they needed to cut themselves some slack. Teenagers often acted their age. "More like running away."

"How is joining the marines running away?"

How often had he run away from those feelings gripping him, threatening to overwhelm him? The fact they'd lost their son—even one he hadn't gotten to know—rubbed him so raw he'd suppressed it, fed himself platitudes.

"Losing the baby changed everything. Tracy changed... I changed. I was sorry about the late-stage miscarriage, but deep down I'm ashamed to admit I was probably relieved. God—" he ran a hand over his scalp "—isn't that a terrible thing to admit?"

"You were both young and tried to do the right thing." She shook her head. "Maybe everything would have worked out. You have no way of knowing and shouldn't beat yourself up over being young."

"So should you. Why is my situation any different than yours?" he shot back.

"Maybe you're right." She heaved a deep sigh. "But I can't believe she divorced you while you were serving your country."

He knew the town had been outraged on his behalf. To his great shame, he'd done nothing to change that. Maybe it was time he did. "That's not totally accurate."

"Oh?"

"History has been known to get rewritten by the folks in Loon Lake."

"Like that children's game of telephone."

He nodded. "Exactly. I came home before deployment, and we pretty much called it quits, so the divorce proceedings were just a formality. Neither of us was happy, and we'd gotten married only for the baby's sake."

"She still shouldn't have done that, in my opinion."

"Don't make me out to be the injured party here. I'm the one who took the coward's way out and left when things got tough."

"Joining the marines for a better future wasn't cowardly. You said yourself how hard it was getting steady employment once the economy took a downturn. You were doing what had to be done to secure a better future."

"I literally abandoned her," he said bluntly. "There's no way to sugarcoat that."

"I hate to say this, but a lot of marriages falter after the death of a child."

"That may be true, but I didn't put enough work into it. Just like playing baseball or going to college, like my pa wanted."

"How old were you when you got married?"

"I had just turned eighteen." He shook his head. "Barely out of high school."

"You did the honorable thing by her. You didn't have to."

"Of course I had to. She was pregnant and…scared."

"Loon Lake might be small-town, but it wasn't the 1950s."

"What're you saying?"

"That I think you acted honorably. And you each

moved on when you realized there was nothing left for you in your marriage. Now you're free to be happy."

She snuggled closer, and pretty soon her breathing had evened out. He lay awake wishing he could be different, be the kind of guy who stuck. For her. And for the kid. But could he ever be the man she wanted him to be?

The next morning, he shifted, trying to ease away from her, but he ended up waking her.

"Sorry about that," he muttered. "You can ignore it."

She laughed. "I thought all guys had a morning—"

He put a finger over her mouth. "This is an Addie one. Not simply a morning one."

She blushed and grinned. "That's nice to know. Are you planning on doing something about it?"

"I thought you might be too sore."

"It's okay," she told him. "Do you have another condom?"

"I may not have been a Cub Scout like Teddy, but I am prepared."

"That's good to know," she said and turned toward him.

Oh God, how he loved this woman, he thought as he pulled her into his arms. His heart began to pound as he realized what he'd just admitted to himself. For a moment he froze, letting that knowledge sink in.

"Gabe? Something wrong?"

He looked into her eyes, saw the worry in them and kissed her forehead.

"No. Nothing's wrong. For once, everything is right." And he set about showing just how right things were with her.

* * *

Gabe was turning onto his street when his phone dinged, indicating a text. He pulled into his driveway and checked the message. It was from Addie, asking him to come ASAP. He frowned. It had been two weeks since their trip to Boston. Despite his fear of letting her down, things had seemed to be going well. They'd been spending all their free time together, doing family things like watching movies on school nights and mini golf on the weekend. He'd even managed to help Teddy with his homework a few times.

The more times they were together, the more he believed he could be in it for the long haul. When he thought about the future, he thought in terms of Addie and Teddy.

With Addie's encouragement, he began studying for his contractor's license.

After parking his Jeep, he didn't even bother to go to his place but let himself into her place. "Addie? What's going on? I got your text."

"In here."

He followed the sound of her voice into the kitchen. She stood by the sink. "I'm so glad you're here."

She looked and sounded relieved to see him, filling him with pride. He went to her and took her into his arms. He patted her back when she sagged against him. "What's wrong? Are you okay?"

She nodded and pulled away. "I just had a bit of a fright."

He wanted to take her back into his embrace. She felt so good, like she belonged, but she backed away. "Tell me."

She took a deep breath. "There's a snake on the step leading to the carport."

"What?" He started to get a queasy feeling in his stomach. He hated snakes. Yeah, a walking Indiana Jones cliché. He'd heard it all before and therefore did his best to keep it hidden. Huh, a lot like Addie with her cynophobia.

"I couldn't find my wallet, and I was going out to see if I'd left it in the car. I opened the door and glanced down, and there it was. Just curled up on the step."

He shrugged. "Sounds to me as if it was simply minding its own business. Not hurting anyone."

"Yeah, well, it can mind its business elsewhere."

"So, you want me to kill a snake because it innocently wandered into your carport?"

"Absolutely not! I don't even like killing bugs. I always feel so guilty after." She stuck out her bottom lip in a pout.

"After?" He had the urge to take that bottom lip between his teeth. *Go for it*, his inner voice urged. Create a distraction and maybe the stupid thing would slither away. Problem solved. "So, you do kill bugs."

"This isn't about whether or not I kill bugs. I'm asking you to deal with the snake."

"Want me to call it an Uber and send it over to Montpelier? Is that far enough away?"

"Go ahead. Make fun."

"You're asking me to risk my life for a snake?"

"Vermont doesn't have venomous snakes… Well, unless you count the handful of timber rattlesnakes over in Rutland County."

"What?" He blinked. "You mean there are poisonous snakes in Vermont?"

"Like I said, there are over in Rut—"

"And I suppose you're going to tell me they respect borders?"

She narrowed her eyes at him, and the speculative glance she gave him had him shifting his weight from one leg to the other.

"Do you have a thing about snakes?" she asked.

He shook his head, unwilling to hand over his man card that easily. "No. I just think they should be allowed their freedom."

"And I agree, as long as it's not anywhere near me." She glared at him, but her eyes contained a mischievous glint. "Ophidiophobia."

He wet his lips and repeated the word. "Hmm. Sounds interesting... What is it?"

She made a noise with her tongue, but a grin lifted her lips. "That's what the fear of snakes is called."

He huffed out a breath. "I am not afraid. It's just a healthy respect."

"Of course," she said and nodded. "Just like I had a healthy respect for dogs."

"That's different," he scoffed, but he returned her grin. His pride wasn't such that he was insulted. Besides, even if he was, she was too cute for him to stay annoyed.

"Oh? How is that different?"

"Snakes don't have fur and big brown eyes."

"Maybe this one does." She pointed to the door. "You should go check it out."

"I'd rather check out something I've been thinking about since your wet T-shirt show."

He leaned forward and brought his lips closer to hers. She parted her lips in anticipation of—

"Addie? Can I—? Whoa." Teddy skidded to a stop in the doorway to the kitchen. "What're you guys doing?"

Gabe closed his eyes and rubbed the back of his neck. Talk about embarrassing. He and Addie had briefly discussed what they were going to tell Teddy about their relationship but hadn't done it yet. Looked like they'd run out of time, but he'd follow her lead.

Addie jumped back and tugged on the front of her shirt. "We—" She cleared her throat. "We were discussing Gabe's fear of—"

"I'm not afraid of—"

"Mr. Gabe ain't afraid of nothing!" Teddy stuck out his chin.

"Gabe's not afraid of *anything*," Addie said.

Teddy looked confused. "That's what I said."

"Gee, it's a relief to see we're in agreement over my lack of fear of snakes." He wasn't above smirking at her.

"I wasn't referring to your fears but correcting Teddy's double negative." Addie narrowed her eyes at him.

"What's a double negative?" Teddy demanded.

"It means you said Gabe wasn't afraid twice in the same sentence."

"Well, the kid knows what he's saying." He'd been trying to lighten the mood, but, judging from her expression, his technique needed work.

"Teddy, your two negatives turn it into a positive."

"Huh?" Teddy scrunched up his face.

"It means he is afraid of snakes."

"Why is it okay for you to be afraid of dogs but not for me to feel the same about snakes?"

The only sound in the room was Teddy's shocked gasp.

* * *

Addie's stomach dropped below her knees. She was sure Gabe had been teasing. Nevertheless, she shot him a quelling glance. But she was afraid to look at her brother for fear he'd see the truth written on her features.

"Addie? Is it true?"

"Teddy, look, I can ex—"

"No!" Teddy shouted. "You lied to me. You said dogs were expensive, but that's a lie. You just don't want me to have one. I don't want to live here anymore. Mom says I can have a dog if I go live with her." He turned and ran out of the room.

A door slamming reverberated through the house. Torn between running after him and letting Teddy cool off, she turned helplessly in a circle.

A hand came to rest on her shoulder, halting her and guiding her toward a chair. Gabe pulled it out with his foot. "Give him a few minutes to cool off."

She sank onto the seat. "I should have been honest with him from the beginning."

She pressed her fist against her mouth. He hunkered down in front of her and pulled her hand away and held it in his.

"I f—messed up, and I'm sorry," Gabe murmured. "Do you want me to talk to him?"

"No. That's my responsibility. I should have taken your advice sooner and been totally honest with him about everything." She sighed and got up. "I'd better go speak with him."

"Want some help?"

She shook her head. "It's my responsibility. I'm his guardian. I'll handle it."

"I'm going to go let Radar out. He's been cooped up all day."

She nodded and went into Teddy's room. She knocked but didn't wait for a response that might never come.

He was lying on his bed, his face in a pillow.

She sat on the bed and touched his back. "I'm sorry. It was wrong to mislead you. I know that now. I'm not wrong about how expensive dogs can be, but I should have explained about my fear. I hope you will still want to live with me. Once I finish my college degree, I might be able to get a job as head librarian and we can see about affording a dog. But I can't make any promises." She patted his back and smoothed a hand over his hair. "I am sorry and I hope you'll forgive me." No response whatsoever.

She sighed and got up to leave. She made it into the hall and was going to close his door.

"Addie?" He turned over.

Addie's heart ached when she saw his face. She could tell he'd been crying. She'd been too afraid to give in to tears because once they started, she might not be able to stop them. "What is it, Teddy?"

"I'm sorry. I didn't mean it when I said I didn't want to live with you." He sniffed and sat up. "Please don't hate me."

She stepped back into the room and he sprang off the bed.

"Oh, Teddy, c'mere. I love you. I could never hate you, no matter what you said." She opened her arms and he ran into them. They clung to one another. Taking comfort from each other.

Teddy lifted his head. "Even if Mom gets better, I want to stay here. Please don't send me away."

"I would never do that. I promise."

"I was just a stupid kid when I got burned. I wouldn't do anything like that again. I promise. Please don't send me away."

"You can be with me forever, sweetie. That's why we have to go to court."

He gazed up at her, searching her face. "Is it still okay to love her? Even if I don't want to live with her?"

"Of course it is, sweetie. She's our mother." She blinked back tears. She'd struggled with some of the same things. Gabe had been right. They should have been honest and talked things out. "You know our mom isn't a bad person."

He shrugged. "Everyone said she's sick."

"In a way, I guess she is. She has a drug problem. Do you know what that means?"

"A policeman comes and tells us about that stuff in school." He nodded and sniffed. "You would never do that, right?"

"No, I wouldn't, but I also shouldn't have lied to you. It's just that when I was your age, I was bitten by a dog. I know you love dogs and probably can't understand that I was afraid of them."

He touched her hand. "I'll bet it's like how I didn't want to take a bath after I got burned. I was afraid to touch the water in case I got burned again."

"I guess you do understand. I'm sorry I wasn't there to help you, Teddy. But I'm working through my fear, thanks to Gabe and Radar. Just like you did with the hot water. We're both brave, right?"

"Yeah. And the social worker lady kept telling me you were too young to take care of me, but I said that wasn't true and that you would never act like Mom. And that's what I'm going to tell them when we go to talk to that judge person."

She hoped so. Because now she couldn't imagine her life without Teddy—or Gabe—in it.

CHAPTER FOURTEEN

ADDIE PACED THE living room waiting for Teddy. She'd agreed to Gabe's plan to let Teddy walk home from the bus stop alone that afternoon. Usually, on the days she was working, he took the bus that dropped him off at the library, where he did his homework, read or helped with the younger kids doing crafts.

She spotted him coming down the sidewalk, but this wasn't his normal gait. Something was wrong. She just knew it.

She flung the door open and ran down the steps. He wasn't wearing his glasses, and his shirt was ripped. He looked as if he'd been in a fight.

"Oh my God, Teddy, what happened to you?" As if she didn't already know. She rubbed her hands up and down her arms, hoping to get the blood flowing. She felt as if she'd never feel warm again. How could she have let this happen?

She hunkered down in front of him. His eye was an angry red and violet, the edges already starting to turn yellow. "Oh, Teddy, look at your eye."

He shook his head. "Addie, you know I can't see it without a mirror."

He has the beginnings of a black eye. She closed

her own. This couldn't be happening. And on the day before their court appearance. She would be standing before a judge with Teddy sporting a giant bruise on his face.

"I'm sorry, Addie." His face crumpled. He held out his twisted glasses in the flat of his palm.

"There, there. Glasses can be replaced." She pulled him close for a hug. She was just glad he was all right.

He sniffed. "I should have taken them off like Mr. Gabe said."

"What do you mean, like Mr. Gabe said?"

"He was showing me some…some defensive moves and said to always remove my glasses so they don't get broke."

Gabe had been showing Teddy how to fight? When the judge asked how he got the black eye, would he tell them that his sister's friend was teaching him to fight? She'd be labeled as a negligent parent, just like their mother. Teddy was in her care; he was her responsibility, not Gabe's. How dare Gabe do this to her? He knew the hearing was tomorrow. He knew how tenuous her situation was.

She groaned. This was all her fault. She should've taken better care of Teddy, listened to her instincts, not let someone else influence her.

"Here he comes now."

Sure enough, the Jeep was pulling into the driveway.

"Teddy, go in the house," she said shortly. "I'll be in, and we'll put some ice on your eye." See if they could mitigate the damage.

"But I want to show Mr. Gabe my—"

"Not now. Go inside," she said, doing her best to keep her tone even.

"But, Addie—"

"Now, Teddy."

He muttered something about fairness, twirled around and stomped into the house.

A car door slammed and she drew in a deep breath, barely able to control her fury. Who did he think he was? He'd gone behind her back and betrayed her. Served her right for ever getting involved in the first place. She'd had misgivings in the beginning. Why had she allowed herself to get sucked in? She was no better than their mother, letting a man come before her duty to Teddy.

"What's going on?" Gabe strolled across the lawn toward her. "Is Teddy okay?"

"No, he's not. He came home with a black eye and busted glasses." She shook her head, striving for calm but not achieving it.

"Is he hurt?"

"It's nothing permanent." She shook her head. "I knew letting him walk home alone was a mistake. The school didn't contact me, so I can only assume this happened at the bus stop."

"Did you ask him?"

No, she hadn't. Not really. Which made her the most irresponsible parent ever. Her one job was to keep Teddy safe and she'd failed.

"Not yet," she admitted.

"Boys get into scrapes." He put a hand on her shoulder, but she brushed it off.

She didn't deserve to be comforted. She'd brought all this on by being lax with Teddy—and letting a man she barely knew take on a paternal role with her brother. *Her* brother, her responsibility. Not his. "Is that what you did? I know you're the big war hero now, but it seems like everyone has a story to tell about the things you did as a teen. Are you trying to turn my brother into a delinquent like you?"

Oh God, Addie, what are you doing, lashing out?

She held up her hand. "Look, I didn't—" But the damage had already been done; Gabe looked stunned and hurt. It was as if the connection between them had been severed by a sharp knife.

He held up his hands, palms out. "You're right. I'm a lousy role model for a kid."

"No. Honest, I didn't mean it." She hated the pleading note in her voice but couldn't help it.

He shook his head. "No, you're right. We should both go inside before we say something we might regret."

Too late. "Yeah, I should go check on Teddy."

He shoved his hands in his pockets. "Tell Teddy I hope he's okay. And don't worry—I'll stay away from him from now on. From both of you."

"If you want…" Tears pricked at her eyes. She couldn't imagine losing Gabe now, but she had to do what was best for her brother. She hadn't meant…

He shook his head. "I'm going inside, Addie. You should too."

She nodded and watched him walk away. He went into his home without a backward glance. She stood motionless for a moment, staring at his closed door. Her world had just ended…not with a bang, but with the closing of a door. She felt dizzy, sick to her stomach. Would she ever be whole again? Not having Gabe in her life would be like not having Teddy.

Teddy. She needed to check on him, get some ice on his eye.

He was in his room, sitting on the end of the bed, staring at his glasses in his lap. She joined him and sat next to him. Picking up his glasses, she said, "I'll see if we can salvage these until we can get new ones."

"I'm sorry, Addie."

She put her arm around him, hiding her face in his hair so he wouldn't see her eyes brimming with tears. "I know you are. Want to tell me why you got into a fight?"

"That new kid, Brandon, was making fun of Sam because he can't talk. I tol' him that not being able to say stuff without his tablet didn't make him dumb. But he kept saying it did, so when we got off the bus I tol' him to take it back, and when he wouldn't, I punched him in the stomach."

She winced but resisted scolding. "Then what happened?"

"He's bigger'n me and he punched me back. I was gonna still fight him, but he ran away."

She sighed and hugged her brother. "You know I don't condone fighting—for any reason."

"I know, but..." He shrugged.

"But I am proud of you for standing up for Sam. You are a good friend."

"I like Sam."

"So do I." She squeezed him and kissed the top of his head before standing up. "We'll put some ice on that eye. Maybe it won't look so bad tomorrow."

"What if it does?"

"All you can do is tell the truth." She squared her shoulders. And that was all she could do too—to Gabe, to herself and to the judge. Even if that meant she lost the man she realized she loved…forever.

After ministering to Teddy's eye and leaving him eating ice cream at the table, she straightened her spine and walked the few steps to Gabe's place.

She knocked on the door and tried to gather her thoughts. How could she make this right? What if she'd hurt him beyond repair?

"Hey," he said when he opened the door. "How's Teddy?"

"Nothing wrong that a bowl of ice cream and some Gorilla Glue can't fix," she said, shifting her weight from one foot to the other.

"Glue?" His tone lacked inflection. His face was as blank as his voice, his body held rigidly straight.

She managed a wobbly smile. "For his glasses."

Radar came over and sat next to Gabe in the doorway. Steadying her nerves, she reached out to pet him on the head. "He's probably looking for Teddy."

Gabe grunted in reply and looked away, refusing to make eye contact.

Okay, well, this might take a bit more than a simple apology. "I shouldn't have lashed out at you like that. I was wrong and I want you to know that."

He shrugged, reminding her of Teddy when he was trying to pretend his feelings weren't hurt. She should have thought before she said anything. Too late now.

"I shouldn't have interfered," he said.

"Teddy's skirmish had nothing to do with him walking alone from the bus stop. I was wrong not giving him some responsibility. He was fighting because a kid was picking on Sam Gallagher."

"The one who is nonverbal?"

"Yeah. Teddy was sticking up for him. I can't blame him for that. And it isn't your fault either. I shouldn't have said what I did. I was angry, but not at you—at myself. I didn't have any right to say those things."

"People sometimes say how they honestly feel when they're angry."

She shook her head vehemently, trying to make him see that she'd just been worried for her brother. "No. This was bound to happen. Maybe it's better to have happened at the end of the street. Teddy might have gotten himself suspended if he'd fought at school. And you're not a bad role model, Gabe. Far from it, in fact."

He rubbed the back of his neck. "What about tomorrow's hearing?"

"There's not much I can do about it except tell the truth and pray. Like you say, boys get into scrapes, and I have to trust that the judge will understand."

"He might not have, if I hadn't encouraged him." He raised his hands, palms out, in front of him. "I'm not a good candidate to be a father figure to a seven-year-old boy. I can't get my own sh—stuff together. How am I supposed to set an example? I can't even stop swearing."

"My brother doesn't need some saint or war hero. Maybe he just needs someone to look up to who's good and kind and decent. It doesn't matter if you make mistakes. God knows I've made plenty."

"It's not just—"

"Except it is! That's exactly what it is."

He shook his head. "I'm not following you."

"Teddy needs to know that someone will be there for him...day in and day out. Someone who won't disappear for hours and leave him to fend for himself. Like our mom," she added bitterly.

Gabe took a step back. "Is that what happened?"

"He won't talk about it. But it's what happened to me, so I have to assume she left him on his own a whole lot too." She wiped her face with the back of her hand, which she waved around. "Look, I see why you don't want to get involved. We're a package deal, me and Teddy, and we come with a lot of baggage."

He ran his fingers through his hair. "I'm the one who is messed up. I already have one failed marriage. I don't want another."

She raised an eyebrow. "Oh, has there been a proposal? Did I miss that?"

"You know what I mean." A muscle ticked in his cheek.

"You were a kid when you got married. How can you blame yourself for that?"

"If things were so great, why did she divorce me?"

It was like talking to a brick wall, but she had to try. "I don't know. Did you ask her?"

"I just signed the papers when she sent them."

"And you're the one preaching to me about talking with Teddy…being open and honest. And you couldn't even confront your own wife?" The words had left her mouth before her brain could catch up. He made her react in ways she couldn't control.

"You're right. I have no right to offer any advice to you or your brother. That's why this won't work. I'm the last person you should be listening to."

Desperation clawed at her chest. She hadn't felt this helpless since that dog had clamped his jaws around her. She laid her hand on his arm. "But don't you see?

That's why you're perfect for us. You're offering guidance you've learned from experience. I didn't have a chance to tell you, but I took your advice and was honest with Teddy. I told him that I didn't want to alienate him from Michelle but that I also didn't trust her."

"He doesn't trust her either."

"Did he tell you that?"

He nodded. "I didn't want to break my promise to him not to tell, but I couldn't let you two go on at cross-purposes."

"And I can't tell you how grateful I am."

"At least something good came out of this."

Her heart began to pound as his words sank in. "What do you mean? You're making this sound like it's the end of something."

"Something that never should have started. I knew better than to get involved with someone like you."

Confusion flooded her mind. "What do you mean, someone like *me*?"

"Someone who expects...expects..." Gabe waved his hands in the air.

"Expects what?" She had an ominous feeling about this. She wanted to cover her ears, block out what he was about to say, but she couldn't do that. She was done with running from the truth—now and forever, whether it was about her family or why she'd feared dogs for so long. And if Gabe didn't want to be with her, even after all they'd shared—well, she'd just have to deal with that too. Just like she'd dealt with everything else in her life.

"Happily-ever-after," he said, sounding as if the concept left a bad taste in his mouth. "I don't do *forever*... Ask my ex. Ask the Corps. Things get tough and I bail."

"I never asked you for happily-ever-after." But she could admit to herself she wanted it. How she longed for it—with him.

"But you expected it."

"No, what I expected was just *ever after*. I can make my own happiness." She swallowed past the clog in her throat and blinked. "You can choose to be a part of it or not."

"I guess I choose not."

She started to leave but turned back. "I'll try to explain it to Teddy. He'll be devastated." She inhaled and struggled to get the next words out. "But you know what they say—kids are resilient, so don't worry about us."

Gabe stood in the middle of the room after she'd left, fighting the urge to go after her.

Why? So he could mess up her life too?

A cold wet nose shoved into his palm. Radar made a new noise. A sort of grumble. "What're you? My conscience?"

Radar whined and Gabe shook his head. "It's for the best."

So why did doing the right thing have to hurt so damn much? Like a big black hole had opened in his chest, sucking up all the oxygen and making it hard to breathe. He staggered to the couch and threw himself down. Slumping over, he rested his elbows on his knees and held his head in his hands.

Are you trying to turn my brother into a delinquent like you?

Addie's words echoed in his head and he groaned. The truth hurt. He shook his head. No, that wasn't true. He'd tried his best with Teddy, but his best wasn't good enough. And that was worse. Knowing he simply wasn't the right man to guide Teddy into adulthood had him wishing that black hole would suck him up, put him out of his misery.

Radar crowded close and tried to lick his face. Gabe lifted his head and absently stroked the dog's ears.

The cold truth was that there was only one reason the thought of losing Addie hurt so much. He was in love with her. It wasn't the kissing or the fantastic sex; it was everything. Sitting on the steps and playing trivia fed something in his soul as nothing else had ever done.

He sighed and rubbed his hands up and down his face. *Great timing, Bishop.* He was in love—the forever and ever kind—with Addie.

And that was why he had to let her go. His heart was screaming at him to go and beg her to forgive him. But he had to be strong. His first instincts had been right. He wasn't the guy for them. They needed a guy who wasn't a screwup, a guy whose past wasn't fodder for town gossip.

For once in his life, he'd do the honorable thing and truly mean it. He'd let them go, let them find somebody worthy of them. A woman like Addie needed her equal in life.

Gabe was still telling himself it was for the best two days later. He'd done his damnedest to avoid Addie and Teddy in the intervening time. He had to assume the court proceedings went well, because Teddy was still next door. If he weren't such a coward, he'd go and ask or call her. But even though he loved them both, he wasn't what was best for them.

Radar jumped from the comfort of his dog bed and ran to the front door. Sure enough, a knock sounded.

Teddy stood on the stoop. His heart flipped over at the sight of the boy's healing black eye behind a new pair of glasses. Radar whined and nudged him as if to hurry him to open the door. The kid was probably here to ask if Radar could play. As much as he wanted to stay away from temptation, he was going to have a hard time telling the boy a flat-out no. After all, he'd come to care for Teddy like the boy was his own son.

Breathing deep, Gabe opened the door. "C'mon in."

Teddy shook his head but greeted and hugged Radar. "I just came to tell you something."

"Oh?"

Teddy took a deep breath and launched in. "You told me that I shouldn't let being scared stop me from doing the right thing, but that's exactly what you're doing. With Addie, I mean."

"This is different." Was it? Was it really any different from what he'd told him? Was he protecting Addie or himself? "Where's your sister?"

"Addie's on the phone. She thinks I'm in my room, playing a game."

Teddy, with hands on hips and a mighty glower on his face, made quite the sight. "What happened at the hearing? Are you and Addie okay?"

"The judge says I can live with Addie forever if I want, but that's not what I came to say. Addie says you and her are taking a break, but my friend Ashley says that really means you're broken up. She said that's what her mom said when her dad left. But her dad never came back to live with them. Is it true that you're broken up?"

Gabe felt a pang of guilt. "It's complicated, Teddy, and—"

"Yeah, that's what Ashley said you'd say."

Gabe jerked his head back. Was his personal life a subject of discussion on the school playground? Before he could recover to form an appropriate response, Teddy started talking again.

"I wanted you to know that standing up to those kids when they picked on Sam was scary, but I did it, and now they leave Sam alone. I got a black eye, and it hurt, but it was worth it and I'd do it again." Teddy sniffed and wiped his nose on his sleeve. "Telling all those strangers why I wanted to live with Addie was scary, but I did it. Seems to me some of the best stuff is the scariest.

"Addie told me that she was scared of dogs because, she said, you said it was the right thing to do. So how come you can go around telling everyone else what to do and to not be scared, but then you hurt my sister because you're a coward?"

Well, this was a novel experience. He was used to military brass busting him, not a seven-year-old. One thing was the same, though. He'd have to swallow his feelings and not lash out. And besides, Teddy was right. "Is that what she told you? That I was a coward?"

"Nah. She said stuff to make you look good, but that's what Addie does. Maybe you fooled her, but you ain't foolin' me. You're scared and you don't want to be, so you broke up with my sister. But guess what— we don't need you."

Hearing those words felt like ice stabbing his heart. "Teddy, I'm sorry, but sometimes—"

"And you know what else? I think the way adults handle things is stupid."

The kid had him there. This wasn't the first time he'd bailed when the going got tough. He tried to tell himself this was different. That Addie was young and had her whole life ahead of her. *And what are you?* his inner voice asked. Sure, he was a few years older than her, but she'd gone through a lot in her young life and was probably more mature than him. She'd been willing to put her life, her dreams, on hold to take care of her little brother.

He believed Teddy when he said Addie hadn't bad-mouthed him. As Teddy said, that was what Addie did. The kid was right about something else too. He didn't deserve someone like Addie, but he was selfish enough to want her. What did that make him?

Radar looked from one to the other and began to whine. Teddy looked as if he might start crying at any minute, but he straightened up and faced Radar. "Gabe will have to explain to you why, if we won't be able to be friends anymore. It's up to him, but you'll always be the bestest dog in the world to me."

He hugged the dog and gave him a kiss on top of his head. Then he turned and left, going back to his side of the duplex and shutting the door quietly behind him. Leaving Gabe's heart broken into a million little pieces. So many pieces, he doubted he'd ever be able to even find them all if he tried.

Radar stood in the still-open doorway and cried. Talk about a pitiful noise. Finally, he gave Gabe a glower to match Teddy's, hung his head and slunk back to his bed. If Gabe didn't already feel like crap, this would do it for sure. He shut the door, wondering if he was shutting out the best part of his life.

Once Addie thought it over, she'd probably be glad to be rid of him. He didn't exactly have a very good track record when it came to relationships. He couldn't even stick with the marines all the way to a full career and military retirement. He could have told her to ask Tracy. Gabe knew people in town tended to blame her for the divorce because they liked thinking of him as some sort of war hero. So of course, it couldn't have been his fault. When, in reality, it rested squarely on his shoulders. Tracy probably thought so.

He'd been reckless when he'd gotten Tracy pregnant. Maybe marrying her had been reckless too. He just hurt everyone he came in contact with—and he cared about Addie and Teddy too much to hurt them anymore.

Gabe spent a restless night, but by the next morning, he'd made a decision. He found Radar in his dog bed, his head on his front paws, looking like he carried the weight of the world.

Gabe jingled the leash, but the dog didn't budge. "So, you're still mad at me? How about if I told you I not only came to a decision, but I also have a plan?"

Radar made noises deep in his throat, a cross between a whine and a growl, but he crawled out of bed and trotted over.

"Let's hope when all is said and done, Addie is as forgiving as you."

CHAPTER FIFTEEN

GABE SHUFFLED HIS feet as Tracy held the door open and stared at him. She looked good. Older, more mature, of course. Her long brown hair that she'd always been so proud of was now chin length. But she was unmistakably still the same woman he'd married—and left—years earlier.

What had made him think this was such a good idea? He'd contacted old classmates until someone was able to give him her current address in a fashionable Boston suburb. He cussed and mentally dropped money into Teddy's swear jar. Except he didn't have the right to do that anymore.

"Gabe? Is it really you? How did you find me?"

"In the flesh," he said, expecting her to slam the door of the modest two-story home in his face. When she didn't but continued to stare at him, he cleared his throat. "Guess you never expected or wanted to see me again."

"Believe it or not, I've wanted to contact you over the years but always chickened out."

"Really?" He would have figured she'd been glad to see the last of him. He wasn't sure how to feel about her admission that she'd thought about him over the years.

"Yes, really." She touched his arm. "Come in. Please."

His first instinct was to tell her this was all a mistake and to run. As fast and as far as he could. But Teddy's accusing voice calling him a coward shouted in his head, and he grabbed the door his ex-wife was holding. "Thanks."

He followed her into an elegant living room. As he glanced around, he thought of Addie and Teddy's living room with its mismatched, flea-market furnishings, a room that was lived-in and charming. A room he wanted to share with the two of them—forever, he knew, if he could figure out a way to make that happen after the stupid stuff he'd said. But first he needed to close the book on the past. He recalled seeing one of those motivational posters that said something to the effect that you couldn't see the future if you were always looking back. Well, he was done looking back. Addie and Teddy *were* his future—if he could get over his own history.

Tracy pointed to an upholstered wingback chair. "Have a seat. Can I get you a coffee or anything?"

He shook his head. At the moment, he wasn't sure he could keep anything down. "No, thanks. I hope I'm not interrupting anything."

"No. My son won't be home from his playdate for at least an hour."

"You have a son?" Why should he be surprised? Of course she'd moved on, because that was what people did. And what he finally hoped to do too.

"Yes. Greg is five. He'll start kindergarten next fall."

"I'm happy for you." And he meant every word.

"What about you? Do you have any kids?"

"Not yet."

She smiled. "That sounds like you have plans."

"I'm hoping so." If Addie would have him and Teddy forgave him. He'd find a way. Marines got things done even when missions went sideways.

"Gabe, I want you to know I regret not reaching out to you before officially starting the divorce proceedings. I know we'd called it quits that last time you came home, but it still felt wrong somehow."

"To be honest, I was pissed when I got the papers, but I was also relieved," he admitted. "For that feeling alone, I think I deserve your scorn. I'm ashamed to even admit it."

"Sorry to disappoint you, Gabe, but I don't hold any animosity toward you. At first I did, but only because you were able to escape and I wasn't."

"Escape?" he questioned but had to admit the word was an apt description. His feelings of relief at getting away from the mess he had made of his life had mired him in guilt.

She shrugged. "We were kids in over our heads. I know that now."

"I was scared but thought I'd done the right thing by marrying you."

"You did the honorable thing, but I'm not convinced it was the right thing. We were too young. And once we lost our child, there was nothing left holding us together."

Tracy's words about honor echoed Addie's. God, how he missed her and Teddy. He could see by Tracy's expression, the tone of her voice, that she was happy. Probably settled in a relationship based on love and commitment. Oh, how he longed for that with Addie and Teddy. He wanted to be there through good times and bad, building a life in Loon Lake, raising Teddy and adding to their family when the time was right.

"Do you have someone special in your life? The way you said 'not yet' made it seem like there is someone."

He sighed. "I did, but, well, it's complicated."

"Do you love her?"

"I do." Huh, that was easy to admit. Why was he able to acknowledge that to his ex-wife and not to the one woman who actually mattered?

"Then I think you should be telling her, not me. I don't know what you did to make you say 'it's complicated,' but you should know, an apology goes a long way."

"This may take more than an apology."

"Want to talk about it? Maybe I can help?"

"You'd do that?" He was surprised. She really had forgiven him.

"Sure." She shrugged. "You're not the enemy, Gabe. You're not even a bad guy. Like I said, we were kids. I hope you haven't been shouldering guilt all this time."

"I was the one who was able to escape and leave you to deal. I'm not proud of that."

"Well, considering I was pushing you away, the fact you left didn't come as a surprise. Even if you'd stayed, I can't say that we would have been able to make the marriage work long-term."

"That may be true, but I still wanted to apologize to you." She might be letting him off the hook, but he needed to follow through on why he came. He wasn't letting himself off the hook. He needed to complete the mission, so he could go back to Addie and Teddy with a clean slate.

"Apologize?" She frowned and tilted her head. "For what?"

Did she truly not blame him? "For running when stuff got tough."

"Why would you think you owed me that? I initiated the divorce. If anyone should be saying they're sorry, it's me." She touched her open palm to her chest.

"But I abandoned you."

She shook her head. "And here all this time, I thought you'd joined the marines."

Okay, she had a point. Why was she so willing to forgive, though, when he couldn't do the same for himself? "But then I went overseas and left you to deal with everything here."

"It wasn't like my waitressing job was enough to support us." She shrugged. "And we had no medical insurance. You did what you had to."

"Then why the divorce?"

"We got married because I was pregnant. When I lost the baby, I didn't see any reason to stay together. I'm sorry. I… I shouldn't have handled it the way I did. I've carried the guilt of that."

"I know it may not have seemed like it at the time, but I did grieve the son we lost," he said softly. They'd barely had time to deal with losing their son when he'd shipped out.

He'd pushed away or stuffed down his grief, but even in Afghanistan, those feelings had sneaked up on him. He'd see local women with their children and be overcome, trying to deal with how raw and hollow he felt.

"Then put him to rest." She reached out and touched his knee. "Took me a while and a good therapist, but

I've moved on and I'm happy. I'd like to think you were too."

"Is that your son? He's cute." He pointed to a picture on a side table. "All I can manage at the moment is a dog."

"Do you have a picture of your dog?"

He raised his eyebrows. "Really?"

"Really. I'm curious because there was a lot of emotion behind your statement." She laughed. "That's what three years of analysis can do."

"I'm sorry about your therapy. I—"

"Getting help was about me. Not you. And it was a good thing, so no need to apologize. Sounds like maybe you should consider it."

He grunted and pulled out his phone. Therapy? Would it help him get Addie back into his life? He'd do whatever it took to work through his issues—as evidenced by the fact he was with Tracy right now. He scrolled through his saved photos until he came to his favorite. He handed her the phone.

"Who is the boy?" She raised her head from the device to look at him before she handed it back.

"My neighbor's kid," he said quickly and glanced at the picture before slipping the cell back into his pocket.

"Oh? Sounds like more."

He shrugged and chuckled. "It's just that it was a case of love at first sight for the boy and the dog."

"You look kinda smitten too."

"Teddy's a good kid. Been through a lot in his young life. He lives with his sister because their mom is a drug addict."

"His sister? How old is she?"

"Twenty-two—no, make that twenty-three. Her

birthday was last month." He couldn't help remembering that night after the opera. He laughed. "Teddy got it into his head that Addie wanted to go to the opera. Not sure where he got that notion, but I bought tickets and went to my first-ever opera."

"Gabriel Bishop at the opera?" She looked at him with amused wonder. "I would have paid good money to see that."

"I went. Turns out she isn't any more of an opera fan than I am." He grinned and shook his head. "We're still not sure what gave him that idea."

"Maybe he was playing a joke on you."

"I wondered that at first, but he was so proud of his suggestion, we knew he'd been serious. Neither one of us had the heart to tell him the truth."

"Sounds pretty serious to me."

He opened his mouth, but the denial died before it made it past his lips. Who was he kidding, except himself? The tightness that had dogged his chest since leaving Loon Lake finally began to ease. He inhaled deeply. "I love them."

"Do they know that?"

"Not yet."

She smiled at his simple statement and took his hand. "You know, I felt guilty for a long time too. Then I met Mitch and decided to forgive myself, to have a family and a future with someone I loved. Isn't it time for you to do the same?"

Maybe it was. All that time spent feeling guilty suddenly seemed like such a waste. Teddy called him a coward. Damn, but the label fit. He'd used his failed marriage as an excuse over the years, when it was really fear that had kept him from giving his heart again.

Teddy was 100 percent right. He *was* a coward...
and would continue to be unless he told Addie and her
brother how he really felt about them.

After he said goodbye to Tracy, he used the key fob
to unlock the Jeep's door and opened it. He stood for a
moment beside the vehicle, looking back at the house.
It looked like a happy home and he was glad for Tracy.

He felt as if a weight had been lifted from his shoulders. One that he hadn't even realized he'd been carrying around all this time. Sure, he'd regretted the way
he'd handled things, but he had done such a good job
of pushing it into the background that his relief came
as a surprise.

Getting in his Jeep, he started the engine.

"I have to do something to make this right."

He pulled away from the curb without a backward
glance. He was through living in the past, through letting old mistakes—especially ones made when he was
a teenager—ruin his future. He'd hurt both Addie and
Teddy, and it wasn't going to be easy to win them back,
but he wasn't going to give up. Failure wasn't an option.

Back in Loon Lake, he stopped at the Pic-N-Save
and purchased a bouquet of flowers. He figured they
couldn't hurt. If she wasn't in a forgiving mood, she
could always throw them in his face.

Checking his watch to be sure he had time to beg
forgiveness before Teddy came home, he knocked on
her door. And he thought he'd been nervous standing
on Tracy's doorstep. This was way worse. Tracy was
his past. Addie was his future.

She opened it, and he could have sworn she looked
glad to see him. At least she hadn't slammed the door

in his face. And she hadn't even seen the flowers yet. Of course, the way he was squeezing those stems, he'd probably strangled the life out of them.

"Gabe."

"Before you say anything, I want to apologize for acting like such a jerk." He swallowed. "And to tell you I went to see Tracy, my ex."

"You did?" She motioned him in.

He nodded. So far, so good. "I did. I needed to face the past in order to move forward. I needed to put that to rest."

"How did it go?" She moved into the living room.

He followed her. "It was hard but easy too. Huh, I guess that doesn't make much sense."

She sat on the sofa and pointed to the spot beside her. "It makes perfect sense. You have a lot of history together."

He sat beside her but resisted the urge to touch. He needed to clear the air first. "We were able to talk about what happened. I guess you could say we were finally able to grieve together for the son we'd lost. She made me understand that feeling guilty was preventing me from moving forward."

He swallowed and shifted, edging toward her. "And I definitely want to move forward...with you and Teddy."

"I want that too. I guess I was dealing with my own guilt over what happened to Teddy and I thought I had to give up my future to atone. I think that's why I have such trouble trusting. But since the judge granted me permanent custody of Teddy, I've tried to relax a bit. Michelle didn't even show for the hearing, so I guess I fretted for nothing." She sniffed and touched his arm.

"I want you to know I have absolute faith in you. Gabe, I would trust you with our future."

She pointed at the drooping flowers. "Were those for something?"

He loosened his death grip on the wilting bouquet. "They were for you, but I swear they looked better in the store."

She gave him a smile that quivered. "Maybe they'll perk up in water. Do you want me to—?"

"No! I mean, I need to say something more first. You can laugh or kick me to the curb, but I need to say it."

"Yes?"

Okay, this wasn't quite as easy as it had been when he'd rehearsed it in his head. He swallowed. "Addie Miller, I love you and...and I love Teddy as if he were my own. I would be honored to call him my son and to make it legal, if you agree."

Her face crumpled and she began to cry. *Oh no, not crying. Please.* What was it about women's tears that lowered men's testosterone levels? He tossed the flowers aside and he did the only thing he could—pulled her into his arms and held her tight. He rubbed his hand in circles over her back as she sobbed against his shoulder.

She lifted her tearstained face to his. "I don't know why I'm crying."

"It's okay. You can let it out. I think you've been holding in a lot of stuff for a long time. You won't have to carry your burdens alone ever again."

He continued to rub her back to comfort her. He hated her tears, but if that was what she needed for healing, then he'd put up with it. But, by God, after today, he'd do his best to never give her a reason to cry again.

As her tears subsided, he brushed the hair off her face and wiped her cheeks with his thumbs. "Sorry I'm not the kind of guy who carries a handkerchief to assist ladies in distress."

She made a sound that was half laugh, half sob. "You're perfect the way you are."

"That's a good start, because you're not getting rid of me. I love you."

She caressed his face. "And I love you."

Several hours later, they sat on the front steps watching Teddy and Radar playing with a Frisbee. It had taken a little convincing to get Teddy to forgive him, but with Radar's help, he'd managed it. A sincere apology hadn't hurt, either.

His chest expanded as if trying to contain all the things he was feeling. Happy and proud that he'd figured out how to put his life back on track before it was too late. He'd made mistakes in the past and, no doubt, would again, but he'd never do anything to jeopardize his family's happiness. His family. He liked the sound of that.

He was still figuring out what he wanted to do, unsure if construction was for him in the long haul. It was good, honest work while Addie pursued her dream of a degree in library science. Thanks to his pa and the time they'd spent tinkering with those castoffs, Gabe had agreed to help Ogle open and run a small engine repair business next to his garage.

He watched Teddy toss the Frisbee for Radar and silently thanked his pa for everything he'd taught him, including how to be a good dad to Teddy.

Addie turned to him. "I have something to ask

you…and you don't have to do it if you don't want to. No pressure."

He took her hand. "Do what?"

"I think you should be the one to accompany Teddy to the Cub Scout lock-in."

"Are you sure?" He squeezed her hand.

She nodded. "It's only fair. I know how hard you two worked on the Pinewood Derby race car. I hate to swoop in at the last minute and snatch all the glory when you guys win."

"You're that confident we're going to triumph?" He joked, but he knew how important this was. Teddy was her heart. She was granting him access to her heart, making him truly a part of their lives. And he wanted to seize the moment with all the joy he felt.

"I have confidence in you," she said and leaned over to kiss him.

He kissed her back, knowing her statement was about more than just the race car.

"Yuck, you guys." Teddy paused his game and shook his head. "Quit the mushy stuff."

Gabe pulled back and laughed. "Never."

EPILOGUE

Six months later

GABE TOUCHED THE box in his pocket as he paced and waited for Teddy. Head on his paws, Radar lay in his bed, his eyes following him as he crisscrossed the room.

Why was he so nervous? Although he and Addie maintained their own places, they'd been practically inseparable ever since their reconciliation. Many a morning he'd left her place before sunrise to return to his side of the duplex. They wanted to set a good example for Teddy—both of them. Although, he wasn't sure who was fooling who. The kid was as sharp as a tack. And Gabe couldn't be prouder of him if he'd been his own son. Which hopefully one day he would be. He and Addie had discussed adopting Teddy, so they'd officially be his parents.

Radar jumped up and ran to the door with Gabe on his heels.

"Hey, Gabe. I'm here like you told me this morning."

Gabe had asked Teddy to come straight to his place after school. He grinned at the boy.

"You are."

"Is anything wrong?"

"No, but I wanted to talk to you about something."

Teddy nodded solemnly, and he and Radar went to sit on the couch.

"You know your sister and I have been…have been…"

"Together?" Teddy supplied and grinned.

Gabe laughed. "Yeah. I'd like to make it, uh, permanent."

Teddy scrunched up his face. "Huh?"

"I'm going to ask your sister to marry me."

Teddy jumped up and whooped, causing Radar to dance around and bark.

Relief swept through him and Gabe laughed at the two of them. "Does this mean I have your permission?"

"Oh yeah! Does this mean Radar and I are brothers now?"

"I guess it does—if your sister says yes."

"She will." He nodded. "Does this mean I could… maybe…like call you Dad?"

Gabe tried to swallow past the sudden lump in his throat so he could respond. Teddy was looking up at him, no doubt waiting for an answer, and he couldn't get his voice to work, so he knelt and opened his arms.

Teddy threw himself at Gabe. "Dad."

"Son," Gabe managed to choke out. He couldn't believe how right that sounded, how it made him weak and strong at the same time. In that moment, as he hugged Teddy, he thanked his own pa for setting such a good example.

Radar pushed his nose between them, wanting in on the action. They both laughed and pulled apart enough to include the dog.

"How about we make the dad stuff official too?" Gabe suggested.

"What does *official* mean?"

"It means I would be your dad forever."

"What about Addie?"

"We'd both adopt you and she'd be your mom."

"Hear that, Radar? I have a real mom and dad now and we're all gonna live together forever and ever."

The doorbell rang and Radar rushed over, barking.

"Radar, stop," Gabe ordered, and the dog immediately stopped barking and sat down in front of the door.

"Hey, come on in," Gabe greeted Des Gallagher.

"Sorry if I'm late." Des came in but didn't shut the door. "Sam's in the car."

"No. Perfect timing."

"What are you doing here, Mr. Des? Why is Sam in the car?"

"I've come to invite you to play miniature golf with Sam and me. Afterward, we're going for pizza. How's that sound?"

"Right now?"

"Sure. That's why I'm here to pick you up." Des turned to Gabe. "I thought you were going to speak to him."

"I did... I am." Gabe shrugged. "We didn't get to that part yet."

"What part?" Teddy asked.

"The part where you come with Sam and me," Des told him.

"But—but it's happening now. I'll miss it," Teddy said.

"What's happening now?" Addie asked from the doorway. "What's going on?"

Gabe started laughing. When was the last time any of his plans had gone off without a hitch? He sighed and got down on one knee. "This is what's happening now."

Des leaned down and whispered something in Teddy's ear.

"Yuck. Mushy stuff. I'm going with Mr. Des and Sam."

Addie watched Teddy and Des leave, then turned back to Gabe, who was still down on one knee.

"Addie Miller, will you marry me?" He took the box out of his pocket and opened it.

She dropped to her knees in front of him and threw her arms around him. "Yes, I'll marry you."

He slipped the simple but elegant diamond solitaire on her finger. She threw her arms around him again, and he hugged her tight and kissed her as pure joy flooded his body.

Radar sat on the floor next to them and woofed. They both laughed. Addie reached out to pet the dog and whispered, "Thank you, Radar."

* * * * *

COMING SOON!

We really hope you enjoyed reading this book.
If you're looking for more romance, be sure to
head to the shops when new books are
available on

Thursday 22nd July